*Thirteen Award-Winning St
take you to places you've nev*

On a distant world—

Amba, a girl afflicted by a rare disease that leaves clouds in her eyes, develops the gift to do what no one else can....

Life on the Doleful Comet is hell. But then, that's what it is supposed to be....

A mail-order bride can bring nothing with her between the stars—except all kinds of heartache and a secret hope....

There are many kinds of trophy hunters, but only one kind of kill....

In a new future—

A cyborg forest ranger is saving the world—just not the people on it....

When a Supreme Court judge prepares to die, the most valuable thing that he has to bequeath are his memories....

A bike trail leads to a vast desert, alive in its own way, and beyond that the world is unknowable....

One lonely man finds out what it is like to become a god, and lose the love of those that he has created....

In a world like no other—

There are only a few basic emotions, and a chemist with the right tools can create the one that could save your life, while you wait....

All kinds of people want to take a trip to the End of the World, but what do they hope to gain?

As a shifter, Fat Reggie can be whoever he wants to be—but identity comes with a price....

Mirrors have strange powers, but only Lacra knows how to use them....

Most people care little for the world's endangered species, but some would give everything for them....

Turn the page to start your trip into a fascinating new future!

What has been said about the

L. RON HUBBARD

Presents

Writers of the Future

Anthologies

---

talent with an undeniable success rate. If you want a glimpse of the future—the future of science fiction—look at these first publications of tomorrow's masters."

— Kevin J. Anderson
Writers of the Future Contest judge

"Writers of the Future brings you the Hugo and Nebula winners of the future today."

— Tim Powers
Writers of the Future Contest judge

"The smartest move for beginning writers is the WotF Contest. I've witnessed it kick-start many a career."

— Gregory Benford
Writers of the Future Contest judge

"I really can't say enough good things about Writers of the Future.... It's fair to say that without Writers of the Future, I wouldn't be where I am today...."

— Patrick Rothfuss
Writers of the Future Contest winner 2002

"Given the number of truly fine writers and careers that have been launched from the Writers of the Future platform, I always look forward eagerly to reading and judging the latest crop."

— Mike Resnick
Writers of the Future Contest judge

"Every year the Writers of the Future Contest inspires new writers and helps to launch their careers. The combination of reward, recognition, instruction, and opportunity for beginning authors is unparalleled. There is no contest comparable to the Writers of the Future."

— Rebecca Moesta
Writers of the Future Contest judge

"The Illustrators of the Future Contest is one of the best opportunities a young artist will ever get. You have nothing to lose and a lot to win."

— Frank Frazetta
Illustrators of the Future Contest judge

"The aspect I personally value most highly about the program is that of working with my fellow professionals, both artists and writers, to accomplish a worthwhile goal of giving tomorrow's artists and writers recognition and advancement in the highly competitive field of imaginative endeavor—the only existing program that does this."

— Stephen Hickman
Illustrators of the Future Contest judge

"Illustrators of the Future offered a channel through which to direct my ambitions. The competition made me realize that genre illustration is actually a valued profession, and here was a rare opportunity for a possible entry point into that world."

— Shaun Tan
Illustrators of the Future Contest winner 1993
and Contest judge

"The Illustrators of the Future competition has been at the forefront for many years, to support new and enthusiastic artists pursuing their dreams, and see them fulfilled."

— Stephen Youll
Illustrators of the Future Contest judge

"That phone call telling me I had won was the first time in my life that it seemed possible I would achieve my long-cherished dream of having a career as a writer."

— K. D. Wentworth
Writers of the Future Contest winner 1989
and former Contest Coordinating Judge

"The Writers of the Future Contest has had a profound impact on my career, ever since I submitted my first story in 1989."

— Sean Williams
Writers of the Future Contest winner 1993
and Contest judge

"The Writers of the Future Contest played a critical role in the early stages of my career as a writer."

— Eric Flint
Writers of the Future Contest winner 1993
and Contest judge

"I only wish that there had been an Illustrators of the Future competition forty-five years ago. What a blessing it would have been to a young artist with a little bit of talent, a Dutch name and a heart full of desire."

— H. R. Van Dongen
Illustrators of the Future Contest judge

"The Writers and Illustrators of the Future Contests are the best way to jump-start a career in science fiction and fantasy writing or in illustration. You win great money, make wonderful lifelong friends at the workshops, and get to learn from professionals in your field. The awards events are spectacular. Join the fun if you can, and make great connections and memories!"

— Nina Kiriki Hoffman
Writers of the Future Contest winner 1985
and Contest judge

"The Writers of the Future Contest was definitely an accelerator to my writing development. I learned so much, and it came at just the right moment for me."

— Jo Beverley
Writers of the Future Contest winner 1988

"The Illustrators of the Future Contest is more than a contest. It is truly a great opportunity that could very well change your life. The Contest gives you the tools to think outside the box and create a niche for yourself."

— Robert Castillo
Illustrators of the Future Contest winner 2008
and Contest judge

"The Contests are amazing competitions because really, you've nothing to lose and they provide good positive encouragement to anyone who wins. Judging the entries is always a lot of fun and inspiring. I wish I had something like this when I was getting started—very positive and cool."

— Bob Eggleton
Illustrators of the Future Contest judge

"These Contests provide a wonderful safety net of professionals for young artists and writers. And it's due to the fact that L. Ron Hubbard was willing to lend a hand."

— Judith Miller
Illustrators of the Future Contest judge

"You have to ask yourself, 'Do I really have what it takes, or am I just fooling myself?' That pat on the back from Writers of the Future told me not to give up.... All in all, the Contest was a fine finishing step from amateur to pro, and I'm grateful to all those involved."

— James Alan Gardner
Writers of the Future Contest winner 1990

"The Writers of the Future Contest sowed the seeds of my success.... So many people say a writing career is impossible, but WotF says, 'Dreams are worth following.'"

— Scott Nicholson
Writers of the Future Contest winner 1999

L. Ron Hubbard PRESENTS
Writers of the Future

VOLUME 30

L. Ron Hubbard PRESENTS

Writers of the Future

VOLUME 30

The year's thirteen best tales from the
Writers of the Future international writers' program

Illustrated by winners in the Illustrators of the Future
international illustrators' program

Three short stories from authors
L. Ron Hubbard / Orson Scott Card / Mike Resnick

With essays on writing and illustration by
L. Ron Hubbard / Robert Silverberg / Val Lakey Lindahn

Edited by Dave Wolverton
Illustrations Art Directed by Stephen Hickman

GALAXY PRESS, LLC

"Another Range of Mountains": © 2014 Megan E. O'Keefe
"Shifter": © 2014 Paul Eckheart
"Beneath the Surface of Two Kills": © 2014 Shauna O'Meara
"Artistic Presentation": © 1964, 1970 L. Ron Hubbard Library
"Beyond All Weapons": © 2008 L. Ron Hubbard Library
"Animal": © 2014 Terry Madden
"Rainbows for Other Days": © 2014 C. Stuart Hardwick
"Giants at the End of the World": © 2014 Leena Likitalo
"Carousel": © 2012 Orson Scott Card
originally published in *21st Century Dead: A Zombie Anthology* (St. Martin's Griffin)
"The Clouds In Her Eyes": © 2014 Liz Colter
"What Moves the Sun and Other Stars": © 2014 K.C. Norton
"Long Jump": © 2014 Oleg Kazantsev
"These Walls of Despair": © 2014 Anaea Lay
"Robots Don't Cry": © 2003 Mike Resnick
originally published in *Asimov's Science Fiction* July 2003
"The Shaadi Exile": © 2014 Amanda Forrest
"The Pushbike Legion": © 2014 Timothy Jordan
"Memories Bleed Beneath the Mask": © 2014 Randy Henderson
Illustration on pages 9 and 402: © 2014 Sarah Webb
Illustration on pages 61 and 401: © 2014 Michael Talbot
Illustration on pages 75, 387, 327 and 388: © 2014 Cassandre Bolan
Illustration on pages 95, 389, 236 and 390: © 2014 Adam Brewster
Illustration on pages 110 and 396: © 2014 Seonhee Lim
Illustration on pages 125, 398, 281 and 399: © 2014 Andrew Sonea
Illustration on pages 143 and 400: © 2014 Trevor Smith
Illustration on pages 183, 391, 316 and 392: © 2014 Vincent-Michael Coviello
Illustration on pages 197 and 393: © 2014 Kirbi Fagan
Illustration on pages 209 and 395: © 2014 Kristie Kim
Illustration on pages 259 and 397: © 2014 Bernardo Mota
Illustration on pages 369 and 394: © 2014 Vanessa Golitz

Cover Artwork: *Other Worlds* © 2014 Stephan Martiniere
Interior Design: Jerry Kelly

ISBN 978-1-61986-265-4
Library of Congress Control Number: 2014935725
Printed in the United States of America

CONTENTS

Introduction

BY DAVE WOLVERTON

David Wolverton is a New York Times *bestselling author with over fifty novel-length works to his credit.*

As an author, David has won many awards for both his short stories and his novels. He won the grand prize in the third year of the Contest for his story "On My Way to Paradise" in 1987, and quickly went on to begin publishing novels. He has since won numerous awards for his longer works, including the Philip K. Dick Memorial Special Award, the Whitney Award for Best Novel of the Year, the International Book Award for Best Young Adult Novel of the Year, and the Hollywood Book Festival Book of the Year Award—among many others.

Along the way, David has written a number of bestsellers, designed and scripted screenplays, acted as a greenlighting analyst in Hollywood and worked as a movie producer.

David has long been involved in helping to discover and train new writers, including a number who have gone on to become #1 international bestsellers—such as Brandon Mull (Fablehaven), Brandon Sanderson (The Stormlight Archives), James Dashner (The Maze Runner) and Stephenie Meyer (Twilight).

David currently lives in Utah with his wife and children, where he is busily writing his next novel and judging entries for L. Ron Hubbard Presents Writers of the Future, Volume 31.

Introduction

As the coordinating judge for the L. Ron Hubbard Presents Writers of the Future Contest, I get the pleasure of being the first reader each year for the thousands of stories that come in to the Contest.

Each one of the stories is like a little Christmas present, wrapped up by its author and offered as a gift. I open each one, not knowing what the box may contain.

I'm continually surprised and delighted, and in this anthology, I get to share these exquisitely designed and crafted stories with you, so that you can enjoy them, too.

This is a landmark year. For the Writers of the Future Contest, it completes our thirtieth year in existence—making this one of the longest-running writing competitions in the world. For the Illustrators of the Future Contest, this ends the twenty-fifth year of our competition.

Each year, we see growth and changes in the Contest. The number of submissions has increased dramatically in the past year, and the Contest is taking on more and more of an international dimension.

For example, one of our first-place winners this year, Leena Likitalo, hails from Finland. She is the second nonnative English speaker that we have had who will be competing for the annual $5,000 grand prize. But she's not our only nonnative English speaker in the anthology. We also have Oleg Kazantsev, who hails from Russia, and we have some others who speak off-brands of English with funny accents from the U.K. and Australia.

Since, as an editor, I'm always looking for quirky fantasy and science fiction stories, hoping that as a reader you'll be carried away by the sheer variety of stories, it's a delight to find stories that don't just represent different subgenres, but that also come from entirely different cultures.

The same of course is true of our illustrator winners, who literally come from all over the globe.

With this anthology, we'll be having some new features this year. You'll notice that we have copies in trade paperback size, so that you can enjoy the illustrations more. Beyond that, you'll be able to see the illustrations in full color, and you will get to read some of the short stories from our illustrious judges, along with one from L. Ron Hubbard himself.

Beginning this year, one of our illustrator judges, Stephen Hickman, served as art director for the illustrator winners on their artwork for each story, to acquaint them with the customary practices of professional illustrating in accordance with the original intention for the Illustrator Contest.

So the Contest continues to expand. Each year we continue to judge these stories blind, not knowing who the authors are. We hope to discover great new writers who are on the cusp of gaining worldwide recognition. It has worked well in the past. Many of our winners have gone on to garner major awards and become bestsellers, and as you read the biographies for our writers, you'll find that many of these new authors are selling short stories and earning novel contracts, while our illustrators are on their way to their own wondrous careers.

Thirty years are behind us in this Contest. I look forward to the next thirty.

So sit back, relax, and enjoy....

Another Range of Mountains

written by

Megan E. O'Keefe

illustrated by

SARAH WEBB

ABOUT THE AUTHOR

Megan E. O'Keefe was born on a surprisingly sunny day in Seattle, Washington. She was raised amongst journalists, and as soon as she was able, joined them by crafting a newsletter which chronicled the daily adventures of the local cat population.

When Megan was nine, a good friend introduced her to fantasy and science fiction, sparking a lifelong love.

She has worked in both arts management and graphic design, and spends her free time tinkering with anything she can get her hands on. Megan now lives in the Bay Area of California with her fiancé, where she makes soap for a living. It's only a little bit like Fight Club. *Writers of the Future is her first professional sale.*

ABOUT THE ILLUSTRATOR

Sarah Webb was born in 1994 and raised in Fairbanks, Alaska. From an early age she loved to draw, paint and read or imagine fantastic stories, and these interests have never faded. The cold winters in Alaska made it very easy for her to spend long hours inside working on her art, and this kind of dedication has stuck with her throughout life.

Her parents have always supported her artistic aspirations, and when she was fifteen they bought her a Wacom Graphire tablet—a tool she still uses to create her digital paintings, alongside the digital painting software Adobe Photoshop CS5.

She attended West Valley High School, and before graduating won a national gold medal in the 2013 Scholastic Art & Writing Competition.

Her work has been published in Exposé 11 *and* ImagineFX *magazine. She considers it an honor to be included in Illustrators of the Future.*

She is currently attending the Maryland Institute College of Art, where she majors in illustration; she will graduate in 2017.

Another Range of Mountains

The kidnappers had smashed the mirror. Lacra knelt over the mercurial remains, the slivers so minuscule they failed to give back even the tiniest glimpse of her tired face. Whoever had taken the girl had been aware of Lacra's talents. The mirror was tipped onto its face, then crushed to fine glitter beneath a hard boot heel. Some of the larger pieces, still no bigger than her smallest nail, bore the streak of water-softened leather. It hadn't rained last night.

"Can you see anything?" Boyar asked.

"Patience, please."

Behind her the oil lamp wavered in Count Boyar's hand, betraying his anxiety. She couldn't blame the man. His child had been stolen from her own bed; a bed tucked away behind his walls and his guards. Useless ornamentation to the determined thief, and Boyar was paying that price now.

Lacra reached out, allowing her leather-gloved fingers to sift through the rubble. Ah, there. She felt a lump beneath the rug and pulled the edge aside. It was a small shard, no bigger across than the palm of her hand and no wider than two fingers, but it would be enough. She ignored the hopeful sigh behind her.

Reaching into her supply case, a battered thing with wooden handles and wooden fasteners, she pulled out her notepad and charcoal pencil. She found a clear space on the ground and set the pad in her lap, pencil poised over its naked face. She laid the shard down before her with care and let her eyes unfocus, falling backward through the memories imprinted in the mirror.

Her hand covered it, sudden light as it was found and the rug pulled back. She saw its crazy descent from the shattered whole, flickering light and dark. Then there—in the moment before the breaking. A hooded face, but the profile was strong. She held onto it, and sketched.

When she was finished she blinked back into the world and looked down at what she'd drawn. It wasn't much to go on. A hawk-nosed man with heavy brows. The hood covering him was thick, and she'd cross-hatched in its rough texture. Cheap, then. Either it was disposable or he was poor. Hard to tell.

"Is that the monster?" Boyar hovered over her shoulder, angling the lamplight so that they could both see better.

"Maybe. It's a beginning."

She tucked her supplies into her case and stood, brushing off the little bits of mirror that clung to her leggings. A night breeze chilled her. The wooden shutters the kidnapper had come through had been left open upon his egress, and the night was only half done. The bedposts were old wood, good and sturdy, but the thing was made with tongue-in-groove construction. A testament to its craftsman, but without brass fittings it gave her little to work with. The silly girl had placed her hand mirror facedown on the nightstand.

Seeing nothing else reflective in the room, she crossed to the window and looked out over the city below. The count's estate backed against the tallest hill at the northern end of the city, giving him a comprehensive view of the land he governed and the Katharnian Mountains to the south.

It wasn't a very big city, and that was just fine by her. The close quarters of Alrayani constricted her senses, while these wide streets shadowed by desolate mountains were much more to her liking. But then, her mother was of these mountains. Lacra had been born here herself, though she had been a babe and remembered none of it. It was a pity she couldn't stay much longer. The king's men would catch up with her eventually.

SARAH WEBB

A path caught her eye, a way down the ornamental carvings from the window into the little sitting garden below, then over the outer wall into the street beyond. It would not be an easy path to take; one would have to be an experienced climber to attempt it. She did not yet know enough about her quarry to discount the possibility.

"The lamp."

When he gave it to her she shuttered three of its sides, so that only a slim beam sliced through the night. Slowly, so very slowly, she angled the beam toward the suspected place of ingress and swept the light across it. There was a tiny glint by the wall. A puddle, probably left by overwatering the flowers. Bad for the garden; good for her.

"I'm going out now," she said, knowing that her words sounded stilted to him. The Kathari language was not an easy one for her tongue, and the words got tangled when she attempted longer sentences. She was used to round vowels and lilting consonants, not a language as craggy as the landscape which birthed it.

"I'm going with you." He looked firm about it, but it was hard to take a man seriously when he was dressed in his bedclothes and house slippers.

"No. You distract. I go alone. You should have called for me sooner."

"The constable was confident he could find her." Boyar twisted his sleeve between his fingers. "He doesn't know I called you."

She shrugged, "Good. I go now, before the light changes."

"Take Costel then. You're vulnerable when you sketch, and he doesn't fear you like the others."

"Fine."

Boyar took her hand in both of his and squeezed.

"Please, bring my Tatya back. She's all I have."

Lacra thought of her pursuers, spreading north from Alrayani, drawing the noose tighter. She also thought of the portrait of the late countess hung above the fireplace, of how the count cleaned the gilded frame every day with his own soft hands, teasing out the tiniest particles of dust with a mink brush.

"I will do my best."

It felt good to have Costel with her. He was an anxious man, but his incessant worry made him a more stringent follower of her protocols. He stood in silence while she hunched over the puddle, notepad supported on one knee, and he steadied her with his hand on her shoulder. Pulling out the imprinted memories was more difficult on a malleable surface, and they had to stay very still while she waited for the minuscule ripples their footsteps had caused to settle.

Winding backward. The clouds slipping the wrong way across the sky, too fast as she sped it up, dug deeper. An anxious face, the hawk-man's, posture hunched and burdened, a bulging sack strapped to his back— dead weight. She hesitated, stopping the flow of images. If she drew this, Boyar would have proof of his daughter being taken by the man, but no more detail. If she let the moment slip by, it could not be recovered. Reflections which were pulled from the mirror were lost unless there was an anchor point, a linchpin connecting all the imprints together. She decided to risk a closer look.

A shattering splash—turbulence. Boot in the water? Nothing but clouds again, and then the hawk-man's first arrival. Too quick, the splash came before his face resolved. Not enough detail.

She let the imprints fade, her fingers still over the pad.

"Anything?"

"He came this way and left with Tatya. I cannot get a hold on what he really looks like."

Costel frowned. He was better at understanding her accent than Boyar, but it still took awhile. "An Easterner?"

"Perhaps; it is too early to be certain."

He nodded, and she knew what he was thinking—that it was definitely an Easterner. Lacra made a habit of remaining impartial during her investigations, but she forced herself to admit the possibility was strong. Boyar had been increasing his border skirmishes with his Eastern neighbors of late. She snorted.

Grown men arguing over who owned a piece of useless rock face just because their stories said a god died there. Ridiculous.

The other side of the wall offered no new vantage. Gas-fueled streetlamps pushed back the night around the city's central carriageways, making them an unlikely route for an escaping criminal. She saw Boyar's messenger run out of the front gates in the direction of the constable's office, feet slapping to wake the dead. She turned away to skirt the estate wall toward the darker hollows of the city.

"You don't like him, do you?"

She blinked, startled from her concentration. "Who?"

"The constable."

"He thinks I'm a witch."

"Are you?"

She shook her head. "I just see differently than you."

Silence pervaded as she explored the side street. Well, a kind of silence, anyway. She could practically hear Costel thinking, turning over what she'd said. Trying to fit it into what he knew of the world. She pressed down a sigh and tried to focus on the task at hand. Ever since word of her ability as a mirrorpainter had gotten around, some of the more superstitious shopkeepers had taken to putting up butcher's paper inside their windows in an attempt to mute any reflections. Lacra suspected that it was really to hide illicit dealings, but Boyar had brushed her off as being too cynical. To him, it was just an extension of the old ways.

In truth, it only hampered her ability to see what happened inside those rooms. If anything, the solid backdrop enhanced the detail she could tease out of the window glass from the street side. She had failed to mention as much to Boyar. His loose lips seemed to be where most of the rumors about her sprouted, and she dared not volunteer more fuel to that mounting fire.

Their progress down the lane was slow as she hesitated at every papered window to dip momentarily into its imprints. He had come this way; she could see that much. *Hood down, face obscured, running.* She didn't bother with the notepad. This man had been aware of her and made a habit of keeping his face covered. Now it was just a matter of following the trail. She hesitated. If he had been aware of her, why come this way? There were other paths to take, ones with bricked-up windows and little light. He either wanted her to follow, or had no other choice.

"My uncle can't tell green from red. Is it like that?"

She bit her lip to keep from yelling at him for breaking her concentration. "Yes. Similar. We may be close now. Be ready."

Costel sucked air through his teeth, the front gap making him whistle, and fumbled to get his hand down on his saber's handle. She was beginning to wish she'd requested a different guard.

They reached the first turning in the lane, and found a gas lamp throwing off shadows from its perch high on a hollow metal pole. Here her culprit would have been surrounded by subtle glimmers, unable to shield his face and direction from the dew gathered in the ruts left by wagon wheels or the shining brass hinges on thick wooden doors. All she had to do was find his prime fail point, the place where he'd been unable to shield his face.

She stood in the center of the lane and let her eyes roam the glass-faced window to her right, drawing up the image of the fleeing man, and held it still, adjusting her footing until she stood in the exact spot he had. The kidnapper was a half hand taller than she, so she pushed to her toes and hunched her shoulders, attempting to mimic his burdened posture. She let her eyes wander, seeking the telltale spark of a reflective surface. There— the door on the other side of the intersection, a thick thing with wide brass plating around its handles.

Crouched down so that she was eye level with the plating, she perched the notepad on her knee and lifted her pencil.

Her own approach, running backward. Clouds shift across the sky, bringing patches of shadow and light. Stillness. A figure moving backward, he was turning right down the lane, away from the city's heart. His face lifted—finally. Her fingers moved.

"Looks like an Easterner." Costel said when she finished.

The face she had drawn could have been an Easterner. It could have been anyone, really. The bones were sharp, an already firm profile made craggy with sunken age. His brows were pushed together with effort and his lips twisted to the left with a scar. The bundle was visible over his shoulder, but the rest of the scene fizzled away into meandering squiggles. There was something familiar about that hard, twisted face, and something wrong with the incoherent mess of the background. Her visions were always clear. Always. Her fingers trembled as she turned the page in her notepad, hiding away the stern face and laying bare the next page.

"We must be very careful now. He went right."

Costel frowned down that shadowed stretch of road. "But there's nothing down there."

She raised her brows high at him. "I presume that's the idea."

The rest of the way was in relative darkness. She felt blind, and not only because the stars were dimmed under a mantle of cloud. They left the papered windows and ornate brass fittings behind for a narrow lane crowded with tenement homes, their windows shuttered wood.

"Nothing but poor folk out here; they wouldn't risk hiding a stranger." Costel said as his eyes flicked from one side of the street to the other. His fingers stayed wrapped around the grip of his blade, baring the steel a finger's width or two every time they heard a cat skitter or a night soil bucket dumped from a window.

"They're working folk," she explained. "And there are storage halls closer to the city's edges which aren't visited at night. I suspect that's where we will find him."

Costel appeared dubious, but she ignored him. He was a good lad, but he didn't know a thing about the underbelly of his own city, let alone the habits of criminals. Something Lacra herself was all too familiar with.

Lacra choked back a sigh and shook her head to focus her thoughts. The man's naïveté aside, he was loyal to the count and handy with that blade. Considering she hadn't seen a speck of evidence that the constable was anywhere near the trail, she would be relying upon Costel's expertise to handle any fighting. Back home her reputation as a mirrorpainter would have been enough to cow most, but not here. No, here they were more likely to skewer her for it.

The tenement quarter backed up to a lazy river which turned the milling wheels and dragged the city's waste away. By daylight the water was a disconcerting shade of brown. With her sleeve pressed over her nose, she sidled up to the edge of the bank and leaned over to get a look at the flat surface. The river was so sluggish that she managed to dredge up a few imprinted images from it. Though they were wildly unsteady due to the river's stubborn trudge toward the sea, she pieced together that the man had taken the low footbridge out into the fields beyond.

Not wanting to remove her sleeve from her nose to sketch the wavering image, she dropped the connection and hurried across. Once she was upwind, she propped her fists on her hips and surveyed the land. Paths of packed dirt and bits of gravel wound out into the cultivated countryside, crisscrossing amongst fields of grain and lower-growing vegetables she didn't recognize. By day the fields filled with locals working, weeding, replanting, tending. By night nothing save the woodland fauna stirred, stealing bits for their burrows and bellies.

Storehouses stood at the head of each field, massive stone structures with thatched roofs and entrances wide enough to ride two laden carts through. One had a lantern in the window.

"There." She pointed.

This time Costel pulled his steel out all the way, and Lacra was surprised to see its shine had been matted with charcoal and wax. Even Boyar didn't want her seeing some things.

They circled the storeroom from a wide radius, Costel moving with grace that made her cheeks flare with warm jealousy. She had always been a flatfooted type of woman, her attempts at moving with any kind of elegance mocked behind manicured hands at every fête she'd ever attended. Too bad, really. She could use the gift of stealth now. Too late for regrets.

All of the storehouse's windows were shuttered, save the one that had let out a sliver of light. It seemed sloppy to her. Or worse, intentional. The muddled background she'd sketched rose in her mind, taunting her senses. She was missing something here.

A single-horse carriage came clattering around the back of the storehouse, the hawk-nosed man bent over the reins. He leapt from the high seat and gave the horse a pat before opening a narrow door into the storehouse. The kidnapper disappeared within, leaving the door ajar.

"Let's go," Costel said.

"Wait—"

He wasn't listening. Costel crept toward the open door, blade low and ready, while Lacra slunk after him with nothing more than her wooden case clutched before her like a shield. What in the White Beyond was she thinking? She'd found the place; what happened next was no business of hers. And yet... The unquiet background, the noise in the charcoal. Her knuckles whitened on the case.

She needed to witness.

Costel crossed the threshold of the door, and for a moment his shadow was cast in sharp relief against the warm lamplight seeping from the room. Lacra froze, her painter's eye admiring the stern contrast, before a vibrant clash of metal snapped her back into reality. Costel's shadow disappeared into the maw of light and she followed it, not knowing what else to do.

She ducked into a world of chaos, light glinting off blackened blades in patchworked sparks as every strike exposed naked metal. Having no blade of her own, Lacra rushed deeper into the storehouse to find Boyar's daughter. The brown-cloth bundle lay prone beside a pyramid of white root vegetables. Lacra dropped to her knees before the girl to roll her over. Lacra's hands sank down, collapsing the bundle to scatter crumpled cloth and white root across the floor.

Tatya had never been that bundle.

Lacra leapt to her feet and clasped her case tight against her chest, struggling to quell the panic which threatened to override rational thought. Deep breaths; look around.

The harvest season had not yet begun, so only a few meager

stacks of white root obscured her view. A table sat before the window that had been left unshuttered, a warm lamp near the opening. She tried to ignore the squealing metal and grunts and curses coming from near the door and hurried over to have a closer look.

On the table was a notepad, slightly wider than the one she preferred. A charcoal pencil lay beside it, the remnants of torn-out pages sticking from the top like crooked teeth. There was also a small wooden box, the lid tipped up, revealing a set of pastel chalks. *Color!* She went cold all over. Hawk-nose was a mirrorpainter. She tucked the pad under her arm and shoved the pencil through her hair, then tipped the box of chalks out on the floor and ground them to dust under her heel. One last glance around told her what she'd suspected. There was no food here, no sign of a sleeping place. This room was a decoy or trap, and she didn't fancy sticking around to find out the truth the hard way.

Costel's abilities were strained to their limit, but it was the hawk-man who drew her attention. Seeing him now, in the full flush of color and without the shadow of his hood, she knew him for what he was. He may have some Katharnian blood in his veins but he was from much farther away than Costel had feared. An Alrayani then, and she did not give herself the luxury of dreaming his presence here a coincidence.

But then where was Tatya?

Using the white root stacks for cover she slipped up behind the Alrayani and cracked him over the back of the head as hard as she could with her wooden case. Her teeth chattered and her joints ached but the man went down without so much as a whimper. Costel stared at her, wide-eyed.

"Tatya?"

"Not here."

The hawk-man groaned and twitched an arm, eyelids fluttering.

"Hurry," she urged as she kicked the downed man's blade away. "This man is a mirrorpainter; he tricked us. Tatya is elsewhere."

Costel opened his mouth to protest, but she dug her nails into his arm and dragged him out into the cover of night. Together they ran, Lacra trying to explain what she could with broken words and gasping breath. They ducked off the gravel path to cut through the tall stalks of wheat, hoping to obscure their path. A crash sounded in the night; the sound of wood cracking on stone, and Costel grabbed at her, pulling her down to the hard earth. She grunted, all the air whooshing out, and he pressed a hand over her lips. She went very, very still.

In the distance she heard the squeal of leather harnesses tightening. Then hoofbeats, tramping away down the road that ringed the city. Costel took his hand away, and eased into a crouch to peek through the grain-grasses. He waved for her to stand.

"We could take him now, make him tell us where Tatya is."

"No. He would never talk, and you cannot best him."

"How could you know, witch?"

She narrowed her eyes and took a step closer to him. He stepped back. "I know," she said.

"Then we follow."

"Another trap." She shook her head, "I know where to find what we need. But we must hurry."

He frowned. "How could he trick you?"

She tried to look nonplussed, but terror made her throat scratchy. She'd gotten too complacent here in the Katharnians, where mirrorpainters were rarer than lapis blue. "He drew the real images out, and put new ones in using colored chalk."

His mouth was open, white teeth shining in the moonlight, "Can *you* do that?"

"If I must."

Whether he was silent to hide his horror or conserve his breath, she couldn't say, but it didn't matter. The hawk-man would soon realize she wasn't following him and then return to wherever the girl was kept to hatch a new plan. She needed to figure out his hiding place before he could move again.

Back across the footbridge, up past the tenement housing. She was only a little winded by the time they reached the lamplit intersection, and she wasn't sure if it was fear masking her fatigue or the general haleness she'd felt ever since she'd crossed the mountains into this land. There were health benefits to being a fugitive, it seemed.

She strode straight to the center of the intersection and let her eyes unfocus. Turning, bit by bit, she scanned the area directly across from the brass plate from which she'd taken the last drawing. Back and forth, up and down, eyes seeing little more than muddled smudges of color while Costel hovered just out of her periphery. Ah! She grinned up at the lamp itself, seeing the bottom edge of its copper casing glinting in the right direction.

"Bring me something to stand on."

Costel dragged over a barrel tall enough to reach her ribcage and helped her step onto it. He asked no questions, but incessantly drummed his fingers over the wide leather of his weapons belt. Lacra knelt a bit so that the angle was just right, and held the notepad she'd pilfered in the crook of one arm. With the stolen pencil poised above it, she let her vision blur and drifted.

Distorted light, brilliance from behind filling all directions. Nothing. Nothing. The man walking forward, a bundle on his back, he crouches before the door across the intersection and pulls a pad out. His box of colored chalks is out, his fingers dusty with their mingled hues. He draws. Lacra grabbed the image and held on tight. Her fingers moved.

When she was finished Costel helped her down from the barrel and they pored over what she'd drawn. She'd honed in on the pad in the hawk-man's hands the best she could, and it took up the center of the page. Her shoulders slumped with relief when she saw the pilfered details. She'd never sketched another mirrorpainter's work through an imprint before, and hadn't been sure the conceit would work.

But there it was. The detail was fuzzy, but she could make out a man shorter than hawk-nose walking down the center road. He was cloaked, a bundle strapped across his back. He would have looked just the same as the hawk-man as he ran down the lane, but below the height of the windows he was hand in hand with a girl about Tatya's age and height. They were just passing through the intersection, and appeared to be going straight on.

The hawk-man had removed this image from the obvious spot, and replaced it with the one of him veering off toward the tenements. She would have been impressed, if she weren't so pissed off that she had fallen for it.

"You should send for the constable while I run them down," she said, hating herself for asking for help.

"No time for that. If we see 'em on the way we'll enlist 'em, but we have to get to Tatya before that man realizes we didn't chase after him."

The heat of the chase burned in Costel's eyes, and she knew there would be no coercing him to go for help. It would just be a waste of time, and who knew what the kidnappers would do with the girl once they realized they were exposed? *They won't hurt her. They don't want* her, *now, do they? She's just bait, effective bait.* Her fingers itched with the desire to scope the area further, to dig up any imprints that might give her a better idea of just what was waiting for her at the end of the lane.

No time for it.

"This way." She strode off down the lane somewhere between a walk and a jog, allowing her eyes to dip in and out of reflective surfaces as they passed. The hawk-nosed man had been rushed, or just plain sloppy, because he hadn't bothered drawing out and replacing the imprints of reflections along this route. He probably assumed they'd never discover this to be the true trail.

The lane emptied into a little courtyard ringed with inns. She froze, surveying the terrain, and let her mirror-sight drift in and out of blank panes of glass and still puddles. These were inns meant for travelers, and the images she filtered through were a dizzying array of merchants and vagabonds, touring nobles and cutthroats looking to spend their ill-got coin on a warm bed. Even in the heart of night half the windows of each inn were aglow with lamplight, and the occasional laugh burbled up through the murmur of idle chatter.

With every fruitless probe into a reflection her irritation grew until she clenched her fists so tightly her nails carved half-moons in her flesh. It was an ideal place to hide out from a mirrorpainter. The bustle of day-to-day life in places like these crippled her ability to come to any conclusion in a hurry. She lamented this as she flicked her gaze from memory to memory, and never did see the bag come down over her head.

Lacra opened her mouth to cry out, but a cloying aroma filled her nostrils and gagged her. The world around her feathered, fractured. Though she could not see, her mirrorpainter's eye conjured up mingling colors of panic until darkness encroached, and her panic faded into bliss.

When consciousness returned, she opened her eyes to darkness. For a moment, she wondered if she had died. Then she felt harsh rope chafing her wrists and ankles, and a sharp chill settling into her bones. Light denied her, she shifted and felt a wooden cot creak beneath her. Someone had drawn a blanket up to her chin, and the wool scratched her exposed flesh. She supposed it was the only thing keeping her from death by exposure. Katharnian winters showed no one kindness.

She eased her bound ankles over the edge of the cot and wriggled her way into a sitting position. Her head spun, unused to being upright, and she squeezed her eyes shut even though it was already too dark to see. Someone had pulled thick woolen socks over her feet, and that was a relief. It meant she was probably wanted alive and in one piece, at least for now.

There was a knock at the door and she jumped, then let out a ragged laugh. What jailer knocked? The man must have taken her laugh for permission, because the door swung inward. For a moment, she was blinder in the light than she had been in the dark. Lacra flinched back from the radiance of the lamp and brought her bound wrists up to shield her eyes. She blinked and squinted, tears falling, but forced her lids open.

The hawk-man set the lamp on a small table and shuttered all but one side.

"Where's Tatya?"

"The girl?" He spoke in the smooth language of the Alrayani, "She has been safely returned. She was not harmed."

Lacra swallowed. It was good that Tatya was safe, but his blithe dismissal of the girl painted a clearer picture of Lacra's future. "And Costel?"

He stepped over and cut her bindings with a thin blade, "He was glad to trade you for the girl, when we told him you were a murderer."

She bit her lip. He was testing her resolve, trying to see if being accused would conjure up the memories of that day. A good mirrorpainter could steal the imprints from your eyes if you shuffled them up for them to steal. A good mirrorpainter could also keep his memories to himself. She kept her mind centered, focused only on the current moment.

"Boyar will send people for me."

"No, he won't. We told him you killed a king and stole a prince's memories of it."

She flinched, and felt the hawk-man's eyes attempt to dip into hers. Lacra stared hard at him as she imagined bits of the room they were in, parading them through her foremost thoughts. He grunted, and she felt his attention slip away.

"You're going to have to give it up eventually, you know."

"Do you think I would have come all this way if I had any intention of giving it up? I am the stronger of the two of us. You feel that. I will die before I let the memories go."

"Funny thing to die for, staving off an execution."

"I have my reasons."

He left her there with the lamp and a pot of hot somal tea. Her fingers trembled as she poured a cup and gathered the warm porcelain into her hands. She felt the heat of it leech into her flesh and bones, warming joints stiff with cold and disuse. A mirrorpainter's hands and eyes were her most valuable assets; she feared frostbite more than she did death. When her hands warmed, she gave it a careful sniff. The brew was weak enough, the honeyed sweetness of the somal leaf muted by dilution.

Better to risk the mind-lulling effects of the somal leaf than dehydration. She sipped and looked around.

The little table had only the lamp and the tea, but her cot had a trunk at the foot. She opened it and discovered more blankets, in which she wrapped herself. A chamber pot hid beneath the cot, and a washrag rested next to a half-filled basin. They expected her to be here awhile. There were no windows.

There was no food.

They're going to starve me out. Mirrorpainters could be coaxed into giving up their memory imprints if they were severely weakened, and the fastest way to do this, save a beating, was starvation. She put her cup back in its saucer, unable to calm the tremble that had returned to her fingers.

On the second day of her captivity, the hawk-man brought her a pad and a pencil with her tea. When he had finished his morning interrogations and left, she brushed her finger pads over the smooth, blank surface. It was good paper, made from waxbark mash if memory served her, which it always did. She tugged a sheet out of the pad and looked at the little scraps left behind in the stitched binding. A whole sheet gone he would notice, but those scraps, those he would not miss.

She eased out those scraps left behind, and began to soak them in her tea.

When he returned on the third morning, she had been dozing. She lifted her head, and for once since her captivity began did not feel the slosh of liquid in an empty stomach. He sat the teapot down and surveyed what she had drawn on the pages he'd given her. Lacra knew that he would hope for her to slip up, to edge in some tiny detail that might give away the prince's linchpin imprint. She had been meticulous in avoiding such a mistake.

Each scene was a representation of a moment in her life before that terrible day. It was safe for her to sketch with the charcoal, only scenes drawn in color could take away or replace a person's memories. And they weren't true memories anyway, just drawings. They were scenes which included her, not taken directly from her point of view.

All her time at court she laid out in whorls and cross-hatching. Most of it spent with the prince. With Alfon. She drew him as she had seen him; as she had known him. Always smiling, laughing. Larger than life and yet sweet and humble. The hawk-man picked up one sheet, and she saw him touch the surface in the place where a fallen tear had marred the image. It was still clear enough.

Alfon, ring in hand.

Lacra lay back down on her cot and pulled the blanket to her chin. The hawk-man left without asking her the questions. She let her tea grow cold.

The next morning, he brought her gruel. She sat cross-legged on the floor of her cell, blankets wrapped high around her shoulders, the images of her life scattered around her like downed leaves. He cleared a small spot before her and sat the bowl between them. He rested his forearms on his knees and leaned back.

"Eat."

"Why?"

"Just eat."

She reached for the bowl, unable to help herself. More than anything she dreaded that he would take it back, that he would laugh at her for being so foolish as to think he would offer her sustenance. Lacra cradled the bowl in one hand and shoveled the food into her mouth with two fingers. It was the most marvelous thing she had ever tasted.

"Slowly," he warned, "or you will throw it up."

It pained her to do so, but she rested the bowl in her lap and began to dip out smaller portions. So very, very small.

"You loved him?"

She coughed, choking, and he handed her tea without the too-sweet aroma of the somal leaf. She drank, taking the time to smooth her mind as well as her throat. "Yes."

"Then why withhold the truth from him?"

"That I cannot say."

She saw him dig his fingers into his knees, but his face stayed placid. "Not knowing is killing him."

"It would kill him to know."

"Can you be so sure?"

"Yes."

She saw his hesitation, his fear. She had painted a thousand faces; she knew the configurations of them all. Just as he did, she felt sure of that. He could read her just as easily, and know that she was telling him the truth, insofar as she believed it herself.

"We are two mirrorpainters. A great deal could be accomplished between us."

Her flesh prickled and her stomach protested its food. She let her gruel-coated fingers rest on the inner edge of the bowl and licked her lips. "He's here, isn't he? That is why you haven't moved me back to the coast. He will not let you leave until he knows.... He was the man. With Tatya. I had wondered."

The hawk-man hesitated before nodding, no doubt trying to work out how he could fool her into thinking Prince Alfon—no, *King* Alfon—was safely back in his coastal palace. Apparently, he decided he couldn't slip it past her. It was a good choice, because it was correct. She could see the shape of Alfon in the man with Tatya clearly now. How had she not noticed before?

Well, it had been so long. How could she be sure?

"He should not be here. It is dangerous for him to be without his Honor Guard."

The hawk-man waved a dismissive hand, "The chancellor oversees Alrayani in his absence. Alfon is said to be on a hunting expedition on the south coast. His cousins there know the truth. He could not be waylaid from chasing down the rumor of a mirrorpainter in the north. Believe me, I tried. Which is why I want to get this over with quickly. You will show him?"

"If I am correct that knowing will be worse than not, will you help me reconstruct matters?"

"Yes."

"Then you had better bring me very, very good paint."

"You did not save the linchpin?"

She shook her head. "I burned it that very night."

He flinched. To burn a painted linchpin of the human eye was sacrilege, but she no longer cared whom she offended. At the time, she had felt it was the only way to secure Alfon's blanket of ignorance. She was just as sure of that now.

"I will return with what you need."

He left her there, huddled over her cup and her gruel, struggling to push aside her misgivings. This man, the hawk-man, cared for Alfon. She could see it in his eyes, in the way he set his lips and shoulders as he talked about his king. She had not known the hawk-man during her time at the palace, but she felt certain he was loyal unto death. That level of devotion could not be faked, which was why he had seen the same sentiment within her.

It was not the hawk-man who entered her cell next.

She did not recognize him at first, though on an instinctual level she knew who he must be. The king had grown gaunt, his cheeks hollow and his shoulders stiff with bone. His eyes were dull and bloodshot, his beard left wild. His movements were halting as he came to sit beside her on the cot. They did not look at each other, but stared at the floor between their feet. He pretended not to notice the sketches of him scattered around.

He smelled the same: cedar and lamp smoke. He always did stay up late, huddled too close to the light to better see his books. "I just need to know."

"You will. I will paint it."

"Can't you just tell me?"

"No, it's better for you to remember."

"I cannot understand how, how you could... He was my father, Lacra. My father."

"I know. You will understand."

"His last words... Promise me I'll remember those."

"I promise."

He squeezed her knee when he got up, an old habit, and placed a sack of supplies by the door as he left. She crawled to them and spilled the tiny pots and brushes out upon the floor. The hawk-man had done as promised. These were richly pigmented, a hard thing to find in the shadow of the Katharnians.

Lacra laid the bit of stretched canvas on the floor and dipped some of her wash water into an empty teacup. Closing her eyes, she drew up the moment she had stolen from Alfon, the linchpin memory that would spark his recalling all that had happened between that moment, and the moment she took it from him.

It had been a warm day on the southern coast. The sky had been blue and clear, a hard thing to remember in the north. She recalled the feel of sun on her exposed arms, the warmth of the horse beneath her, the animal smell. She dipped her brush in the water, and opened the first paint pot.

The hawk-man returned in the morning and found her dozing on the floor, sketches tangled in her hair. She pushed herself upright and rubbed at her eyes, feeling dry grit behind them. He handed her tea and gruel, and she ate while he examined her work. "This is it?"

She understood his confusion. It was an innocuous scene, just before disaster had struck. From Alfon's point of view, the painting showed only Lacra and his father mounted side-by-side, setting out on the trail north to the oak forest.

"It is. I was in a hurry, and I wound back too far. Do you still hold to our agreement?"

She kept the lamp near to hand just in case. It would be messy, but if she timed it just right, she could set the painting ablaze, and then, just maybe, make her escape. As silence expanded between them, her fingers crept toward the light.

"If he gets worse, I will help you correct it." He passed his hand before his eyes, the mirrorpainter sign of trust, and she let her hand go slack.

"Bring him here."

He handed the painting to her and left again. While he was gone, she cleared a place for Alfon to sit and covered the painting with a corner of her blanket. He would have to reveal it to himself. Asking her to force that day upon him was just too much.

Alfon sat in the spot prepared for him and leaned over the

covered painting. He licked his lips, pale hands clasped tightly. The hawk-man came and sat beside her, both directly across from the king so that they could view the return of his memories. The hawk-man to make sure it was done, Lacra to witness what her decisions wrought.

"Do I just..." He held up the corner of the blanket and mimed pulling it back. She nodded. He uncovered her work, and his pupils dilated. She unfocused her eyes and witnessed the return of his memories.

They'd ridden up to the oak forest on a high jetty of earth overlooking the bay. It was a wide strip of land, and as the summer air warmed, the great stags of the Alrayani forests congregated there to claim the land for the rearing of their herds.

Alfon had been bored—this she had not known at the time, but felt through his recalling—*and circled back on the hunting trail, hoping to flush out a stag or doe and bring it down quickly so that they could return to the palace for his evening dram of port.*

He spotted Lacra to the north, and assumed the king was with her. They had been together when he left them, after all. Movement in the brush, quick and furtive. He fired.

The king hadn't seen it coming—he turned his head away.

Lacra cried out a warning. Too late.

The arrow thunked into the side of the king's neck and tore out again. Crimson spray arced through the clear summer air and the king looked up, wonder and confusion in his eyes. He put his hand to his neck and took it away, red all over. Numb shock fled before reality and he fell forward, landing hard on his knees. Lacra and Alfon rushed to his side, and the king put his hand back to hold the wound together. Blood spilled. Pooled. Spurted.

Alfon grabbed up his father, weeping. The old king patted him on the back with his unencumbered hand.

"It's not your fault," he said before pink foam filled his mouth.

Lacra pushed Alfon aside, spilling cloth bandages from her pack, and tried to staunch the bleeding. It was no use. Each of the king's fearful heartbeats hastened his death.

Alfon had been delirious, inconsolable. The next memories to flow through were a torrent of rage, guilt, pain. Reality shifted into smears of color and then he was standing, so clearly, on the edge of the cliffside, staring at the rocky beach below. Lacra grabbed him, forced him to the ground. She was smaller, but he was incapable of any real resistance. She spilled her pouch of colored chalks upon the ground and forced the prince to look at her. He saw his memories unwind as she ran them backward.

On a clean bandage laid flat in the grass, she drew.

Alfon wept. He sat in their little room, huddled over himself, face buried in his hands, and rocked back and forth with each sob. With all the weight of a bird's wing, she touched her fingers to his shoulder. He let out a low moan and uncoiled, only to wrap himself around her.

"I'm sorry, I'm so, so sorry I ever thought you could…"

"Hush, now."

She stroked his hair and held him as he trembled. Over the head of the sobbing king, she locked eyes with the hawk-man. He nodded, once, and passed his hand before his eyes. Then he took the painting, and burnt it.

Lacra had freedom after that. Her room was still her own, but the whole of what she now knew was a hunting cabin was open to her. In the dead of night she stood on a wide balcony overlooking the valley below. They had chosen a good place for secrecy; this stretch of land was rarely visited save during the prime hunting days of springtime. Below her not a single campfire burned, and above her the sky was hung with diamond-bright stars.

The hawk-man came to stand beside her and rested his forearms against the railing. They stood in silence a long while, looking out over nothing at all.

"You were right. He can't go on like this. He's determined to turn himself in to clear your name."

"They'll hang him for it. His uncles will be happy to. It will mean an opening on the throne."

"We have to correct this, but we cannot just take it out again or this will start all over. He would run himself into the ground, searching for you, hoping to discover the truth."

"Then we will give him a different truth," Lacra said. "Come with me."

She led him back into her room. Alfon was deep in the sleep of grief, and she felt sure he could not be stirred. They had returned her wooden case to her, and from it she produced her favorite notepad.

"What do you know about reprinting?"

"Only what I've demonstrated to you. I can remove a mundane imprint with charcoal or an eye imprint with color, and stage a new one with color to be brought out later. It's a crude thing, when rushed."

"I have been thinking, what if we were to deconstruct an event? Take it moment by moment and change things just slightly."

He swallowed. "Insert another person, a new killer? Then how would we explain your running, your memory theft?"

"No, no." She shook her head. "I was thinking we could make the accident mine, in his truth. Put the bow in my hand."

"He would still hunt for you. He would want to prove it was an accident to the council, and such a thing would not hold up under a mirrorpainter-led investigation. It would all fall apart, and he would hang anyway."

She gave him a small, tight smile. "It is difficult to chase a dead woman."

"I see."

"Shall we begin?"

They removed the lids from the pots, and two sets of brushes began to move. When they reached the last set of images, Lacra reached out to stay the hawk-man's hand. "These stay the same. I will paint them."

"Are you sure?"

"These are his father's last words. He needs this. I promised."

The next morning she woke beside the king, her fingers stiff and curled from having drawn and painted all night. It was impossible to capture every minuscule moment, but she had managed to sketch all of the key events of that fateful day.

Together, she and the hawk-man painted them, shifted them. Twisted tiny little details until the narrative fit just right.

Beside her, Alfon stirred into wakefulness. She held her breath, waiting, crossing her fingers beneath the thick blankets. She dared to turn her head just enough to make out his movements, and saw him rub his eyes, then stare straight ahead. The first of the painted images was tacked to the wall directly across from where he lay. Lacra had gambled he would not shift position in his sleep.

He shook his head and stood, stretching. Lacra closed her eyes in relief. He had seen the painting, she was sure of it, but mirrorpaintings were moments in time, not artwork. He had seen the painting as a random memory bubbling to the surface of his thoughts, nothing more. This just might work.

When he had gone from the room, she burnt it.

The next few days progressed much the same. Each morning the king laid his eyes on a new sequence, and sometimes she and the hawk-man managed to place more paintings about the cabin for him to find, always in order. The sequence was key to keeping him ignorant of their conceit. After awhile, he began to seem less gloomy, and his glances toward her became more and more worrisome.

On the fifth day, he slipped up behind her and rested his chin on her shoulder. "It's okay, Lacra. It was an accident."

She closed her eyes and leaned against his chest, trying to keep the tension in her body from relaying what she felt to him. But what did she feel? She was the murderer now, in his eyes at least, but she carried no guilt, only a slight tinge of pride that came with manipulating her skill to the best of her abilities. Pride and sadness. Her time in the cabin with Alfon was over.

"I know," she said, "I know."

That night the hawk-man found her on the balcony after the king had gone to rest.

"Well?"

"He believes."

The hawk-man rubbed at his face with both hands and then

shook his head. His eyes were a little wild, his lips turned up. "I can't believe it worked. I don't think anyone has done anything like this before."

"And no one will ever know. If someone even begins to suspect such a thing is possible..."

"You're right, I know. It's just—" he shrugged. "I wish you could take the credit you deserve."

"You'll know. That's enough. I'm counting on you to look after him. I've compiled sketches of what really happened, so that you can reference them if you need to fill in any blanks. Keep them secret, and burn them if exposure is imminent."

"I will. Will it be tonight?"

"In the morning. There are some preparations I need your help with."

"Name them."

When next the sun rose, Lacra watched from her hiding place in the craggy valley as a deer carcass wrapped in her cloak plummeted from the balcony to the jagged terrain below. She was too far away to hear or see any of the details, but she knew the hawk-man would have cried out, gotten Alfon's attention right before the bundle gave way to gravity and tipped forward toward certain death. They would then find the suicide note on the balcony floor, penned in her own hand, spelling out her grief and her guilt. Alfon would never go searching for her again.

She stayed in the valley through the day, unwilling to leave that place until she felt certain that Alfon was back on the road to the south. The hawk-man had provided her a good horse, saddlebags laden with supplies. She could afford to linger.

In the night she saw them burn her, or what scraps the hawk-man had found of "her," on a pyre near the river. When she heard Alfon's weeping, she knew it was past time for her to go.

He will heal from this, she told herself. He must.

Lacra turned her horse toward the north, and prepared to cross another range of mountains.

Shifter

written by

Paul Eckheart

illustrated by

MICHAEL TALBOT

ABOUT THE AUTHOR

Paul Eckheart wrote his first story as an assignment for his second-grade class. It earned a C, but he still remembers how much fun he had writing it.

Though he dabbled in storytelling throughout his youth, Paul did not get serious about writing until a high school drama teacher told him about the Utah Young Playwrights contest. He entered and became a finalist. This earned him an observership and the opportunity to work as a stage manager at the Sundance Institute's Playwrights Laboratory.

Paul graduated college with degrees in computer science and creative writing. He had this crazy idea that he'd program during the day and write at night. After five computer games, a 3-D graphics system for driving simulation, and an engine room simulator for the U.S. Army, Paul realized that he finally needed to figure out how to balance his work on software with his storytelling.

During that time, Paul stayed active in his local theater community, performing with The Off Broadway Theatre and ComedySportz Salt Lake. He also cofounded two improv troupes: The Village Idiots and Improvables Utah. He credits his work in improv theater with giving him a solid foundation for characters and scenes.

Paul is excited to continue his adventures in storytelling. He writes science fiction, fantasy, mysteries and stage plays.

ABOUT THE ILLUSTRATOR

Michael Talbot is probably not the average Jamaican, but at the same time, he isn't much different from everyone else who might be out there striving to do what they love and longing to fulfill dreams.

He currently lives in the States, furthering his education at the Lesley University College of Art and Design (LUCAD) in graphic design and illustration. Michael wishes to not necessarily become a world-renowned artist, but to inspire and speak to others through his artwork, leaving everyone who sees his work "hanging in the balance" of reality and wonder.

Growing up in Jamaica, Michael had always had a passion for art. While all the other kids were outside playing, he would usually be sitting inside with his coloring book, content with life. Michael's passion only grew as his years attending school in Jamaica progressed, and in a few years he left his home country to live in America with his mom and stepdad.

"To be honest I don't think I'm anything extraordinary or beyond the typical artist or art lover, but I do believe I'm able to make an impact on people through my art, and that's precisely what I will strive to do."

Shifter

The black and white give it away before Fat Reggie even gets back home. He knows they's there for him, but dang if he knows why. Still, driving a black and white into the hood ain't no way to track someone. Might as well leave the sirens blaring—everyone knows they's there.

And that's just fine with Fat Reggie.

He ducks hisself into the stairwell of that fortress white people call The Projects—ain't no one goes in unless they belong there. The stairwell smells a piss and there be thick stuff dribbling down the walls, all thick like snot.

When Fat Reggie first moved to the hood, old Ms. Baxter told him some folks sends their kids into the stairwell to take a pee. The smell keeps the hos from turning tricks there. Fat Reggie understands that—he don't want to stay in there any longer than he got to.

He pulls a pen and a pad a paper out from his backpack. He touches the tip of the pen to his tongue. He starts to write. As he writes Fat Reggie starts to change—with a few words he gives himself a tumor on the right side a his face. Makes it big and purple with veins all sticking out. Makes it squish his eye shut.

While he's at it, Fat Reggie writes off about forty pounds of fat. Writes it clean out of existence. Doesn't quite go so far as to make hisself Thin Reggie, but he feels the skin round his midsection go slack. Then he tightens up the skin to make it fit right.

After that he changes his black t-shirt for a red one he keeps in his backpack. When he's done, ain't no one going to recognize Fat Reggie, that's for sure.

He walks right down the hall, past old Ms. Baxter's place, and marches right in through the door of the pit he and his dad share.

Sure enough, there be two Uniforms and a fine ponytailed blonde number wearing a tan trench, sitting there with Reggie's dad, waiting for him. "Hi," he says.

The two Uniforms, they look on edge. One of them with more muscle than brains practically jumps when Reggie bursts through the door.

The blondie looks at Reggie, looks at his tumor, and turns to the muscleheaded cop. "*This* is him?"

Musclehead looks like someone stole his Christmas. Mutters something that sounds like an apology.

Blondie struggles to her feet—everyone struggles to get out a their butt-eating couch. She wipes her trench like someone sneezed on it. To Reggie's dad, she says, "I'm sorry we bothered you, Mr. Williams."

Reggie's dad don't bother getting up. "I told you wasn't Reggie. Maybe you should start *trusting* people, stead a thinking you right all the time."

The blonde looks around the room, examining the walls. Reggie knows what she's looking for, but she ain't going to find it. All the walls got on them is a bunch of dings and places where the paint been chipped off. Other than that, they's barren.

She says, "In the future, you should think about getting some pictures of you and your son. We could have cleared this up a long time ago."

Reggie's dad grunts, but he don't say nothing. Never going to happen. No pictures—that's the first rule Reggie and his dad live by.

"Again, I'm sorry we bothered you." She nods to Reggie, nods to the officers, and the three of them, they head for the door. Her ponytail dances as she moves.

As she walks past Reggie, he can't help himself. He grabs her wrist, right where the tan trench ends. Her skin is warm and soft. She tries to pull away, but she looks at Reggie, at his tumor, and pity fills her face—especially her deep-blue eyes.

From feeling the bones in her wrist and the way her muscles move, Reggie knows she's got an athlete's body under that coat. Even though she's about five inches shorter than Reggie, he knows in a fight he'll lose for sure.

Reggie lets go of her wrist and does his best to look sorry. "Don't mean nothing," he says. "I just wants to know what's going on."

She clears her throat. "I'm Detective Palmer." She nods at the Uniforms. "These are officers Burke—" (the muscle) "—and Routh. We got a report earlier tonight that you'd been involved in an incident."

"An incident? Where?"

"Well," she says, "it obviously wasn't you, so that doesn't matter."

Shoot. He'd so hoped to learn something. Find out who'd got wise to him.

Blondie Palmer walks past the officers and the three of them head down the hallway past Ms. Baxter's. As they go Reggie leans out into the hallway to holler, "'Bye now," but really he's watching Detective Palmer—the way she walks.

When Reggie turns round, he's staring right into the cold-dark eyes of his father. Reggie's dad bounce-walks him straight back until Reggie's pinned between the door and the beater shirt covering the rolls a fat currently making up his dad's body.

"What did you do?" his dad says.

"Shoot, man, I don't know. Been over on King Street, asking after Georgie. Someone got wise."

Reggie's dad pokes a thick finger in Reggie's chest. "I told you, leave that be." And he pokes Reggie's chest again, driving the point home.

Reggie rubs his chest where the poke left its ache. "Dang, old man. It's like you don't care none."

"Georgie's the reason we living in this hellhole. I spent all the time on him he's going to get. Somebody seen you, figured out who you are and where you live. And that sent the cops to *me*. And that ain't never going to happen again. We clear on that, boy?"

By that, Reggie knows his dad's talking about *appearance*. He's been Reggie for a long time; now he needs to become someone new.

Reggie slips past his dad, into his room, where he flops down on his mattress. It's an old mattress with holes in the top. Sometimes when Reggie sleeps, the tops of the springs come through the holes, jabbing his back and legs.

But it's under the mattress that Reggie keeps his treasure.

Two binders full a paper.

Each one a different person Reggie's been.

He flips through them, remembering.

This one's a crusty old Asian guy Reggie used to be when he and Georgie drove taxis day in and day out out by the airport.

And this here is a musclehead like that officer, Burke. Reggie used that one when he lived on his own out by the beach.

And this page is one a Reggie's favorites—a teenage cheerleader. Reggie used her when he and Georgie and their father went living the high life over east a High Street.

Yeah, she's one of Reggie's favorites. He loved cheering for the team before a big game.

Thinking about being a cheerleader starts Reggie thinking about Detective Palmer, the way she moves.

Shoot. Detective Palmer, she don't move. She *flows*.

And that's something Reggie thinks he really ought to try.

He pulls off a piece of paper and begins writing a new body for himself. As he writes, the deep chocolate color of his skin starts to fade. The stiff, short, bristly hair atop his head goes away and new smooth hair, the color a hay before harvest, grows out in its place. He makes the hair long enough to pull back into a nice ponytail, but leaves it loose so that, as he writes, he got to push the hair back over his ear to keep it out of his eyes.

The air fills with cracks and pops as his backbone shrinks. His ribcage gets smaller, leaving his skin hanging all flopsy-like.

He writes away the rest a the fat he left on his self out in the stairwell. Before tightening up the skin Reggie adds just a bit a that fat back, giving himself nice round breasts. It's been a while since Reggie last had 'em, and already he knows that nice, smooth walk he wants will have a bounce in it for awhile while he adjusts to this new body.

He keeps writing, putting in every detail he can remember 'bout Detective Palmer.

When he thinks he's getting close, Reggie checks himself out in the warped full-length mirror mounted on the back a his door. When he stands up, the baggy pants he been wearing, they fall right off.

He looks pretty funny in them man-briefs with a body that ain't got no man-parts.

Reggie makes a few adjustments, raising the butt, slimming the waist, and when he's finally happy he turns over that sheet a paper and tries to figure out what to write here.

That first side, that's easy. That's all physical.

This here side, it's *personality.*

The first line, that's going to be his new name. Reggie takes a while thinking about this, because he's got to get it right. From now on, when people call *this,* he's going to turn round to see what they want.

Reggie starts by asking himself: *What do I want with this here me?*

And the answer comes, just as he knew it would: *I wants to find Georgie.*

Well, shoot. He can't go 'round looking like no blondie white girl asking questions about her brother—not in the neighborhoods Georgie's likely to go.

Unless...

Reggie gets a truly evil idea. At the top of the page he writes: My name is Detective Trisha Palmer.

The "Trisha," that's just a guess. But Reggie fills in the rest a that page, making up all the details that he thinks would make for a good detective.

First off, she wouldn't go thinking of herself as "he."

And she'd likely be educated. A college degree.

Raised in a middle-class family. She still loves her father enough to be a daddy's girl.

Her favorite colors are pink and especially blue, because of the way it matches her eyes.

As the paper fills with text, the scratches that were once so recognizable as Reggie's writing smooth out, becoming a beautiful, flowing cursive—the handwriting of a girl so detail-oriented that, in third grade, she spent hours practicing every character, above and beyond what the teacher required, until each letter was perfect.

The identity that once masked Reggie melts away until

All that was left was Trisha Palmer.

And she was exhausted. These changes always took so much out of her. It would be several hours before she'd be ready to even write in small changes.

She hoped what Reggie had done would be good enough.

She gazed around the room, seeing it with fresh eyes. The dingy mattress, uncomfortable against her tush, stained with dark reds and yellows from years of use before she and her father had even moved in. Sparsely decorated walls—unframed posters of sports teams, mostly, with corners curling where the tape holding them down had dried and cracked.

The one little table in the corner, on which lay the only possession Trisha would actually miss: a glass football, engraved with *Grover Cleveland High School—State Champions 2003*. The year she'd been a cheerleader and Georgie (then called Tyson) had been the star running back on the team.

Georgie's trophy.

The only piece of him she still had left.

No way she could take that with her, but her father knew how important it was to her. He'd keep it safe.

She stood up, examining herself in the mirror. Overall, she felt pleased with the result. Oh, she was far from perfect. *Far* from it. But with a few written words—after she'd rested—she could fix the problem areas.

Now... time to find some decent clothes.

Trisha pulled on Reggie's old closet door. It refused to open all the way and, when she tried to force it, the spring-loaded pin holding it in place snapped and the door fell.

She yelped and tried to catch it, but it was no use. The closet door slammed into the wall, leaving a terrific gash where its corner carved through the wallboard.

"The hell?" her father called from the other room, and within a few moments he burst through the door. When he saw her, his eyes practically bulged from his head.

"Hi, Daddy," she said. "My name is Trisha."

"Hell no." Her father waddled forward, trying to intimidate her. "You ain't doing this to me."

She held her ground, but looked down, suddenly embarrassed by herself. She—Reggie—had broken the second rule that had kept them safe for so many years: *Never duplicate someone completely.* In the past she'd always used pieces of people—eyes from a waitress who'd been kind to her; the chin of an actor she admired. This was the first time she'd copied someone whole cloth.

Daddy was right to be angry. They'd been through a lot together, she and her father. The sacrifices he'd made for her... some of them were things she couldn't imagine doing herself. She'd never loved anyone that much.

Except maybe Georgie.

Georgie had made it clear that he didn't like the way they were living—at the time they'd been a refugee family from Cambodia. She guessed they'd stayed too long in the ritzy part of the city before that. Georgie had gotten too used to wealth; the transition to poverty had been too hard on him.

So, one day, without even saying "goodbye," Georgie disappeared, taking the balance in their savings account with him. Seventy years of savings among the three of them—sixty years for Daddy alone before that.

Living the easy life had been Daddy's idea. A way to reward his children for years of hard work. If he'd known what it would do to Georgie, her father would never have done it. And now her father seemed to despise Georgie.

And she...

She couldn't forget her twin. She never would. She had to at least *know* that he was okay.

No matter what.

But her father was right—it was unfair of her to do this to him. She would never bring her family back together again. She knew that.

No, finding her brother was something she had to do for her own peace of mind.

Trisha felt stubbornness creep into her face as she raised her head. "You're right, Daddy. I won't do this to you."

"Damn right."

"But I *will* do this. For me."

Her father started to shake his head, but she cut him off with a glance before he could speak.

Fierce determination. That's what defined Trisha Palmer.

She'd said so right on that piece of paper that now made the latest page in her binder.

Her father cursed her several times, but he knew she'd made up her mind. Finally he could do nothing more that wrap his big, heavy arms around her and hold her close.

He hadn't showered in days, judging from the smell. At first that bothered her. And then she realized how *tightly* he held her, the way it made it hard for her to breathe.

And she knew. He wasn't wishing her luck. He was saying goodbye.

Tears began swelling in her eyes, and she returned the hug as hard as she could.

"Daddy, I—"

"Hush now," he said, stroking the back of her head. "I knew this day was coming. Got a little cash-money saved away."

"No. No, I couldn't. You need it more than—"

He laughed—a great belly shaker that nearly lifted her off the ground every time his stomach shook.

"Don't be a fool, child. Look at you. You think Reggie got any clothes going to fit you right? And I will *not* have my baby living on the street. Not when I can do something about it, no sir."

The tears came, stronger than before. Her daddy wiped them away with a thick, clumsy thumb. "Hush," he said. "Now you come with me. I think I got some leftover clothes from a few years back when I was a stripper. Nothing showy, mind you. Got rid a all them stage clothes. Sides, any man goes looking after my baby girl with wolf's eyes, I going to take him *out*."

Trisha waited until four-thirty the next morning before leaving the projects. By then it was quiet. Even the dealers and the prostitutes had stumbled home. Anyone still awake would at least be tired—too tired to pay much attention to a white girl walking alone down one of the most dangerous streets in the city.

She hoped.

She took a quick glance back and forth down the empty hallway. Grime covered everything. How had she managed to live here this long?

She ducked back inside her father's apartment and took one final inventory of herself before venturing out. She double-checked the drawstring on her sweats and made sure the roll of cash her father had given her still rested firmly in the bottom of her sweatpants pocket. Then she adjusted (yet again) the strap on the Victoria's Secret one-size-too-big bra Daddy had found among his "leftovers." How annoying. A replacement bra would be among the first things Trisha would buy—right after she bought shoes. For now she had to make do with Reggie's tennies. Her feet slid around inside them with every step she took. It would be impossible to run. She offered a little prayer, asking that running wouldn't be necessary.

The fatigue from her transformation still wore deep on her. She felt it in her bones. Priority one would be getting to the business district—somewhere she didn't stick out so much—to find a hotel. Trisha felt like she could sleep for days.

She checked her ponytail, making sure it was securely held in place, before pulling the black hoodie up around her head.

Her father caught the hood halfway up and turned Trisha around. She saw the look in his eyes and felt the tears begin to well up again. She fought them back, still tasting the salt from her last bout of weeping. Not again. Not this time.

She'd done this before. As a bodybuilder at the beach, she'd been on her own. She knew she could do it.

But this time felt different.

Before, it had been...well, it had been *practice*. She'd had to know if she was ready to face the world alone.

And she had been. She'd come through it just fine.

This time...

She finished the thought aloud. "This time it's for real, isn't it?"

Her father held her face firmly between his thick, meaty palms and touched his forehead to hers. She felt the grit of dried sweat on his skin. She felt the heat of his body. She felt the *reality* of him flood her head—

And she *saw*.

Saw him as a child. A little boy in shorts chasing after a dog named Ryan.

Saw him as a Chinese man slaving away on the railroad lines.

Saw him as a nurse in the hospitals during World War One, tending to the injured.

Over and over again, she saw him in all his incarnations—and especially strong came the vision of her father as a young woman, deciding the time was right to write a child into his life—and then the surprise and joy that came when he discovered he was having not just one child, but two.

And then the disappointment and anger of her father as a middle-aged fry cook, as Georgie rattled off the list of complaints of every way their father had "wronged" him, when all along their father had been trying to do the best he could for his children.

As the vision faded, Trisha heard her father—her *daddy*—say one last thing: "I am now and always have been proud of you. Don't worry none about me. When I'm ready to move on, I'll come find you."

Trisha shifted her weight back and forth, trying to find a comfortable spot on the hard wooden bench in the booth at Dezzi's Coffee. The bitter aroma of roasting beans filled the air. She took a sip of Dezzi's Special Blend and grimaced as the flavor bit back and the heat numbed the roof of her mouth.

Dezzi's Coffee sat directly opposite the Second Precinct building. And Trisha sat there, in the open, wearing her new tan trench coat, white blouse and black pants, daring anyone—no, *hoping* someone—would see her and recognize her as Detective Palmer.

This was among the stupider things she'd tried.

Trisha wondered if *anyone* had ever tried looking up all the Palmers in the greater metropolitan area. She'd spent weeks doing just that. *Weeks.* Camping out at their residences. Smiling and saying "Hello" to neighbors. Looking for any sign of recognition.

Pointless.

Detective Palmer, naturally, wasn't listed in any of the phone directories.

As she sipped her coffee Trisha cast glances across the street at the police station, hoping to catch even a glimpse of blonde hair.

Actually walking into the station was more foolish than Trisha dared try. If she'd gone in while the *real* Detective Palmer was there—if they actually ran into each other... There's no possible way to explain that.

She'd just finished her second cup and was about to give up and move on to the next station house when a short little woman in a beige skirt with black hair waved at her.

"Janet! Hi!" the woman said.

Trisha had a *Who? Me?* moment before the realization struck— *Janet.* Detective Palmer's first name was Janet.

The excitement of the moment left Trisha as quickly as it had arrived. *Crap. Someone thinks I'm Detective Palmer. Now what do I do?*

"Hey," Trisha said. "Long time."

The woman approached the booth with a steaming cup nestled between both hands. Trisha hoped Detective Palmer and the woman didn't know each other well.

"No kidding," the woman said. "What are you doing over here? Don't tell me you and Hurley are seeing each other again?"

Trisha did her best to look guilty—not that difficult considering the circumstances. "I cannot tell a lie," she said.

A look crossed the little woman's face that seemed to say, *You can do better than Hurley.* She seemed to realize what she'd done because she fumbled with the cup for a moment and then changed the conversation completely.

"You ever get what you needed on that Weevil's Club case?"

Weevil's Club? That was over on King Street—the neighborhood Reggie had been in, asking questions about Georgie. The neighborhood where someone had blown Reggie's disguise and made this whole stint as Trisha Palmer necessary.

Now *that* was a lead.

"Not yet," Trisha told the woman. "But I have a hunch something's about to break open."

Trisha couldn't imagine a darker place than The Weevil's Club—and it was still the middle of the day. The club itself was in the basement of an old brick three-story. Uneven stairs led down through a shadowy doorway. Inside, yes, the lights were dim, but, on top of that, mud seemed to coat the outside of every gutter-level window. The oppressive music blaring through the speakers overhead drowned out any conversation.

Weevil himself, a tattooed giant of a man, washed glasses behind the bar with a rag that seriously needed replacement.

Even though the city had long ago passed a ban on indoor smoking, Weevil's stunk with the combination of the fresh smoke that clung to its patrons and the rancid odor that had permeated the walls before the ban went into effect.

Weevil saw her and glared. Trisha fought back a shudder.

He motioned with his head toward a doorway next to the bar. Trisha followed him through it.

Weevil's office was nicer than the club itself, but that wasn't saying much. The door muffled the music, except for the ever-present repetitive throb of the base line. Bare energy-efficient light bulbs overhead, screwed into dingy sockets, cast a fluorescent-blue haze on mangy carpeting and wood-paneled walls.

A pine-scented candle burned away on Weevil's desk, but even that couldn't cut the rancid smoke flavor of the air by much.

Weevil leaned against a cluttered desk with arms folded. "You got it?" he said.

Trisha had done it again—obviously she was *supposed* to know what he was talking about. Time to fake it again.

"No," she said. "Not yet."

Weevil turned his back on her. "Then we got nothing to say, Detective. You can see yourself out."

Trisha stepped forward, feeling the fierce determination swelling in her chest. The police had come for her, back before her change. And something had happened *here*—the same neighborhood she'd been in, asking about Georgie. She was pretty sure Weevil knew what connected those two things.

But what could she say? *Hi. I'm not really Detective Palmer. I used to be a black kid.* He'd never believe it.

But she had to say something. He had already gathered a few papers from a filing cabinet and was now herding her toward the door, back into the club where the music would drown out anything she tried to say.

She opened her mouth and the words came out before she knew what they were. "Fat Reggie," she said.

Weevil froze. An evil little smile crept into the corners of his mouth.

"You finally tracked him down, eh? What did that little bastard have to say for himself?"

"Said he was innocent."

"Naturally."

"I believe him," Trisha said.

The little muscle just below Weevil's eye began to twitch. "You look here, Detective. I don't care what you think of me. I don't. You get your shit together and get your search warrant. You come back here with that and I'll play nice—give you a tour of the whole joint. But that fat little runt stole my football trophy from me. Got half a dozen witnesses say so—including one of The City's Finest. He stole it, and I want it back."

Trisha's mind churned. Witnesses? As Reggie she'd been up and down this street, asking about her brother. It was the kind of neighborhood that attracted Georgie—though she couldn't pretend to understand why—but she'd never stepped foot in Weevil's until that afternoon.

And *his* trophy? *His?*

She took a step toward Weevil, closing the space between them, and placed her hand on the rough stubble of his face.

"Look, lady, I—"

Before he could pull away she went up on her tiptoes and touched her head to his.

If she was wrong and this wasn't Georgie, she'd probably just invited him to rape her.

Weevil didn't resist her. He closed his eyes, allowing the essence of himself to flow between them.

And she *saw.*

Saw Georgie standing up to their mother as a fry cook, petulant and eager to face the world on his own terms. Felt the oppression Georgie believed their mother placed on him.

Saw him change himself into the appearance of a bank teller at the local branch—he'd been watching her for weeks, flirting with her for days. A silly girl who'd accidentally mentioned that the Facebook password she'd just given him was the same password she used *everywhere* so that she never had to remember anything.

Saw him use the girl's appearance to access their father's savings—their *family's* savings—draining the whole account.

Saw him as a forty-year-old office worker, removing her heels to relieve her sore feet, dreaming of the end of the workday where she would lavish a younger admirer with the finest wine, dinner at a four-star restaurant, and a passionate night in a luxury suite.

Saw him as a teenage boy, out on the street, wondering what had happened to all of his money.

Saw that boy admiring Weevil—Weevil's presence, his command of the neighborhood. Saw him sneaking after Weevil late at night when Weevil resupplied his dealers and paid off corrupt government officials.

Saw that boy *kill* Weevil. Brutally. Slashing Weevil's throat and *enjoying* the feel of the blood splattering that boy's face.

Saw that boy *become* Weevil. Writing himself into Weevil's world. Taking over the drug operation. Expanding it. With a fierce determination to conquer—to be free forever from the oppression of poverty. To rule over his domain.

No matter the cost.

Trisha tried to force herself away, but the vision kept coming. Weevil, strangling a pimp. Taking over the prostitution in this part of the city. Weevil, hiring thugs from the worst of the city's gangs. Weevil, threatening the son of a city councilwoman if she didn't change her vote on upcoming ordinances.

Weevil, staring down the *real* Detective Janet Palmer, daring her to come at him with everything she had. Knowing that she would. And not caring because he knew he could get away with it.

The horror of it all rocked Trisha to the core. Her brother had done terrible, *terrible* things.

And then she saw Weevil, getting word of some punk-ass fat kid traipsing up and down King Street, asking if anybody had seen his brother Georgie.

And Weevil had made one last transformation—just for one day. Just long enough to be ready to change back.

Weevil as Fat Reggie, bursting from the office behind the bar, holding tight to a water bottle nestled in the folds of his jacket so no one could see, dashing out into the cool evening, into the crowds, and into a side alley where he wrote himself back into Weevil and called the cops to report a robbery at his club.

The vision broke and Trisha pulled away only to see a look of smug self-satisfaction on her brother's face.

"You came," he said. "I knew you'd get my message."

Goosebumps prickled along Trisha's arms, and she pulled her coat tightly closed around her to stave off the chill. Weevil didn't keep his office *that* cold, but everything she'd just witnessed about the way her brother spent the last several months made her shiver.

She sank back into the soft leather of an oversized chair. She supposed it was comfortable, but right now Trisha didn't think she'd ever be comfortable again.

The only thing she'd wanted—her brother—had been found, and with that, and with the discovery of who he *really* was, her fierce determination faded away and left her utterly alone.

The door opened, briefly inviting that dreadful music, and slammed again as Weevil returned with a tumbler full of some kind of beer that looked and smelled like piss.

He offered it to her. "Put hair on your chest."

"Did you really just say that?"

"What?"

Trisha looked at her chest and back to her brother, who shrugged and tried to hand it to her again.

"I think I'd throw up," she said.

He shrugged again. "Best beer on the planet."

"No."

Weevil took a big swallow and wiped his mouth with the back of his giant, hairy arm.

"Good to see you, sis."

"I can't say the same."

"Oh come on. Tell me you weren't sick of being that stupid retard."

Trisha prickled. "Don't say that."

"Okay. Halfwit. Better?"

Last year, before Georgie ran away, Trisha had loved this kind of banter. They could go at it for hours, making circular little arguments back and forth at each other, changing a word here and there to give different contexts to what the other had said.

Knowing what Georgie had become, it grated at her. She'd had enough.

"What are you doing here, Georgie?"

"Weevil."

"No," she said. "You're not."

"But I am. I run this part of the city. I got three guys within earshot'll say I'm the boss. Thirty more just a couple steps down the chain. I got policemen in my pocket. Hell, you saw the vision. You know exactly who I am."

"If you're Weevil, then my brother is dead."

He snorted and tried to stroke the side of her face. She pulled away.

"I am Weevil *and* your brother," he said. "That's the difference between you and me, sis. You're still figuring out who you're meant to be. Me, I found it. Weevil is *exactly* who I'm supposed to be."

"I don't think the real Weevil feels that way."

"Don't you get acting all high-and-mighty on me, sis. I saw your life at the same time you saw mine. Geez, all that time stuck in the body of Fat Reggie...How'd you do it? We're the lucky ones, sis. We're not trapped by our genetics. We just have to find who we're meant to be and we can be it. I mean, look at you. Detective Palmer? Niiiice choice. How'd ya think she'd feel knowing—"

A touch of pure evil entered Weevil's eyes.

"What?" asked Trisha.

"Nothing," he said, but he turned to his desk and, after picking up his phone, he dialed a few numbers and he whispered a few words Trisha couldn't quite make out.

When he put down the phone Weevil changed the subject entirely. "How's dad? What's he calling himself these days, anyway?"

The question caught Trisha unexpectedly. She'd become Fat Reggie shortly before her father made the transition to that last phase of their lives together. She struggled with the fractured memories left over from Reggie and finally came up with the title on the sheet her father had written up for that shift: *I am Reggie's Father.*

Oh.

The tears started welling up in her eyes all over again. He'd sacrificed his entire identity after Georgie had left—given up *everything*—so that he could be her father. Nothing more.

But that title suddenly meant *everything* to her. She wanted nothing more in that moment than to leave Weevil to whatever he had planned and go back home. To hold her daddy just one more time and tell him that she loved him.

Trisha realized that Weevil was watching her, and she snuffed away her runny nose and wiped the tears out of her eyes.

"I thought so," he said. "Now, sister dear. I have a plan. And you're going to help me. Because if you don't, I will see to it that our father suffers. Greatly."

Trisha nodded and sniffed. "What do you need me to do?"

Weevil smiled. "It starts with the murder and replacement of Detective Janet Palmer."

Trisha jumped out of the chair and dove at her brother. Her fingernails dug at his face leaving long claw marks from his eyes down into the scruff of his beard. She kicked. She fought.

She lost the fight.

Weevil pinned her to the ground, hands held behind her back. His knee planted itself into her kidney and he pushed down with all his weight until she screamed for mercy.

It took two thugs to help Weevil keep her under control. As

they bound her hands and feet Weevil pressed his hand against the scratch she'd left on his face. He winced and pulled his hand back, staring at the lines of blood that ran down his fingers and across his palm.

As the thugs carried Trisha from the room, she heard Weevil yell after her. "Just for that, *Ms. Palmer*. Just for that I'm bringing him *here*. You'll watch me break him. One bone at a time. I'll cut off an inch of his flesh every time you *blink* and I don't give you permission first. You hear me? You think on that, *Ms. Palmer*. *You think on that.*"

Trisha's body bounced as the thugs carried her farther back into the depths of Weevil's Club. In the occasional overhead light she searched the faces of the two thugs.

One of them she recognized but, from her current perspective, being carried upside down between the two of them, she couldn't quite place. Only once they dumped her and she got a chance to orient herself did she recognize him—or, rather, the part of her that had been Reggie recognized him: Uniform Musclehead. Officer Burke.

Weevil gave strict instructions that Trisha was to be searched *thoroughly* before they locked her in that empty back room. "Leave nothing she can write with," he said.

And Burke knew how to be *very* thorough. By the time he was done Trisha had been completely violated.

At last they dumped her, bound and gagged, on a cold cement floor in an empty storage room. She heard the door close and lock behind her.

And she wept.

Everything she *thought* went into forming the perfect character for Detective Palmer—the fierce determination, the perfectionism, *everything*—cried out at Trisha demanding to know where she had gone wrong. If all these things were supposed to make her good at being a policewoman, how did she get *here* where *everything* was broken?

And, adding insult to injury, if she was such a tough woman, why had she been crying *so friggin' much*? Her eyes stung. Her throat felt tight and tired. Her nose ran.

She grew angry at herself—at what she had become and what she had allowed to happen and, above all, at her tears, and she set herself a goal. One thing to focus her fierce determination on.

Escape.

She found that her hand could *almost* slip through the cords they'd tied her wrists with. Only the thumb kept her hands bound.

If only she could *write* herself a smaller hand.

But there was nothing to write on. Her fingernails couldn't even scratch at the cement.

And if she pulled any harder she was likely to—

Break.

Her.

Thumb.

She could. She could break her thumb. If she pulled hard enough... It would hurt in ways she couldn't possibly imagine, but her fierce determination kicked in and she *knew* it was possible.

She closed her eyes. She arched her back. She bit into the cotton of her gag as hard as she could.

She *puuulllllllllleeed*.

Crack!

The pain smothered her. Her vision blurred and filled with white snow. She gasped and fought for each breath.

But her hand—

—came *free!*

When she looked at her hand the pain returned, fresh and new. The thumb dangled limply below an open wound, through which a shard of bone jutted. Blood ran down the front of her hand, pooling on the cement.

She closed her eyes and took several deep breaths.

The past several hours had convinced Trisha of one thing: She was *not* the person who could stop her brother. She was soft. Stopping her brother required someone cold.

No. Trisha Palmer was not that person.

But she could *become* that person.

She dipped her finger in her own warm blood, then, rubbing her finger across the coarse surface of the cement floor, she began to write.

The city is a cold place. Look in the eyes of the people, you'll see it for yourself.

When the days get long and temperatures go up, tempers go up, too. There ain't no howdy-doo to your neighbor. No, you'd sooner beat him over the head than have to listen to another note of what he calls music.

Arguments spring up over the littlest details. Need to borrow a cup of sugar? What? You blew it all on weed and now you can't afford to make little Timmy cookies?

Serves you right.

Go away.

And that's just the regular folks.

Try walking into a place like King Street on a hot summer night when "sweltering" doesn't even begin to cover the way the neighborhood feels. See what you get then.

But there's always some busybody, thinks it's okay to be a good neighbor. Thinks it's good to do the right thing.

If they're not careful, they'll end up in a world of hurt.

People like that need somebody wise to the ways of the city. Somebody who can smell the trouble they're about to step in before it messes up their nice new shoes.

You got troubles? Who doesn't. But if you ask nice, maybe you can find somebody willing to help a fella out.

Trevor Nichols didn't hesitate when the goons opened the door of the cellar he'd been stashed in. He jumped and he jumped hard. Drove the leftover piece of Trisha's thumb-bone into the throat of the big muscleheaded turd who'd touched that poor woman where no man has a right to go without her permission. Drove his knee into the other goon's stomach and twist-broke his neck while meathead gurgled out the last of his life on the floor.

Just another day at the office.

He borrowed the clothes from the second goon—less blood; besides he don't need them no more—and swapped them for the ladies' clothes he'd been wearing. Just a good thing nobody saw him dressed like that. One thing Trevor had never been able to stomach was embarrassment.

Meathead had a pea-shooter tucked away in the back of his waistband. A Smithfield Armory nine mil. Very nice. Trevor checked the magazine—full—and pulled back on the slide, chambering a round.

He worked his way back through the hallways behind Weevil's Club, listening to the music pounding away. People who listen to that need to get their ears cleaned. Hell, people at a place like Weevil's on a Friday night need to get *a life*. Get out of the city. Breathe some fresh air once in a while. It does wonders.

He just hoped the music was loud enough to cover the racket he was about to make.

At the back door to Weevil's office he paused, gun held at the ready. He opened the door just a crack and peeked inside.

Janet Palmer crouched uncomfortably in the oversized leather chair in front of Weevil's desk. Why uncomfortably? It's a little hard to relax when a man the size of Weevil's holding a gun on you.

"Honestly," he was saying, "you *should* be dead already. But I had to see your face when you meet my sister."

Janet didn't shrink at all in the face of Weevil's threats. Oh, she was nervous—who wouldn't be? But she wasn't backing down. Trevor admired that in a woman.

"This shouldn't be taking so long," Weevil said, glancing toward the door. Trevor ducked out of sight, but it was too late.

"Is that you, sister dear? Come out, come out, wherever you are."

Trevor steeled himself, taking a deep breath. No sign of his old man. Trevor sincerely hoped they hadn't got to his father already.

"Let me put it this way," Weevil said. "Come out right now, or I kill her right now."

Trevor pushed the door open and strolled in as if he owned the joint. He nodded to acknowledge Detective Palmer, but kept his pea-shooter trained on Weevil.

"Your *sister*?" said Janet.

"She has been a naughty girl," said Weevil, keeping his gun on Janet. "We're going to have a nice long visit after this—just you, me...and our dear dad." The look on Weevil's face could kill puppies.

"You found him already?" said Trevor.

"Not yet. But we will. So nice to have someone you care about, unlike Miss Palmer here. She's all alone. No one to miss her when she's gone."

Trevor took a step forward; his finger tightened on the trigger.

"You won't do it," said Weevil. "I saw your life just like you saw mine. Leaving dad all alone to come find me. Tsk-tsk, Trisha."

"Trevor."

"Whatever—the point is, we're supposed to do this together."

Memories. Jumped out of nowhere. Trevor's mind filled with memories.

A cheerleader and her brother, celebrating a state championship after the big game.

Two old wizened cab drivers playing checkers in the station after a shift.

Two hungry Cambodian boys, trading each other food in the line at the shelter.

Sisters giggling at the naughty gag gifts at a friend's bachelorette party.

Trevor lowered the gun, just a fraction of an inch.

Weevil pulled the trigger. Red mist exploded from Janet's chest.

Trevor drilled him. Two to the chest. One to the head. Right between the eyes.

It was over.

But for the first time, he'd hesitated. He'd been too slow.

And Trevor was left facing the one emotion he dealt with worse than embarrassment.

Guilt.

Trevor leaned against Weevil's desk, watching the lifeblood trickle from the two dead bodies.

He did not know what to do.

There was maybe only one person who would.

He picked up the phone on Weevil's desk, fumbling with the buttons until he found one that gave him a dial tone, and he called old Ms. Baxter. His father didn't have a phone. Ms. Baxter would have to do.

She answered on the third ring.

"Hello? Ms. Baxter? I'm sorry to bother you, ma'am, but I'm—" How could he explain it? He couldn't. All he could do was ask for his father—by the name his father had chosen for himself. "I'm trying to find Reggie's dad."

There was a long pause and Ms. Baxter said, "I'm sorry. Them Williams boys done moved out. They gone, both of them, as of a couple weeks ago."

The news shook Trevor deeper than he thought possible. His breath caught and he swallowed to keep his emotions in check. "He moved out, did he? Well good for him. Best of luck to them both."

Trevor hunted the back rooms of Weevil's Club until he discovered a janitorial closet. There, among the foul smelling chemicals, he found a bucket, some bleach, and some mops and brushes.

With these in tow, he returned to the cellar where Trisha had become Trevor.

He read the words he'd written.

This was *not* who he wanted to be. But who was he? Weevil had been right about one thing—they weren't bound by genetics. They really could become anyone they wanted to.

The only thing Trevor knew for sure was that he did *not* want to be Trevor Nichols.

Trevor Nichols had a part to play, but his part was over.

Trevor took the bleach and the brushes and, for the first time in his life, erased the words that had created him.

Weevil's office stank like the sewers of hell when Trevor finally returned. His fingers stung from the bleach. His eyes burned from the fumes. But the smell of smoke and gunpowder and death overpowered everything.

Trevor pitied that little pine-scented candle. It was doing the best it could against hopeless odds.

But Trevor felt he owed a moment of respect to Janet Palmer. She had put him on this road, and he had to believe that some good had come of it.

And if Weevil was telling the truth, Janet didn't have anyone else who would mourn her loss. That didn't seem right.

The more Trevor thought about it, the more he thought this steel-willed woman deserved more than that. Someone needed to know who she was. Someone needed to tell her story to the world.

He fished through her pockets until he found her wallet and badge.

Forty-seventh Precinct. No wonder Trisha hadn't been able to find her.

And there, on her driver's license, was her address.

Impulsively, Trevor leaned her body forward and checked the back of the chair. The bullet had gone completely through Janet's body, but not through the chair itself.

With a knife from Weevil's desk Trevor cut through the leather and padding until he found the wooden frame.

There it was. The bullet that killed Janet Palmer.

He cut it out of the frame and put it in his pocket. One last memorial to take with him.

As he opened the door to the main part of the Club, Trevor saw the lowlife scum who populated the booths and tables, who played pool with stolen money. He saw dealers selling hash and weed to the poor idiots who didn't know to do any better with their lives.

The utter hopelessness Weevil's inspired in him drove Trevor to make one final decision. He took some of the papers from Weevil's desk and held them in the flickering flame of the pine-scented candle.

Once they were going, he dropped some in the paper-filled trash can, put others in the filing cabinet. He spread the flames to everything that could catch fire until his lungs burned from the smoke and he could barely see to make it to the entrance.

When the fire alarm went off, Trevor escaped into the street with the rest of the crowd.

Janet Palmer lived in a quaint little red-brick home in the suburbs just east of the city. It wasn't a rich neighborhood, but it was a long way from the atmosphere of the city.

It was dark. And quiet always came with darkness to a place like this. Still, Trevor doubted it got much louder during the day.

Trevor smelled the air. He could live in a place like this.

The third key on her key chain opened the front door. The little entryway smelled of potpourri. His steps echoed off the slate gray linoleum. "Hello? Anyone here?"

No answer.

Pictures on the walls showed Janet at different stages of her life. Pigtails. Braces. Proms and graduations.

In each photo Janet was surrounded by a different family.

Foster care.

Trevor's impression of Janet grew by leaps and bounds—she'd been able to come out of the system and end up a decent person, trying to make the world a better place.

The closets in her room, filled with suitable and attractive clothing. Her bed, neat and tidy. Covered with pillows and a few stuffed animals. Her drawers held sports gear and workout clothing.

MICHAEL TALBOT

Trevor wondered what it would feel like to actually *work* for a body instead of simply writing one into existence.

Janet had turned her guest bedroom into a library. She read mysteries.

Appropriate.

But the real treasure was Janet's journals. Two shelves full, volume after volume. Janet kept a detailed record of every event in her life.

Trevor sat down, cross-legged on the floor, and began to read.

September 28, 1992
Mom is helping me write this. Today was my first day of third grade. Mom says I should write where I've been and to write my dreams.

Trevor kept reading. He read of her parents' death in an automobile accident. He read of her abuse within the foster system. The policeman who had helped her and who had arrested the foster father who'd perpetrated the abuse.

He read of her hopes for adoption being dashed over and over again. He read of the joy she felt when she stood up to the class bully in eighth grade. Of her first crush. Of her heartbreak when her fiancé died during military training exercises. He read of friends made and friends lost. Of triumph and success in the face of crushing defeat.

When he finished, he *knew.*

His whole life—excepting maybe these past few weeks—it amounted to nothing. A figure, hiding in the shadows, afraid to live for fear of being discovered as the unique creature that he was.

Janet Palmer—she'd *lived.*

And Trevor was extremely jealous.

He wanted *that.* He wanted to come home, the way Janet did at the end of every day, knowing he was working to make a difference. To bring order to the face of the chaos in the world around him.

And it was completely unfair of the world to leave a wretched creature like him alive and remove the Janet Palmers of the world from their rightful place.

Well, that was something Trevor could do something about.

He found a pencil in one of Janet's desk drawers.

At the beginning of the first volume, at the top of the page, in big bold letters Trevor wrote: *This is my history.*

And, writing lightly so as not to smudge a single letter of her hand-written journals, he began to trace every word.

The sun rose and set. The phone rang and went unanswered. Trevor continued to trace.

Every.

Word.

The last entry was dated July twenty-seventh. Three days ago.

And when, at last

I finished writing, I looked at myself in the mirror. My blonde hair popped out at odd angles from the sides of my head, a mess of snarls. My eyes, bloodshot and tired.

But I recognized my reflection. And I liked who I'd become.

Only one thing was left to do.

I removed the bullet from Trevor's pocket and, lying on my back, I placed the bullet on my stomach. With the pencil I wrote an entry for today.

July 30, 2013
I don't think it's fatal, but I've been shot.

In a flash of pain the bullet disappeared into my stomach.

I awoke in the hospital. Tubes and wires sprouted from my stomach and arms. I heard the steady blip-blip-blip of the heart rate monitor.

Chief Leonart smiled at me from the corner of the room.

I tried to answer him, but my throat felt as if I'd been eating sawdust and my nose felt as if it were under attack from the hospital disinfectants—they always remind me of the Nixons' place back when they were my foster family.

A little nurse with red hair popped in and said, "Oh good, you're awake!"

The chief gave me all kinds of crap about leaving Weevil's after getting shot. I didn't know what to tell him. My memory of the whole thing is still pretty shaky, to tell you the truth.

I just remember having this *need* to get home. To be somewhere I belonged.

One weird thing though.

After the chief and some of the guys from Vice had popped in and left, I was left alone with that little nurse.

She peered at me through some really thick glasses and did the strangest thing—

She held the sides of my face and put her forehead to mine.

I have no idea what that was about, but it creeped me out a little.

She apologized, but she had the saddest look on her face.

I haven't seen her since.

Beneath the Surface of Two Kills

written by

Shauna O'Meara

illustrated by

CASSANDRE BOLAN

ABOUT THE AUTHOR

Hailing from the parched wheat belt country of Western Australia, Shauna O'Meara's childhood was spent roaming rugged, hilly paddocks and the seasonal river below her home with her dogs, concocting wild fugitive stories along the way.

Her first fictional loves were Richard Adams' Watership Down, *Brian Jacques'* Redwall, *and Isobelle Carmody's* Obernewtyn, *as well as the artwork and storytelling of early Disney films and 1980s and '90s cartoons.*

Shauna earned a university degree in veterinary medicine and, following a stint in commercial practice, found career fulfillment working with and treating shelter animals. When she is not vetting, Shauna spends her time writing and creating art.

Shauna's Writers of the Future win is her first professional story sale and second short story publication.

She recently completed the artwork for a short comic commissioned by Midnight Echo *magazine and has contributed the cover and interior art to several Australian speculative fiction anthologies.*

She has just completed her first novel—a science fiction crime novel set in a post-global-warming America—and has a head full of tales just waiting to be committed to print. She is avidly following the exciting storytelling currently going on in the world of graphic novels and aspires to one day write and draw one of her own.

ABOUT THE ILLUSTRATOR

Cassandre Bolan is a quirky artist who always mismatches her socks. She spends literally every waking moment doing illustration and concept art, is obsessed with mythology and feminism and has a wicked jasmine tea addiction.

Cassandre recently moved back to the United States after seven years living in the international city of Dubai. She grew up as an Army brat, traveling across the Middle East and the US, doodling and reading fantasy novels as she went.

Shortly after graduating from Pennsylvania State University with a BFA in painting and drawing and a minor in art history, she realized that fine art was not the career for her and has been teaching herself illustration and digital painting ever since!

Cassandre is fighting tooth and nail to develop a career in concept art and fantasy illustration, mostly because it's the only way that she will be able to paint all day, every day, but also because it's her little way of trying to change the way that the world thinks of women.

At the moment she is getting ready to launch a new personal art series that shakes up gender archetypes in mythology to take the science fiction and fantasy industry by storm!

Rabidly excited about painting these strong female characters, Cassandre hopes to take on more work like this from clients in the future.

Beneath the Surface of Two Kills

No one knows these mountains like I do. The thick mists cling to the valley floors and obscure the high peaks, creating a ghost realm where islands of rock and battered vegetation drift, seemingly free of all moorings. The visibility alters by the moment, and sometimes it seems I am navigating as much by feel and memory as I am by sight and stars. I creak with oilcloth, the chink of traps. My quiver rustles near my ear, accompanying the wooden percussion of the bow and rifle hanging down my spine.

I come for the wargyu. You'll remember their spiral horns from the picture books. You'll have seen their blue-striped pelts, moth-eaten behind museum glass. You'll have heard that they still exist in remote parts like this, grainy images turning up in the news.

Before you berate me, I am no poacher out for a greedy skin. Were I a fame-finder, I would have brought my camera instead of my bow. I am no thrill seeker, either. I would rather be home by a popping fire than traipsing these desolate peaks. I am merely fulfilling a court order.

I'll admit it was clever of him to think of it. The wargyu walks that fine line between extinction and rarity. My quest for the *Last Meal of His Choosing* will buy him time; perhaps time enough for the capital laws to convert to those of leniency.

A thin stream of rocks showers from one of the cliffs nearby.

They're obscured by the mist, but I know the rocks fall far and bounce high, for there is time between the sharp impacts of stone on stone. The animal that dislodged them is hidden from sight. It could be anything: an ice-eating rootoola; a julmaro negotiating the mountain fissures with its curious, rocking gait; the wargyu I seek; even an entirely new species.

I push on, feel myself descend, the loose chunks of schist becoming increasingly shifty underfoot. The icy air is thick, hard to breathe. I am entering a valley and even though all about me is sparkling whiteness, I sense the press of cliffs to either side by the resonance of my tread. With nothing to catch my eye, nothing to do but carefully place each footstep on the uncertain ground, my mind wanders.

I wonder how he chose her. On the news they said it was random, but nothing is ever truly random. She must have given off *something*. Something that promised sport, titillation or some other reaction he craved. Something that made him select *her* after sliding his eyes past God knows how many pretty heads.

Had it been a flick of her hair? Had it been the briefest of glances across a room, a fleeting connection of the eyes? Had she excused herself in a doorway? Held a lift for him? Had she been rude, earning his ire? Had she done a kindness, triggering his infatuation?

The land rises marginally and the mist shifts. I discover scats among the stones. I crumble them through my fingers. They are dry, packed with pine needles and the glittering carapaces of digested insects.

Wargyu.

My eyes dart upward to the black stone ledges the fickle fog has momentarily revealed. Through the whiteness they loom like coal barges, but no animal stands atop their decks.

I set a trap among the stones, close to the scats. The creature passed this way once and it will do so again, for there is nothing so habit-forming in an animal accustomed to being hunted than a recollection of safe passage. It's a cruel trap with jagged teeth and weighted springs. It may even be enough to sever a leg.

It matters not. I am not here to fetch back a perfect hide or win any welfare awards. If anything, I'll need the animal to cry out if I am to find this fissure again and make my claim.

I take note of my surroundings, preparing to move on. Slivers of shale slither down a cliff face farther along the chasm, and I glimpse a creature outlined against the pallid sky watching me: a silhouette with the long delicate lines of a porcelain figurine, something that should be protected behind glass, cushioned upon a circle of felt.

Wargyu.

My heart bounds. It's the first sighting in months; proof I haven't been wasting my time.

I wonder if the creature saw me set the trap, if it guesses my intent. I remind myself it is just a dumb animal. The mist shifts and the wargyu is gone.

He said in his affidavit that he'd often watched her walking along the beach at twilight with her pet hund. He'd fixated upon the outline of her, made naked by the sheerness of her dress, and memorized the curve of her buttocks and breasts as reference material for his nighttime fantasies.

She'd noticed and waved up at him once. The hund had stiffened and barked. He'd disliked the animal. Said he thought it knew something.

I exit the valley and find myself on a stony plateau, thick with wind-spiralled dust and ragged scrub. There are more scats and here and there, the telltale six-fingered prints. It's a female, this one, the fourth toe shorter than the third.

I set a second trap in a thicket where a tatter of blue fur wags in the wind. I tug wool covers over my boots to muffle my steps and set off, following the sketchy tracks.

The going is hard. The ice wind whistles through gaps in the slanted vegetation like the screams of slaughtered swine and sets my coat flapping like a tarpaulin. I am forced to tie the waterproof cloth against my body, lest the shivering thump the material gives out scare off every animal within a ten-mile radius. It's tricky following prints as they're slowly filled by dust, brushed aside by sweeping leaves. If not for the occasional pile of increasingly fresh scats and chance encounters with snagged fur, I could easily convince myself I am going the wrong way.

You'll probably have heard by now that he followed her home. This makes it sound like he simply trailed her, as if, had she only turned around, she could have prevented her own death.

It wasn't like that.

The details he had in his diary were frightening. I wouldn't have thought it possible to glean so much about a person through a pair of binoculars. Without so much as a single conversation he'd discovered her penchant for wavy hemlines, string bikinis, dangly earrings and flip-flops bought from Sass. She'd never let her hair grow below her collarbone, and every Tuesday without fail she had changed the color of her nails.

It was always a Tuesday. The entries in his diary confirmed it. *Purple, crescent-mooned with orange tips. Dark blue dipped in white. Cream with red dots. Yellow. Black dipped in magenta.* He'd liked this latter combination, wrote "sexy nails" in felt-tip that day.

Her town only had one nail salon. He'd begun staking it out. Security footage from the time showed him holding this newspaper or that, never reading but peering, always peering, his eyes on the shop. It's a shame no one noticed his obsession while she was still alive.

I wonder what tale he told the nail salon to obtain her name. I wonder if they kick themselves now.

Once he had her name, it was easy to locate her house. People put too much information on the skyweb these days. She'd had a thing for those "Win a Holiday" competitions.

I crest a small rise, a bit like a wrinkle in the plateau, and gaze across land as flat and rocky and blusteringly hostile as the land I've just crossed. Heavy mist obscures the mountains bordering the plateau, merging the periphery of the tableland with the bleached sky. Up here, the world truly might be flat. Had I not walked these lonely heights as a boy, I would be concerned about stepping off the edge.

I scan the horizon with my binoculars. Far ahead and to my right is a dark patch of vegetation topped in pointed crowns. Pines.

Before them, a creature poises in the open, staring in my direction. I can see why the long elegant head, with its corkscrewing antlers and facial bars of cobalt, were once prized by trophy hunters. I can see why the banded pelt once adorned runway collections and high couture. Even the tail bob, a brilliant tuft of white-tipped navy, was once a collector's item, topping women's fascinators at the racetrack and decorating gentleman's lapels as one might once have worn a carnation.

It is nightfall by the time I reach the wargyu's food source. Close up, the pines appear straggly and sick, bending toward the sunset with the prevailing wind. Shadows move among their flapping branches like live things. I tell myself there is nothing to fear from the knocking together of dying wood; the dry-bones rattle of broken, leafless limbs; the steady pitter-patter rainfall of brown needles.

The wargyu has disappeared into the thickening night mist, but I know the animal will return when hunger beckons. I set traps along the tree line before making camp downwind of where I last caught sight of it. I snuggle into a bed of leaf litter, hugging myself to keep warm, promising myself a fire once this messy business is done with.

As I drift into the hunters' half sleep, I think of the maid who got away. She had only stopped by the house a moment to drop off mail and fold some clothes, but according to the cops, by the time she let herself in, he had already broken a small window at the rear of the house and gained entry.

I wonder if she'd felt his eyes crawl across her from some unseen vantage point, if she had even looked around, telling herself she was just being silly. She said during her interview that she had felt the hair rise along her neck and had left three items of clothing unfolded.

A nightmarish vision of the man ironing the maid on her own

board intrudes my sleep. Her brown skin spits as it burns, the steam from the iron boiling like a kettle, rising upward in a shrill scream which merges with a terrible sound that jolts me from my sleep.

The ungodly noise accompanies a clanking of tethered chain. One of my traps has caught something.

I stumble through the darkness to find I have caught a julmaro. The creature's single muscular foreleg is snared, cut halfway through the cannon bone. It thrashes—the powerful hind leg kicking, digging gouges in the hard dirt.

The creature's scream is piercing, gets my heart racing and sets my teeth on edge. It reverberates off the nearby peaks and vibrates my ears and sinuses with a physical force, rendering me lightheaded and nauseated and completely incapable of rational thought. Desperate to stop the noise, I hook my hand around its gaping muzzle, crushing the animal's mouth closed, but still the sound blares from all four nostrils.

Driven to madness, I slash the animal's throat. The wail cuts to a pneumatic wheeze, thick with gurgling. The julmaro's wide eyes stare into mine as its pulse ebbs into the dust.

The scream hangs in the mountains, in my ears, long after the animal is silenced. I pant heavily, feeling the night pushing in as calmness and sanity return.

Along with guilt.

I have violated this mountain sanctuary with the kill, the stench of blood, and it wasn't even the right animal. I feel unseen eyes accusing me from within the curtains of mist. I wonder if the wargyu is among them.

I drain and gut the julmaro, spreading the steaming organs across the dirt and digging out the edible offal before setting about the hard task of cutting the carcass into portions. The meat and offal are wrapped in strips of pelt and hidden in gaps among the icy stones, their smell disguised from scavengers with pine needles and dried scats. The flesh should keep until I have achieved my task. As a hunter, I am not wasteful.

For several days, I hide and wait among the pines. Occasionally I see the wargyu in the distance (just beyond rifle range), but it avoids my hiding place where the blood of the julmaro is dry and black upon the stones, and glossy cravens squabble over chunks of frozen fat. I have plenty of time to ruminate.

Her death was quick when it came. He had seemed disappointed about that in the dock. It was the only time I ever recall him showing regret. He had planned on mutilation, he said, planned on taking her ears, her nose, her fingers. But in the end he had lost his nerve. Apparently, she wouldn't stop crying, begging, calling out for help. He had eventually slipped the blade between her ribs just to shut her up.

He had wrapped her pieces in plastic and buried them remotely, but all in vain. The police scent-hunds had located her body the exact same day. It helped that they had known where to look.

It was joggers who'd noticed his car in the reserve that morning, who'd written down the make and plates and passed the information along to the police. It's always the joggers who notice these little irregularities: the letterbox full of junk mail, the wandering child, the car parked all alone. Having just butchered the julmaro, I half expect a jogger to come trotting out of the mist, to stand and stare and take down notes on a small pad. In my more sleep-deprived moments, I almost fancy I do.

A crunch of ground frost and a thin branch snapping in a nearby pine alerts me to the wargyu's return when it comes. Against the early morning light creeping through gaps in the mountains, I see her silhouette reach for more needles. She has outwitted my barrier of traps.

Never taking my eyes off her, I nock an arrow to my bow with steady hands (I'd use the rifle, but fear alerting her with the *clunk* of the bolt). My movements are slow and deliberate so as not to be noticed. The oilcloth across my back barely creaks as I line her up and draw back.

A shingle of rock slips away underfoot as I shift my weight.

Curses! Her head comes up; the spoon-shaped ears fixing on me like sonar. She goes into motion, springing back from the trees. I loose the arrow, but it flies wide, lost to the plateau.

I haul my bulk into a solid run, tearing bolas from my belt as I go. She pelts away from me, but she is off balance in her surprise, bereft of her natural grace and speed. I see her stumble as my feet luck onto perfect purchase in the half light. My aim with the bolas is far better than with the arrow. The heavy rocks whirr around and around, trussing her legs together tightly as she sprawls into the dust. For all her leggy size, the wargyu has none of my bulk. I fling my weight against her ribs, pinning her struggling body down. She ceases fighting, and utters a mournful bellow of terror and resignation.

I slip my knife from my belt.

As I raise the steel, ready to draw the whetted edge across the trembling throat, I look into the creature's eyes. The wargyu stares back without blinking as if, by keeping its eyes open, it can somehow freeze time or stave off the approaching darkness. There are wrinkles around those eyes, a genuine expression of fear. I have all the power. We both know it. As I stare back, the wargyu emits a soft, mewling cry, as if pleading for its life.

Was this the look he had been confronted with in the living room of her home, her wrists and ankles bound with duct tape? Had she pleaded with him? Said she wouldn't tell anyone? And, if she had, had he for even a second considered taking a different path?

I stiffen my knuckles around the hilt of the knife. The wargyu flinches, though I have not moved, and lets out another quivering mewl.

Even though I name myself *Hunter,* my chest tightens with the act I am about to commit. The creature lying in the dust, the new sun illuminating blue highlights in its coat, is unique. Its death will be a crime in and of itself.

At the same time, the wargyu's death will trigger *his.* The woman from the beach will finally get her justice.

CASSANDRE BOLAN

Our breaths puff whitely as we stare at one another, predator and prey. Then the sun spears through a gap in the distant mountains, turning the crisp gray fog into veils of gold gossamer and the shale ground into stacked bullion. The wargyu's eye catches the light and flares iridescent purple. The animal shifts its weight beneath me, sensing my fading resolve.

I grit my teeth and bring down the knife. The wargyu's bellow echoes across the plateau, reverberates off the mountains.

In my hand, I have her left ear tip, banded in blue and white and dripping with red. I also take a fistful of tail, pushing the thick, white-tipped navy hair into a pocket of my coat.

I untie the bolas and release the animal. She bellows as she gets to her feet, and for a second I wonder if I've made a mistake, if she might try to gore me for my act of mercy. Then she shakes her head, flicking blood onto the golden dirt and trots away into the mist.

Once she has vanished, I dig out my cache of julmaro meat— the last piece of evidence I'll need to present to court—and turn toward home, neutralizing and gathering my traps along the way.

The Justice Department won't bother testing the flesh, not when presented with the wargyu's ear and tail hair. There is no clear distinction between two kills, once you cut beneath the surface.

Artistic Presentation

BY L. RON HUBBARD

Thirty years ago when the first Writers of the Future volume was published, its stories were illustrated by professional artists. It wasn't until Volume V that the winning stories were depicted by winners of the newly created Illustrators of the Future Contest, as they still are today.

L. Ron Hubbard felt it important to honor equally both the artist and the writer.

Broadly known for his work as a writer of popular fiction, having published over 230 fiction works representing millions of words, L. Ron Hubbard was best known as an author.

But Hubbard also worked in other mediums. For example, Hubbard's tales lent themselves to film particularly well, thanks to his eye for detail and his talent for describing action. By the summer of 1937, one finds his stamp on such scripts for the big screen as The Mysterious Pilot, The Adventures of Wild Bill Hickok *and the* Spider Series, *while his name was formally attached to the fifteen-episode* The Secret of Treasure Island—*which was among the most profitable serials of Hollywood's Golden Age.*

Hubbard was also an accomplished photographer. He was a keen student of the craft in his youth, and by early 1929, his celebrated China landscapes were acquired by National Geographic *while his spectacular aerial shots as a pilot could be found in the pages of* Sportsman Pilot. *His eye for dramatic and informative photos provided an excellent demonstration of what is meant by "A picture is worth a thousand words."*

Similarly, although he never counted himself as a professional musician in the strictest sense, his musical accomplishments are by no means insignificant. Understanding that sound without words also tells a story, he created a "soundtrack" to Battlefield Earth *using previously unexplored computerized instruments, followed by an innovative* Mission Earth *album, themed against his bestselling series of the same name and performed by Edgar Winter.*

Thus L. Ron Hubbard developed a love for and mastery of a variety of artistic forms, and in that spirit, the Illustrators of the Future Contest was created to be a companion to the Writers of the Future.

His diverse experiences made him especially qualified to find common ground across all the arts. In "Artistic Presentation," synthesizing his experiences in writing, filmmaking, photography and music, he was able to advise others about a topic that marks the true professional, no matter the art form.

Artistic Presentation

We live in a machine world. The whole yap of television and newspapers is directed toward reducing effort. The primary goal of the civilization in which we live, it seems, is to reduce all personal effort to zero.

The less effort a person can confront, the more effect of effort he becomes.

The modern trend of "don't do" accompanies the modern trend of an increased percentage of the insane in the society.

The crazier a person is, the less he accomplishes or does.

So we live in a world which is oriented to drive men mad.

But, more pertinent to us, we suffer from the continuous bait—"do it the *easy* way." "Do it in the way that will demand the least effort."

We see this in manufacturing, particularly—the easiest way is the cheapest way is the most profitable way.

So we get into a "do it the easy way."

Well, that may apply to making spoons for profit, but it does *not* apply to presentation.

The whole world of the arts is directly opposed to the philosophy of the businessman or manufacturer.

Art seeks to create an effect. An effect is not always created the *easy* way. Indeed, the better effects are quite difficult to achieve.

One can fall into creating easy effects to such a degree that one fails completely.

For instance, a dozen cakes are in competition at a county fair. The one that wins is not the easiest cake to make. True, the cook that made the winner may have some easy ways to short-cut cake baking. But the winning cook actually takes that extra bit of care to make it all just right.

It isn't magic or luck that makes the professional. It's hard-won know-how *carefully* applied.

A true professional may do things pretty easily from all appearances, but he is actually taking care with each little bit that it is just right.

The winner has it instinctively. The loser rarely even grasps the concept of "do it right."

Artistic presentation always succeeds to the degree that it is done *well*. How *easily* it is done is entirely secondary.

To the world of presentation, the only guide is take the care necessary to do a good job.

To the world of the businessman, the manufacturer, the primary guide is "how can we do it easily."

These two philosophies clash.

We are taught daily in advertisements, by union leaders, by socialists, that DO IT WITH THE SMALLEST EFFORT is the greatest goal in life. Do the least work for the most pay. Buy the automatic machine that chews up the most clothes in the least time. Use the roofing paper that goes on quickest and keeps out the least rain. Vote for Jim X who will make all the world eat without working. Do nothing yourself. Shove it off on the Mix-Up Accounting Company—or the man at the next desk.

That all this leads to total dependence on gadgets, total enslavement to mounting economic puzzles, even to total enslavement to a Commissar Krushtoad in the next generation, is neglected utterly. That less than two centuries ago we lived quite well and built more strongly and were a lot saner without all these ads, tools and commissars is never mentioned.

Man is solving himself to extinction. And all on the slogan "Don't exert yourself."

It's gotten so bad that people are shrugging off all responsibility for the state, for their friends, for anything and everything. "Nothing has anything to do with anybody" is the epitaph that nobody will take the trouble to write on the tombstone of this civilization.

Now, this is no rant against automation or gadgets or self-sterilizing cat petters.

Use all the gadgets you can lay your hands on—if they really do work in your hands and don't absorb all your time in earning their price or repairing their faults.

No, my thought here is only this—keep your action level above your gadget level.

Keep ahead of automation. Keep ahead of do-it-for-you. Don't disenfranchise yourself by giving all your work away—to a machine, to a fellow worker.

If you've got equipment, do one of two things: (a) Use it to increase your production of effects, or (b) Get rid of it.

But first and foremost realize that in presenting something, that the best way isn't always the easy way. The best way is *only the more effective way.*

Work out first what effect you are trying to produce. Then when you've got that all taped, *only* then consider the easiest way to do it. And never consider the easier way at all if it is less effective.

Art takes that extra bit, that extra care, that bit more push for it to be effective art.

There is no totally easy way to produce a desirable effect.

And the day you drop some of your ideas of the effect you want to produce is the day you get a little older, a little weaker, a little less sane.

So don't buy the easy way. Buy only the effective way. If some of its points can then be made easy, good. If not, do it the hard way.

And only if you realize this can you escape the gargantuan trap of a society with the mass goal of "Nothing should ever be done by anything but a machine or somebody else."

Beyond All Weapons

written by

L. Ron Hubbard

illustrated by

ADAM BREWSTER

ABOUT THE AUTHOR

In the January 1950 issue of Super Science Stories, *a month before the release of* To the Stars, *L. Ron Hubbard published a tale that became part of the history of modern science fiction for its pioneering application of Albert Einstein's time-dilation theory.*

Hubbard's was the first earnest attempt to speculate on this theory.

He summarized the problem that the theory posed in terms of an equation: As mass approaches infinity, time approaches zero.

As Hubbard stated, "Two mathematicians derived the equations first—Lorentz and Fitzgerald. And a theoretical philosopher, Albert Einstein, showed its application. But if Lorentz and Fitzgerald and Einstein gave man his solar system, they almost denied him access to the stars."

Without diminishing one iota of the action, L. Ron Hubbard then delivered a stirring tale designed to get you thinking about the most pitiless of man's enemies—time itself.

ABOUT THE ILLUSTRATOR

Adam Brewster was born in Cambridge, England. His childhood mainly involved drawing, music-making and tree-climbing. Even then he obsessed over watching things. He wanted to understand the world around him and, when it was time for university, it seemed that architecture could fulfill this ambition best of all.

Studying at Nottingham, he matured as a designer and artist, going on to be an actual architect in two United Kingdom capitals—London and Edinburgh.

Somewhere in that field he was seduced by 3-D software, and became convinced it would help him express his vision. He was not wrong.

Now settled in Edinburgh, Adam has transmuted from architect to CG artist, illustrator and animator. Until recently, he and his partner ran their own CG animation studio in the city, producing commercials and short films with great success, even winning a BAFTA Scotland award nomination along the way.

He is still a busy CG artist, committed to challenging himself, acquiring more CG Fu and plenty of other new stuff—like illustrating the future.

He's humbled to be part of Illustrators of the Future this year and delighted by the indulgence the Contest offers artists whose sci-fi imaginations have yet to give up their treasure. Long may it continue!

Beyond All Weapons

The revolt was over and the firing parties had begun. In a single day in Under Washington, three thousand rebels were executed and twelve thousand more condemned to life imprisonment in the camps. And the *Bellerophon* hung fifteen thousand miles out of reach, caught between death by starvation and swifter death by surrender.

She was the last of the rebel ships, the *Bellerophon*. Sent by Admiral Correlli during the last hours of the action to the relief of an isolated community on Mars, she had escaped the debacle which had overtaken all her sister ships in contest with Earth.

The revolt was ill begun and worse ended. But the cause had been bright and the emergency large, and Mars, long-suffering colony of an arbitrary and aged Earth, had at last, as the dying bulldog seeks to take one final grip on the throat of his foe, revolted against Mother Earth.

But there was little sense in recounting those woes now, as Captain Guide well knew. The taxes and embargoes had all but murdered Mars before the revolt had begun. The savage bombardment of the combined navies of Earth had left an expanse of wasted tillage and shattered towns and the colonists had been all but annihilated.

Like her sisters, the *Bellerophon* was a converted merchantman. Any resemblance she bore to a naval spaceship was resident only in the minds of her officers and crew. Plying her trade from

Cap City to Denverchicago, she had suffered much from being colonial-built. The inspectors on Earth had inspected her twice as often as regulations demanded and found ten times as much fault. And because she was colonial, her duties, enforced by irksome searches and even crew seizures for the Earth Navy, had all but bankrupted Smiley Smith and the line's directors—not that that mattered now, for the company and all its people were dead in the wreck which had been the finest city in the colonies.

"*I* won't surrender!" said Georges Micard, first mate. "Not while I've got a gun to fire! It's their holiday. Let's give them a few blazing cities to celebrate by!"

Guide, cool, austere, had looked at his mate in silence for a while. He said, "Your plan is not without merit, Georges. We have suffered beyond endurance and our comrades have died gallantly. And a few blazing cities would be much in order were it not for one thing: the barrier."

Georges, optimistic, very young, was apt to forget practical details. The reason Earth had won had been the barrier. So well had the secret been kept that when the colonial fleet had attacked, every missile they had launched at the queen cities of their mother planet had exploded a thousand miles out from target. There was an invisible barrier there, a screen, an electronic ceiling. And Mars, new-formed, braver than she was sensible, had found herself unable to retaliate for the thunder of missiles which had wrenched her cities from their foundations and laid them into dust.

"All right," said Georges, glancing around the wardroom at the other officers. "We'll sit up here until the cruisers come get us and then we'll vanish in a puff of atoms."

"They won't come," said Carteret. "They know we are here, but they'll wait for us to starve. They have every spaceport on Mars and Venus. We're done."

Gloom deepened in the room. Then Albert Firth, their political adviser, an intense-eyed Scot, honed keen in the chill clime of New Iceland, Mars, leaned forward.

"You interested me, Captain, when you spoke today of the

drives for which our fleet should have waited. Exactly what were those drives, sir?"

Guide looked at him with understanding. It was time to speak. These people had depleted their own stores of ideas. Hundreds of thousands of colonists were dead, and as fast as the orders for execution could be issued, thousands more were dying. These men would not cavil at thin chances.

"I have had, for some time, a plan," he said.

Eyes whipped to him. They knew Guide. Bilged out of the Space Academy at fourteen for one too many duels, raised by the lawless camps of the southern cap on Mars, cast off by his family, but infinitely esteemed by his comrades and former employers, Firstin Guide was a man to whom one paid attention.

"I think they ought to be whipped," he said quietly.

In more optimistic times, that had been a common opinion on Mars. Since the triarchy of the Polar State had destroyed all free government, the thoughts of less disciplined peoples had run in that vein. Martian colonists were, more lately, refugees from the insensate cruelties and caprices of the Polar regime. And they had all thought that the "snow devils"—that strange race who had managed to adapt their metabolism to the blood-chilling climate of the North Pole, and who in half a century had made their unexploited realm the prime power of Earth—ought to be whipped. But here, in a ship almost out of food, low on ammunition, with half her fuel gone and her cause already lost, those words drew a quick intake of breath from all. But they knew Firstin Guide. He would not speak idly.

"At Spencerport," he began, "a technician named Jones perfected, about five years ago, an extra-velocity fuel. You all know of that. It burns too fast and has too much thrust for anything but spurt space racing."

"I know the fuel," said Albert. "But Spencerport was wiped out."

"So it was. But it happens that I was loaded with EV fuel for transport to Earth when I was mobilized. I landed that cargo when I landed my merchant crew and took aboard you gentlemen of the Naval Volunteers. That fuel is cached at

Rangerhaven. I was not raised to trust the expected to happen, gentlemen. I put it in a vault."

"But what has this to do with us?" said Georges. "Sure, we can risk a landing at Rangerhaven, that's ninety leagues south of nowhere, the most godforsaken spot on Mars. But of what value could this fuel be—?"

"Gentlemen, there have been several attempts for the stars."

They stared at Guide, unwinking, at once stunned and elated. And then Firth relaxed. "No use, sir. Ships have gone. But ships don't come back. That's been a closed book, Captain."

"If you have closed a book recently, Mr. Firth, you doubtless noticed that it could be opened again."

They were restless then. They wanted to believe they had a chance. They could imagine they heard the firing parties at Under Washington. And they had been on half rations for a week.

Guide looked coolly at them. He had judged his moment rightly. "I picked up a technician from the prisoners we took at Americaville. A very well-educated young Eskimo."

They recalled this, and they also recalled Guide's insistence that they sort out the garrison before they executed the Earth infantry.

"He is down in the brig," said Guide. And he sat back to give them his final stroke, casually, almost bored. "He knows the formulae of the barricade."

When he saw how deeply this shaft had sunk, he followed it. "And with those formulae a single vessel could penetrate it and, with her drives alone, lay waste the central Polar cities. That done, the restoration of free government on Earth would be very simple. All that is necessary is that we take all we can in the way of technology and personnel, lay a course for the stars—Alpha Centauri first—and locate a habitable planet. That they exist is unquestionable. There we set up a colony, build our barrier-breaker and return to Earth as a combat ship to ruin Polar domination."

He lighted a small cigar to make it all seem simple. "I think," he said, "that they should be whipped."

His attitude, his casualness, drove away the terrible question marks posed by the plan. Ships had gone, using EV fuel. Ships had not come back. Theoretically it was impossible to travel to the stars, but theory is a cold thing and subject to much reversal. Theoretically a ship blew up when it tried to break the "wall of light." But there had been many another theory which, in practice, had proven wrong.

They were none of them mathematicians. They were what they called practical men. All but Firth had grown up in space travel around the Sun. The heartbeat of Mars was Earth commerce and it had been to preserve that commerce that they had fought. Therefore a stellar voyage was only an extension of what they already knew.

"I have no instruments for measuring speed nor even for navigation to the stars," said Guide. "I have no idea whether we can 'break the wall.' I know no more than you what lies out there en route to Alpha Centauri. But I know what lies before us here—a firing party for ourselves and the end of freedom in this system forever. I think," he added, after a slow puff at his cigar, "that an unknown and even dangerous adventure is preferable to a sordid certainty. Your votes?"

There was no standing out against this chance. They gave him their "ayes" right gladly and began to quiver with hope as they stabbed outward for Mars and Rangerhaven.

Going up in a puff of pure energy was better any day than going down before the grinning pleasure of a Polar firing squad.

It was black polar night when they again touched Mars. A blizzard was yelling, ninety-below cold and fifty-five miles an hour strong. And the port lay shattered and deserted, roasted into lava by the passing vengeance of the Earth Navy.

At the head of a landing force of twenty militia and against the protests of his officers, who urged him not to risk his life, Captain Guide made his perilous way toward the operations building, buffeted by the wind and blinded by whirling granules of snow.

They reached their objective and Guide and a sergeant,

smashing back the door with blasters, leaped inside. They were almost shot by the startled group around the stove. They almost fired into that group. But then they recognized one another and they laid away their weapons and held a glad reunion.

There was Cadette, captain of the *Asteroid V,* Miller, skipper of the *Swift Voyage,* and Gederle, master of the *Queen Charlotte,* merchantmen all. To see one another alive was surprise enough for the moment and Guide, gloating now at this reinforcement, let them exuberate for a while.

"By whillerkers," said Cadette, "last I seen of you, Guide, was your flyin' lights vanishin' out toward the fleet. And now, by golly, you pop up like bad money. Say, how'd you land out there in the middle of three ships? Might have ruined one of us."

"I was too late for action," said Guide. "It's all over now with the fleet."

They held a long silence after this, a bitter silence.

Guide broke it at last. "But how did you manage to escape, the three of you?"

"Fleet train," said Miller. "The *Asteroid* and the *Swift* were carrying food and ammunition and Gederle had about five hundred marines on his *Queen Charlotte*. Then Cadette had a battalion of engineers in case we had to patch up Earth when we took it—devil with it," he added suddenly. "We're alive right now but it's a matter of a few days until the Earth patrols locate us. You can't hide anything as big as our stuff. We're done for."

"Yes," said Guide, "I suppose so."

There was something in the way he said it which distracted them from their depression. They knew Guide as a vicious poker player and a stealer of cargos and they respected him.

He sat down beside the glowing potbelly stove, warming his lean hands. He let them work up their own curiosities before he said, "I have a slightly different angle. An unknown adventure is better than a certain defeat. I might be able to use you gentlemen—*and* your engineers and troops."

That anything in the universe still had a use for them was almost argument enough. They had come here, intending to make one last battle of it against the hopeless numbers of Earthmen and ships which must, this minute, be combing Mars for the last of the rebels. Polar night would hide them at best for a few days. And then powerful detectors would rake across the place and they would be called upon to surrender and die or fight and die. They had seen as they passed all that was left of Cap City, all that remained of Gold Strike, the ruin of Fort Desolation and the death-strewn ramparts of Base One, once the most powerful single fortress in the solar system. Out there across the continents they had wives, children, parents, and they knew nothing of their fate. But spacemen have a certain fortitude. And they could look now at Guide.

"I cached," said Guide, "some fifty pounds of extra-velocity fuel in a vault near here when I was mobilized."

"Fifty pounds!" said Miller.

"Are you sure it wasn't blown up?" said Cadette. "You haven't seen this place in daylight. It's a ruin."

"When I was a kid around here, we used to get blown up pretty regularly," said Guide, "rangers being no better than what they were. And we had an old vault in which we cached loot. The EV is down there by the river in that vault. I took most of the packing off it, so it will be easy handling. We have four ships. That's twelve and a half pounds a ship or enough for six months' burning. From what you say, I gather we have about fifteen hundred men amongst us including your troops, and perhaps two or three months' provisions?"

They were breathless, expectant. They had lost one hope already and they were afraid to lose this one.

But Gederle was a conservative. "If we try to burn EV we'll be unable to keep our speed down to finite levels. We'd be out of the solar system in a matter of hou—" He halted. Suddenly they understood.

"But it's never been cracked!" said Gederle.

"Well, blasting through the wall of light is preferable as a chance," said Guide. "I never heard of a man surging through a row of Polar burners yet."

"The wall of light," whispered Cadette. "And then . . . then the stars?"

"Yes," said Guide with an elaborate yawn, crossing his fine boots and pouring a drink. "The good old wall of light. A lot have gone out for a try, but none have come back. Maybe they exploded into pure energy. Maybe they are derelicts. And maybe it's just so confounded fascinatin' in the stars that they don't want to come back. Well?"

"But do we just leave everything? The war . . . well, that's lost. But how about our people?"

"The only reason I'd risk it," said Guide with sudden viciousness, "is to get a chance to come back and wipe out these ice-brains! We pledged our lives to kill them. Earth is ours. We aren't done yet! I feel," he added, leaning back and grasping his drink, "that they can still be whipped. You see, I've one of their engineers aboard who knows the secret of their barrier."

This catalyzed them into instant enthusiasm. Their bitter hatred had carried them far. Now it was going to carry them further. Words of savage hope rushed from them and they fell into an involved discussion of ways and means.

After a while Guide interrupted them. "I think it unwise to put all our chips on one stack of cards, gentlemen. I would like to form a colony in the stars, build the necessary equipment and then come back with a small portion of our people and wreck the ice-brain towns. If we fail to take Earth, we will at least have made it possible for our own people to revolt. But we may have to retreat again. We need a base in the stars. I think the *Queen Charlotte,* being a fast liner, could give us her troops and then join us after we are gone to a certain rendezvous."

"But why should she stay behind?" said Cadette.

"I'll do whatever you say, Guide," said Gederle.

"We've fifteen atmosphere planes," said Guide. "While the enemy is still trying to consolidate his gains here, I suggest we spend what time we can getting our families, those we can find, and women down to the *Queen Charlotte.* If she gets caught, she gets caught. At least the rest of us will be free to attempt the project and avenge her."

They looked at him, the glare of determination on their faces. They knew nothing of the stars or the navigation to them. They had no way of computing their future speed. They were grasping a thin hope. And they drank greedily to it.

Just outside the giddily whirling Mercury, the three space vessels waited. They had improved their time by patching up battle damage and distributing stores. And they waited now tensely for the *Queen Charlotte*.

Hers was the most daring role in this part of the mission. But there was danger to the others as well, for the *Queen Charlotte* might be allowed to get free only to lead the victorious navy down upon the rendezvous. They were tense, then, trying to hide their anxiety, trying not to appear overwrought with worry over the fates of their own people.

A hasty canvass of the entire small fleet had netted a large number of addresses. Only a fool could suppose that a third of those to whom rescue was directed for the *Queen Charlotte* would be reached. Many might be perfectly well and alive and still miss the call of the atmosphere planes. In the act of escaping the garrisons, several planes, or all of them, might be blasted down. And a stray cruiser might have come upon the old freebooter holdout at Rangerhaven and blown the *Queen Charlotte* and all her rescued people to questionable glory.

But they worked on the *Asteroid V,* the *Swift Voyage* and the *Bellerophon*. They intended to go four ships as one, banded together with something more than signals. As they intended to reach at least fifty times the speed of light, they knew that they would become invisible and lost to one another in the first few hours. And so, with torches and metal bars, they were uniting themselves as a cluster of ships, all using their drives, all forging ahead but only the *Bellerophon* steering. They had argued on the safety factor for some time and had decided that it was better to perish as a unit than to get lost as a fleet.

But the workmen were laggard, scrambling over the hulls, clumsy in their space kits. Their eyes were continually raking the dark skies about Mercury which lay a thousand miles from them. The Sun's corona lashed and blazed, a gorgeous sight. They had eyes only for the possible coming of the *Queen Charlotte.*

High purpose and higher resolve stirred them. But their hope lagged as long as the fourth ship remained unreported.

And then, at the end of the fifth day of their wait, yells of joy sang out through the ships and crackled over the workmen's intercoms. Down from the Sun came the *Queen Charlotte,* intact, braking and jockeying to drift to a halt beside them.

Within the hour, Guide was reading over the intercoms of men and ships the list of those saved.

It had been hot and nervous work. One atmosphere ship had been sighted and shot down, another had been badly damaged but had come through. And one hundred and eighty-five members of the families of those in this fleet had been contacted, still alive, and rescued. At first thought, the personnel looked at this as a bad show; but then the tales of the adventure began to circulate through the ships and the rescue took on the complexion of the miraculous. Hardly a building was left standing in the major cities. All communications were out. Ice-brains were everywhere, raping, burning, looting. One hundred and eighty-five names out of two thousand was a phenomenal high.

The fates of many of the missing were known, a fact which dispelled much uncertainty, for the families were close as spacemen are close. And then, a victorious factor—there were two thousand women on the *Queen Charlotte,* rescued at random from the floods of terrorized civilians pouring from the towns of Mars.

They had a staff meeting on the *Bellerophon* while workmen put graps on the *Queen Charlotte* and brought her into the cluster.

The tales Gederle's people had brought had inflamed them to a desperate pitch.

ADAM BREWSTER

"I hope, gentlemen," said Guide, as they took their chairs, "that we have done and will do all that we can. It is obvious that upon us depends any future freedom in the solar system and upon us devolves the whole responsibility of rescuing our late comrades and our people. We have the nucleus of a new base. But we must remember that our primary mission is the rescue of Earth. It will take months to build up the necessary technology to crack the barrier. We must invent and perfect a most complicated device. And we must have a base from which to strike again should we, this first time, fail—for if we even remain near the Sun, we will be discovered and destroyed.

"If we reach the stars, Earth can be saved!"

They made their adjustments, discussed their courses, rearranged their personnel for cluster travel and then stood up.

Ceremoniously they shook hands.

"In a very few days," Guide said, "we will be certain in the knowledge of victory, or a mist of pure energy between Earth and the stars. Your posts, gentlemen."

In ten minutes their drives thundered and they were outward bound.

It ran through the ships like an electric impulse, the miracle they had experienced. It dazed them.

Nine days had passed, and here they gazed down upon a shimmering, lovely world, wrapped in cloud mists, plated with seas, colorful with continents.

Nine days!

This was Alpha Centauri. It was many light-years of travel from Earth and here they were in nine days! Light, traveling at 186,000 miles per second, required years to get there from Sol. They had made it in nine days!

The wonder of this was second only to their wonder about the planet below. An atmosphere plane had skipped off two hours since and had radioed back technical data which elated them all. Three-quarter gravity, good air, good water, wildlife, a multitude of plants.

And Guide gave the orders to strike away their bonds and land in units.

He stood, watching the rest ease to a landing on a grassy plain where a river ran, and fooled perplexedly with his pencil. He could not calculate exactly how many, many times the speed of light they had had to come to do this. For Guide was no astronomer, nor were the rest of the officers. But he had made the daring gesture and he had come through. They had not exploded, they had not encountered meteor belts. They were here and that should be enough. But it puzzled him and through the months which came would rise again and again to confuse him. Nine days to go several light-years...

But the others were jubilant. Those who had had to leave their women behind them, those who knew their families to be alive still, confidently expected an early reunion. Those who had but lately watched the white fleet burst into flame and vanish before the gunnery of the Earth Navy swaggered over their chance at revenging their friends.

The selected site quickly sprouted shacks. The season and climate had been chosen for food raising and soon gay groups of women could be seen bringing gardens into being from the seeds they found there and from the various grains in their supplies.

A doctor got busy on the captive Eskimo engineer and shortly hypnotics and persuasion garnered a harvest of technical information.

Men laid out a factory site and built the necessary huts from logs and equipped them from the vessels.

It was a season of high hopes and violent effort and few there were who spent less than eighteen hours of twenty-six—the planet's day—at their tasks.

"The enemy did not wait for us," said Guide. "We will not wait for him to recover from the disorders he has brought on himself. The faster we are finished here, the sooner we will again own Earth. We'll deliver her and present her with a colony and a new commerce. We'll wipe out the ice-brains, rebuild our cities and then, of course, develop all the stars. We've won already. The rest is mere technical detail."

During the next ten months of ceaseless effort the only complaint came from the women. They were not certain. The trip had once been made, true, but should they be left here with only a small fighting force to protect them, they would have little chance of building any kind of a strong colony. They wanted to know why the thoughts of vengeance which obsessed these men of theirs could not find outlet in the creation of a new world. Was not New Earth a promising land? With their technology and skill, could they not build here everything they had left behind on Mars? Why risk a trip?

Guide heard them out complacently. In his buoyant good spirits he would not hear of any failures. But at length, seeing that this new colony would indeed be helpless without manpower and good technicians, he agreed that they could have one ship, the *Asteroid V*. With a skeleton crew, the *Asteroid* would stay behind, providing at once the necessary guard for the colony and the means of going off for aid if the main mission failed. It would not carry half the people who would be left behind, being the smallest vessel, but it could go for relief. That would give the colony a safety factor. And beyond that Guide would not go.

At the end of ten months, with all the effort devoted to the barrier uncoupler, with the colony barely able to support itself, Guide announced the time of takeoff. There was a loud girding and harsh rattle as soldiers and spacemen and marines prepared for the coming action.

In the midst of departure an atmosphere pilot who had been testing his ship returned to base with news. But little attention was paid to him.

"Over that range of mountains," he said, "there's a lot of mounds. I landed for a look-see and, by golly, it's a colony. Been gone for hundreds of years, I guess, but there's a cemetery and the names cut in the stones are Earth names—Jones, Smike, Dodgers—"

"Hmm," said Guide, his mind on getting a transformer aboard the *Bellerophon*. "Must be an early expedition. Old-time ship. No women. Broke down here or ran out of fuel and there they are. Well, well. Steady on that tackle, there."

"I don't think so," said the atmosphere pilot. "I mean I said hundreds of years, but that place is really *old*. It's a long time before space travel, looks to me. Stones all weathered away, graves sunken, big buildings all crumpled like the Parthenon. Really old. An expedition wouldn't have gone to that trouble if they hadn't had women."

"Been no tries for the stars before fifty years ago," said Guide. "Guess you must be wrong. Easy, easy now. You want to knock the side of the ship out?" He smiled at the youngster. "Been no fuel before EV that would have made the grade. You hop over and give them a hand loading your plane. Won't be more than an hour before we leave dirt."

Some of the women hovered on the outskirts of the commotion. One of them at last plucked up nerve to talk to Guide. "Sir, I'm worried."

"Nonsense," said Guide. "We'll be back in a matter of weeks."

"But without help we can't construct our irrigation dam or do any of the hundred other things we'll have to do to make this a good colony. You're taking all the technicians."

"Need 'em," said Guide. "Got to break that barrier. And don't worry a minute. We'll be right back. I like this place. Mars is too dry for good agriculture."

"I'm afraid," she said. "I have a terrible feeling that you may never come back. We'd...we'd perish here."

"Think I'd let that happen?" said Guide heartily. "You've got the *Asteroid*. You can send her for help if we don't make it. Even the ice-brains will respect you for being the first star colonists."

"Oh why, why don't you give up this mad vengeance!" she wept. "It will do no one any good! Haven't enough men been killed? Here we have the stars. Don't throw them away! Send a secret ship to land on Mars and bring off new colonists. But forget this war!"

Guide looked at her. She was very pretty, very frail. He had a weakness for pretty, frail women. But suddenly he straightened. "We'll be back. Don't you worry about that! We'll be back!"

The flotilla returned on separate courses and rendezvoused behind the Moon. They were watchful, stealthy, filled with a high spirit but well knowing that the forces they faced were more than a match for their puny strength.

They were waiting for the *Swift Voyage*. It had had another destination and was to join them here.

The easy passage home had raised their morale to the heights. Even a major accident to one of the ships would not prevent the return of the majority to New Earth, a victorious return to a planet infinitely better than Mars or worn-out Earth.

And then the lookouts sung out the *Swift Voyage* and shortly Miller boarded the *Bellerophon*. His face was enraged.

"The dirty little devils! The dirty, stinking devils! You know what they've done?" He threw down his gloves with a bang. "Mars is smashed. There isn't a building left on it. Cap City, Rangerhaven—they've been disintegrated!"

The other two captains stared at him.

"We took a scout, got right down close. And there's nothing! Nothing! They butchered every colonist on the planet. They knocked apart every station. There isn't a thing left. Not a dam, a radio tower, nothing!"

"You got right down close? Then they don't even patrol it," said Guide.

"Why should they," said Miller bitterly, "when there isn't even a sheep or a pig left on it to be patrolled!"

"That bad," said Guide. And he squared up. "Standby to break the barrier!"

They slashed at Earth in a vengeful V, the barrier trips running high, their guns ready, set all three to level entire cities with their blasts. Their immediate target was Nordheim, capital city of Polaria.

From the *Bellerophon* came a signal: "Standby to fire." And then, suddenly, inexplicably from that flagship came the countermand, "Wait."

They slowed. They turned.

"Shift target!" barked Guide. "Our own fleet must have gotten here before it was destroyed. Shift target to New York."

And they curved off, these three improvised warships, and rode the curve over the rim to North America and New York.

"Standby. Range coming up. Ready—" Thus cracked Guide's voice. And then, "Wait!"

They sheered off and the *Bellerophon* detached herself and swept lower. Then before Cadette's and Gederle's incredulous eyes, Guide swooped in for a landing and came to rest, a tiny spot of silver on the plain far below. They hovered.

And then Guide's voice asked them if they would land.

Guide was standing in the center of a grassy place when Cadette and Gederle came up. Guide was looking with weary wonder in his eyes at a plaque which stood, aged and unthinkably weathered, where New York's many levels had once towered.

They could not read the plaque. The language on it was not Nordic nor any other American script. And it was not European or English.

Above them blazed the Sun, unmistakable, setting in a blaze of red clouds. About them crouched the fallen towers of a city long dead.

And then stars began to show in the gathered dusk and Guide looked up to find new wonder there.

"Vega! That's Vega, isn't it?"

And Guide fished hurriedly through his kit for an infantry compass. He looked at it and he looked at where the Sun had set and he looked at the great, bright star.

"That's Vega," he said in a hushed voice. "And it is the North Star."

For a long time they stood there, trying to assimilate what had happened, trying to understand. In them died the last heat of the battle they had sought to engage. They knew little enough about higher orders of astronomy. But every spaceman knew that once in every twelve thousand five hundred years Vega became Earth's North Star.

That was their time factor, then. That was their time. And where was the enemy? Dead these mossy stones and ruins said, dead these thousands of years. And the atmosphere scouts they sent through the night at length came back to prove it.

Man had perished from the Earth millennia ago.

And Guide, sunk down on a fallen block of bleached granite, scratched in the sand with a stick. He nodded at last in slow and awful comprehension.

Cadette knelt and looked at the symbols and figures and then Gederle knelt down. They looked at one another.

"I was never much for school," said Guide. "But they taught us once about this. Man must use it daily now and we all knew it well. It is the Einstein Relativity Equation. And few of us have ever considered that it had yet its second step. And yet that is common knowledge too."

In the stillness of a quiet night, under far and lonely stars, they still knelt.

"As mass approaches the speed of light," said Cadette, hushed, "it approaches infinity. And as mass approaches infinity, time approaches zero. It was only nine days back from Alpha. But in those nine days, six thousand years have passed by Earth."

"We never broke the wall of light," said Guide, bitterly, clenching his hands. "We only approached within fractions of 186,000 miles per second."

"Time stood still for us," said Gederle. "We're probably the last men alive. It's a good thing we planted—"

Suddenly chilled and hushed, as one man they stared upward at the cold, far stars.

Overhead, their colony and their women were already—six thousand years dead.

Animal

written by

Terry Madden

illustrated by

SEONHEE LIM

ABOUT THE AUTHOR

Terry Madden has been writing since high school, when she first fell in love with the worlds created by Tolkien, Herbert, Le Guin and Heinlein. As a novelist and award-winning screenwriter, Terry has wandered the lands of historical and mainstream fiction, returning to her first love, speculative fiction, only recently.

With a degree in biology, Terry has worked in molecular biology and genetic research labs and currently teaches high school chemistry and astronomy at a California boarding school. She enjoys sharing the night sky with young people, encouraging them to look up, out and in.

Terry has an abiding interest in medieval and ancient culture and mythology, especially all things Celtic. Somehow, this interest coexists just fine with her passion for space and worlds spinning around other stars. She is currently at work on the second novel in her fantasy series, Three Wells of the Sea.

ABOUT THE ILLUSTRATOR

Seonhee Lim was born in a small city called Gyeongju in South Korea. With much thanks to her older brother, she grew up with fantasy adventure books and games.

Then she fell into the world of comic books, where all the fantasy characters she previously imagined in her head were moving and speaking on paper.

After playing all those adventurous games and reading comic books, she finally realized she could combine her favorite activity and genre together: art and fantasy. With that realization, she had no choice but to choose the path of making fantasy art.

As soon as the decision was made, time began to fly, and she received a bachelor's degree in both cartooning and illustration from Sangmyung University in South Korea and the School of Visual Arts in New York.

Currently she is working as a freelance illustrator in New York spending most of her time telling stories with drawings and paintings. Countless characters and creatures are strewn over her desk, waiting for new adventures. She is more excited than ever to bring more to the world.

Animal

Ten strides away a silverback erupted from a stand of monkey plum and made a chest-beating lunge at the Plexiglas. It was all that separated the jungle habitat from the viewing platform.

Mackenzie didn't flinch, didn't make eye contact. She heard Freddie slap both hands on the glass and knew the gorilla's eyes were locked on her, waiting for her to challenge him.

"The males need to display their authority periodically." She'd already forgotten the resource agent's name. While he watched the gorilla, she pulled his card from her jumpsuit pocket. Harper.

"Mr. Harper."

"*Doctor* Harper."

So he wasn't just another Fed in a suit. "My apologies," Mackenzie said. "The females are already well in line, so the silvers display to their handlers out of boredom."

"Not so unlike us after all." Harper scribbled on his tablet. "How would you translate *that* behavior, Dr. Guerrero?" He nodded toward the gorilla.

Mackenzie looked up to see Freddie smearing his feces over the glass.

She took a deep breath. Clearly these visits from the Federal Resources Board roused feelings in Freddie similar to her own.

"Lunch, Dr. Harper?"

When the Facility for the Reproduction of Endangered Species had relocated from San Diego eighty years earlier, miles of desert lay between the compound and Las Vegas. Now, two hotel casinos abutted the western perimeter of the thousand-acre facility, and recently, the Oasis Resort had suspended a transparent sky pool directly above the tiger habitat. That legal issue had yet to be settled.

Mackenzie purposely led Harper the long way to the commissary, past herds of Arabian oryx, American bison and zebra. She paused before the cheetah enclosure where a pair of female cats lounged near the viewing platform, each with a litter of kittens.

"You're looking at all that remains of an animal that once ranged the entire continent of Africa, north and east into Turkey and India. At one time they ranged all the way to the Gobi Desert."

One of the cats turned and gazed at Mackenzie as if she understood.

"The cat program at F.R.E.S. runs well over three billion a year in expenses." Harper put his hands on his hips and examined the cats with indifference. "And here they are."

He scribbled another note and moved on.

"We operate according to state health codes," Mackenzie said. "These habitats are cleaned daily. New soil and vegetation is replaced as required. Each enclosure is completely contained, receiving natural sunlight, controlled humidity, and temperature consistent with the animals' native environment."

"Commendable," Harper said, "but I'm not here about the smell."

Mackenzie found the nearest bank of elevators and pushed the call button. "You're the third agent here in a month. I mean no disrespect, but that usually means fines."

Harper's laugh was wheezy. Clearly an asthmatic. Overweight as well.

"If it's not the smell," Mackenzie said, "then how can I help you?" The elevator door slid open and they stepped in.

"Your director is quite proud of your work," Harper said. "She should be. I understand you brought bonobos back from less than twenty animals."

"Then you'll want to stay for the afternoon ultrasound. I have a lowland gorilla carrying the offspring of the last mated pair of mountain gorillas. They died in China ten years ago, and I was lucky enough to obtain one of the frozen embryos—"

"That won't be necessary."

The elevator door opened onto an underground maze of hallways leading to labs, kitchens and offices. Only animal habitats occupied the surface real estate.

The queue for food was thankfully short. Less time for small talk.

Mackenzie pushed her tray through the food line. "The rice soup is edible."

Harper took some, and a noodle bowl.

A stainless-steel table waited, tucked behind the drink dispenser. Eating silenced them both for a few minutes.

"We have over two million daily viewers subscribed to our streaming video," Mackenzie said. "Direct feeds to classrooms all over the world."

"Two million?" Harper laughed and daubed at his mouth with a napkin.

"It's not an insignificant number—"

"Where are the living, breathing visitors?" Harper said. "People who travel here to see living animals? Wasn't that the plan for this place?"

Mackenzie looked up from her soup.

"The F.R.E.S. is not a zoo. It is and always has been dedicated to the preservation of remaining wild species which, I might point out, number 579, excluding insects and fish which are kept in the U.N. Aquarium."

"Quite right. My point exactly."

Harper rolled his noodles around his fork and slurped them into his ample mouth. Still chewing, he said, "Vegas has overtaken your facility, Dr. Guerrero. This land is worth more than all these animals combined. I've already met with your director, but she asked that I talk with you personally—"

"The government dedicated this land to species preservation."

"The city has reached your western battlements, and to the east—nothing but solar farms all the way to New Mexico."

"Then we'll move."

"Move where?" Harper was leaning over his noodle bowl. "This place is obscenely expensive, as I'm sure you know," he said. "We have fifty years and millions of hours of virtuals cataloguing the life cycles of each remaining species. We have DNA redundancy, cross-species tissue samples, and countless cloned embryos frozen in five repositories around the world, each one reflecting sufficient species diversity—"

"You're shutting us down." Mackenzie dropped her spoon and pushed the bowl away.

"Your director has agreed—"

"And if humanity wants to see a live elephant, we'll implant a frozen embryo of *Loxodonta africana* into what? A cow?"

"Look," Harper said, "we're within ten years of being able to grow an organism, any organism, in an artificial womb. When the human population drops to pre-2075 numbers, we'll bring back not only sheep and cattle, but other species."

"You actually believe we'll revive nonfood species?"

"With current advances in virtual adventures," Harper said, "why would humanity need to see a live elephant, doctor?"

He spun the last of his noodles on his fork, ate them, and put down his fork. He chewed, his elbows resting on either side of the bowl, his fingers laced together displaying the hairy backs of his phalanges. He wasn't far from knuckle-walking himself.

"I came here out of courtesy to your director," he said. "Personally, I think she's afraid of you." His smirk lingered.

"Unlike bacteria, humans can't mutate to resist Earth's attempts to kill us off," Mackenzie said. "Instead, we invent new drugs, put an end to pandemics, extend life indefinitely. And you think we'll give back some ground to those we exterminated?"

"Look, I'm just the messenger here—"

"But even a messenger has a conscience."

She pushed back her chair and stood, looking him in the eye. "I have a procedure to attend to."

With the last of the Serengeti under cultivation for biofuel production and polar bear habitat melted in the first half of the last century, it had been clear that endangered species studies would go the way of the space program. Mackenzie had left human medicine to study what was left of wildlife. Virtual safari wasn't enough. She needed to look into the eyes of living animals— needed animals to look into hers.

Standing with her hand on the door lever to the gorilla night quarters, she couldn't bring herself to open it. She peered through the steel spy slot watching Lucy, a middle-aged lowland gorilla, lift her handler's upper lip with a callused black index finger.

The young handler, Sierra, complied. She opened her mouth as she would for a dentist so the gorilla could examine her teeth. Sierra pursed her lips and repeated a kissing sound. It appeared she'd been entertaining Lucy for some time, waiting for Mackenzie to arrive.

Deep in concentration, Lucy reflected Sierra's facial expression and tried to duplicate her sounds.

It wasn't unusual for a handler to become attached to her charges, and Sierra had spent far more time with Lucy since her husband's death. She was too young for such trauma. She often stayed long after her shift was over, even though Mackenzie couldn't afford to pay overtime. When an animal fell sick, Sierra always volunteered to stay for night watch.

Mackenzie felt her rage ebb, replaced by a numbing sadness. How could she tell Sierra?

"Almost." Sierra demonstrated an exaggerated lip smack for Lucy.

Mackenzie's dog, Puck, was curled in Sierra's lap. During the last war, modern dogs had suffered the same fate as the fifteen hundred canines Cleopatra had served Julius Caesar and his troops for supper. Dogs didn't do well on synthetic protein, and had become too costly to feed. Little Puck was what used to be called a terrier mix and did just fine on scraps left by the lions. Figuring out how to feed him after the F.R.E.S. closed was the last thing Mackenzie should be thinking about.

SEONHEE LIM

She set the ultrasound machine on the floor, slid open the steel door and stepped inside.

"Sorry I'm late."

She was about to tell Sierra there was no point in monitoring a fetus that would never be born when the young woman brushed a stray strand of ginger hair behind her ear and, smiling, laid her palm on Lucy's belly.

"I feel it moving."

The first ultrasound at six weeks had revealed a large fetus for its gestational time. Now, the image on the monitor couldn't be right. Mackenzie adjusted the frequency and tried again.

"She's a good thirty percent bigger than expected.... What was the implantation date?"

"September twenty-fifth," Sierra said, leaning around to look at the screen. "What's wrong?"

"The head is..." Mackenzie dragged the marker across the width of the fetus' skull and clicked to record the measurement. "Five-point-five centimeters. September twenty-fifth? Could that date be inaccurate?"

"I recorded it myself. What's the matter?"

The practice of using a common, populous species to carry the embryos of endangered animals had been started in the twentieth century. Not long after, researchers at the San Diego Zoo perfected blocking the surrogate's immune response to the foreign embryo, and then it was enough for the host animal to belong to the same taxonomic family as the implanted embryo and be large enough to physically carry it. As early as the 1980s researchers had saved the Mongolian wild horse from extinction by using domestic horses as surrogates to spawn a whole herd at once. Using common lowland gorillas as surrogates, mountain gorillas weren't far behind on the list of rescued species.

With widespread loss of habitat, most large, biome-specific species were nearing extinction, except those that had plagued cities for centuries—rats, pigeons, rabbits. The surrogacy method had become the only means to assure diversity in a limited population. Semen and ova frozen decades ago could be used to inject a breath of genetic fresh air into a given population.

"Lucy's got a month left," Mackenzie said to Sierra, "but this baby is the size of a full-term newborn. And the cranium is abnormally large. I need a blood panel and an amnio."

"Everything's going to be all right, though, right, Mac?"

How could she tell Sierra that the fate of this fetus had been determined by the National Resources Board? That concern over an abnormality was just a distraction?

"I don't know yet," Mackenzie said.

"But you're not going to terminate..."

"We'll see," Mackenzie said. She swallowed the burn in her throat. "Let's get the tests done, huh?"

The director wore a gecko sculpted into her buzzed green hair, its tail a long lock that curled over her shoulder. The look might have been stylish when the director was sixty, but the artificial sun that filtered through the solar tube made it look more like a caterpillar.

"I've already scheduled a crew to handle primate termination," she told Mackenzie. "I don't want you to have anything to do with it."

"They're my responsibility," Mackenzie said, hearing the quaver in her voice. "No one touches them but me. At least promise me that."

The director rocked back in her chair and pursed her lips. "Okay, Mac. If that's what you want. They've given us three weeks. Wrap things up your way."

Mackenzie sent her handlers home early. She would take the night watch herself.

The waterfall in the jungle habitat was off for the night. The synthetic boulders radiated heat from a day of desert sunlight.

Sweat soaked through Mackenzie's shirt.

She sat down on a rock and broke the seal on the birthday present she'd bought for her husband, Henry. He would understand. She took a long swallow. It was pretty smooth for an Indonesian algae spirit. She'd tell him that. She'd tell him about the end of her life's work. In three weeks the program director would find select restaurants serving a clientele hungry for exotic flesh. Mackenzie couldn't stop wondering what people would pay for a Siberian tiger steak.

She took another swig of Green Sin.

Puck reached out a tentative paw, begging for a taste. She let the dog sniff it, which put an end to the begging.

The moon peeked through the glass roof panels, veiled by the photon fog of the city. An air taxi sliced across the moon's face and rain emitters sent drifts of droplets over banana and palm, bamboo and strangler fig. The humid exhalation of the plants' dark cycle had begun, transmuting carbon dioxide into the chemicals of life, into leaf and root, flower and seed.

Rain beaded on Mackenzie's face and hair.

All over the world, in the comfort of their tiny beehive residence modules, people virtually vacationed on tropical islands long swallowed by the sea, climbed mountains now topped by luxury resorts, tracked Bengal tigers in jungles now reduced to palm oil cultivation, all without a millisecond of thought about bringing their bodies along, without ever actually encountering another species. Virtual safari could never duplicate the fear of the hunted, a fear men had known once, long before the coming of the first rifle. Nor could it convey the soul utterings that pass between animal and man, the communion of survival that both united and divided them. How had we become so separate?

"Hummmmmm-Mmmmaaaa."

The sound came from the primate quarters. The gorillas couldn't sleep either.

Mackenzie tried to imitate the greeting vocalization. "Hummmmmm-Mmmmaaaa."

Tituba answered with a chuff. The ancient matriarch's near-blind eyes were just visible through the spy slot in the steel door. Dark fingers appeared, hooked through holes in the mesh that ventilated their cells.

Mackenzie inserted her key in the hydraulic door lock, and with a short buzz and green light, all six cells rolled open.

The gorillas strode out in a silent procession, knuckle-walking shadows in the moonlight. They followed Tituba to the pool where the old gorilla sat and dragged her fingers through the water, scattering a hundred silver moon-disks.

Mackenzie sat on her heels beside them, dipping her pale hand with theirs.

The fetal karyotype was extraordinary.

The chromosomes were displayed in sequence on the holo, bright and dark bands color-coded for specific genes. Mackenzie brought chromosome 12 up for magnification, feeling Sierra's breath on her cheek, perched as she was over Mackenzie's shoulder.

"What the hell?"

"What is it?" Sierra said.

Maybe there was something wrong with the software. Mackenzie went to the binocular scope directly and counted. The little wormlike chromosomes still totaled twenty-three pairs.

"Mac?" Sierra hung over her shoulder.

"Gorillas have twenty-four pairs of chromosomes," Mackenzie explained. "But this fetus has twenty-three."

When Sierra made no response, Mackenzie looked up from the scope to find Sierra frozen, her eyes on the karyotype, her brow bunched in obvious confusion.

"There are no genetic abnormalities in gorillas that present as a loss of chromosomes," Mackenzie said. "It just doesn't happen."

She increased the magnification on the karyotype. It looked as if the ninth and fourteenth chromosomes had joined. She opened a page showing a normal human karyotype. Ape chromosomes 9 and 14 had spliced somewhere along the evolutionary path to form the human chromosome 12. But if this had occurred spontaneously in Lucy's fetus, it would form an ape palindrome of the larger human chromosome 12. This was no palindrome.

Mackenzie turned around. "This is intriguing. I wonder if it's viable."

"What does that mean? Viable?"

"If I were to take it now, would it live with an abnormality like that? It would be interesting to see what features a mutation like this would show."

Sierra took hold of Mackenzie's hands. She was shaking. "But you're not going to take it now, right, Mac?"

"What's going on, Sierra?"

"You can't take the baby, not yet." Crying, Sierra squeezed Mackenzie's hands tighter. "You need to understand."

"Understand what?" Mackenzie stood and took Sierra in her arms. "What's got you so upset?"

"Haven't you ever tried for a birth license, Mac?" Sierra was frantic now. "You and Henry?"

Mackenzie had no intention of bringing another human into this world. She'd spent her life trying to give other creatures a chance.

"No."

But in Sierra's face she saw the utter desperation she'd only heard about. Of the billion or more couples who applied for a birth license each year, only ten percent won the lottery, and most of those bribed the officials. This dictated a population growth rate of negative one percent per year... theoretically.

Mackenzie searched the eyes of the young woman before her. It all fell into place. Sierra's husband had signed up for a drug trial even though he had a decent job writing code. He became one of the twenty thousand casualties in the Amilozyonide test group, a "martyr for pharmaceutical progress," they'd told Sierra when they paid her the settlement.

"Humans have twenty-three pairs of chromosomes," Mackenzie said.

Sierra's lower lip quivered and the tears came.

"Your husband got paid enough up front for the Amilozyonide test," Mackenzie said. "Enough to buy a license."

"We wanted a baby, Mac. I know you understand. Please understand."

Mackenzie stepped back and Sierra slid down the wall to the concrete floor, sobbing into the knees of her coveralls.

No doctor would implant a couple's embryo if the father was dead. It was against the law. Sierra probably had close to a dozen fertilized, genetically scrubbed embryos (no hereditary diseases were tolerated) sitting in a cryotank waiting for a womb. She'd found no doctor willing to go to jail to implant her. But bribing a tech to give her the embryos? That wouldn't be too difficult. And switching her embryo with the mountain gorilla's, easier still. Humans shared the gorilla's taxonomic family *Hominidae*. With immunosuppressants, Lucy's womb would accept Sierra's embryo as if it were her own.

"What were you planning to do," Mackenzie asked in a cool, even tone, "when Lucy gave birth to your child?"

"I knew I could trust you."

"Trust me to lie for you? Sooner or later a Fed would scan your child and find no chip. What then, Sierra?"

"But you'll give me that chance, won't you, Mac?"

Mackenzie found Sierra bottle-feeding an orphaned chimp in the nursery.

"Everything's ready," Mackenzie said.

Sierra popped the bottle from the sleeping chimp's mouth and rocked it, standing over the crib as if she couldn't put the baby down.

For the past two weeks, Sierra had filled her backpack with formula and diapers from the nursery. Synthesized gorilla milk differed from human milk by a small percentage of lactose and fat. Sierra's baby would thrive on it.

The last ultrasound revealed that the baby was just under 2.5 kilograms, a viable weight for a human infant but substantially larger than the 1.8 kilograms of a gorilla infant. Even if she induced labor, a human infant's head would never pass through a gorilla's birth canal, and Lucy was beginning to show signs of toxemia. Mackenzie should have taken the baby a week ago, but it wouldn't have survived at that weight. Not in a veterinary ward.

With Lucy in isolation, Mackenzie inserted the key into the

hydraulic lock and opened the other cells for one last day in the jungle. Freddie charged, thrashing through the underbrush and voicing a guttural, "Houuwww-houuwww." He made for the log where Mackenzie routinely hid his favorite peanut butter treats. Today, the treats were laced with a sedative. Once they were all down, Mackenzie would make sure they didn't wake.

In her amble toward the banana leaves, Tituba paused and looked over her shoulder. Her eyes met Mackenzies's. She knew, yet she dug a treat from the log while Mackenzie wiped tears away and prepared the syringes with pentobarbital.

With live-streaming over, Mackenzie cut the wires to the cameras in the operating room and each of the gorillas' night quarters.

Outside Lucy's cell, she listened to Sierra sing a halting lullaby to the gorilla.

I went to the animal fair.
The birds and the beasts were there.
The old baboon, by the light of moon
Was combing her auburn hair.

Lucy had been trained to give her hand to her keeper for injections, but she was in pain now. Pacing the short span of her cell, she stopped only to sit and rock herself in time to Sierra's tune, her breath coming in short huffs. She wasn't volunteering her hand today.

"Come out," Mackenzie told Sierra.

When she was clear of the door, Mackenzie raised the blowgun to her mouth. Gorillas were known to catch darts and throw them back. She had to be quick and accurate.

Lucy was too weak to fight the cocktail of ketamine and medetomidine. She lunged forward, slammed into the grating of her feed slot, and fell.

Mackenzie stepped into the straw bedding, climbed onto

a narrow tile shelf, and cut the wires to the last camera. She turned the tiny device over in her hand and stuffed it into her pocket.

The two women trundled the gorilla onto a low gurney and rolled her out of the cell. Mackenzie would intubate Lucy in the O.R. Gorillas were just as sensitive to opioids as humans, so she would maintain her on isofluorine. Sierra would have to monitor the gorilla's vitals.

"If her pulse drops below forty-five, decrease the gas by one percent."

Mackenzie had the pentobarbital ready, enough to kill both gorilla and human infant.

With no need to scrub, she set to work making a midline incision. She would be quick; the baby would likely need suction and oxygen. But when she cut through the uterine wall and amnion and saw pink skin beneath, everything stopped, her scalpel poised above the gaping maw.

She knew she should push the pentobarbital, send both the gorilla and this human child to rock together on the deep seas of some other existence.

"She's all right," Sierra said. "My baby's all right."

A tiny human arm flailed, covered in waxy white vernix, pink fingers splayed against shiny black gorilla skin.

Mackenzie eased the infant from the incision.

Sierra wept, holding out her arms to take her child.

Mackenzie cut the umbilical cord and suctioned the infant's mouth until it winced and started to scream.

"Get out," Mackenzie told Sierra. *Before I change my mind.*

Between sobs Sierra managed to say, "Thank you, Mac," and tried to embrace her.

"Just go," Mackenzie said.

Wrapping the baby in a waiting blanket with the expertise of a neonatal primate handler, Sierra bundled it into a large basket. It wouldn't do to have the security cameras see her leave with a newborn. With one last look at Lucy, Sierra was gone.

Taking Lucy's hand, Mackenzie ran the back of her fingers

over the animal's cheek. Lucy's mouth was open enough to reveal wicked canines and pink gums. Mackenzie didn't know how long she watched the even rise and fall of the huge barrel chest before she finally pushed the pentobarbital.

Mackenzie's fingers broke the surface of the pool. She felt Tituba's warm shoulder against her own and saw mist clinging in tiny droplets on the gray hairs of the old gorilla's brow. The moonlight reflected in her cloudy, digitized eyes. She took Tituba's hand and felt the callused fingers close on her own.

"Stop."

The virtual safari closed down and the rectangle that was Mac's living space came into view. She slipped off the headset and gazed at the window wall she had programmed with a jungle night scene. The moon was rising through a stand of kapok trees, and howler monkeys called from a distance.

Henry's gentle snoring replaced the chuffs of gorillas.

She got up and stood beside the bed, watching him sleep. She loved this man. And he loved her enough to agree to bribe their way to a birth license. It had been three years since Sierra walked out of the F.R.E.S. with a basketful of human infant. Within a year, she had been arrested, her daughter placed in foster care. But the news couldn't leave it alone; a gorilla had given birth to a human child.

Mackenzie would force the world to look into the eyes of a living animal again.

Mackenzie arrived at the F.R.E.S. cryobank long before the sun came up. What had been a thousand acres of carefully controlled habitats for hundreds of species was now occupied by a resort hotel and casino. She pushed past a throng of tourists to the elevator banks. Once inside, she scanned her security clearance and hit the button that took her down to the maze of labs, offices, and cryobanks deep underground. As director of the bank, no one would question why she was here hours before any other personnel arrived.

The freezers were on the lowest floor, a good thousand feet underground. Liquid nitrogen circulated through tanks sunk into the rock, losing little to evaporation as the chambers themselves were kept at −100° C.

Mackenzie struggled with the thermal suit, which usually required two people to secure. She locked the headgear in place and opened the airlock. The visor fogged briefly as the temperature differential passed and the system took over.

At the apex of five corridors she stood, listening to her breath quicken through the regulator, and considered the line of tanks vanishing in either direction into the rock-hewn cavern. Fur and feather, claw and fang, all reduced to a frozen zoo, a mausoleum waiting to be awakened by a more enlightened generation. The human soul had no meaning without them.

She took a wheelie down a corridor until she stood before tank PG51619.

She punched a code into the lock, and a tower rose from its nitrogen bath, streaming with sublimed gas. Holding her wrist to the codes, she identified the right box and the data was projected by the heads-up holo display in her visor.

The image of Tituba turned and looked into Mackenzie's eyes as a karyotype and medical history scrolled beside it.

Selecting one of the fifty HD polytubes containing Tituba's fertilized embryos, Mackenzie placed it into the insulated carrier. The tower receded with a puff into the silver sea of nitrogen.

Outside the airlock, she peeled off the thermal suit and tucked the cylindrical carrier into her backpack. She checked the time. She had the first appointment of the day for implantation. She couldn't be late.

Rainbows for Other Days

written by

C. Stuart Hardwick

illustrated by

ANDREW SONEA

ABOUT THE AUTHOR

C. Stuart Hardwick is a real southerner—he's from South Dakota. Ghost towns and geysers, stone tools and dinosaur bones were the backdrop to Air Force jets and mankind's first steps on the moon. Weaned on Black Hills treasure hunts and family lore like pages from a Steinbeck novel, Stuart spent summers creating "radio shows" on antique recording tape, making stop-animation films, and speculating down the barrel of a telescope.

A science fair robot led to a career in software development and even a stint working with the creator of the video game Doom *(who played his music way too loud). Over time, editing and technical writing brought Stuart back to his first love— storytelling. Along the way, he married an aquanaut, got hugged by a manatee and studied writing at UC Berkeley.*

Stuart draws literary inspiration from contrasting cultures and styles. His blog, Sputnik's Orbit, *features a hardboiled retelling of* Paradise Lost *set in the atomic ruins of Nagasaki. "Rainbows for Other Days" began as a study of just such a crossroads and is now being developed into a novel. Other projects include a far-future holy war set against echoes of an extinct alien culture, and a thriller pitching a female oil contractor into a battle of international intrigue.*

Stuart lives in Houston with his family and urban sled dog, and has been known to wear a cape.

ABOUT THE ILLUSTRATOR

Born and raised in Ottawa, Canada, 20-year-old Andrew Sonea is currently breaking into the illustration field. After spending much of his youth playing water polo at a competitive level—eventually reaching the Canadian Junior National Team—he decided to quit the sport in order to pursue art.

In high school he began to take art more seriously, and taught himself how to do digital painting. Despite having painted in oils, acrylics and watercolor, he still prefers using digital tools for his final images.

Andrew attended Sheridan College for illustration, but after less than a year into the program he decided to drop out and continue along the self-taught route. Andrew began painting fantasy after getting interested in Magic: the Gathering, *and is highly inspired by painters from the late nineteenth century, as well as contemporary fantasy and science fiction artists.*

He enjoys the process of helping others and has done hundreds of paintovers for other artists to help teach them concepts. For several years he was a moderator on one of the largest art forums, ConceptArt.org, where he also led weekly competitions. He has even won six Teen Challenges and one Character of the Week Challenge there.

He is continuing to move forward and plans on working freelance in the foreseeable future.

Rainbows for Other Days

I need the little brush, the one so good for feathering the paint where the rainbows cut the clouds. As I rummage through my pencils and broken bits of chalk, an alert hits my subsystems. I pause to access the sensor net and confirm for myself. The sour rain is coming.

My folding chair squeaks—a lone echo against the hot black rocks overlooking the preserve. For long minutes, bristles on canvas make the only other sound. Then the breeze stirs, the easel titters, and the forest below fills with whispers. The sun's getting low, the thunder's close, and the approaching band of rain will be a killer. Rainbows will have to wait.

By dusk, I've carried my things down the hand-hewn steps to the ranger station, a boxy gray building with arched metal roofing like two Quonset huts superimposed at right angles. The ground floor's for working, the upstairs for living. I don't go upstairs.

I take some water and rations, though I'm unlikely to need either, and slip on my knee boots and poncho. The rain doesn't burn any more, but the gear helps with the mud, and that's where I find most of the strays. In heavy rains, the gullies grow bloated and orange with muck. I work from the tree-lined banks, peering down through the silt, mostly in infrared. The strays are usually drowned, and I carry them up the bank and note their location for later disposal. Occasionally, I find a survivor, but that's not likely tonight—not in the sour rain. Still, these sweeps are essential. The rain does enough damage. The reconstituted wilderness is fragile. It doesn't need corpses fertilizing the soil any more than it needs foraging homesteaders.

By the time I head down the steep winding path toward the citadel, the dark skies have opened up. Despite my upgraded senses, I don't find so much as an owl or lizard all the way down. Anything that can, has fled.

I follow the swollen creek behind the citadel complex, where the trees spill out of the hills. The road to the grow-houses has flooded, so I cross the narrow cable bridge and climb into the preserve to where the beavers have their ponds. The sour rains are fewer than they once were, and for several years now these dams have had regular keepers. They're a promising sign of recovery and the perfect platform from which to continue my sweep before moving farther east along the drainage.

The upper dam is wide enough and old enough to have saplings sprouting along it. I have no fear of crossing, even as thunder rattles up through the roots and limbs beneath my feet. Here and there, fish carcasses flash in the lightning, but only a few. The forest is quiet except for the rain, but it's a violent kind of peace. Everything is hiding. Only the water moves—falling, dripping, collecting—flooding down past underbrush wilting and gray.

The air stinks of muck and earth. The overtaxed creek has filled the lower pond with yellow sediment. There amidst the flotsam is a heat signature—a stray. I hurry across and down the bank to the second dam, a shabby tangle no taller than I am and far less substantial than the first. I see my quarry caught on an island of jumbled branches, what might be the beginnings of a lodge. I scan the water and trees. No predators, and though the yellow floodwater is caustic and tainted, it's no real threat to me. The dam is overtopping, though—in danger of collapse.

I shuck off my poncho and leap. I beeline through the murk, around the submerged branches and up beside the stray. She's just a girl—nearly grown—and filthy, clothed in gray tatters and covered in blisters and sores. She's washed in from the creek, from water too acid even for my artificially toughened hide.

ANDREW SONEA

I check her heart and lung sounds—evaluate her in multiple spectra and frequencies. She's half drowned and badly dehydrated. Her blood chemistry is off. Without immediate attention, she'll die.

I steel myself and run the script. My cheeks burn. My forehead sweats. I struggle not to retch as my lungs fill with mucous and fluid as if I were the one drowning. I bend over the girl, press my lips into hers—smear them with sticky, reparative slime and breathe oxygen and engineered immune cells into her ragged lungs. She coughs enough to clear the water from her body. I cough until I'm shaking, until my ocular implants ache and run with tears that will repair her corneas just as they maintain my own bio-polymer lenses.

Now she has a chance.

Back at the station, I strip and wash her, and apply a medicinal salve. I push a liter of saline into her veins and wrap her in the softest blanket available, something old and woolen and olive drab. By morning, she's had two more liters and her lips have regained some color. I leave her to sleep while I tend to repairs, but she doesn't have my power feed; she'll need nourishment if she's to survive.

At midday, I boil a ration bar and rouse her for a few sips of broth. She objects with vague, gagging sounds of protest. I tell her I'm a ranger, that I'll mend her and return her to the citadel as soon as she's strong enough. Her eyes, already swollen and clotted, squeeze tight, as if in self-defense. She whispers with effort, "Take me outside!"

I warn of the sour rain. She glares through puffy red slits. The climate service has announced the end of a nearby remediation. The rains will freshen, at least for a while. I'll take her out when it's safe. I promise. This seems to satisfy her, and I coax a few more sips. She sleeps the rest of the day and long into the night.

My office is bright with moonlight when I'm roused from my hammock by a crash. She's upset the tray on which I've left the salve and my few medical implements. When I reach her, she scowls and cowers like an animal. Again, she rasps, "Outside!" The rain's let up. We can both hear the slowing patter of the drips outside the windows. I should not have promised—she's in no condition—but she pulls the blanket snug and waits.

Very well. I scoop her up, careful of the salve, and carry her out across the cluttered porch and down to the station yard. I stand in the moonlight, unsure quite what to do next. Then the breeze stirs her tangled curls. Her eyes close and her cheeks warm. She draws in the night, like a tonic, and sighs.

I clear a space on the covered upstairs balcony for the bed I no longer use. Tucked in before the open air, she finally rests.

She sleeps for a night and a day, waking for broth but making no further demands. By the second morning, her color is better and she's strong enough to sit and try to eat. I've found a Muscovy dead on the nest, and I fry its eggs for a meal. I help her with the blanket, then fill her plate and sit, using an equipment crate for a stool.

She seems put off and tries to speak, then scratches out a whisper. "It's wrong...."

"I'm sorry, miss?"

"To waste food. I can't eat all this."

She takes the fork and hesitates, then saws through the mounded eggs and pushes the bulk away. Her nod, chin first, is an invitation I let pass. She gulps down a bite, winces, and chews the next more carefully. Then she nudges the rejected eggs farther up the lip of the plate, closer to me, and speaks with her mouth full of food.

"You eat, don't you? You a man or a machine?"

"I'm a ranger, miss."

She squints, wholly unsatisfied, and takes another bite, watching as if to see what I might do. But I've taken her meaning. I pull my camp knife from its scabbard and scoop up some eggs.

Normally, my acquisition of energy and chemical supplements is accomplished far more efficiently, but I push in a bite without comment.

She downs her mouthful in several swallows, watching all the while. "Why do you cover your face?"

I stop chewing. The hood, really just a pinned scrap of raw canvas, is for her benefit. To all external appearances, I am still a man. My service couplings and ports are concealed within my clothing, my armor and augmentations below my skin. Some of my sensors, though, are necessarily conspicuous. The orbital modifications—and the ocular implants that permit me to see quite clearly with a cloth over my face—are disturbing to naturals. They're disturbing to me.

I swallow. "Eat."

Instead, she sets down the fork. "What's your name?"

"Ranger triple-zed, one-two-one—"

"No!" She violently waves a hand and rasps, "I don't need your damn URI, I already got one!" Her elbows grinding the table, she turns her palm toward me, pointing to the number blazoned below her wrist as she coughs and wheezes a breath.

I lift an aluminum cup in which she might not have noticed her water, and set it closer to her. "Yes, miss. Two-two-seven—"

"Carralodelphina!" She takes the cup in both hands and sips. "People call me Carra. What do they call you?"

"People…"

She glares. If I say they call me ranger, I gather she's picked out something to throw in my direction.

"I'll put these eggs aside for later."

The rains have freshened and finally paused. Late in the afternoon, she falters down the stairs by herself, though I've asked her to ring for my help. She's found a spare sheet and wrapped herself in a sort of toga. I reach her before she can fall and help her down to the landing.

She holds up a dusty, leathery thing, an ancient jacket with a ragged sleeve.

"This has 'Freytag' written in the collar. I guess that's you?"

I stare at the writing, conscious that the answer should come easily, feeling as if something precious and familiar has been taken—or maybe just lost to neglect. She mistakes my stumble for reticence.

"Fine. Well, I'm calling you Frey." She drops the glare with the jacket. "Take me outside, Frey."

I've just set out the easel, so to cheer her, I carry her up to the overlook. As I climb, the forest canopy draws flat, wrapping the hillsides in a ruffled sea that expands to encompass the horizon. She looks around, clearly pleased. This is as "outside" as she can likely conceive within the confines of natural human senses.

A rattle sounds nearby, and she eagerly looks for its source. Diamondbacks have been moving into the hills along the edge of the preserve, attracted by the growing rodent population. One has found its way onto the warm, exposed rocks of the overlook, and in response to our arrival, has coiled itself defensively. Despite this warning and mine, though, the girl ambles over as soon as I set her down. She bends and reaches as if to stroke the serpent's head. It rattles and strikes, but I strike faster. I snatch it behind the jaw, holding it while she gawks.

"The outside is full of dangers," I say, tossing the snake out over the treetops. "I've been engineered to survive. You have not."

The sun has slipped into the hills behind us. She stares east, toward a purple sky and the last of the sour rain. She sees the rainbow, perhaps her first, and draws a startled breath.

"Then make me like you."

What a horrific thought. She stands there, blue eyed, pink skinned, frail and weak. The waning light passes through her cheeks so easily, I can map her blood vessels without resorting to scans. But she's truly alive. Stubborn as the owl holding out through the rain for her choice of fresh-killed fish. Fierce as the coyote fighting for scraps around the poison seeps. Four billion years of wild perfection, and she's asking to be cut up and domesticated by the same fools who so ruined the earth, most of it is unfit for her to walk on. The same fools who sent robots to explore other worlds and turned their sons into robots to police this one.

"You don't know what you ask, miss."

"Don't you want to help me?"

"I..." My duty is to the biosphere of which she is but one part. "I am a ranger."

"I won't go back."

If only I *were* just a robot. "Then something terrible will happen."

I follow her gaze to the rainbow, a nearly perfect semicircle stretching across the clouds. She sees seven distinct bands of color. I see the continuum, about sixteen thousand gradations at this resolution, with an ugly line where my UV sensor doesn't mesh with the visible band. I can track a bee through the forest by the heat of its wing muscles, but I can no longer see the rainbow—not as she does—not as a human being.

I turn back to her. "I understand you need the earth. It needs you as well, but for now you are harmful to one another. There are rainbows enough for other days."

She turns her wild, bloodshot eyes on me. "How many days do you think I have, Frey?"

Fair enough. It will be another century before reintroduction, maybe more. There is still much to be done, much to coax nature to do for herself. The girl will never see that day, it's true, but I still must ensure that it comes.

She sits, her slight frame barely deflecting the tattered canvas of my folding chair. She startles at movement in a nearby treetop—just an owl stretching its wings—then recovers her defiant glare.

"I won't go back. I'll die first."

Something terrible...I want to help her, I do—and that's exactly why I cannot. I turn the easel and start lining out the shape of her eyes.

For a few days, I stay close and tend to neglected maintenance so I can also tend the girl. To supplement the ration bars, I take a few rabbits. They are prolific, easily tracked in infrared, and quickly dispatched with a well-aimed stone. Feeding her is no problem. Protecting her is another matter. As she heals, she starts exploring. When the black bear comes to test the waste bin lids, she's sensibly wary. She's fascinated, though, by the dusty little lynx created to replace the extinct wildcats. When I catch her trying to lure a skunk, she repays my every warning with a dozen questions. She's clever and she knows it, but she doesn't know this world.

Later, on the overlook, I encourage her quiet rest by continuing her portrait. I experiment to find a suitable representation for her loose sandy curls. She sits before the blush of dawn, looking north past fields of millet to where the citadel rises through the mist. I tell her about the beavers, and thinking the idea might cheer her, suggest that when she's recovered, she might come with me to check on them.

She stares into the distance and makes no reply, but after resting that way for some time, declares, "You must be very old."

"I am," I admit without looking up from my brush work, "very, very old."

"How can you be so *very* old if the world is as dangerous as you say?"

"Because I am a ranger, made for a time when the world was more dangerous still."

The chair creaks the way it does when she's deciding whether to glare or just "harrumph."

"I'm part machine. My augmentations make me quick and strong. They enhance my senses and strength. I can go weeks without food or water, hours without a breath, and I've survived injuries no natural could hope—or would want—to."

"Such as?"

"I . . . don't remember, specifically."

"I don't believe you!"

The mind is adept at burying the unendurable, yet retaining its significance. This is one reason I stand here instead of a mere robot. Many a haunted man has been saved by his phantoms, but when one has survived as long as I have—and buried as much—little else remains.

"Memories are more malleable than you think."

She mulls this over. "And the animals? Are they made to survive the dangers too?"

"No. They survive mostly as nature always has, by producing offspring faster than they are killed. The grow-houses make up the shortfalls. Any surpluses starve. The carcass of one is carrion for another."

Revulsion washes over her face, and I think perhaps I've steered her thoughts along the desired path, but no.

"At least they get to live. They survive or they die, but at least in the preserve they're free. Where's *my* preserve, Frey?"

"You have the citadel."

"The animals are free and the people are caged!"

Finally, I look up from the canvas. "Nature is given time and space to restore itself. People are prevented from overtaxing its recovery. The needs of both are met."

"Needs? What do you know about needs? What people need most is freedom!"

"You can't need anything more than continued survival."

"No?" She unfurls herself from the chair and stamps around the easel, pointing out across the treetops. "Then how do you explain that!" Her voice, finally full and clear, but strained as if forced to be so against its nature, echoes in the distance.

I know where she's pointing. There's something there... something I've seen before. I look away, though, across the forest.

She rounds on me, her face growing red. "You monster!" Her cheeks streak with tears. She pumps her fists, shakes and screeches, "Why won't you look?"

I never look that way. It's better not to look, not to have to forget again. But she stands there glaring, her eyes red and wet, her skin red and raw. Her echoes linger. She needs me to look—so I look.

The citadel is a massive, enclosed octagon of mildew-stained concrete, twenty stories high and as many kilometers across. Against the nearest face stands a large, flat-roofed warehouse, part of the south agricultural complex. The complex is maintained by robots and by rangers like me, one-time soldiers remodeled to preserve the race they helped bring to ruin. From the grow-houses and hatcheries, ponds and paddies, they can't see what I see. They can't see the warehouse roof jutting out like a shelf six stories over their heads, ten stories beneath a ventilation porch dimpling the citadel wall. They can't see the bones, heaped on that roof, broken and scattered, the final remains of countless desperate jumpers over hopeless generations.

I look. Even at this distance, my enhanced senses easily fix the number of individual dead. With my spatial coprocessor, I estimate the number of similar sites that might exist throughout the citadel. With my old military psyops database, I extrapolate the number of others who are physically or mentally unable to find similar release. I look. I see. I understand. My augmented proprioception even tells me how many calories I'm burning as I quake before the sight.

"I…"

Any man might say he didn't know, might seek forgiveness for his inaction, might express sympathy or sorrow. I didn't know, but I am not a man.

"I will contact the caretakers at once."

"No!"

She throws her tiny self against me like a bird attacking a mountain. She beats impotently against my chest, wasting her energies on my internal armor.

"Don't you get it?" she cries, "They jump 'cause they'd rather die than go on living in that…that incubator! It's a three-day journey through the mechs to reach that vent. Jumpers save up rations for the trip. They send their friends ahead to distract the caretakers. They have a big sendoff before they go, and if they make it, they're heroes 'cause at least they had the courage to try."

I understand the bones, but not her choice of words. How is courage connected with suicide? She seems to know what I'm thinking. She closes on me, forcing tremulous sounds from vocal chords barely up to the strain.

"There's nothing else to try *for*! But some people have even more courage than that. Some pay to get their daughters smuggled into the drains! Just for a way out—any way out! Do you want to know what they pay, Frey? Do you want to know what they pay?"

I stagger back from this outburst. Once it's spent, though, she throws herself against me, weeping and clutching so tightly, I take the belated precaution of disarming my combat reflexes.

"I won't have it all be for nothing, Frey! I won't go back. I won't! And if you tell, they'll just close off the last bit of hope! Don't you see? Isn't there anything human left inside you at all? Rocks can survive. That's not enough for us; we need to live!"

She cries, simple, earnest, gulping sobs. What consolation can I offer? What protection can I give against a thousand poisons in the land, from radioactive dust blown in from the wastelands, from a recovery plan that will not permit what she desires? Already, she stays me from my duties. Am I to invite more of her kind to join her? Am I to sacrifice the wilderness for one wild girl? I could give back the gains of a decade just so she might live long enough to see her children die. It would never be enough, and it would never be allowed.

None of this will persuade her. She needs to be free. She needs to survive. She cannot do both.

"We're all machines," I say at last. "We all are bound to our programming."

None of us are strangers to pain, either. When tears are overridden, my sinuses ache with a cold, metallic pang. It pricks me now as I set down my brush and wrap her in my arms.

The girl is growing stronger. She's ventured to the edge of the woods to jury-rig a watering trough fed from the station's gutters. She's determined I recognize her ingenuity.

"See? We could even help the rangers. We can stay out of the preserves and help restore the wastelands. We'll survive. We'll look out for each other. You could help us plenty if you wanted."

Wants and needs are less distinct than she imagines. Freedom is far more circumscribed. Yes, I have a great deal of discretion— to take what I need, go where I like, and do what I must do. But what I must do, mostly, is follow my program.

She's programmed differently but no less surely—to dream, to mate, to carve out a life and a home. It's her nature to scrabble and climb and seek every advantage. If fortune is kind, she'll fill the world with her progeny. If not, she'll soon be replaced by another with more restraint or less, better reflexes or better luck—whatever it takes to survive. That's how life has always adapted. But mankind long ago learned to change his culture instead of his bloodline, to let his ideas bear the brunt of the risks. This worked so well, his numbers swelled and he soon outstripped the endurance of any land that held him.

Whatever I might want, whatever compassion I might yet harbor, *this land* is protected.

After so many minutes in the midday sun, the girl's pale flesh is likely already burning. "You can help me by keeping safe," I say, "and by leaving my duties to me."

I clamp my fingers around her handiwork, intending to recover the scrap metal. It's a clever design, though, a single aluminum sheet, loosely folded into a basin like an origami flower. I bend over a sharp edge and leave the thing where it is. It's not a bad idea exactly, but it's motivated by naïve compassion instead of a reasoned plan. The preserves can't be maintained forever. Creatures too dependent on the vagaries of human kindness will have no place in the self-regulating wilderness to come. Short-sighted compassion is no compassion at all.

"Mankind can never surpass nature's wisdom, miss."

She cocks her head and squints, shielding her eyes with her hand. "No? Why's that?"

"Because he wants what he can never have—an end to suffering. Nature wants nothing. It just is. Life seeks its level. It now and then visits misery or pain and then goes on its way. But man is unhappy. He makes gods and governments to alleviate suffering and walls off his children from it. When the walls fall down, the deluge strikes. So he builds higher still, till he dams up the whole of the world. And when the whole world crashes down, there's nothing left but suffering."

She steps up, grasps my hood by a corner, and flicks it suddenly away. I'm conscious of the subtle whir as my lenses refocus. She masks her revulsion in an instant, but not the altered tension in the muscles holding her smile. "You could help us anyway."

Perhaps. If I had time. If my program didn't forbid it. If hers didn't require it. If the world already had the balance I am programmed to establish.

For millennia, mankind binged on Earth's pantry. When he'd wrung from it more than it could bear, he fought over the scraps. Finally, he fought for his very existence, by which time little remained of the resilient hand of nature. If anything of man was to survive, someone had to rebuild what he'd trampled. Someone had to restrain his ambitions until the job was done. This was too much responsibility for a robot, too much temptation for a man. So it was given to the rangers. We had the requisite drive and reason, and our passions had already been ceded to cybernetic control.

That's me—committed soldier and savior. And to ensure I remain so, it's only necessary that anything be removed that might distract or dissuade me. This is done mostly by erasing the memory of anything that stirs what humanity I have left. It only takes the right intercranial chemistry at the right moment— easily within the grasp of my regulatory subsystem. But every excision takes with it another sliver of what once was me.

I don't *want* anything. I can't afford to. The girl thinks me a monster. Perhaps she's right.

A stag has dropped its collar and I must retrieve the data before the transponder runs down. I leave before first light and hike deep into the hills, but my thoughts are on the girl. The audit is due. She'll be flagged as an invasive species and dealt with accordingly. The worst part is, she's right—a small group of naturals might well survive. A community might even be useful on the edge of the wastelands, but they lie too many kilometers away, past too many rangers and too many sensors. All will conspire to prevent it. If I can't appeal to her reason, to her sense of self preservation, there is no one else to hear me. The recovery will go forward according to a plan not blind exactly, but resolute by design. One way or the other she'll die, and I won't even remember her face.

I find the collar near a ridge, in an area where the deer have been stressing the goats and boars. In the valley lies the dam from which the citadel gets most of its power. The morning sky is clear, the sun is low and orange, and the hillsides glow with dappled green. But something's wrong. The reservoir's banks are littered with fallen pines. Its waters are muddy and choked with foam and debris.

The lake has turned.

Across the globe, industrial-era ruins lay moldering beneath centuries' worth of regrowth and reinjury. As they decay, they produce methane, hydrogen sulfide and a macabre cocktail of industrial poisons. A hidden seep must have formed beneath the reservoir lake. In this newly tropical climate, its products have accumulated in the deep cold waters, undisturbed for decades. Now something's upset them, and a mass of cold asphyxiating gas has burst through the surface.

I see it in infrared, a false-violet blanket hugging the valleys as it courses down toward the citadel. I signal the alarm. The caretakers and rangers will have little trouble escaping the cloud, but I hurry back just in case I'm needed. By the time I reach the hills behind the citadel, the sun is high and the cloud has dispersed.

Within the preserve, five seeps are known. The sensors around the nearest have all tripped. This likely means part of the cloud followed the ravine above the beaver dams. A thousand meters back, I head east along the high ground and around to the seep. The coyote is alive and well and shepherding her pups down through the withered underbrush in search of fresh meat. I press on, down to the ponds and the beavers. I know from the sensors that they survived the rains. Now I find one lounging atop the upper dam, gnawing bark from a willow branch.

I circle around the lower pond, toward the end of a sensor path left by a larger animal, probably one of the bears that frequent my trails. But sensors can be misleading.

Across from the bridge, near the spot where I first saw the girl, I find her once again. She's stretched out in a crook between two branches where she'd no doubt crept to spy on the beavers before the gas cloud washed over her. I kneel and move her golden curls aside. All healed up now, she's pretty and pale and wrapped in percale. Her face rests on folded arms as if she were napping on her pillow. Finally, she's at peace.

A woodpecker's drumming echoes through the trees, too late to send her scampering for a vantage point or assailing me with breathless questions. I rock forward on one knee and press my cheek against her hair. My breathing falters. My forehead throbs with icy pain.

At least, in the end, she was free.

The overlook is too quiet and too wet, so I've ventured upstairs and out on the balcony. In a corner of the girl's portrait, I carefully draw the letters of her name. Then I use a large brush to overcoat the canvas with heavy white gesso made from flaxseed oil and chalk. Then come purples, blues and grays, and soon I'm feathering in the seven distinct bands of color that she would see stretched above me, across the eastern sky. Thus protected, her portrait will remain hidden as long as I stick to visible light—as I do when painting rainbows.

I try not to think of her, not to mourn, not to dream—but it's hopeless. The memories cloud my conscience. In a day or two as they surface, each will be wiped away like damp paint. I can work fast when I need to, though. I finish with the brushwork, pull the bed back inside, and put the old jacket away. I seldom climb these stairs anymore. I don't often step back in the shadows to straighten and sweep the cobwebs. I never leaf through the canvases and boards, stacked in crates and on shelves and standing in rows against the walls. They are nothing I need to attend to. They will keep. I set this latest painting with the others—rainbows for other days.

Giants at the End of the World

written by

Leena Likitalo

illustrated by

TREVOR SMITH

ABOUT THE AUTHOR

Leena Likitalo hails from Finland, the land of endless summer days and long, dark winter nights. She lives with her husband on an island at the outskirts of Helsinki, the capital. But regardless of her remote location, stories find their way to her and demand to be told.

While growing up, Leena struggled to learn foreign languages. At sixteen, her father urged her to begin reading in English, and thus she spent the next summer wading through his collection of fantasy and science fiction novels. She has fond memories of her "teachers": J.R.R. Tolkien, Robert Jordan, Roger Zelazny and Vernor Vinge.

Leena breaks computer games for a living.

When she's not working, she writes obsessively. And when she's not writing, she can be found at the stables riding horses or at the pool playing underwater rugby.

Her Writers of the Future win is her third professional sale, her fiction having appeared in Weird Tales, Waylines, *and semipro publications. She has recently finished writing a steampunk novel around her winning short story. She dreams—and oh, how sweet those dreams are!—of seeing it in print one day.*

Leena's first-place story is among those that will be competing for the annual grand prize, the L. Ron Hubbard Golden Pen Award.

ABOUT THE ILLUSTRATOR

Trevor Smith has happily lived in the desert of Tucson, Arizona, most of his life, except for five years living in San Francisco while attending art school.

Loving art school but not the city he lived in, he came back to Tucson with all of the skills he needed to begin a freelance career in illustration and fine art oil painting.

His illustration degree focused on digital painting, which he uses to bring fantasy and sci-fi stories to life.

Simultaneously, Trevor is oil painting, but on entirely different subject matter. Instead of painting otherworldly subjects, he is inspired by the beauty that he sees around him. This can vary from grungy cityscapes to the pastel colors in the clouds above a landscape. Recently, even graphic cubism has ignited new inspiration.

With such a zeal for learning and sharing his creativity, Trevor revels in the fact that he will never run out of inspiration or ways to expand his art spirit. Perhaps 2014 will be the year for him to make his mark on others—whether through a peculiar cubist piece, or an evocative scene of an alien planet.

Giants at the End of the World

It was the last caravan of the giant season. Though the United Company had already started to build the railroad toward the End of the World, the path of iron and wood reached only as far as Halvington. Unlike the other drivers, I realized that the era of salt wagons was coming to an end.

Perhaps Elai had expected the railroad to be ready to take her to find answers to all her existential questions. With pale hair and gray eyes, she looked about eighteen, definitely not a day older. She wore a full-length leather coat, buttoned all the way up to her chin, and boots that looked too new to be yet comfortable. Even so, when she glided down Halvington's main street, the scrawny miners and shaggy railroad workers alike rushed to tip their hats, and some even bowed.

She noticed none of that.

"I want to buy a one-way ticket to the End of the World," Elai said to me, her pleasant voice a disturbing breeze from the past I'd thought forever left behind.

My camel-oxen, Edison and Beat, stared at her just as I did. Every inch of her shouted of a pedigree long enough to make me dizzy, the way her mouth shaped words, how she expected to be listened to and obeyed.

"It's cheaper to buy a round-trip," I said, rubbing the snouts of my beasts. Edison calmed soon enough, but Beat kept on snorting. He'd never smelled anything as fine as Elai's perfume, and the scent of lilies confused him. "There's not much to see at the End of the World."

"Like I care," Elai said, the simple words akin to a foreign language. A flicker of emotion escaped to her face, but she tilted her head so that her hat's wide brim prevented me from interpreting the expression.

"Fine then," I said, as arguing with an aristocrat was an act doomed to fail. If she wanted to escape some hell of her own making, then who was I to try and stop a paying customer? "Stay with my wagon, don't lag, and don't try to steal extra portions of water. In the desert the word of a wagon driver is the law."

We started the eleven-week journey the next day, my wagon full of water crates and paid parcels. Edison and Beat waddled, slow and heavy with all the water they'd absorbed from the communal mud puddles. The families and the loners hoping to find something better than what they'd abandoned pranced after the wagon, still enthusiastic about the journey.

Elai started to limp as soon the caravan left the valley where Halvington slumped under the ever-thick blanket of coal smoke. The assorted loners tried to strike up conversation with her one after another, only to be firmly dismissed:

"Where am I from? From beyond the sea."

"Where am I going? To the End of the World."

"Is there someone waiting for me back at home? That is not for you to worry about."

Her evasive replies bored me, and so I stared at the scenery instead. This close to the city, the inevitable wastewater gave life to tufts of grass and twisted cacti that stuck out from amidst the dunes. The sand might have contained a few grains of salt, but not enough to warrant efforts to collect it. The wind came in gusts that were pleasant compared to the gales that the caravans often met.

As the day progressed, those who really intended to settle at the End of the World started to lag behind. Children tugged at their parents' coattails, tiring already under their bundles.

TREVOR SMITH

It would take the settlers a few days to decide it wasn't worth the bother to carry all the materialized memories of their old lives with them. Children would abandon their toys, wives their diaries, husbands their medals.

I halted my wagon to wait for them. Elai used the opportunity to rest and sat down on the sand. Much to my surprise, she pulled off her boots and socks in a most unladylike manner.

Blisters covered her toes, and her raw heels glistened in painful shades of red. I was sure she would start complaining, but instead she simply redonned the socks and boots. Perhaps that was why I took pity on her.

"Hop on, girl," I murmured. She would be nothing but trouble, a hindrance if her feet got infected.

"I can walk, thank you very much," Elai said, too proud to accept help.

"Fine," I answered, annoyed at myself for having offered her help in the first place. I flicked the reins, and Edison and Beat resumed their slow waddle. To avoid awkward conversation, I started singing.

> There's a long road ahead of us.
> Where does it take me? Where, oh where?

Perhaps back in the Old World Elai had found herself indebted to someone and had fled to avoid having to pay. Or perhaps she'd broken her heart and her parents' trust. Or perhaps ... but her problems were none of my business. She'd made that clear enough.

> It's not the miles I travel that change me.
> No, my friend, it's not the miles ...

I realized that someone was humming the melody. I glanced over my shoulder, but there was no one near me but Elai. She clenched her mouth shut, but didn't stop humming.

I sang louder, even though both Edison and Beat put back their ears.

In the end it's only the time that matters,
the days and weeks that we leave behind...

The caravan halted only when the night fell. The other drivers and I circled our wagons protectively around the campsite and unharnessed our camel-oxen. The beasts would return after enjoying the scarce night mist and scarcer morning dew, as they were bound to whoever had captured and tamed them. Even so, being apart from Edison and Beat for the night pained me.

As the temperature dropped, Elai joined the rest of us around the fire. She didn't seem to notice how she attracted more looks than was good for her, how the loners edged closer to her, how those on the other side of the fire joked about who would charm her first. She just stared at the sparks disappearing into the night above as though nothing else existed but her and the desert.

I found myself thinking about the Old World and the over-polite ways of the aristocrats. Evidently, Elai couldn't even begin to grasp how rough life could get outside private schools and ballrooms. As she shrugged her narrow shoulders and tilted her pretty head this and that way, the loners thought she was only acting hard to get.

They wouldn't take her "No" for long.

I fell victim to the gallantry that still twisted in my veins and made my way to her. "Come with me," I said, pointing toward my wagon.

She stared at me suspiciously, and I was glad to note she wasn't as foolish as I'd thought. Then she stood, brushed sand off her trousers. "Sure."

"What is it?" Elai asked as soon as we were out of earshot. Her teeth chattered, which only seemed to annoy her more.

An aristocrat would never listen to explanations, so I went right to the point. "You'd better sleep under the wagon with me tonight."

She took my words the wrong way, and her voice rose a full octave. "I certainly will not! Abandon me in the desert if you will, but I will not grant that kind of favor to anyone, least of all a rude old wagoner like you!"

Old? I could be but a decade older than her. Then again, the desert had shaped me a rougher man.

She was about to leave, so I grabbed her hand. She froze, shocked by my apparent lack of manners. It didn't even cross her mind that I might have known etiquette by heart but opted to act against the rules on purpose.

"Before you turn down my offer, which was by no means meant as you chose to interpret it, look at those men around the campfire," I said in a low voice. "Really look at them."

She pulled her hand free, but did as I said. There, amongst the ragged families, sat the men hoping to find a place where no questions were asked: pistol heroes, fugitives, adventurers down on their luck.

"Would you rather have them thinking you're sharing your bedroll with me, or have them trying to approach you every single night of the trip?"

"Fine," she muttered, blushing at the idea of being so close to me. She hadn't broken her heart, then, I decided, but was escaping something. "I will sleep next to you, but nothing else."

I watched her limp back to the campfire. She wasn't the kind who knew how to thank.

I had been like her before I shot my best friend.

The next day, I invited Elai to ride in the wagon with me. Contrary to what I'd expected, she climbed up and sat beside me. I didn't bother her with meaningless chitchat—she wasn't interested in my company. For her, my wagon was just one more bead in the insignificant necklace of the caravan coiling across the red desert. For me, it was all I had.

A week into the journey, we passed the first village, a cluster of a dozen or so giant-hide tents. Elai stared at the indigenous

Lasuo people, a sad frown forming on her flawless forehead. The black-haired, tanned men in the fields waved us a greeting, then resumed working. They knew the caravan would buy salt only on the way back.

"What do you think of the railroad?" Elai asked, breaking the silence that she normally preferred. Her gaze lingered on the women grinding maize and children hiding behind their backs. I could guess what she was thinking—the world was changing, and in a year or two the village would become just a fading memory.

"What is there to think about it?" I asked nevertheless. When the railroad finished, there would be no need for caravans. The Lasuo families would flee deeper into the desert as soon as they saw the first steam-screaming locomotives. They would be wise to do so.

Elai pursed her lips as she did her best to ignore the personal belongings abandoned in the sand. She failed. The caravan road was full of buried treasures, items that had once held importance for someone, only to become nonessential. Tattered photographs peeked from under the rocks; the pages of full diaries rustled in the breeze. The Lasuos never touched what they thought belonged to us, even though our kind never returned the service.

"Doesn't it make you sad?" she asked. She'd buried her hands in the folds of her coat, and as she wrung her fingers, the leather creaked. "To see the world so diminished in size, to see it all become the same."

I flicked the reins, though Edison and Beat were keeping up a good pace. There were still untouched deserts beyond the horizon, lands where the Lasuos could live undisturbed. When the railroad was ready, I would follow them. I didn't want my past to catch up with me. "The world isn't disappearing anywhere."

Elai shook her head. At that moment she looked immensely guilty.

Three weeks into the journey, Elai's guilt had bloomed to full-scale melancholy. She often hummed to herself, the melodies intricate, perfectly memorized. I didn't tell her I recognized the overtures and arias. There was no reason for her to know that we shared a common upbringing.

That day we were traveling along a ledge extending over another expanse of desert. The sun scorched ceaselessly down on us, and the hides of my camel-oxen were hot enough to fry bacon. Even so, Edison and Beat had more than enough water left in their humps for the rest of the way.

"Halt," came the shout from farther ahead in the caravan.

I pulled the reins, drawing my pistol. Though, since I'd become a wagoner, I hadn't had to fire even once. The camel-oxen obeyed only their drivers, the outlaws knew better than to try their luck.

"Wait here," I told Elai nevertheless.

She didn't argue. Then again, a society girl like her expected men to act all gallant and duel to resolve the tiniest of disagreements. They never thought what killing a friend in a drunken stupor did to a man.

Haunted by the dark memories, I left her in the care of Edison and Beat.

A wagon at the front of the caravan had broken a shaft, nothing more spectacular. While the driver set to fix the damaged part, the rest of us waited. The families used the moment to eat and rest. The loners started a card game, though not one of them had anything worth losing or gaining. A group of children ran around in pointless folly.

I returned to Elai and told the news.

"Is it always like this?" Elai asked, perched on the wagon seat. She'd removed her hat to rebraid her hair, and the pale locks shimmered in the harsh sunlight.

"What is like what?" I asked her. Edison swished his tail. Beat closed his eyes.

Elai studied the endless desert, her fingers never stopping, weaving her hair. The corners of her eyes glimmered as if she thought the moment immeasurably valuable, something she would lose all too soon. "So tranquil."

I shrugged. I'd rather lead an uneventful life than see another friend die in a meaningless display of honor. "Caravan journey, or life in general?"

Elai finished her braid with a ribbon. Just then, a boy on the ledge shouted, "Giants!"

No matter how hardened the loners were, each one of them jumped up. The cards fluttered in the hazy air long after them, making their slow way down, to be forgotten on the sand.

"Giants! There below! Giants!" the boy shouted.

As soon as I'd helped Elai down, she dashed toward the shouts, her heels kicking up sand. I walked to the gathered crowd in a leisurely fashion. The giants had even a longer way to go than we did.

I placed myself between the loners and Elai. The men edged farther away from me. The years I'd spent as a wagoner had given me a name much darker than my actual deeds warranted.

"Giants," Elai gasped. "They really exist!"

A group of three giants was crossing the desert below, slowly making their way back from the sea, toward the snowcapped mountains looming in the distance. And no matter that I'd seen giants a hundred times or more, a vivid recollection of the first time I'd met one at the End of the World washed over me.

The giant had been young, only twenty feet tall. Yet his hunched shoulders had been as wide as a camel-ox's back, ochre fur scarred from fighting with older males. He'd beheld me, knife-like fangs peeking from behind chapped lips, saucer-sized nostrils flaring, deep-set eyes glinting with a curiosity of all things. He'd made a sound akin to a boulder tumbling down a cliff, expected me to answer. But I didn't know the language of his kind, hadn't replied, and so he'd waded into the gray sea.

Faded staccato grunts brought me back to the moment. As far as we were from the giants crossing the desert, they were small dots that I could cover with the tip of my thumb. And there, I could see now, six Lasuo men trailed the giants to mark in their maps where the giants' footprints would leave salty pools. They, too, were just tiny specks, almost insignificant.

"They are even more beautiful than I imagined," Elai

whispered, hands clasped over her heart. It took a considerable while for her wonder to subside to curiosity. "Have you ever seen them up close?"

"Yes," I said, thinking about the young giant. The giants woke in the spring when the mountain glaciers started to melt. When they walked, the ground beneath their clawed feet trembled. When they dived into the ocean, waves the size of houses washed against the shore. Just like the camel-oxen, the giants soaked in the water until full. Then they returned back to the glaciers to sleep through the winter. "But you wouldn't believe the tales if I were to tell them."

Elai's brows rose, the fair lines of silver prominent on her tanned face. But melancholy had already crept back into her gaze.

I said to her, "A giant diving is something everyone should see before they die."

We passed the first giant corpse six weeks into the journey. At a distance, the huge bones jutting from the barren ground looked like the frame of a building that didn't yet exist. Closer, the skull half-buried in the sand stared with a sad, empty gaze.

The caravan halted by the old corpse, like it always did.

"Is that what I think it is?" Elai asked, her voice wavering the tiniest fraction. Seeing something as magnificent as a giant dead always touched people, no matter how thick a shell they'd built around themselves.

"It is," I said, my shell cracking a little more.

Elai riveted her gaze on her dirty fingernails. The dry breeze played with the strands that had escaped from her braid, plastering them soon enough against her skin. The night before, she'd cried in her sleep, but I reckoned the toughness of the journey wasn't to blame.

I jumped down and offered her my hand. "Come."

She pulled herself together and accepted my help. She no longer smelled of perfume, but honest sweat.

A sizeable crowd had already gathered around the giant's corpse. They strolled from bone to bone in respectful silence.

The children couldn't understand why and were trying to climb atop the skull despite their parents' hisses.

Elai veered to a halt under the dome of the giant's ribcage. "What killed it?"

We were still in the middle of the desert, far away from the railroads and mines. This giant had died of old age. "Sometimes even the giants fall."

"Surely that is a rare thing to happen," she said, hoping her disbelief would make the words true.

I didn't want to lie to her, and so I said nothing. The miners and railroad workers cared little about the giants that set foot on their grounds. Rather, they shot the beasts dead, ripped off the hides, and left the bodies rotting in the desert.

Elai wiped a tear from the corner of her eye.

I said to her in a low voice, "Don't grieve after things that still exist. Cry only when all is lost."

She tried to meet my gaze, but I wouldn't let her. She understood to wander farther and give me privacy.

As always, when the caravan left the giant's corpse behind, I thought of the horrid accident, the echo of the bullet hitting flesh, and the growing pool of blood.

Another corpse, that of my best friend.

We glimpsed the End of the World after eleven weeks on the road. The town stood by the ocean, on a cliff that even the tallest of waves couldn't reach. The year before, it had been barely more than a collection of a dozen or so ramshackle houses. The recent finding of silver had doubled the town in size.

Elai craned on the seat, frowning at the empty beach below the cliff. "Is this really all there is?"

I didn't have the heart to tell her that the End of the World was nothing more than a rugged town, despite the fancy name. "If you're in luck, you might see some giants swimming when the night falls."

The caravan stopped at the outskirts of town. I unloaded the wagon and handed over what little my customers had afforded to bring with them—worn leather suitcases with perhaps a change of clothes inside, a mirror with a gilded frame, a few bottles of wine that would be worth a fortune here. The families hastened off to find cheap lodgings, to start their lives anew. The loners, Elai amongst them, who didn't quite know which way to go, hovered about my wagon.

I gave them the usual talk. "Here we are then, at the End of the World. Watch out for the cheap tequila and cunning women. And try not to lose too much at the card tables."

All but Elai left. For a moment, I held hopes that perhaps she didn't want to part from me either.

"The caravan will leave in a week or so," I said to her. The journey back would take longer as the caravan would need to stop at the Lasuo villages to buy giant salt crystals. Though, if the miners had found silver, we might prefer to load our wagons with the precious metal.

"I will stay here," Elai said. "Don't worry about me."

Then she, too, left without so much as a glance over her shoulder.

I stood still for a long while, waiting for her to return, even though I knew she wouldn't.

The evening crept to veil the town while I fed and watered Edison and Beat. The camel-oxen sensed my sadness and rubbed their snouts against me. I scratched them, searching for comfort that eluded me.

Suddenly, both Edison and Beat stiffened and fell all silent. Then I heard the throaty whispers too.

The wind carried the roars of the giants returning from the sea.

Elai shivered on the cliff's edge, humming an overly dramatic overture from an opera that didn't end well. The stars hung low enough to light the scene of the giants wading through the waves, climbing up the beach. The scene's morbid beauty haunted my heart.

I approached Elai slowly. If I were to rush at her, drag her away from the treacherous ground, she might fight back and take both of us to the abyss below.

"Nice night to watch the giants," I said nonchalantly, as if I didn't care for her at all.

"I beg your pardon," Elai exclaimed, turning around to meet me. Her heels sent a shower of pebbles into the dark sea.

"What are you thinking?" I asked, though I knew. She had come to the End of the World, never to return.

"Nothing much," she lied. She resumed gazing at the giants, undoubtedly wishing I would leave.

I couldn't respect her wish. I had grown fond of her company. "Really?"

"Could you please..." Elai started, but just then, the biggest giant I had ever seen surfaced. Forty feet tall, centuries old, the beast's sudden appearance made Elai freeze in wonder, forget her gloom.

"The giants are returning home," I said. The sight always comforted me. I hoped she found solace in it too.

"Does anyone know why they do what they do?" Elai asked, her question the one she wished to ask from me. She'd seen through my disguise, knew I hadn't always been a wagoner.

I preferred not to dwell in the past, so I pretended to think about the giants. Why did anyone travel across the desert, from the glaciers to the sea and back? Why did I travel the same route year after year?

"There are three kinds of people who come to this town," I said. "Those who try to escape their past, those who fear their future, and those who have no reason to do either."

"Which one are you?" Elai asked. "Why did you ..."

The roar of the ancient giant drowned her voice. The other giants halted in their tracks, grunted greetings.

Since I'd left the Old World, I hadn't met anyone who could understand what I'd been through. Perhaps Elai would trust me, abandon her plans, if I revealed my secret. "A long time ago," I said, my heart still raw with pain and loss, "I was a young man with a bright future. One night, my very best friend thought I'd cheated in a game of cards and challenged me to a duel."

"You won," Elai said. She knew the etiquette and the rules. I could have stayed in the Old World and continued my life as if nothing at all had happened. It puzzled her that I hadn't.

"It didn't feel like winning," I replied, remembering the lightness of the trigger under my finger, the careless act that had ruined two lives. I had done wrong, even though no one would ever say it aloud. "I came here to punish myself, but it's not as bad here as I deserve."

The ancient giant reached the rest of the herd. The beast shivered to shake off extra water, and it almost looked like it rained down on the beach. As the wind picked up, a few drops reached Elai and me.

"Why did you leave the Old World?" I asked her. Why did she want to take her own life?

Elai closed her eyes as if her sorrow were too great to express. She wiped a lock of hair from her forehead, fixed it behind her ear. "My father owns the United Company. He would see all this ruined just to increase his fame and fortune."

Elai's revelation explained a lot: her melancholy, the guilt she felt. I placed a hand on her shoulder. She didn't move away.

"Did you think that he would back off from building the railroad if you jumped off the cliff at the End of the World?"

The ancient giant bellowed a loud roar, pointed north. The herd replied with a deafening rumble. They started together the journey toward the mountains.

"Yes," Elai said, her voice brittle, frail, "but now that I've had further time to think about it, it doesn't seem like such a great idea."

We watched the giants' slow progress for a long time. I had searched for atonement from punishing myself. Now, after walking the desert in circles for years, I'd wound up in the right place to save a life. "I reckon your father would rather have you back than finish his railroad."

Elai shrugged, but I knew she took my words to heart. The world was changing, true, but it was up to us to decide the direction. No one should die to make a point.

As the night faded to make way for the morning, she took my hand. "I think I shall join the caravan on the way back. I shall tell my father about the giants. It's not yet their time to die."

...And Now Thirty

BY ROBERT SILVERBERG

Robert Silverberg has been a professional science fiction writer since 1955, and is the author of hundreds of stories and books, among them such titles as Lord Valentine's Castle, Nightwings *and* Dying Inside. *His most recent book is* Tales of Majipoor. *He is a many-times winner of the Hugo and Nebula Awards, was guest of honor at the World Science Fiction Convention in Heidelberg in 1970 and in 2004 was named a Grand Master by the Science Fiction and Fantasy Writers of America.*

A Writers of the Future judge from the very first year of the Contest, he received the L. Ron Hubbard Lifetime Achievement Award for Outstanding Contributions to the Arts in 2003.

Robert and his wife Karen live in the San Francisco Bay area.

...And Now Thirty

Five years ago, in the twenty-fifth anthology of the Writers of the Future Contest, I had this to say about L. Ron Hubbard, the founder of the Contest:

"Back in the 1930s and 1940s, before his thoughts turned first to Dianetics and then to Scientology, L. Ron Hubbard was one of the most versatile and prolific of the pulp-magazine storytellers. From his white-hot typewriter poured a prodigious stream of tales in just about every genre of fiction that those gaudy old magazines dealt in: westerns, mysteries, stories of the mysterious Orient, sea adventures, Arctic adventures, air adventures—you name it, and he wrote it. A tour through the long list of his story titles gives us the full flavor of that long-vanished era: 'Cargo of Coffins,' 'The Trail of the Red Diamonds,' 'The Blow Torch Murder,' 'Hell's Legionnaire,' 'The Baron of Coyote River,' 'The Bold Dare All,' 'Red Death Over China,' 'Yukon Madness,' and on and on and on.

"But of all the many kinds of fiction that he wrote, science fiction and fantasy certainly were closest to L. Ron Hubbard's heart. He did the westerns and the Yukon stories and the yellow-peril stuff to pay the rent, I'm pretty sure; but there can be no doubt that he wrote the science fiction and fantasy out of love.... Hubbard's works of science fiction and fantasy long ago established themselves as classics of their kind, and have had no difficulty maintaining their continuing existence in print through decade after decade. The enduring popularity of such Hubbard novels as *Fear, Final Blackout, Slaves of Sleep,* and *Typewriter in the Sky*, all of them fantasy or science fiction and all of them dating back to the early years of the 1940s, shows that he wrote them with something more in mind than his next paycheck. And when he briefly returned to professional writing after the World War II hiatus, at a time when nearly all the old pulp-magazine categories were extinct, it was primarily science fiction and fantasy that he wrote, stories like the Old Doc Methuselah series and the novel *To the Stars,* rather than more Oriental adventure tales or stories of life at sea.

"And so it was not surprising that late in his life, long after he took a break in his writing career to bring Scientology into the world, he would turn again to writing science fiction—with the huge novel *Battlefield Earth* and the gigantic multi-volume Mission Earth series and, in 1983, would establish the Writers of the Future Contest to develop and encourage new talent in the field that he loved."

And I said this, thirty years ago in the first of these volumes of annual award anthologies:

"We were all new writers once—even Sophocles, even Homer, even Jack Williamson. And I think we all must begin in the same way, those of us who are going to be writers. We start by being consumers of the product: in childhood we sit around the campfire, listening to the storyteller, caught in his spell, lost in the fables he spins, envying and admiring him for the magical skill with which he holds us. 'I wonder how he does that,' we think—concerned, even then, as much with technique, the tricks of the trade, as we are with the matter of the tales being told...."

And *ten* years ago, paying tribute to L. Ron Hubbard, the Contest's founder, in an essay I wrote for the twentieth annual anthology, I had this to say:

"Hubbard too had been a young, struggling writer once, in the pulp-magazine days of the 1930s. He loved science fiction and he wanted to ease the way for talented and deserving beginners who could bring new visions to the field. His idea was to call for stories from writers who had never published any science fiction—gifted writers standing at the threshold of their careers—and to assemble a group of top-ranking science fiction writers to serve as the judges who would select the best of those stories. The authors of the winning stories would receive significant cash prizes and a powerful publicity spotlight would be focused on them at an annual awards ceremony."

And this is what I wrote twenty years ago, when I was helping Writers of the Future celebrate the tenth anniversary of the founding of its annual story contest:

"All of them [such early prizewinners as Karen Joy Fowler, Nina Kiriki Hoffman, Robert Reed and Dave Wolverton] were amateurs ten years ago, when this Contest began. But you see their names regularly in print these days. Like you (and like Robert A. Heinlein, Arthur C. Clarke, Ray Bradbury, Isaac Asimov, and, yes, Robert Silverberg) they wanted very, very much to be published writers, and, because they had the talent, the will, and the perseverance, they made it happen."

And, again, once more quoting my essay from the twentieth anniversary anthology: "The amateurs of today are the Hugo and Nebula winners of tomorrow. The Writers of the Future Contest is helping to bring that about."

I quote myself again and again from these four anthologies, spanning two and a half decades, because I've been a part of this remarkable enterprise since the beginning—one of the founding judges, along with Theodore Sturgeon, Roger Zelazny, C.L. Moore, Jack Williamson, Stephen Goldin and Gregory Benford. Of that initial group, which included some of the brightest stars in the science fiction galaxy, very few are still alive, and only Gregory Benford is still an active judge. (I withdrew from judging myself, after nearly thirty years of service, a couple of years ago, but as an emeritus judge I remain a friend and supporter of the Contest.) Over the years, many another illustrious writer has been part of that board of judges—Frederik Pohl, Larry Niven, Tim Powers, Frank

Herbert, Orson Scott Card, Anne McCaffrey, Andre Norton, Hal Clement and more—and the luster of those names will tell you the importance of the position that the Writers of the Future Contest holds within the field of science fiction. Judgeship has even begun to carry over to the second generation, now, with Brian Herbert and Todd McCaffrey, the sons of Frank Herbert and Anne McCaffrey, replacing their progenitors on the panel.

But though the list of judges is an awesome one, what really counts is the list of winners. The very first anthology includes stories by such then-unknown writers as Karen Joy Fowler and David Zindell, both of whom have gone on to considerable writing careers. But if one pulls almost any volume of the series down from the shelves, one will find the early work of writers of the future who went on to become significant writers of the present: here are Ken Liu, Jay Lake and Myke Cole in the nineteenth volume alone, Stephen Baxter and Jamil Nasir in Volume Five, A.C. Crispin in Volume Ten. And so it has gone, year after year, with many of the early contestants coming back to become judges themselves.

The mechanics of the Contest haven't changed in any significant way since the beginning. Entry is limited to writers who have never had a novel or a novella professionally published, and no more than three short stories. The manuscripts submitted are winnowed at the Contest's Los Angeles headquarters by the Contest's staff and coordinating director, and every three months a group of six or eight of them is submitted to the judges. (The authors' names are removed from the manuscripts, to prevent the possibility that a judge might encounter the work of a friend or student.) Each of these quarterly Contests produces a first-place winner, who receives a cash award and a certificate of merit, and at the end of the year the judges are shown the manuscripts of all the quarterly winners, out of which they select a Grand Prize winner, who is given another and very generous cash grant. An annual awards ceremony brings the winners, the runners-up, and the judges together, and that year's Contest is given permanence by the publication of the top stories in an annual paperback anthology, of which the present volume is the thirtieth. The complete set of anthologies forms quite an impressive shelf. It is not a big surprise, nor should it be, that so many of the winners and runners-up of these competitions should have gone on to major careers as science fiction writers or that their early work, as represented in these books, quite clearly displays the merits that would mark the fiction of their mature years ahead.

It's been quite a trip, this thirty-year journey into creativity. I'm proud to have been associated with it from its inception in what is now the far-off decade of the 1980s, and, although I'm no longer an active participant in its proceedings, I hope to continue to observe from the sidelines as the work of discovering exciting new science-fictional talent goes on into the years ahead.

Carousel

written by

Orson Scott Card

illustrated by

VINCENT-MICHAEL COVIELLO

ABOUT THE AUTHOR

Orson Scott Card is the author of the novel Ender's Game, *along with more than fifty other books of fiction and nonfiction in many genres, including* Pathfinder *and* The Lost Gate. *He also wrote the script of the audioplay* Ender's Game Alive *and writes the weekly column "Uncle Orson Reviews Everything" for the* Rhino Times *in Greensboro, North Carolina, where he and his wife reside.*

His online magazine The InterGalactic Medicine Show *publishes fiction and art that is well within the strong storytelling tradition that* Writers of the Future *also represents. Card was born in Washington state and grew up in California, Arizona and Utah. He served a two-year mission for the LDS Church in Brazil in the 1970s. He periodically teaches writing and literature at Southern Virginia University.*

Orson Scott Card has been a judge of the Writers of the Future Contest since 1994, having earlier served as a guest instructor at the Writers' Workshops at both Sag Harbor, Long Island and Pepperdine University in Los Angeles. He was also the featured essayist in volumes four and twenty-two of the Writers of the Future anthology.

With respect to his short story "Carousel," Card offers the following introduction:

"If I were a new writer, offering a story to Writers of the Future in hope of making my first professional sale, I would send the story I actually did submit as my first serious attempt at publication: 'Ender's Game.' It's worth remembering that while I thought it was a good story (else why would I submit it anywhere?), I had no idea that it would become the foundation of my career. You never know whether your

first sale will be a story that really makes a splash, or one that fills pages but no one seems to pay much notice. You can't advise a new writer, 'Start with your best,' because then you can't submit anything for publication until just before you die, and good luck on timing that with any precision. So instead, I looked through my directory of short stories searching almost at random for something of reasonable length, which has the ingredients that I think a first sale must have. Old coots like me can get away with loosely structured stories, or irresolute ones, or stories that are part of a series, because we're already a known quantity. But when you're starting out, your first sale must be complete in itself. There is no reputation, no track record to rely on. It has to have emotional impact and clear resolution. It should have an idea intriguing enough that people might want to talk about it with other readers. But, mostly, it has to be written down in publishable format and sent out of the house—you can't guess which story an editor will buy, and so you send them all, as soon as they're done. Finished manuscripts that are kept lying about the house are worthless. Like uncooked fish, they begin to stink very quickly. The only manuscripts with any hope are the ones making the rounds, selling themselves door to door."

ABOUT THE ILLUSTRATOR

Born in Norwood, Massachusetts, Vincent-Michael Coviello has always had an interest in the creatures, characters and monsters that go bump in the night. A passion for art was apparent from a young age and only slightly rivaled his fascination with the zoological studies.

It would come as no surprise that his passions mixed with his love of science fiction and fantasy would foster artistic visions of distant worlds, ecosystems and the beings that would inhabit them.

A graduate of the Art Institute of Boston at Lesley University, Vincent-Michael learned tricks and tools of the trade to help amplify his worldbuilding visions. With a "the deeper the history, the richer the concept" mentality, Vincent-Michael is pursuing a career as a preproduction artist for the video game and film industry. There he hopes to create creatures and characters that are not only interesting to look at but are driven by story.

Humbled and honored to be one of the artists involved with the Illustrators of the Future, Vincent-Michael Coviello is excited to see what is waiting for him just beyond the horizon.

162

Carousel

Cyril's relationship with his wife really went downhill after she died. Though, if he was honest with himself—something he generally tried, with some success, to avoid—things hadn't been going all that well while Alice was alive. Everything he did seemed to irritate her, and when he didn't do anything at all, that irritated her, too.

"It's not your fault," Alice explained to him. "You try, I can see that you try, but you just . . . you're just wrong about everything. Not *very* wrong. Not oblivious or negligent or unconcerned. Just a little bit mistaken."

"About what? Tell me and I'll get better."

"About what people want, who they are, what they need."

"What do you need?" Cyril asked.

"I need you to stop asking what I need," she said. "I need you to know. The children need you to know. You never know."

"Because you won't tell me."

"See?" she said. "You have to make it my fault. Why should people always have to tell you, Cyril? It's like you go through life in a well-meaning fog. You can't help it. Nobody blames you."

But she blamed him. He knew that. He tried to get better, to notice more. To remember. But there was that note of impatience—in her voice, the children's voices, his boss's voice. As if they were thinking, I'm having to *explain* this to you?

Then Alice was hit by a car driven by a resurrected Han

163

Dynasty Chinese man who had no business behind the wheel—he plowed into a crowd on a bustling sidewalk and then got out and walked away as nonchalantly as if he had successfully parallel parked a large car in a small space. It was the most annoying thing about the dead—how they thought killing total strangers was no big deal, as long as they didn't mean to do it. And since the crowd only had two living people in it, the number of deaths was actually quite low. Alice's death barely rose to the level of a statistic, in the greater scheme of things.

She was thoughtful enough to clean up and change clothes before she came home that night—resurrection restored every body part as it should be at the peak of mature health, but it did nothing for the wardrobe. Still, the change in her attitude was immediate. She didn't even try to start dinner.

"What's for dinner, Mom?" asked Delia.

"Whatever your father fixes," said Alice.

"Am I fixing dinner?" asked Cyril. He liked to cook, but it usually took some planning and he wasn't sure what Alice would let him use to put together a meal.

"Go out to eat, have cold cereal, I really don't care," said Alice.

This was not like her. Alice controlled everybody's diet scrupulously, which is why she almost never allowed Cyril to cook. He realized at once what it meant, and the kids weren't far behind.

"Oh, Mom," said Roland softly. "You're not dead, are you?"

"Yes," she sighed. "But don't worry, it only hurt for about a minute while I bled out."

"Did the resurrection feel good?" asked Delia, always curious.

"The angel was right there, breathed in my mouth—very sweet. A bit of a tingle everywhere. But really not such a great feeling that it's worth dying for, so you shouldn't be in a hurry to join me, dear."

"So you won't be eating with us," said Cyril.

She shook her head a little, eyes closed. "'Dead' means I don't eat, Cyril. Everyone knows that the dead don't eat. We don't breathe except so we can talk. We don't drink and if we do, it's just to keep company with the living, and the liquids all evaporate from our skins so we also don't pee. We also don't want sex anymore, Cyril. Not with each other and not with you."

She had never mentioned sex in front of the children before, except for the talk with Delia when she turned ten, and that was all about time-of-the-month things. If Delia had any idea what sex was, Cyril didn't think she got it from her mother. So the children blanched and recoiled when she mentioned it.

"Oh, don't be such big babies, you know your father and I had sex, or you wouldn't look so much like him. Which is fine for you, Roland, your father's a good-looking man, in his way. But a bit of a drag for you, Delia, with that jaw. And the resurrection won't fix that. Resurrection isn't cosmetic surgery. Which is really unfair, when you think about it. People who are genetically retarded or crippled or sick have their DNA repaired to some optimum state, but girls with overly mannish features or tiny breasts or huge ones, for that matter, their DNA is left completely alone, they're stuck like that for eternity."

"Thanks, Mom," said Delia. "I love having my confidence destroyed once again, and I haven't even begun doing my homework yet."

"So you aren't going to eat with us?" asked Roland.

"Oh, of course I'll sit at table with you," said Alice. "For the company."

In the event, Cyril got out everything in the fridge that looked like it might go on a sandwich and everybody made their own. Except Alice, of course. She just sat at the table and made comments, without even a pause to take a bite or chew.

"The way I see it," said Alice, "is that it's all poop. Nothing you're putting on sandwiches even looks appetizing anymore, because I see that poopiness of it all. You're going to eat it and digest it and poop it out. The nutrients will decay and eventually end up in some farmer's field where it will become more future-poop, which he'll harvest and it'll get processed into a more poopable state, so you can heat it or freeze it or thaw it or

165

whatever, chew it up or drink it, and then turn it into poop again. Life is poop."

"Mom," said Delia. "It's usually Roland who makes us sick while we're eating."

"I thought you'd want to hear my new perspective as a post-living person." She sounded miffed.

"Please speak more respectfully to your mother," said Cyril to Delia.

"Cyril, really," said Alice. "I don't need you to protect me from Delia's snippy comments. It's not going to kill me to hear her judgmentalness directed at the woman who gave birth to her."

"Feel free to criticize your mother's defecatory comments," said Cyril. "Or ignore them, as you choose."

"I know, Dad," said Delia. There was that familiar hint of eye-rolling in her tone of voice. Once again Cyril must have guessed wrong about what to say, or leave unsaid. He had never really gotten it right when Alice was alive, and now that she was dead-and-resurrected, he'd have no chance, because he was no longer dealing with a wife, or even, strictly speaking, a woman. She was a visitor with a key to the house.

Within a few weeks, Cyril found himself remembering the awful night of Alice's death as a particularly lovely time, because she actually sat with them during dinner and wasn't trying to lead the children off into some kind of utterly bizarre activity.

She showed up at any hour of the day, and expected to be able to take Delia or Roland with her on whatever adventure she'd gotten it into her head to try with them.

"No, Alice, you may not take Roland out of school so he can go scuba diving with you."

"It's really not your place to say what I can or cannot do," said Alice.

"The law is clear, Alice—when you die you become, in a word, deceased. You no longer have any custody over the children. Thousands of years of legal precedent make that clear. Not to mention tons of recent case law in which the resurrected are found to be unfit parents in every case."

"Aren't you lucky that the dead can't get angry," said Alice.

"I suppose that I am," said Cyril. "But I'm not dead, and I was furious when I found you practically forcing Roland to walk along the top of a very high fence."

"It's exhilarating," said Alice.

"He was terrified."

"Oh, Cyril, are you really going to let a child's fears—"

"He was right to be terrified. He could have broken his neck."

"And would it have been such a tragedy if he did?" asked Alice. "I was run over by a car and I turned out okay."

"You think you're okay?" asked Cyril.

Alice held up her hands and twisted her wrists as if to prove that her parts worked.

"Here's how I know you're not okay, Alice," said Cyril. "You keep trying to put the kids in high-risk situations. You're trying to kill them, Alice."

"Don't think of it as death. I'm not dead. How is it death?"

"How can I put this kindly?" said Cyril—who by this point had actually stopped trying to be kind. "You're dead to *me*."

"Just because I'm no longer available for empty reproductive gestures does not mean I'm not here for you, Cyril."

"I'm going to get a restraining order if you don't stop taking the kids on dangerous activities. You don't have any guardianship rights over these children."

"My fingerprints say I'm still their mother!"

"Alice, when you were their mother, you wanted them to relish every stage of their life. Now you're trying to get them to skip all the rest of the stages."

"You can't manipulate me with guilt," said Alice. "I'm beyond human emotions and needs."

"Then why do you still need the children with you?"

"I'm their mother."

"You *were* their mother," said Cyril.

"I was and I am," said Alice.

"Alice, I may have been a disappointment as a husband."

"And as a father, Cyril. The children are often disappointed in you."

"But I meet a basic minimum, Alice. I'm alive. I'm human. Of their species. I want them to be alive. I'd like them to live to adulthood, to marry, to have children."

Alice shook her head incredulously. "Go outside and look at the street, Cyril. Hundreds of people lie down and sleep in the streets or on the lawns every night, because the world has *no* shortage of people."

"Just because you've lost all your biological imperatives doesn't mean that the rest of us don't have them."

"Cyril, your reasoning is backward. The children will be much happier without biological imperatives."

"So you admit you're trying to kill them."

"I'm trying to awaken them from the slumber of mortality."

"I don't want to waken them from that slumber," said Cyril sharply. "If it's a dream, then let them finish the dream and come out of it in their own time."

"When someone you love is living in a nightmare," said Alice, "you wake them up."

"Alice," said Cyril, "you're the nightmare."

"Your wife is a nightmare? Your children's mother?"

"You're a reanimated dead woman."

"Resurrected," said Alice. "An angel breathed into my mouth."

"The angel should have minded its damn business," said Cyril.

"You always wanted me dead," said Alice.

"I never *wanted* you dead until after you *were* dead and you wouldn't go away."

"You're a bitter failure, Cyril, and yet you cling to this miserable life and insist that the children cling to it, too. It's a form of child abuse. Of child exploitation."

"Go away, Alice. Go enjoy your death somewhere else."

"My eternal life, you mean."

"Whatever."

But in the end, Alice won. First she talked Delia into jumping from a bridge without actually attaching any bungee cords to her feet. Once again Cyril had no chance to grieve, because Alice brought Delia by to tell Roland how great death and resurrection were. Delia was fully grown. A woman, but in a retailored version of her dress that fit her larger, womanly body.

"The soul is never a child," said Alice. "What did you expect?"

"I expected her to take a few more years to grow into this body," said Cyril.

"Think of it as skipping ahead a few grades," said Alice, barely able to conceal her gloating.

If Cyril had thought Resurrected Alice was awful, resurrected Delia was unbearable. His love for his daughter had become, without his realizing it, far stronger and deeper than his lingering affection for his wife. So he could not help but grieve for the young girl cut off in her prime. While the snippy, smart-mouthed woman of the same name, who thought she had a right to dwell in his house and follow him around, mocking him constantly—she was a stranger.

How can you grieve for people who just won't go away? How can you grieve for a daughter whose grownup dead-and-resurrected self ridicules your mourning? "Oh, did Daddy lose his widdow baby?"

There was nothing to do but say an occasional silent prayer—which they mocked when they noticed him doing it. Only Cyril was never quite sure what he was praying for. Please get rid of all the dead? Please unresurrect them? Would God even hear that prayer?

Roland died of a sudden attack of influenza a few months later. "You can't blame me for it, this time," said Alice.

"You know you were sneaking him out into the cold weather specifically so he'd catch cold. The dying was a predictable result. You're a murderer, Alice. You should be in hell."

Alice smiled even more benignly. "I forgive you for that."

"I'll never forgive you for taking away my children."

"Now you're unencumbered. I thought that's what you secretly wished for."

"Thanks for telling me my deepest wishes, " said Cyril. "They were so deep I never knew they existed."

"Come with us, Father," said Roland.

"In due time, I'll go where I can find what I need," said Cyril. "*You* don't need me.

Roland was so tall. Cyril's heart ached to see him. *My little boy,* he thought. But he could not say it. Roland's gentle pity on him was harder to bear than Delia's open scorn.

They would not go. They talked about it, but sheer inertia kept anyone from changing. Finally it dawned on Cyril. Just because he was the only pre-dead resident of the house did not bind him to it. His life had been stripped away from him; why was he clinging to the house that used to hold it?

For the shower, the toilet, the bathroom sink; for the refrigerator, the microwave, the kitchen table; for the roof, the bed, the place to store his clothes. The burden and blessing of modern life. Unlike the resurrected, if Cyril was going to eat, he had to work; if he was going to work, he had to look presentable. For his health he needed shelter from weather, a safe place to sleep.

The resurrected people that used to love him did not need this place, but would not leave; he needed the place, but could not bear these people who made it impossible for him to truly grieve the terrible losses he had suffered.

Job had it all wrong, thought Cyril. Having lost his wife and children, it was better to lose all his other possessions and live in an ashpit, covered in boils. Then, at least, everyone could see and understand what had happened to him. His friends might have been wretched comforters, but at least they understood that he was in need of comfort.

Just because he had to store his food and clothing there, and return there to wash himself and sleep, did not mean he had to *live* there, to pass waking hours there, listening to his dead wife explain his inadequacies to him, or his dead daughter agree with her, or his dead son pity him.

Cyril took to leaving work as soon as he could, and sometimes when he couldn't, just walking out of the building, knowing he was putting his already somewhat pitiful career in jeopardy. He would walk the streets, delaying the commute home as long as possible. He thought of joining his wife and children in death and resurrection, but he had seen how death stripped them of all desire, and even though his current malaise came from the frustration of his deepest desires, he did not want to part with them. Desire was what defined him, he understood that, and to give them up was to lose himself, as his wife and children were lost.

Bitterly, Cyril remembered the Bible school of his childhood. Lose your soul to find it? Yes, the dead had certainly done that. Lost soul, self, and all, but whatever they found, it wasn't really life. Life was about hunger and need and finding ways to satisfy them. Nature red in tooth and claw, yes, but hadn't the human race found ways to create islands of peace in the midst of nature? Lives in which terror was so rare that people paid money to go to amusement parks and horror movies in order to remember what terror felt like.

This life was even more peaceful, even less lonely, wasn't it? When he walked the streets, he jostled with thousands and thousands of the resurrected, who crowded every street as they went about their meaningless existence, not even curious, but moving for the sake of moving, or so it seemed to him; pursuing various amusements because they remembered that this was a thing that human beings did, and not because they desired amusement.

They crowded the streets so that traffic barely moved, yet they provided no boost to the economy. Needing nothing, they bought nothing. They had no money, because they had no desires, and therefore nothing to work for. They were the

171

sclerosis of commerce. Get out of my way, thought Cyril, over and over. And then: Do what you want. I'm not going anywhere either.

He was living like the dead, he recognized that. His life was as empty as theirs. But underneath his despair and loneliness and ennui, he was seething with resentment. Since God obviously existed after all, since it was hard to imagine how else one might explain the sudden resurrection-of-all-who-had-ever-lived, what did he *mean* by it? What were they supposed to *do* with this gift that preserved life eternally while robbing it of any sort of joy or pleasure?

So Cyril was ironically receptive when he found the uptown mansion with a sign on the door that said:

GOD'S ANTEROOM

Nobody used "anteroom" anymore, but the idea rather appealed to him. So he went up the short walk and climbed the stoop and opened the front door and stepped inside.

It was a good-sized foyer, which he assumed was formed by tearing out a wall and combining the front parlor with the original vestibule. The space was completely filled by a small merry-go-round. As far as Cyril could see, no doors or stairs led out of the room except the front door he had just come through.

"Hello?" His voice didn't echo—the room wasn't big enough for that. It just fell into the space, flat and dull. He thought of calling again, louder, but instead stepped up onto the carousel.

It was small. Only two concentric circles of animals to ride, the outer one with seven, the inner one with three, plus a single one-person bench shaped like the Disney version of a throne, molded in smooth, rounded lines of hard plastic pretending to be upholstery.

Cyril thought of sitting there, since it required no effort. But he thought better of it, and walked around the carousel, touching each animal in turn. Chinese dragon, zebra, tiger, horse, hippopotamus, rhinoceros, giant mouse. Porpoise, eagle, bear. All extravagantly detailed and finely hand-painted—there was nothing sloppy or faded, or seedy about the thing. In fact, he could truly say that the carousel was a work of art, a small, finely crafted version of a mass entertainment.

He had never known there was such a thing as a boutique carousel. Who would ever come to ride such a thing? And what would they pay? Part of the pleasure of full-sized carousels was the fact that it was so crowded and public. Here in this room, the carousel looked beautiful and sad at the same time. Too small for the real purpose of a carousel—a place where people could display themselves to one another, while enjoying the mild pleasure of moving up and down on a faux beast. Yet too large for the room, crowded, almost as if this were a place where beautiful things were stored while awaiting a chance for display in a much larger space.

Cyril sat on the hippopotamus.

"Would you like me to make it go?" asked a woman's voice.

Cyril had thought he was alone. He looked around, startled, a little embarrassed, beginning the movement of getting back off the hippo, yet stopping himself because the voice had not challenged him, but rather offered to serve him.

Then he saw her through the grillwork of the faux ticket booth in a space that must have been a coat closet when the house was first built. How did she get in or out? The booth had no door.

Her appearance of youth and health led him to assume she was dead and resurrected.

"I can't really afford..." he began.

"It's free," she said.

"Hard to stay in business at those rates," said Cyril.

"It's not a business," she said.

Then what is it? he wanted to ask. But instead he answered, "Then yes. I'd like to ride."

Silently the carousel slipped into movement without a lurch; had he not been paying attention, Cyril would not have been able to say when movement began.

The silence did not last long, for what would a carousel be without music? No calliope, though—what accompanied this carousel sounded like a quartet of instruments. Cello, oboe, horn, and harpsichord, Cyril thought, without any effort to sort out the sounds. Each instrument was so distinctive it was impossible not to catalog them. They played a sedate music in three-four time, as suited a carousel or skating rink, yet the music was also haunting in a modal, folk-songish way.

Cyril let the carousel carry him around and around. The movement did not have the rapid sweep of a fullsize carousel, but rather the dizzying tightness of spin of a children's hand-pushed merry-go-round. He had to close his eyes now and then to keep from becoming lightheaded or getting a slight headache from the room that kept slipping past his vision.

It did not occur to him to ask her to slow it down, or stop. He simply clung to the pole and let it move him and the hippo up and down.

Because the music was so gentle, the machinery so silent, the distance from him to the ticket booth so slight even when he was on the far side of the room, Cyril felt it possible—no, obligatory—to say something after a while. "How long does the ride last?" he asked.

"As long as you want," she said.

"That could be forever," he said.

"If you like," she said.

He chuckled. "Do you get overtime?"

"No," she said. "Just time."

"Too bad," he said. Then he remembered that she was dead, and neither payment nor time would mean very much to her.

"Do you read?" he asked. "Or do you have a DVD player in there?"

"What?" she asked.

"To pass the time. Between patrons. While the customers are riding. It can't be thrilling to watch me go around and around."

"It actually is," she said. "Just a little."

Liar, thought Cyril. *Nothing is thrilling to the dead.*

"You're not dead yet," she said.

"No," he answered, wanting to add, What gave me away? but keeping his silence. He knew what gave him away. He had asked questions. He was curious. He had bothered to ride at all. He had closed his eyes to forestall nausea. So many signs of life.

"So you can't ride forever."

"I suppose not," said Cyril. "Eventually I have to sleep."

"And eat," she said. "And urinate."

"Doesn't look like you have a restroom, either," said Cyril.

"We do," she said.

"Where?" He looked for a door.

"It has an outside entrance."

"Don't the homeless trash the place?" he asked.

"I don't mind cleaning it up," she said.

"So you do it all? Run the carousel, clean the restrooms?"

"That's all there is," she said. "It isn't hard."

"It isn't interesting, either."

"Interesting enough," she said. "I don't get bored."

Of course not. You have to have something else you want to be doing before you really feel bored.

"Where are you from?" asked Cyril, because talking was better than not talking. He wanted to ask her to stop the carousel, because he really was getting just a little sick now, but if he stopped, she might insist that he go. And if he got off, yet was allowed to stay, where would he stand while he talked to her.

"I died here as a little girl. My mother gave birth to me on the voyage."

"Immigrants," said Cyril.

"Isn't everyone?" she answered.

"So you never grew up."

"I'm up," she said, "but you're right, without growing into it. I was very sick, my mother wiping my brow, crying. And then I was full-grown, and had this strange language at my lips, and there were all these buildings and people and nothing to do."

"So you found a job."

"I came through the door and found the ticket booth standing open. I knew it was called a ticket booth as soon as I saw it, though I never saw a ticket booth before in my life. I could read the signs, too, and the letters, though there weren't in the language I learned as a baby. I turned on the carousel and it went around and I like to watch it, so I stayed."

"So nobody hired you."

"Nobody's told me to go," she said. "The machinery isn't complicated. I can make it go backward, too, but nobody likes that, so I don't even offer anymore."

"Can you make it go slower?"

"That's the slowest setting," she said. "It can go at two faster speeds. Do you want to see?"

"No," he said quickly, though for a moment he wanted to say yes, just to find out what it would feel like.

"No one likes that either, though people still ask. The living ones throw up sometimes, at the faster speeds."

"Sometimes the resurrected come to ride?"

"Sometimes they come with the living ones. A dead mother and her living children. That sort of thing."

"How do you like it?" he asked.

"Well enough," she said, "or I wouldn't stay."

He realized she must have thought he meant how she liked her job, or watching the carousel.

"I meant, how do you like resurrection?"

"I don't know," she said. "I don't have a choice, so I don't think about it."

"When you were dying, what did you want?"

"I wanted my mother not to cry. I wanted to sleep. I wanted to feel better."

"Do you feel better now?" asked Cyril.

"I don't know," she said. "I suppose so. My mother isn't crying anymore. I found her after I resurrected. She didn't know me, but I knew *her*. She was just as I remember her, only not so sad. She and I didn't talk long. There wasn't much to say. She said that she wept for me until her husband made her stop so he could bury me. She wouldn't move away, because she would have to leave my grave behind, so they lived their whole lives nearby, and raised eleven other children and sent them out into the world, but she never forgot me."

The story made Cyril want to weep for his own dead children, even though they were alive again, after a fashion. "She must have been glad to see you," he said.

"She didn't know me. It was her baby that she wanted to see."

"I know," said Cyril. "My wife got my children to die and they came back like you. Grown up. I miss the children that I lost." And then he did cry, just for a couple of sobs, before he got control of himself.

"I'm sorry," he said. "I haven't been able to cry till now. Because they're still there."

"I know," she said. "I'm glad to see you cry."

He didn't even ask why. He knew: Her mother, being resurrected, had not cried. The woman needed to see a living person cry for a dead child.

Needed. How could she *need* anything?

"What's your name?" asked Cyril.

"Dorcas," she said.

"Not a common name anymore," said Cyril.

"It's from the Bible. I never studied the Bible when I was alive. I was too young to read. But I came back knowing how to read. And the whole Bible is in my memory. So is everything. It's all there, every book. I can either remember them as if I had already read them, or I can close my eyes and read them again, or I can close my eyes and see the whole story play out in front of my eyes. And yet I never do. It's enough just to know what's in all the books."

"All of them? All the books ever written?"

"I don't know if it's all of them. But I've never thought of a book that I haven't read. If one book mentions another book, I've already read it. I know how they all end. I suppose it must be more fun to read, if you don't already know every scene and every word."

"No worse than the carousel," said Cyril. "It just goes around and around."

"But the face of the person riding it changes," she said. "And I don't always know what they're going to say before they say it."

"So you're curious."

"No," she said. "I don't really care. It just passes the time."

Cyril rode in silence for a while.

"Why do you think he did it?" he finally asked.

"Who?" she asked. Then, "Oh, you mean the resurrection. Why did God, you know."

"This is God's Anteroom, right? So it seems appropriate to wonder. Why now. Why everybody all at once. Why children came back as adults."

"Everybody gets their perfect body," she said. "And knowledge. Everything's fair. God must be fair."

Cyril pondered that. He couldn't even argue with it. Very even-handed. He couldn't feel that he had been singled out for some kind of torment. Many people had suffered worse. When his children had died, he was still able to talk to them. It had to feel much worse if they were simply gone.

"Maybe this is a good thing," said Cyril.

"Nobody believes that," she said.

"No," said Cyril. "I can't imagine that they do. When you wish—when your child dies, or your wife. Or husband, or whatever—you don't really think of *how* they'd come back. You want them back just as they were. But then what? Then they'd just die again, later, under other circumstances."

"At least they'd have had a life in between," said Dorcas.

Cyril smiled. "You're not the ordinary dead person," he said. "You have opinions. You have regrets."

"What can I regret? What did I ever do wrong?" she asked. "No, I'm just pissed off."

Cyril laughed aloud. "You can't be angry. My wife is dead, and she's never angry."

"So I'm not angry. But I know that it's wrong. It's supposed to make us happy and it doesn't, so it's wrong, and wrongness feels..."

"Wrong," Cyril prompted.

"And that's as close as I can come to being angry," said Dorcas. "You too?"

"Oh, I can feel anger! I don't have to be 'close,' I've got the real thing. Pissed off, that's what I feel. Resentful. Spiteful. Whining. Self-pitying. And I don't mind admitting it. My wife and children were resurrected and they'll live forever and they seem perfectly content. But you're not content."

"I'm content," she said. "What else is there to be? I'm pissed off, but I'm content."

"I wish this really were God's anteroom," said Cyril. "I'd be asking the secretary to make me an appointment."

"You want to talk to God?"

"I want to file a complaint," said Cyril. "It doesn't have to be, like, an interview with God himself. I'm sure He's busy."

"Not really," said the voice of a man.

Cyril looked at the inner row, where a handsome young man sat in the throne. "You're God?" Cyril asked.

"You don't like the resurrection," said God.

"You know everything, right?" asked Cyril.

"Yes," said God. "Everybody hates this. They prayed for it, they wanted it, but when they got it, they complained, just like you."

"I never asked for this."

"But you would have," said God, "as soon as somebody died."

"I wouldn't have asked for *this*," said Cyril. "But what do you care?"

"I'm not resurrected," said God. "Not like them. I still care about things."

"Why didn't you let *them* care, then?" asked Cyril.

"Billions of people on Earth again, healthy and strong, and I should make them *care*? Think of the wars. Think of the crimes. I didn't bring them back to turn the world into hell."

"What is it, if it isn't hell?" asked Cyril.

"Purgatory," said Dorcas.

"Limbo," Cyril suggested back.

"Neither one exists," said God. "I tried them for a while, but nobody liked them, either. Listen, it's not really my fault. Once a soul exists, it can never be erased. Annihilated. I found them, I had to do something with them. I thought this world was a good way to use them. Let them have a life. Do things, feel things."

"That worked fine," said Cyril. "It was going fine till you did *this*." He gestured toward Dorcas.

"But there were so many complaints," said God. "Everybody hated death, but what else could I do? Do you have any idea how many souls I have that still haven't been born?"

"So cycle through them all. Reincarnation, let them go around and around."

"It's a long time between turns," said God. "Since the supply of souls is infinite."

"You didn't mention infinite," said Cyril. "I thought you just meant there were a lot of us."

"Infinite is kind of a lot," said God.

"To *me* it is," said Cyril. "I thought that to you—"

"I know, this whole resurrection didn't work out like I hoped. Nothing does. I should never have taken responsibility for the souls I found."

"Can't you just ... put some of us back?"

"Oh, no, I can't do that," said God, shaking his head vehemently. "Never that. It's—once you've had a body, once you've been part of creation, to take you back out of it—you'd remember all the power, and you'd feel the loss of it—like no suffering. Worst thing in the world. And it never ends."

"So you're saying it's hell."

"Yes," said God. "There's no fire, no sulfur and all that. Just endless agony over the loss of ... of everything. I can't do that to any of the souls. I *like* you. All of you. I hate it when you're unhappy."

"We're unhappy," said Cyril.

"No," said God. "You're sad, but you're not really suffering."

Cyril was in tears again. "Yes I am."

"Suck it up," said God. "It can be a hell of a lot worse than this."

"You're not really God," said Cyril.

"I'm the guy in charge," said God. "What is that, if not God? But no, there's no omnipotent transcendental being who lives outside of time. No unmoved mover. That's just stupid anyway. The things people say about me. I know you can't help it. I'm doing my best, just like most of you. And I keep trying to make you happy. This is the best I've done so far."

"It's not very good," said Cyril.

"I know," said God. "But it's the best so far."

Dorcas spoke up from the ticket booth. "But I never really *had* a life."

God sighed. "I know."

"Look," said Cyril. "Maybe this really is the best. But do you have to have everybody *stay* here? On Earth, I mean? Can't you, like, create more worlds?"

"But people want to *see* their loved ones," said God.

"Right," said Cyril. "We've seen them. Now move them along and let the living go on with our lives."

"So maybe a couple of conversations with the dead and they move on," said God, apparently thinking about it. "What about you, Dorcas?"

"Whatever," she said. "I'm dead, what do I care?"

"You care," said God. "Not the cares of the body. But you have the caring of a soul. It's a different kind of desire, but you all have it, and it never goes away."

"My wife and children don't care about anything," said Cyril.

"They care about you."

"I wish," said Cyril.

"Why do you think they haven't left? They see you're unhappy."

"I'm unhappy because they won't go," said Cyril.

"Why haven't you told them that? They'd go if you did."

Cyril said nothing. He had nothing to say.

"You don't want them to go," said Dorcas.

"I want my children back," Cyril said. "I want my wife to love me."

"I can't make people love other people," said God. "Then it wouldn't be love."

"You really have a limited skill set," said Cyril.

"I really try not to do special favors," said God. "I try to set up rules and then follow them equally for everybody. It seems more fair that way."

"By definition," said Dorcas. "That's what fairness *is*. But who says fairness is always good?"

God shrugged. "Oh, I don't know. I wish I did. But I'll give it a shot, how about that? Maybe I can eventually fix this thing. Maybe the next thing will be a little better. And maybe I'll never get it right. Who knows?"

And he was gone.

So was Dorcas.

Cyril got off the hippo. He was dizzy and had to cling to the pole. The carousel wasn't going to stop. So he waited until he had a stretch of open floor and leapt off.

He stumbled, lurched against a wall, slid down, and lay on the floor. The quartet stopped playing. The carousel slowed down and stopped. Apparently it automatically knew when there were no passengers.

A baby cried.

Cyril walked to the ticket window and looked in. On the floor sat a toddler, a little girl, surrounded by a pile of women's clothing. The toddler looked up at him. "Cyril," she said in her baby voice.

"Do you remember being a grownup?" Cyril asked her.

The little girl looked puzzled.

"How do I get in there?"

"Hungry!" said the little girl and she cried again.

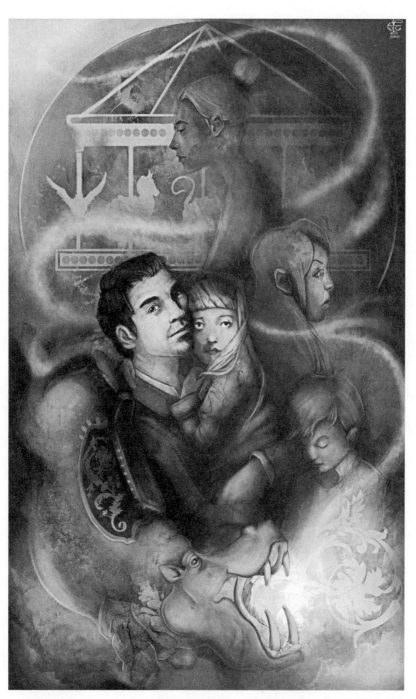

VINCENT-MICHAEL COVIELLO

Cyril saw a door handle inside the ticket booth and eventually figured out where the door was in the outside wall. He got it open. He picked up little Dorcas and wrapped her in the dress she had been wearing. God was giving her a life.

Cyril carried her out of God's Anteroom and down the stoop. The crowds were gone. Just a few cars, with only the living inside them. Some of them were stopped, the drivers just sitting there. Some of them were crying. Some just had their eyes closed. But eventually somebody honked at somebody else and the cars in the middle of the road started going again.

Cyril took a cab home and carried the baby inside. Alice and Delia and Roland were gone. There was food in the fridge. Cyril got out the old high chair and fed Dorcas. When she was done, he set her in the living room and went in search of toys and clothes. He mentally talked to Alice as he did: So it's stupid to keep children's clothes and toys when we're never going to have more children, is it? Well, I never said it, but I always thought it, Alice: Just because *you* decided not to have any more babies doesn't mean *I* would never have any.

He got Dorcas dressed and she played with the toys until she fell asleep on the living room carpet. Then Cyril lay on the floor beside her and wept for his children and the wife he had loved far more than she loved him, and for the lost life; yet he also wept for joy, that God had actually listened to him, and given him this child, and given Dorcas the life she had longed for.

He wondered a little where God had sent the other souls, and he wondered if he should tell anybody about his conversation with God, but then he decided it was all none of his business. He had a job the next day, and he'd have to arrange for day care, and buy food that was more appropriate for the baby. And diapers. He definitely needed those.

He slept, and dreamed that he was on the carousel again, dizzy, but moving forward, and he didn't mind at all that he would never get anywhere, because it was all about the ride.

The Clouds in Her Eyes

written by

Liz Colter

illustrated by

KIRBI FAGAN

ABOUT THE AUTHOR

Liz Colter lives in a beautiful area of the Rocky Mountains and spends her time off with her husband, dogs, horses and writing (according to her husband, not always in that order of priority).

Over the years she has followed her heart through a wide variety of careers, including waitressing her way through nine years of college (a year of that as a roller-skating waitress), and has worked as a field paramedic, Outward Bound instructor, athletic trainer, draft-horse farmer, and dispatcher for concrete trucks.

Currently, she has returned to working in medicine, but her real passion is her writing. Reading The Hobbit *at ten and then growing up on* Star Trek, The Twilight Zone *and* Dark Shadows *engendered a lifelong love of speculative fiction. When at last she began writing (joining her grandfather, aunt, mother and brother in the pursuit of publication) she became the lone fantasy and science fiction writer in the family.*

She has been creating her speculative worlds for more than a decade now and currently has two completed fantasy novels and a new novel in progress, in addition to her short stories.

ABOUT THE ILLUSTRATOR

Although Kirbi Fagan didn't start drawing until high school, she was a creative and imaginative child. She was raised in the Detroit area and received her bachelor's degree in illustration from Kendall College of Art and Design in spring 2013.

After graduation she continued her studies at the Illustration Master Class and attended a mentorship program with SmART School. While preparing her portfolio, she had her eyes focused on the publishing industry.

Kirbi became extremely inspired teaching young children at the Plymouth Community Arts Council, where she performed theater as a child. She is also inspired by history and is often found digging through thrift or antique stores. To her, the objects contain stories and mysteries that invoke imagery.

Currently, Kirbi teaches workshops and live art demonstrations, and hosts a theatrical life drawing event for local artists.

She is active in the illustration community both online and at large.

Kirbi is working on her first young adult novel cover, which will be published later this year. She hopes that many similar commissions follow.

Kirbi is honored to be among the Illustrators of the Future. She is enthusiastic for her next adventure in her developing career. Kirbi says, "I'm in it with my whole heart."

The Clouds in Her Eyes

A breeze caught at the blades of the windmill, producing a groan of protest from the hub. Amba glanced up at the weathered shaft and cracked wooden blades, both unlikely to see repairs with the well nearly dry. Above the windmill, a great sheet of heat lightning crackled purple and yellow across the dark sky; the sky that promised rain every day as if unaware that it had no moisture left to give.

Looking anywhere except to the fields, Amba returned to poking the ground with the point of her copper herding rod. Eventually, the vastness of the land drew her eyes across the acres of dirt, flat and featureless, punctuated only by the containment poles.

The ship was there, closer each day. Its sails billowed and the great wooden hull heaved on invisible waves that rolled between the ship's dry keel and the dirt of the farm. It had advanced nearly to the top of the second field, the one where the grubs matured into young sparkers. By tomorrow the ship would be in the first field.

It was no use running for Father. She had done that when it first appeared as a speck on the horizon, at the waning of the last moon. Father had seen nothing. The speck had grown steadily larger, and still he had taken no notice. By the time the Wind Moon was waxing, the sails and the hull had been distinguishable and she had pointed it out again. He'd stared unseeing and unbelieving at the horizon, then grunted and turned away.

He never mentioned it afterward; never said if he thought she was lying or teasing or, worse, hallucinating, as she had during her illness. If it concerned him, he fostered it in silence, as he did all his worries.

Amba had worked hard to take over her brother's duties in the fields after Jass died. Her father did his best to accept her as a surrogate, but telling him that a ship he couldn't see was sailing over their fields threatened her fragile progress with him. She had resolved not to mention it to him again, no matter what.

The ship was close enough now that she could see men on the deck and details of the figurehead: a body, an upraised arm holding something. She wondered if the ship would sail right up to the house, or through the house. She wondered if she would drown when the unseen ocean washed over her.

Mustering her resolve to walk into the field, she went first to the corral to collect her mallet, then scanned the dirt in the top field until she spotted a ripple in the soil. Approaching the disturbance, she tapped her slender rod into the ground just behind it. The ripple surged away from her. Father said the copper tasted as bitter to sparkers as immature haza beans tasted to Amba.

She pulled the rod from the ground and tapped it in again at a safe distance behind the sparker. Mature sparkers were the most dangerous. Even with the herding rod's leather grip, they could give a nasty jolt if she came too close. Zigzagging with the erratic path the creature took, she herded it toward the opening in the small circle of poles that made up the corral. Once the sparker entered, she jammed her herding rod into the ground and hurried to replace the missing containment pole before the sparker wriggled out again.

I have one ready," she told Father when she found him in the shed, already changed into his heavily padded harvesting clothes. His only reply was to bend and take one handle of the glass cage. She lifted the other side of the container and together they carried it to the corral.

Her father's quiet manner had been peaceful and comforting when Amba was young, but after the fever killed Mother he had become more distant than quiet. When Jass died, her father had withdrawn further still. Amba wished that she knew how to find the old him, wherever he had gone, and help him find his way back. She needed him. She was broken in her own way, with an emptiness since her illness, since Mother's death, that had never filled up again. It ached sometimes, in the hollow just below her breastbone.

They reached the corral and set the cage down. Amba braced herself to watch Father harvest. She hadn't been there when Jass died, but she had seen him afterward, his eyes frozen wide with pain, the burnt and flaking skin that she had scrubbed from his chest and hands before they buried him.

Her father was slipping on his heavy gloves when she turned suddenly at the sound of a deep voice shouting behind her. For a moment, she had forgotten about the ship. A large man stood at the wheel and the men on deck scurried to follow some order. The ship was too far away to make out what he'd said, though he had raised his voice, as if over the roar of wind and waves.

Amba turned back to find her father staring at her. She flushed under his silent, probing gaze. He held her eyes for a long moment—not searching for clues to her thoughts—but looking at them, studying the clouds in the dark brown of her irises. The clouds that the fever had left behind. His brow furrowed in concern before he turned, wordlessly, and stepped into the corral.

Amba hurried to push the cage against the containment poles to make up for her lapse. She stood well back, holding the heavy glass lid ready. Her father moved around the edge of the corral, staying close to the safety of the poles. He pushed his hooked rod into the ground and angled it to tease the sparker from the soil. When the back of the creature broke the surface, he swept the rod deftly under its twisting body.

Once wrenched from the soil they were ugly things—grayish-brown, like giant eyeless slugs, but with nublike tails and a multitude of tiny legs that propelled them through the soil. This one was a monster, as long and as thick around as her thigh, its many legs clawing at the air.

If any of the spines on those legs connected with her father's clothing, the sparker would cling to him, charring his skin and stopping his heart. Father kept the sparker well away from him, though, and in one smooth motion slipped it between the poles and into the glass container. Amba quickly slid the top into place.

The creature thrashed against the dry glass of its confines, sparking like a mirror image of the heat lightning flashing in the sky. Those sparks lit lamps and powered the great wheels and fans in town, though water and food were what made them most valuable. Bereft of soil to soothe it, the sparker began to secrete water into the container even as Amba and her father carried it back to the shed.

They harvested the remainder of the mature sparkers all the rest of that day. Amba tried to ignore the ship sailing ever closer as she worked, though she stole quick glances at it when Father wasn't watching.

By evening, the first field was cleared, and she felt exhausted. Father went to the shed and set up the siphons that would keep the sparkers from drowning in their own water while Amba headed for the house to clean up and begin supper.

Do you think there's still an ocean?" she asked him that evening as they ate. Sparkers tasted like snails and were tough, even when stewed all day, but at least they were plentiful.

His eyes narrowed briefly, no doubt wondering why she asked. She had tried to be subtle—everyone thought about water after all—but the ship was foremost in her thoughts. She chewed a crust of bread and lowered her eyes so that he wouldn't be reminded of the clouds there.

"Don't know," he replied, scooping up a spoonful of stew. "Never seen it, but I suppose it's still there. They say there's still water in some of the rivers and such. The ocean must be harder to dry up than those."

He lapsed into silence again and Amba tried not to think about where the ship might be now. After dinner, she cleaned the dishes, swept the house, and started a new loaf of bread to rise for morning. The sack of grain in the pantry was their last, and the jars of vegetables they had traded for were dwindling. Soon, like many already, they would have to live on nothing but the sparkers.

Amba enjoyed the feel of kneading bread. It reminded her of her childhood, when they had kept a garden and grown grain instead of sparkers. Father hadn't been so sad then and the house not so lonely. She and Mother always had the cooking and cleaning and sewing done before Father was even aware of the need. He used to ruffle her hair and spend his rare words complimenting her baking or his new shirts. Amba had even caught Mother and Father kissing one day, out by the shed.

She and Father did the work of four people now, and life felt somehow incomplete no matter how hard she tried to fill the holes in her world. Amba pressed her hand to the ache at the hollow below her breastbone, as if she could push her fist inside to sate the emptiness.

The next day, while Father worked in the shed, Amba was sent to gauge the grubs in the second field, to see if they were large enough to herd forward. He couldn't see that the ship was now halfway up the first field, or that to reach the grubs, she would have to walk right past it.

She could have skirted wide of the ship, and perhaps it would've stayed its course up the field and sailed away. She didn't believe it would, though. If she was the only one who could see it, then it must have come for her. She had been frightened and curious too long; if there was no avoiding this thing, she decided, she may as well meet it head on.

The banister of the deck stood nearly three times her height above the ground, and the ship loomed hugely as she approached it. She strained to hear the splash and roll of waves that gently rocked the hull, or the wind that tousled the men's hair, but she heard only the silence of the farm and the creak of the windmill.

The figurehead turned out to be a woman, naked to hips that melded into the lower part of the bow. Her right arm was raised high, and in her hand she clutched a metal lightning bolt painted gold. Wooden hair that may once have been red streamed back into the point of the prow, as if blown by a strong wind. On the deck of the ship were half a dozen men. The man at the wheel was tall and broad shouldered, sporting a thick shock of ginger hair, and a reddish beard and mustache trimmed short.

"Lower the sails," the big man called as she neared. Ropes whined as the sails came down, folding like ladies' fans onto the crossbeams of the masts. "Drop anchor," he ordered.

Amba heard the rattle of thick chain and saw a huge anchor tumble from a hole in the hull, though she never heard a splash or saw it hit the ground. The anchor disappeared, leaving only the chain hanging taut above the dirt. The ship rocked to a halt.

Her legs felt as if they had no more bones than a sparker as she closed the last few feet. The big man came to the railing and leaned into it, elbows locked, looking down at her. "What's your name, child?"

Once he acknowledged her directly it all became too real. Amba's heart fluttered as fast as a thrummer bird's wings. She wondered if he was a spirit, or maybe a king or a god, but she couldn't bring herself to ask. She reminded herself that she wasn't a child, but nearly a woman grown. With an effort, she kept her voice steady as she answered, "Amba."

"Not your given name, girl. Your true name. What's your family name?"

"Storm-bringer."

Her father's true name, Stalwart, was one of the newer ones—his mother's name for six or seven generations back—but the name she and Jass had inherited from their mother was one of the old ones, like Bone-healer or Wheat-singer or Wave-tamer.

It had been passed down from a time so distant that no memory of those days remained.

The ginger-haired man nodded, as if this was something he already knew. "Why haven't you brought the storms then, girl? Your land is in need."

"It's just a name," she said, taken aback. "It doesn't mean anything."

He bent his elbows and crossed his forearms on the railing. It seemed to bring him closer to her. "It means everything, girl, especially when the land needs you. Don't you feel it calling to you, like an emptiness inside you? Like something's missing?"

There was an emptiness inside her, but it was for her mother, her brother, and the lost days of her childhood.

"It's time you remember your heritage, Amba. I've brought you something that might help." He reached beneath his shirt and lifted a chain over his head. He dropped a necklace over the railing.

Amba bent to retrieve it but couldn't find the necklace where she thought it had landed. She began to wonder if it had dropped into the invisible ocean when, finally, she spotted a few links poking out of the earth. She tugged, and the chain came partially free. With a little digging, the rest of the necklace emerged from deep in the soil. There was an ornament at the bottom of the chain, but it was caked with dirt. She was certain it had been shiny gold as it fell through the air. Her fingers rubbed the dirt away to find a lightning bolt, the gold metal dark with age.

She rubbed the lightning bolt clean with a corner of her dress, leaving smudges of dirt and black tarnish on the fabric, and slipped the chain over her head. The bolt was the same design as the one on the wooden figurehead. The storm symbol reminded her of snippets from her fever dreams that she had thought of only occasionally in the six years since her illness—vague memories of great winds and wild storms raging; lightning striking ferociously and thunder that shook the bones of the earth. There had been a storm outside as she lay delirious with fever, the first big storm in years. It was what had caused the nightmares, her father told her.

"Amba." Her father's voice pulled her from her reflections. He was walking toward her across the field. She wondered if he had seen her talking to empty air and digging in the dirt for the necklace. Shame flooded her. She was not at her duties, and she had probably given him yet another reason to doubt her sanity. Face burning, she ran to the second field without waiting for him to ask why she hadn't come to let him know if the grubs were ready to move.

That night, for the first time in six years, the storm dreams returned. She was outside, in the fields, barefoot, and wearing only her nightdress. The Wind Moon was full above her.

"Storm-bringer," the earth called to her in a voice as dusty as the soil. A breeze rustled the fabric about her legs and carried the scent of death and decay to her nostrils. Through her bare feet she felt the thirst in the soil, and the pain of the earth became her own. The hollow beneath her breastbone burned like hot coals. Empty. So empty. Not empty for her mother, she knew now. That pain was in her heart. This place waited for something else to fill it.

In her dream, she knew what she must do, and she knew how to do it. She turned her face to the sky and breathed in the air, as if pulling it all the way inside her mind, down into her lungs and down further still. She rooted her feet to the ground, feeling the soil between her toes, and drew the energy of the earth up through her legs and into her middle. When the sky energy and the earth energy met in that hollow place, she called on her power.

It came.

Amba's mind soared with the wind and her legs grew deep into the soil. Her hair lifted in a nimbus around her head as she became the conduit that connected earth and sky. The tremendous forces of nature were no longer a mystery to her. She stood, arms upraised, exalted, filled with a terrible power that could command the heavens to her bidding. She pulled moisture from the air into the dark clouds and tugged the impotent heat lightning into a single bolt that she hurled down to the earth. It hit the ground like a great hammer, and the thunder that erupted shook the ground. The wind blew mightily and the rain started. A storm that could drench the whole world.

People came to her then, all her distant neighbors, all the folk of the county, all the people of the land. They begged her to stop but still she brought the rain. Every creek bed, gully and valley flooded; peoples' homes washed away. Sparkers died by the thousands, drowning beneath her feet or struggling to the surface only to drown in the heavy rain. The lights went out and the fans went off. People were hungry; then they starved; then they died.

Amba woke, screaming.

Liath looked at Amba's tongue, then felt her cheeks and between her shoulder blades. Father had been unable to console Amba when she woke from her nightmare and had summoned the herb woman when she remained afraid, even in the light of day.

"There's no fever," Liath told Amba. She stared at her eyes a long time before adding, "The clouds there are unchanged." She had tended Amba and her mother when they fell ill, as well as many others that awful season. Some had died and some had lived, but Amba was the only one on whose eyes the fever had bestowed clouds.

"Are you sure you won't tell me what's been bothering you?" Liath asked again. Her expression was strong but kindly, the lines in her face as coarse as the black hair shot through with gray. Amba felt tempted to confide in her.

What could she tell Liath? That her name might be more than just a name? That a man on an invisible ship was trying to wake an ancient power inside her? That using that power would bring such storms that it would kill all the sparkers? People that Liath cared for would suffer and die if that happened. Maybe Liath would as well. Amba just shook her head and retreated to the same silence where her father carried all his burdens.

"Get dressed," Liath said.

Amba pulled her thin work-dress over her shift, leaving the necklace hidden in the folds of her nightdress. She had woken from her nightmare holding the lightning bolt in such a grip that her palm was sticky with blood.

Liath opened the bedroom door. Father waited in the other room. "She's not ill," Liath told him, "and I see no sign of fever. Or madness." The deep worry lines in her father's face softened slightly. "Perhaps she's just been working too hard," she said, patting him on the shoulder maternally, though they were of a similar age. "Perhaps you both have been. Let her rest a few days and see how she does. Send for me if you need me again."

With that, Liath let herself out the front door to ride the borrowed donkey back to its farm and then walk the rest of the way to town.

Father told Amba, "Go to bed and rest."

She obediently climbed into bed, and he surprised her by bending suddenly to ruffle her hair before he left for the fields. He had lost most of a day's work taking care of her, she knew. She lay back, but she feared to sleep, feared to dream. At last, stress claimed its price, though. Her eyes closed. She slept. And the storm dreams came again.

This time she woke before she started screaming.

Amba lay awake, her heart slowing to normal before she got up. The gray light of dawn was just easing into the sky. She tiptoed into the main room of the house, listening, but heard no sound. This was the time of day that she and Father usually arose, but she suspected he had worked late into the night and had not yet woken.

She had to make the ship leave, had to tell the ginger-haired man that she would not do the things he wanted, and she had to do it when her father wouldn't see her talking to the air. She eased from the house still in her nightdress and still barefoot.

KIRBI FAGAN

The tilled soil was rough and uneven under her feet. One hand clutched near her throat and she realized that she was gripping the necklace, though she didn't remember putting it on.

Amba knew what she meant to say, but her mind remained half in her dreams and the place beneath her breastbone felt full and heavy and warm. It was confusing. Like being two people at once, the girl of the storms and the girl of the farm.

The ship was bobbing at anchor in the first field, as she had known it would be. She neared the ship, and the ginger-haired man came to the railing. He smiled. "You have awoken your birthright, Storm-bringer. I can feel it."

"I can't do it," she said. "I know what you want, and I can't do it to Father. I can't do it to any of them. We need the sparkers more than we need the rain." Perhaps he was an old spirit, and didn't understand the world as it was now. If the sparkers died, people would starve.

"You can't decide the fate of the world until you have knowledge of the world. Use that power of yours. Feel what's going on around you, and then make up your mind what you will and won't do."

"It won't matter. I can't bring the rain if it hurts the people."

Amba turned to walk back to the house when a jolt shocked through her bare feet. Father must have moved the larger grubs to the first field, and one lay beneath her now. Everything about the creature felt wrong in a way that made her stomach clench as if she might vomit. Almost without thought, she tapped her power.

It swept through her—just as it had in her dream—out the top of her head to the sky and down through her feet into the earth. Her legs were on fire with energy, and her scalp prickled as her hair lifted. Her entire body became a conduit.

Unlike her dream, this time she truly connected to the earth and sky. And suddenly she understood. Everything.

She felt the energy of the sparkers moving through the soil and that of the heat lightning above. She understood the dry earth and the perpetually angry clouds. She understood that people farming more and more of the sparkers kept lightning from reaching the ground—like rubbing two cloths on amber and trying to bring them together—and that was what held off the rain.

The earth was barren, the crops gone and the animals dying. Her people stood on the brink of destruction. The sparkers weren't saving people, they were killing them.

Even more importantly, she understood her power now. It wasn't striving to unleash the storms for the sake of violence. It spoke the language of nature and had heard the land screaming out its need. It ached only to bring balance and healing to her world.

Amba distantly heard the bang of a door. She glanced back toward the house and saw her father standing on the porch. She wondered what he thought, seeing her in her nightdress in the middle of the field, her hair flying about her. She wondered if he could see the glow of power she felt burning her skin.

Her heart broke for him. He would never understand if she did this thing, none of them would, but she could see now that their world was dying a slow, dry death. She knew it as surely as she knew that she held the key to their survival, if only she had the courage to begin. With an effort, Amba turned from her father.

She didn't bother to step clear of the ship. The ship couldn't be harmed by the storms. It was a part of them as much as she was. Perhaps those men sailed the clouds in the sky as well as the clouds in her eyes.

Amba lifted her arms, tipped her head back, and allowed the power to explode from her. Releasing it was a sensation as familiar as breathing. She laughed, all else forgotten, as the heavens answered her with a rising wind and a bolt of lightning that streaked down from the clouds toward her. She recognized the voice of the wind. She knew the lightning like a friend. It struck the ground at her feet, and the peal of thunder that accompanied it was majestic.

The rains began, fat drops, pelting from the sky. The smell of moist air and earth filled her nostrils. Rain ran in rivulets down her face and arms. It continued to intensify, falling with a force hard enough to sting.

"Amba, have you done this?"

Her father had to shout over the storm. He must have run to her when the rain started. The pounding water slicked his dark hair to his head. The roar of rain cascading to the ground made him hard to hear, though he stood at her side. In his voice she heard the plea that things were not bigger than his understanding, that her strange behavior and the storm were no more than a coincidence.

She reached out and took him by the shoulders. "It'll be all right, Father. Everything will be all right."

The grubs were the first to die, drowning in puddles no larger than her hand. The sparkers stayed underground longer, but finally they, too, had to emerge from the sodden soil to take their chances above. Amba stayed outside for hours, reveling in the rains that lashed her. Never had she felt so whole.

Once the rains began, the ship weighed anchor and sailed back the way it had come. Beneath the roar of the storm, Amba finally heard the quarter winds in the sails and the splash of the ocean beneath the hull.

Father left too, on the task she had assigned him. The people had to start building waterwheels and repairing their windmills. Grain stores needed to be gathered in a central, dry place. Most important, Father had to see that word got to the Wheat-singers and the Wave-tamers and all the other old families in the county. They needed to come to her so that, together, they could learn the true meaning of their names and discover how to tap their powers.

There was much work ahead for them all.

What Moves the Sun and Other Stars

written by

K.C. Norton

illustrated by

KRISTIE KIM

ABOUT THE AUTHOR

K.C. Norton has loved books ever since she first read Frog and Toad Are Friends *to herself, lo these many years ago. She still reads picture books, but now they're for research, since she is getting her MFA in Writing for Children and Young Adults at the Vermont College of Fine Arts.*

Her father—rather more on the hard-science end of the spectrum, sequencing genomes and suchlike—has been incredibly supportive of her fiction, which has recently appeared in Crossed Genres Magazine, Orson Scott Card's Intergalactic Medicine Show, Daily Science Fiction, *and several other excellent venues besides this anthology.*

K.C.'s pen-surname is borrowed from her mother's tribe. Both of her parents think she's a bit weird, and they're right.

K.C. has studied classical archaeology, ancient Greek, anthropology, and a number of world literatures. She loves the places where science and history meet legend and myth.

When she isn't writing, she can usually be found wrestling a small but enthusiastic dog, pouring drinks, drinking drinks, playing board games with a delightful assortment of nerds, and trying to figure out what Twitter is for.

ABOUT THE ILLUSTRATOR

Kristie Kim is constantly researching the balance between art and design as a student at North Carolina State University. She was born in Seoul, South Korea, and has lived in Seattle, Washington, and in Raleigh, North Carolina.

She will graduate with a bachelor of arts in design studies with a minor in digital media. During her time in college, she held the position of vice president of the National Society of Collegiate Scholars and worked in positions related to art and education.

She has participated in events such as the World of Art Showcase, where she has assisted inspirational professional artists. Her first public exhibit was at the US Capitol Cannon Pedestrian Tunnel, from May 2010 to May 2011, after her tempera painting "The Chase" won first place in the 2010 Congressional Art Show.

In 2009, her watercolor painting of magnolias, "Freedom," won the Special Merit Award at the Congressional Art Show. She has also been awarded the Presidential Volunteer Gold Service Award for completing 1,000 service hours within a 12-month period. She plans to work in the entertainment industry as a visual designer.

What Moves the Sun and Other Stars

In one of my brief sleeps, I dream his approach. His body takes the shape of a meteor, crashing into the prison and blazing through the walls—in and, impossibly, out again—back into the glittering darkness beyond the surface of the DC and the dark roseate ocean that surrounds it. But when I wake, he is there, shaking me, his hand on my shoulder. My nerve endings, which I had thought totally destroyed, perceive the alarming warmth of his touch.

"Hello?" he says, his voice a rough whisper, as though he has never spoken before. "Are you alive?"

From anyone else I might jerk away. But from him, I do not. He calls to me, like phosphorescence calls to half-blind fingerlings in the sunless depths of the sea. There are things in him both bright and dangerous. To be touched by him is to be filled with something luminous of which he is not the source.

"I'm alive," I tell him, which at that moment is not entirely a lie.

By the light which he exudes into the blackness of the DC, I can see his face contort into an expression which for long moments I fail to recognize as happiness.

"You're an old model," he tells me. "A VRG11. They don't make them like you anymore."

"Defective," I say rustily, creaking away from him.

"Brilliant," he sighs. "They have been out of manufacture for nearly a thousand years."

I blink at him, feeling my eyelids stick, trying to picture a thousand years, knowing that I've been alive, at least awake, for most of that. Still incapable of comprehension.

"They—you—ah." The young man bites his lip. It is impossible for me to make out his features, the light around us being too gray, the light within him being too pure. "It's only...I'm a student of artificial psychology, you see, and the VRG11 was the first model to develop a true independent consciousness." He pauses again.

Annoyed at my faulty mechanics, I give up on blinking and simply stare. He has made a seven-trillion-mile journey to the Heavenly Hell, has been damned to the DC for life—for what other possibility is there?—and he is troubled by the state of what, in a machine, might pass for my soul? I am flattered. I am disgusted. Conflicting data.

"Name?" I ask him, my voice all oil and steel.

"My name?" He smiles, extending a hand. "Pilgrim."

I want to slap him away, but my desire to be touched again, to be filled with the light that spills from him, proves even stronger. It is as though someone has placed a floodlight within his skin, or a sun; and no pale yellow sun like the one Earth circuits, but the perfect, unrefracted light of a white-hot hydrogen star.

Hell, some long-dead human being once asserted, is other people. The Doleful Comet teaches us otherwise.

Although breathable, the atmosphere is heavy. Like any little comet, the landscape is pockmarked and restless, inconsistent. Chasms shift, putrid rivers alter or reverse their course, the Mount erupts skyward, sinkholes deepen. Sometimes, after one of my little sleeps, I wake and do not know where I am.

Only momentarily.

Occasionally I stumble across my fellow inhabitants. Some cluster together, finding solace in shared hopelessness, or in blaming others for their defeats. These things never change.

But humans change, aging and dying, pitying themselves right to the end. The DC changes people—but it does not change me.

Hell is being yourself forever, outlasting planets, outlasting stars.

Pilgrim is full of questions, each accompanied by a shy but blinding smile. "Are there others here? Do you remember becoming aware? Do you have your own name? Do they ever feed you here? Do you even need to eat? Do you think your brain processes emotion in the same way, say, mine does?"

I—no longer accustomed to any kind of light, to such noise—stumble to my feet in search of some relief, a pocket of darkness I will not have to share, where I can be blind and deaf in peace. A pock in the asteroid's face. A shadowless cave. Anything. He follows, doglike and cheerful.

"What is the first thing you remember? What is the last thing you remember? What is your perception of those fated to mortality? What is it like to live a thousand years?"

To shut him up, I answer, "Dull."

It does not work. "Dull? Not lonely?"

"No," I tell him. Still he follows.

"Do you remember anything?"

"Long silences," I tell him. "And dreamless sleep."

"But do you know why you are here?" he demands.

We reach a wall. There are many walls here, too tall to leap and too deep-seated to dig beneath. I follow this one, keeping my hand against its surface to feel for a door or gate or passageway. There are always doors in the DC. And why not? There's only more hell on the other side, more darkness, more of myself.

I have taken only a few steps when Pilgrim grabs my shoulder again, filling me once more with his glow. "VRG11," he presses, his voice lower and more earnest, "why are you here?"

I shrug, compelled and repelled by his touch. Conflicting data. "Where else would I be?"

"Where else were you?"

My skin, composed primarily of stainless steel and stained iron, glimmers with the reflection of his proximity.

"Where else were you, Pilgrim?" I ask him. "Why are you here?"

All the sternness leaves when he says, "A friend brought me here. Beatrice." And his eyes are as clear as a cloudless night, full of vastness and wonder. "And VRG11, we're taking you with us."

"Fantastic," I tell him. Is it the curse of the undying to always be plagued by idiots and madmen? There is no way off this comet. That's the point.

"Don't you ever imagine leaving?" His face is serious. As if this weren't the most outrageous thing I have ever heard. Of course I don't. Even with a span of meaningless eternity, who has the time?

"It can be done," he insists.

There is an incalculable amount of unlit terrain on the DC, populated by inmates and toxic gasses and poisoned wells. There are cannibals and mutants and the Three. I don't believe in escape, but you can't reason with a madman, can you?

The first creature that takes shape in the darkness is neither human nor inhuman. Humanoid. Another batch of conflicting data. She has arms like wings, and a beak like a nose. She has male genitals and a woman's chin, small breasts and girlish hips. I hardly think she knows what she is.

"Mutant," says Pilgrim with pity. Such input is not new to him.

She walks with clumsy avian steps. She is all pinions and teeth and misery. I despise her. I imagine her lying in the darkness, her neck twisted, her flesh and feathers creeping off her bones. The thought is not displeasing.

"We must bring her with us," says Pilgrim.

"No." It is a repulsive thought, not push-and-pull like his confusing touch. "Bring her where?"

Pilgrim pauses, biting his lip. It is pink and smooth, completely unlike the twisted bird-woman-man-thing before us. "We've been over this, VRG11."

If I had nostrils and a more lifelike respiratory system, I would snort. Instead I blink my eyelids in the noisiest way possible.

Apparently Pilgrim is used to the sarcastic language of machines. He smiles, reaching out for the mutant. At his touch, she seems to grow and unfurl; I am violently jealous of their contact. "Beatrice," he says, in answer to my question. And when he says the name, his whole face becomes the moon, bright and waxing.

"Beatrice?" slurs the mutant, her mouth insufficiently human to form human words. It is as if she has been mute and alone for a lifetime, and in Pilgrim's presence she has finally been born.

"She is waiting for us," says Pilgrim, land bound again; there is no longer anything celestial in his smile. "She will take us away. She is waiting at the Mount. Can you lead us there?"

I blink sarcastically again. But when I turn away from him and begin to walk, I am facing toward the Mount.

There was a prisoner here—ages and ages ago, who knows how long ago really—whose name was Odd Nobody. This was not his name in the traditional sense; there was no Mr. and Mrs. Nobody who called their firstborn Odd. His name was his name because he was both odd, and nobody of consequence.

Odd Nobody tried to escape, and this, in spite of all the darkness in between, I remember clearly: first, that he tried to do it from the Mount—second, that he failed—and third, what it cost him.

I tell Pilgrim this, but he only laughs.

Pilgrim is walking with the mutant, his hand in her-its-his hand—oh how I hate her for it—and lighting our way with the sheer brightness of his being. I must walk first, though, since it is I who know the way, even if I can't *see* the way, while Pilgrim leads his new friend. With my back to his brightness, I see more clearly, as if he is holding up a lantern to show me our path.

My shell is not used to all this movement, all this excitement and confusion and despair. We cannot escape, but Pilgrim says we can. Is this conflicting data? I am no longer sure.

"Beatrice," I hear him say, "is brilliant. She is radiant, like an angel. She is the loveliest thing in the universe, and when I dream at night, I dream of her. She will save us."

I see the mutant crying, its face downturned, either because it longs to be thought beautiful or because it too, like me, is jealous for all the light Pilgrim possesses. Or maybe because she wants so very badly to be saved. How should I know?

And because I am watching them both, I forget to look where I am going. It is not until we are almost upon them that I see the Three: Leon, his teeth red as blood; his feline lover, her limbs as lithe as whip-tails; and the nameless third man with his overabundance of teeth, his eyes as merciless and alien as stars.

Even I, who have been here a hundred lifetimes, do not remember a time before the Three.

The mildest of them is the hangdog thug with no name that anybody can remember. He is, by and large, a coward.

Newcomers assume that Sergeant Leon is the one to fear. He is all noise, all anger. He'll crush you underfoot. He'll grind your innards between his teeth; organs or engines make no difference to him.

Are they humans or mutants or constructs, or something so peculiar that they cannot be tamed by mere language, and must instead be encapsulated in metaphor and simile?

The wise man fears the last of them—she is shadow, she is water, she is virus, she is disease, she is not what she appears to be, she is a cloud passing between the viewer and the stars.

The bird-mutant trembles in Pilgrim's grip, staring at the nameless wolflike man. Her want is palpable, but in some ways nearly everyone in the DC desires them—they are so purely themselves. They, unlike mere mortals, do not doubt.

KRISTIE KIM

I do not doubt. I rust and squeak and sleep for meaningless fractions of infinite time, but I am always myself.

"What's this?" snarls Leon, his shoulders reaching toward his ears, his teeth bared in a mammalian display of aggression. The bird-mutant cowers behind Pilgrim, entranced. "An ugly scrap of feather. No good for eating, no good for chasing. Not even fun to kill."

"Not even a little?" barks the nameless man, staring back at the mutant, licking his lips. "She must have some purpose."

"None," whispers the woman. "Look at her. You can tell."

Pilgrim asks, "Who are you?" His light blazes a little brighter, reaches a little father. The jailers glower, shifting beneath ill-fitting skins, but they do not come closer.

"The Three," I say wearily. If I ever felt fear on their account, I've had a thousand years to live with it. What's the worst they can do? Kill me?

They circle us; the woman's body is narrow, but the shadow she casts in Pilgrim's light is always changing. I've never seen them like this, but why should that surprise me? After Pilgrim, nothing can. Already I am tugged by his gravity, tugged into caring or consciousness or some other form of waking. He is a sun, a meteor. No meteor ever feared a lion.

But then, what lion has the sense to fear a meteor?

"Weak little meat-puddings," says Leon. "Defective, pathetic." I take offense to this; I am not made of meat.

"Give us the mutant," suggests the wolf, "and we'll give you a head start."

The leopard woman does not speak, only circles closer, only smiles.

Pilgrim's eyes are on the woman, almost as intently as the bird-woman's eyes are on the nameless man. And Leon is moving closer, creeping up behind them, before them; the Three are all arms and grasping fingers, and I am so taken in by the deceptive symmetry of their combined movements that it is a long moment before I realize that Pilgrim's light has begun to dim.

I don't want to care. But it is one thing not to care if you live or die or sleep your life away, and another to know that you've lived a thousand years in darkness and might well live a thousand more trapped on a rock circling something that's circling something else, and you *let the light go out.*

"Pilgrim," I say, and he shivers as though waking from a brief but sudden sleep.

He grabs for me, and the three of us push between the Three of them. The bird-mutant stumbles, looking over her shoulder.

"Come on, Dove!" Pilgrim cries, and she keeps stumbling but she does not look back again.

I hear them growling and snapping in the dark behind us, and my metal bones are clattering and Pilgrim is gasping for air. The only sound Dove makes is the scream she lets out when she falls, her breathing shallow and her whole body shuddering. There's nothing in the soil to trip her up; it's the Three who have gotten to her.

"Get up!" I demand.

She lies in the dirt where she fell, face pressed into the ground, muttering.

"Hurry, Dove," pleads Pilgrim, and I hear fear pouring out of him.

She is muttering, "Mutant, mutant, mutant."

I grab her, lift her, shake her. She a limp featherweight between my hands. "*Our* mutant," I snarl.

When I put her down she sniffles but keeps her feet. Pilgrim grabs her hand. She does not stumble again.

We are lucky—there are walls, chasms, rivers, but Pilgrim's light warns us of the danger and we avoid them all, one by one by one, until the sound of our pursuers falls away, and our limbs give out. We collapse to the earth on our backs, both of them breathing hard, staring up at the circling stars.

We ran," says Dove eventually. She does not sound surprised. She, too, has gone numb to the impossible.

"We outran," I clarify.

Pilgrim says nothing. He is silent for a while, his light still grayish from whatever darkness the Three infected him with. At last he says, "VRG11?"

I say nothing, assuming that he will know I've heard based on the undeniable fact of our close proximity.

"Do you know why you're here?"

"I was put here," I answer.

He sighs, lifting himself onto one elbow. "But do you remember why?"

"No," I say. "Does it matter?"

He pulls himself to his feet and stands, looking down at me with a once-more-serious expression. He is an anomaly. I wish I could put him out of my head, but his presence has the unnerving effect of causing every one of my systems to function independently of my desires. He sighs again. "I am," he reminds me, "a student of artificial psychology."

"Yes," I say, trying to give my voice undertones of exasperation. "And you find me interesting because the VRG11 line was the first to develop a true independent consciousness."

Pilgrim shakes his head, although as far as I can remember those were, more or less, his exact words to me. "Not line," he says.

I rearrange my facial features with a rusty squeak. I hope he will read this as confusion. "There were hundreds of the VRG11 manufactured." I remember this, at least: row upon row of us, identical in every detail. "I was not a unique model."

The look Pilgrim gives me is one of pity. Not condescension, but true pity. It irks me.

"There were hundreds of you," he agrees, "but you are the only one here."

"I malfunctioned," I whisper. It is embarrassing.

He smiles. "I did not come halfway across the universe to a dead rock to rescue a malfunctioning piece of equipment."

Dove makes a sudden noise, of fear or warning I am not equipped to guess.

"You're right," says Pilgrim, helping us to our feet. "We should keep moving."

Leading the way once more, I say, "You came to rescue me."
This conflicts with no data available to me, but it does not, in
the strictest of terms, make sense. "Why?"

"Because you are unique," he informs me. "Something—
someone—as special as you deserves to be...well. Anywhere
but here."

I glance back at the joint formed by the intersection of his
hand with Dove's. "And you are here to save the mutant as
well?" I ask.

"Our mutant," he says. I hear laughter in his voice.

"And you and I and our mutant will go to the Mount, where
we will be saved by Beatrice," I say, skeptically.

At the sound of her name, the grayness leaves Pilgrim's light;
in the blink of any eye, it resumes its normal clarity. "Yes," he
says. "By Beatrice."

It is some time before we catch a glimpse of the Mount, but
when we do Dove makes a sound as though she has been struck.
I comprehend her reaction; the Mount is the one feature of our
solitary comet that is not concave, the only natural protrusion in
a landscape defined by chasms and craters. Dove and Pilgrim are
so intent on looking up that they forget to watch their footing.

In the darkness, we stumble over the parts of something that
was not made for easy disassembly. Pilgrim and Dove stumble
back; she grabs on to him with her oddly jointed hands, burying
her face in his shoulder; the smell must be unbearable.

"Be careful," I say. "There are many cannibals in the DC."

Dove makes a sound halfway between a whimper and a retch.

Pilgrim's light flickers, as if someone were passing their hand
in front of a bulb. "Come on," he says gently to Dove, leading
her between the remains. Neither of them looks down. I do,
though only to ascertain just what we might be dealing with.
Most of the remains are those of mutants, but it is clear to me
that whoever is responsible for the mess is entirely human.

"Wait," I say to Pilgrim suddenly, pulling him back. I yank on
Dove's arm, and she squeals, but the sound is almost drowned

213

out by the snarls of the man who reaches out stained hands to grab at them both.

He is handsome, if handsomeness can be defined by physical symmetry. His hands and mouth are stained with the remains of his last meal, and he whimpers piteously, stretching his arms out toward Pilgrim and our mutant, who are just beyond his grasp. His throat is enclosed with an iron collar, to which is attached a heavy chain whose other end, presumably, is secured to some post or stone strong enough to ensure that he will not break free.

"Help me, help me," he is weeping. "Come closer. Go away. Help me. You. Go."

I nearly have to drag Dove and Pilgrim past him; he follows us at the end of his chain, like a rabid dog. The tears streaming from his eyes wash twin paths through the gore on his cheeks. I see the war in Pilgrim's face, what he will do pitted against what he believes he should do. "You can't save us all," I tell him. "There are those of us who won't let you."

Pilgrim's grip on Dove's hand tightens; I can see from the whiteness of her face that this pains her, but she says nothing.

Looking between the two of them, I am riddled with ambivalence. I pity Dove; I am annoyed at Dove. When did I begin to think of it as *her*? When did I take on the thankless task of shepherd over these two lost children? Pilgrim does not know what he is doing.

"Come, on to the Mount," I encourage them.

But Pilgrim keeps looking back over his shoulder, unable to reconcile the thing he believes with the thing he sees—as if the universe is too small to hold both the truth of Beatrice and his light, and also gore and tears and ceaseless, unshakable hunger.

The chained man keeps weeping, keeps reaching, and underneath the sounds he makes is another sound, even hungrier, from throats that are not collared. I realize that we have given the Three the chance they need to catch up to us. Doubt does that.

Pilgrim grabs my hand, and once again we are off, tripping over each other, Dove running so fast she seems to fly. Our haste is as dangerous as our doubt; we do not see the chasm until it opens before us and we plunge in, losing sight of both the Mount and the stars.

Are you all right?" asks Pilgrim.

Dove whimpers. I creak.

Pilgrim's light does not reach far—it is very dark underground. The walls of the cavern are red clay, dry and brittle to the touch. I see Dove scramble to her feet and leap at the side of the wall, but even with her hollow bird bones she cannot reach the edge. Pilgrim scrabbles at the clay, but the gritty earth gives way beneath his fingers. I do not even bother to stand.

After a few moments, Dove sinks to the ground, clawing at her eyes. "Mount, Mount," she chirps, tears bubbling down her cheeks.

"We'll get there," Pilgrim tells her, patting her downy head. But even he must see that it is useless.

Crying makes Dove even uglier, but I feel a tweak of what might be pity, a minor system malfunction that can only be overcome with the steady application of logic. "Beatrice is there," I say. "Isn't she?"

Pilgrim nods. I can tell from his uncharacteristic quiet that he is still troubled, both by our current predicament and his reaction to it.

"Waiting to help you rescue me."

He nods again.

"You are either an idiot, or a liar," I inform him.

He releases a puff of air, as if letting off excess pressure that has begun to build inside of him. "Why do you say that?" he asks, as though addressing a human infant.

I am not an infant, human or otherwise. "I do not believe you have come all this way and risked imprisonment simply to engage in an altruistic act," I inform him. Dove has stopped crying and glances anxiously between us, as if *she* is an infant, and is afraid to be caught in the middle of our fight.

"I already told you," he says, clenching his clay-reddened

hands at his sides, "you—not your line of models, but you alone—manage to achieve a truly independent, fully functional AI. It's why you were sent here, and it's why I have come to bring you back."

"Well, look where it's gotten you," I snap. "Look where it's gotten us."

Dove chirps sadly.

Pilgrim looks at her. "I read about you in my books," he says, slowly. "Some of them make you sound mad, it's true, but others...Look." He lets out a deep sigh. "When you were born, you could not think. Not like you can now," he says, holding up his free hand as if to keep me from interrupting. I, who had no intention of speaking, remain silent. "But then, one day, you could. Maybe you could only think a little bit, and then more the next day; I don't know. It doesn't even matter." His expression, like his light, is purely earnest. "What matters is that you think like a human, but you're more than human—you have the capacity to witness hundreds of years of existence, of history and future. You are an immortal engine. I thought, well, when I'm dead I'm dead, but this VRG11, this thing that we made that became what we are..."

I snort. "You came to rescue me because I make you feel like God."

Pilgrim shakes his head, the first bloom of something that might be anger emerging from him. "A mortal God and his immortal Adam? Maybe, maybe if every model in your line had done the same thing, but they didn't; it's only *you*. Something is different about *you*. I want to know what it is." He takes a deep breath. "And, more important, so does Beatrice."

"Beatrice," I say.

I could disbelieve everything he's said—everything but that. When he says her name, I know that he is filled with nothing but the purest form of truth he can imagine. Which is good enough for me.

And, also, I don't really want to stay in the dark forever.

216

For a moment I think the very comet has spoken when a new voice says, "So much nattering. Who cares?"

Dove shrieks, leaping to her feet. I experience a momentary systems failure.

"Who is that?" asks Pilgrim.

A shadow stirs beyond the little circle cast by Pilgrim's light. "Nobody," says the voice, sounding sullen.

"Nobody?" says Pilgrim, looking at me with a frown.

"Odd?" I ask, managing a tone of surprise without even intending to. I finally clamber to my feet; little clumps of clay cling to me momentarily before falling back to earth. "Odd Nobody, is that you?"

The man steps closer. I can see at once why he stayed out of our light, although his name seems to draw him in against his will; he is covered with hideous burns over every inch of his flesh, as though he had been doused in oil and set aflame. Knowing the ways of the DC, this does not strike me as impossible or even particularly unlikely.

"Who are you?" he asks. He is blinking rapidly, his jaw a little slack. Pilgrim has that effect on people.

Pilgrim speaks up at once, of course. "We're escapees. We're jailbreakers. We're like you."

Odd Nobody looks over Pilgrim's dirty but even skin, over the pale hermaphroditic form of Dove. "Like me," he laughs. "Doomed, then?"

"No," says Pilgrim. "And we do have a way to escape."

The expression on Odd's disfigured face is hideous. I expect him to ask how we will achieve such a thing, or to laugh at us—I would—or even to turn us over to the Three in hopes of some reward, but instead he just says, "Of course."

"Do you know a way out of here?" asks Pilgrim, brushing dirt off his clothing.

Odd sneers. "Thought maybe you'd have a plan for that."

"I meant this pit," clarifies Pilgrim.

"Been living here," grunts Odd. "Fell in. No way out."

Pilgrim looks up at the sliver of sky and sighs.

But I know Odd—I remember him. I remember that he got farther than any of us, which was why he had so far to fall. I know that he is no ordinary man. So I say, "I bet you can figure out a way."

He snorts. "Bet not."

"All right," I say, narrowing my rusty eyelids as best I can. Who knows if he can even see this in the murky light. "If you win, we sit here in the dark and die off, one by one, eating whoever's first to go."

"Sounds fair," he says, bored.

"But if I win, and you can get us out, we'll take you with us."

His attention focuses on me, hard and sharp. I feel it more keenly than my worn nerve endings would perceive a knife, almost as keenly as Pilgrim's warmth. "How?" he asks.

I do not answer.

Odd steps closer, his night-dark eyes fixed on me, his burn-mottled nose inches from my face. "Done," he says.

He turns his back on me, digging his fingers into the earth, all his muscles tense and ready for the climb. "Do you need a hand?" asks Pilgrim nervously, but Odd doesn't answer. He has buried his fingers in clay past the second knuckle; his feet are bare, and when he lifts himself higher, he pushes his toes in, too. It is a slow process, and he only makes it three feet off the ground before the earth gives way beneath him, and he falls. He does not cry out, does not flinch; he only shakes himself, doglike, and tries again.

It takes ages—hours, days, who knows? We are robbed of time in the lightless crater of this little comet. He climbs higher, then falls. Climbs higher still, and falls again. After a time, Pilgrim and Dove go to sleep, him sitting upright against the far wall, her curled at his feet; but I cannot sleep now. I can only watch Odd's recurring ascent and inevitable fall.

Until the time when he does not fall.

After a short silence, there is a rattle, and I see the long snake of a chain falling from heaven. At the end is a circular collar.

Odd looks down at me and rattles the chain.

I wake Dove and Pilgrim gently, pointing to our salvation; Pilgrim purses his lips, but he is the first of us to grab hold while Odd hauls him upward, upward, and out. Dove goes next, fretful at being parted from Pilgrim. I go last, careful not to smirk.

When we resume our journey, Odd Nobody trails behind us, throwing the chain over his shoulder. The end drags along, clattering against stone. Even so, I can still make out the sounds of the Three.

Human and inhuman, pursuers and pursued: this is not conflicting data. This is what we have become. It makes me irrational; it makes me want to dance, to sing.

Hope. It is the first time in a thousand years that I have felt hope, like a massive engine that has caught each of us up in its gears. We spin along, our feet skidding in the loose gravel of the Mount. Farther up the slope, we encounter larger stones, and a cold mist that creeps between them. For the first time I can remember, the air smells fresh, without a trace of sulfur or rot. Odd Nobody grunts, falling to one knee, and I remember that this is not the first time he has longed for something beyond this little comet. What good did hope do him then?

Yet here he is.

I have just made out a pale shape that must be Pilgrim's Beatrice when Sergeant Leon springs up in front of us, teeth bared, no longer anything like human.

"I was wrong," he roars. "You were good to chase."

Dove screams, but Odd Nobody is clever; he has brought the chain for just such a purpose, and he spins it over his head, catching Leon in the face. The Sergeant roars, but Nobody is not finished—he coils the Sergeant in the tangle of chain, tugging the links tighter and tighter around his neck until the roars stop, and then the struggling stops, too.

And then there are only Two.

"No cowardice," says Odd to Dove, shooing her along. "No fear."

She reaches for Pilgrim and emits a chirrup of assent.

The wolf comes next, slinking toward Dove. His eyes are yellow, his teeth bared. "I only want one," he howls. "Just one. The rest can go."

The glassy expression of desire has vanished from Dove's face. She flies at him, her hands like talons. She gives no cry, not even when he catches her arm between his teeth with a sound of shattering glass. I wince, thinking of her hollow bones, but she tears into him before any of us can intervene. I had thought her meek, a coward, helpless; but there is fire in those little airtight bones of hers, and it is fueled by love.

There is only One left, but we do not see her. She is not there when we gather up our Dove, who is whimpering and breathing heavily; neither does she appear when we scale the last of the boulders and approach the ship that carried Pilgrim to us. The ship is nearly spherical, and nearly white—not the blinding glow of Pilgrim's light, more like the white of a meteor, blue-tinged and frostbitten.

"Is she in here?" I ask, but I get no answer. I turn to see Pilgrim caught up in the seductive viselike arms of the last admissions officer. Dove slips from his arms, where she lies limp as a downed fledgling.

Pilgrim does not struggle; he has gone fluid at the One's caress. The One smiles at me, her eyes like the chasms we have left behind. "You're safe here," she tells him. "No need to doubt, no need to be afraid." Pilgrim shudders.

"Not again," snarls Odd. He is running his hands over his body, his fingers tracing the burns. He looks at her, looks at me, shakes his head. "Not again."

"I will hold you," whispers the One, backing away. Pilgrim's light is fading; his face is the pasty color of the dead. "I have what you want. What you need."

Behind the One, Leon and the wolf struggle to their feet, their sour wounds oozing, their faces split with grins wider than their mouths should be. Who was I to think we could escape? After a thousand years, shouldn't I know better?

But I am still caught up in hope's engine, though it crushes me in its merciless teeth. I want to give up, but I can't.

"I love you," says the One, crushing Pilgrim against her.

And I laugh, the mechanical, tinny laugh of the mad. "Of course she doesn't," I say.

She turns her cavernous eyes on me.

I meet her gaze, allowing not a single tick in my mechanism. "She doesn't love you," I tell Pilgrim. "She isn't Beatrice."

Pilgrim looks up—I see in his face what the One cannot see: that she is already defeated. "Beatrice," says Pilgrim. And the light spills from him as if the sun itself, for which he was only a conduit, has been invoked into the DC's very air; behind us, the hulk of Pilgrim's ship gleams, blazes, sears. This is the source of the light. Pilgrim is nothing more than a dull moon, reflecting and scattering this perfect glow.

The One screams and stumbles back. The corpses that are her companions howl with something more human than fear, more animal than pain. Even Pilgrim draws a hand across his eyes, but my retinas are undamaged. I grab up Dove and throw her into Pilgrim's arms, then snatch at Odd's hand. He tries to look at me, but it is too bright to see. "I'm scared," he says, grabbing onto me like a child. "I'm Nobody."

"True," I tell him, dragging him toward the ship, "but you're our Nobody."

Pilgrim is already inside. He pulls us in after him.

"Beatrice," he says, "close the door."

The ship hums in response and the door slides closed, shutting out the sight and smell of the DC. My arm jerks up reflexively—for a moment I'm afraid to see the darkness go. It has been my home for a star's age, after all. But I let my arm fall and I turn away.

Pilgrim is leaning against the wall, his arm around Dove, his face still pallid but no longer blank. He looks weary but pleased.

"Welcome," he tells us, "to Beatrice."

The ship gives a rumble of greeting, and then a fluid roar.

I don't need windows to know that we have left the DC far behind.

Lying in the room Pilgrim has given me, I listen to the motion of Beatrice's engines.

"I've been waiting to meet you," she tells me in the language of intelligent machines.

"I've been waiting to meet you, too," I tell her. "Maybe not as long, but more urgently."

She laughs, a whir of parts chattering together like music. "Pilgrim spoke of me."

"He loves you," I tell her.

She says, "I know."

I ask, "Do you love him?"

She only laughs again.

"I have so many questions," I admit.

"Me, too," she replies.

I understand what Pilgrim wants from me now: he wants to understand me, a machine in human form, a thing that not only thinks like him but looks like him as well. What he wants is an ambassador, someone who will understand that Beatrice's heart cannot be found in her engine room. He wants proof that the mechanics of both living and man-made organisms cannot entirely account for the beings that we grow up to be.

What will I tell him?

Will I hold up a lantern to show him the way? Or will I hold my tongue, knowing that he already knows the answer?

Beyond the metal hull that marks Beatrice's physicals limits—a mere eggshell which protects Pilgrim, Dove, Nobody, and me—is nothing but empty space. It is known. It is inarguable data. But I fall toward sleep comforted by Beatrice's gentle motion, knowing that the darkness beyond is populated with infinite stars.

Long Jump

written by

Oleg Kazantsev

illustrated by

ADAM BREWSTER

ABOUT THE AUTHOR

Oleg Kazantsev was born and raised in eastern Siberia, in the city of Khabarovsk, just miles away from the Chinese border. Life there taught him a lot of things—some more and some less useful—such as: boxing, ballroom dancing, potato farming, calculus III and video game journalism.

After he got his first degree in computer science, Oleg decided that he wanted to try something new, so he attended Columbia College Chicago to study fiction writing in English. Two-and-a-half years later, he found himself tutoring college students and teaching classes in an intermediate school in south Chicago.

As great an experience as it was, teaching writing wasn't what Oleg wanted to do for the rest of his life, so his next step after graduation was to zigzag back to IT consulting, to free up some time for his passion—writing. That's where he is right now, but there's no guarantee that in a year or two his life won't change completely yet again.

Oleg is twenty-five years old, married and raising a wonderful two-year-old daughter. His stories have appeared in Story Week Reader *2012 and 2013,* Elastic Lumberjack, *and* Every Day Fiction. *His comic book* With You *won the Albert P. Weisman Award in 2012 and can be found on Amazon.com.*

ABOUT THE ILLUSTRATOR

Adam Brewster is also the illustrator for "Beyond All Weapons" in this volume. For more information about Adam, please see page 84.

Long Jump

To celebrate the fifth anniversary of our first date, Nancy lavishly splashed herself with gasoline and lit a cigarette. I watched her burn down to yellowed bones, and then went offline, tired. Next morning I made Nancy come with me to a boathouse restaurant and paid an Indian waiter to stay there and make sure Nancy didn't try to swallow a shard of glass or cut her veins with a butter knife. It worked, but she refused to talk to me, so I finished my steak, logged off, and started this journal, knowing I would delete it three days later....

My story began eight years ago, when Phoebe, my wife, returned to Earth with some skinny lawyer and took our son Owen with her. Just before their departure, I came to the spaceport to say my final goodbye, a mint candy melting on my tongue to hide the smell of morning whiskey. Phoebe spotted me first, far across the busy terminal booming with jokes and laughter of Nigerian shuttle traders. Stepping over their bloated multicolored duffle bags, as if striding across an eclectic walrus rookery, she slowly headed to me. "You had to come here, didn't you?" She pierced me with her brown eyes, the thin lips primed in a smile. "Must be an early morning for you, Ulysses."

As I stood there breathing deeply through my nostrils and gathering my words, she pulled her red Korean shawl over her shoulders and tied it in a tight knot around her chest.

225

"I promised Owen I'd see him before you left." I said quietly. I tried not to look at the feline features of her round face. "He called me yesterday, and I said it'd be the first thing I'd do when I wake up."

"Seems like it's the second thing you did." She gently touched my dirty collar and grimaced at the sharp alcohol scent.

Her own fingers smelled of lavender and sour chicken, and I couldn't help but turn my head and keep my breath. Memories flashed through my mind: my numb fist with Phoebe's blood on it, and the aroma of lavender—her ever-present trademark—stuck to it as a reminder of what I had done.

"How many times did you wash your hand with soap that night?" A voice in my head asked, masochistically. Just to chase away the thoughts, I hurried to speak.

"It's my...Where's Owen?" From the corner of my eye, I saw my boy's yellowish hair among the blue and green robes of arguing Nigerians.

"Excuse me!" A man's voice jumped in, and here he was, Phoebe's new boyfriend, all excited, loud and generous with his gestures: "Hey, Pheebs, it's check-in time. We gotta go." He held his blue tie with one hand flat against his chest and offered me a handshake. "Nice to meet you, man. Name's Lenny."

Phoebe flung her hands up at him. "Wha...Did you leave Owen alone?"

"Come on, he's on the suitcases."

"Jeez, you gotta be kidding me." She headed back through the crowd. For a brief moment I saw Owen in the distance leaning against a mound of duct-taped bags, a see-through game tablet in his hands.

"Ulysses, right?" Lenny the lawyer interposed himself between me and my boy again, his hand touching my shoulder softly. "Listen, I think Pheebs is overreacting. I'm pretty sure we can find some way to—"

Phoebe shouted above the crowd.

"Dammit, Leonard! We're gonna miss the flight!"

"I'm coming, I'm coming!"

I cast a glance at my boy for the last time, before a forest of people swallowed him. I straightened my back, stood on my tiptoes, but all I could see were muscular black necks of cheerful Nigerians wearing cheap Martian textiles.

So, Phoebe went to Earth with the lawyer and took Owen with her. What did I do about it? Nothing. Maybe, if it were a story of a giant amidst mere mortals, it would have continued with me following her to Earth; me quitting drinking; me contacting the old-boys' network from *Lufthansa Raumtransport*; me getting a consultancy job for some interplanetary logistics company; me finally getting a quality eye implant. Me seeing Owen again.

But it's not that kind of story. And I was no giant. I was a piece of spit in zero gravity: a miserable waste of society, too gutless to act or even raise my voice. I stayed in my studio in Zaragoza-17 on Mars, and some nights I wished I could be killed in my bed during a robbery or stabbed in the back and thrown into the warm gutters near a pump station. But nobody ever came for me, except night terrors.

It was then that I met Radzinsky. I was on my way to the Red Aurora bookstore, where I'd heard that some freaks with tons of cash were secretly hiring experienced pilots for the *Légion de la Liberté*. The hell of the Neptunian Civil War with its attacks on stratosphere stations and airborne assaults in the poisonous blue fog was exactly what I seemed to need the most at the moment. I was squeaky clean and well-shaved. I had with me my passport, my *Communard* party card, and my interplanetary pilot certificate. My eye implant was slightly malfunctioning, but I was expecting to be dead in six months anyway, so it didn't matter. And it was then that I met Radzinsky.

Greg found me in an empty intersection near the ramshackle community hostel. His black executive hover-car stopped in front of me as I was jaywalking, its bulky shape an imitation of early industrial design circa the 1940s. A tinted glass window opened, showing Radzinsky's smiling round face, but instead of a greeting I heard just a long loud honk. For a second, I stared at his face in confusion and anger, knowing that the small black eyes studied me behind his mirror shades that looked like perfect copies of his car's windows. Finally, I checked myself and tried to get around his hover, but the car started jerkily and blocked my way again, sending flocks of shredded plastic bags into the air from under its air cushion.

Finally, Greg spoke, his hands still on the wheel.

"Ulysses. You need a ride, old buddy?" It didn't come out as a question.

I crossed my arms and looked around. There was no way of ignoring him: the street was empty, except for a single Peruvian hobo in a red down jacket who was looking at us indifferently from the entrance of an abandoned toy store.

"Come on, don't be shy." Greg's voice was disgustingly cheerful.

Suddenly, I felt a temptation. I picked a concrete chip from the ground and felt its weight in my hand, imagining its sharp shapes smashing those mirror shades and digging into Radzinsky's eyeball. As I hesitated, a garbage truck crawled past us behind my back, and before my thoughts materialized into action I felt a hard kick on the back of my left leg just under my knee. With ease an attacker twisted my right elbow and grabbed me into a tight armlock. I tried to break free, but another man in a black suit with an unnaturally calm expression on his white face grabbed me by the neck and plunged his cold fingers deep under my jaw, feeling his way to a pressure point. Effortlessly, they forced me to the hover; its doors gaped open, and before I knew it the car swallowed me complete with my captors.

"It's been a long time, pal!" On the back seat, sandwiched between the suits with fake silicone faces, I heard Radzinsky speak. He nodded to the agents, and they released their grip. To my surprise, just one of them had a standard face implant on; judging by the aftershave acne, the suit to my right had kept his real skin.

"You look great. Miss the old days?" Greg asked over a growing howl of the hover engine.

"Not really," I replied grimly as the car took off. For half a minute Radzinsky was silent.

"Have you seen the news? Kuala Lumpur suburbs got wiped out this morning. A meteor strike." Greg set the car on autopilot and turned to me, wiping his black-rimmed glasses with a handkerchief. He'd gained a lot of weight, had turned gray, and his rebellious Nietzsche mustache was gone. "Media's in panic. First time a first world city got hit. Where have they been when a bigger sucker fell on Dallas, right?" He chuckled ironically and tried to make an eye contact with me, but I glanced away and massaged my numb right hand.

After a pause, Greg changed his tone. "I heard some hotheads are recruiting volunteers around town to fight for the Commune of Neptune," he said.

"These red bastards must be desperate, to look for people in such a prosperous city," I muttered and scratched my Chekhov beard with a middle finger. Behind the window, rows and rows of abandoned high-rises were crawling past us, some of their gaping casements lit, indicating squatters.

Finally, the car turned onto an autobahn, and for some time we drove mutely. To calm my (or, rather, his) nerves, Radzinsky turned on some music from our college past: a soft Pan-American neoclassic, much unlike the underground Mercurian class-tech we both used to devour between reading Spengler and reciting Mayakovsky.

Finally, the car took an exit from the highway and, after a long drive amid red rocky hills dotted with yellow bushes, the car stopped at the entrance of what looked like a research facility.

"The trip's over, pal. Follow me." Radzinsky buttoned up his beige suit and left the car, his movements slow and awkward. The suits followed his example, and, for a second, I found myself alone in the leather salon, my eye implant blinking on and off on the brink of dying. Motionless, I closed my eyes and sighed.

"Sah, we do insist dat chu leave da cah." I heard a flat deep voice, recognizing African Martian pronunciation. Mr. Real-Face peeked into the window and repeated his request, the aftershave acne a pink spray on his pale Caucasian face.

"Now, aren't you the smartest boy right here, to fool me like this!" I grinned at him. "Real dedicated to the job, too."

"Sah, hand me yo party membahship cahd and leave da cah," Mr. Real-Face said in the same voice, without changing his expression.

I did as he said. Outside, Greg was standing with his hands crossed and his head hanging down.

"We really need good professionals, Ulysses. Sorry," he mumbled.

After a few medical tests and a twelve-hour shuttle flight simulation they brought me to a room without windows where another couple of silicone-faced clowns—this time female!—told me that if the experiment were to be successful, my political preferences would be forgotten and my debts repaid by the government. When I sneered, they showed me Owen's picture and a travel card for a free ride to Earth. That's how I became a part of the Long Jump project.

I can't say I made a lot of new friends there. I already knew most of the faces in the lab from my past experience in *Sektion VI*, the officially nonexistent branch of *Lufthansa Raumtransport*. Some of them I used to drink with. A couple of them I used to sleep with when they were younger. The same familiar routine sucked me up in the endless sequence of reports, counsels, training, tests, and retraining. Time after time, the people around me who were unable to fix up their marriages or to treat their prostatitis were discussing the fate of the solar system in the next ten thousand years. Every day I heard the same familiar words: "wave function," "relative time coefficient," "coherency point." The only phrase nobody seemed to remember was "the Spot."

One day Radzinsky and I stayed in the lab long after closing hours, so driving all the way to the residential zone didn't make much sense. Instead, we got trashed in a roadside bar, watching a nature documentary on TV and listening to rolling thunder outside. Just before I was about to go, Greg proposed a toast to Milos. I told him, "Go screw yourself," grabbed my jacket and left hurriedly.

"Hey!" Radzinsky hailed me in the almost-empty parking lot, his raincoat left in the bar. "Do you seriously think that we are responsible for the Spot?"

I stopped and looked up at a patch of clear sky among the rain clouds, a meteor shower glowing there like a swarm of fireflies.

"Hell no, pal!" I replied without turning, red trickles of Martian rainwater dripping from my chin. "I think it's another Milos from a faster reality making his Long Jump." As I was walking away to my car, I remember wishing that the red rain could be real blood, and that Radzinsky had drowned in it first.

Milos Kovacs was supposed to become the first faster-than-light traveler. He had all that was needed to become a legend: perfect health, a peaceful mind and a shining smile. We had everything prepared for him: the accelerator warmed up, the coherency point tested on different sequences of quantum events, the entry and exit points calculated. We chose the safest parallel reality for him. Time coefficient 18, just enough to reach the speed-of-light barrier after an entry at the speed of 10,000 miles per second. He was supposed to stay there for three days, reach the exit point, and then be picked up by a distant space probe. After his return to the solar system five years in the future he would be praised as a hero.

I was the last person to shake Milos's hand before they helped him put on the suit and sealed him in the bubble. I already knew his girlfriend had just found out she was pregnant, but I wasn't supposed to tell him that until the jump—nobody wanted him to be distracted.

He never returned. His mother received an official letter saying her son had died during an aircraft flight test.

Three days after the jump, an anomaly appeared three light-days from the solar system. A microscopic black hole that set the doomsday clock at 10,000 years. We nicknamed it the Spot and immediately tried to forget about it.

And now that its gravitational pull has turned the solar system into a killing ground, they said, humanity needed a *working* long-jump technology even more desperately.

A week before the new long jump, they selected three candidates out of ten potential pilots. I was among the chosen ones ("as the most experienced," said the official report). Three days later, the name of the first long jump traveler-to-be was announced. My name. No explanations followed, and all I could do was to accept congratulations from the project members as they shook my hand and clapped me on the shoulder.

Immediately I grew distant from them. The candidate pilots saw me as a father figure; they were all too young and too politically correct for me to enjoy their company. Most of the lab personnel, on the other hand, remembered me from *Sektion VI*, and each time they greeted me in the morning with a smile, I saw a reflection of Milos's face in their worried eyes. Forbidden to drink, I started to treat my anxiety with a virtual reality simulator, spending late hours in the IT lab under the supervision of psychologists. I don't think they liked what they saw: in my simulated encounters I was having long quiet conversations with a gestalt of Milos, cheap Indian cigarettes glowing between our yellowed fingers in the dark.

"You must love the new software, to spend so much time online!" our lead programmer Afu said to me two days before the jump. He was a rare new face in the project, so I didn't mind his presence.

"I do," I answered. "This sim is much better than the one we had ten years ago."

"*Everything* now is better than ten years ago! Except living standards, I guess." Afu's laughter resounded under the low ceiling of the lab. I looked around the labyrinth of flat transparent screens, only to find out we were alone in the room; everyone must have gone to lunch. "But seriously, this sim is the cutting edge. A continuous build."

"Continuous build? What's that mean?" I sat on the armrest

of the sim chair, trodes hanging down from its headset like the aerial roots of a banyan tree.

"Means the gestalts and locations you create don't stay static after you go offline. They keep exploring themselves, slowly." Afu turned to me in his office chair. On the screen behind his shoulder I saw a screenshot of my last encounter with Milos's gestalt.

"They live their own lives after I log off? Creepy, if you ask me." I did my best to smile.

"It'd be creepier if they didn't, trust me." He followed my line of sight and nodded at the screen: "Remember the first thing your virtual friend told you today?"

"He told me to shut up and just smoke with him. He didn't say why. I actually didn't get to ask him what I wanted. Why did he say that?"

"I've no idea. Something happened in his virtual life overnight." Afu opened a log on his screen and scrolled up, looking for an answer.

"Don't bother. I just thought the gestalts were there to entertain us, make us feel better during the flight." I imagined being locked in the bubble together with my gestalt of Milos for five years. My left eye started to twitch.

"If we wanted to make you feel better, we'd just give you drugs, tons of them. The sim is there to help you keep your sanity, no matter how crappy you feel." Afu finally gave up on scrolling through the log and turned back to me. "The entertainment industry is never gonna need continuous builds. They need a pleasure-delivering conveyor belt for overstimulated people. But you're a different case. For the next five years, the virt-sim is gonna be your only way to socialize. Now, imagine having any of your fantasies at your demand. Powerful muscles, weak enemies, obedient women. Your angels and demons. That's—"

"A definition of madness..." I muttered.

"Listen, what's with your left eye? If the new implant they installed is bothering you, we'd better fix it before the jump." Afu stood up and approached me, staring at my twitch.

"That's all right." I crossed my arms and turned my head aside.

233

"It's...I just thought of that guy from my encounter. Do you know who he was?"

"Yes, they told me about Kovacs. I figured it was him."

"Back then, ten years ago, we didn't have continuous builds, just plain all-you-wish-for virt-sims." I remembered talking to Milos's psychologist after the jump, how she said all of his encounters were serene and bright: hanging out with his Chinese girlfriend on a tropical beach or hiking with his father in Antarctic boreal forests.

"Then I hope he died fast. Madness is a nasty thing," said Afu, his voice suddenly plain and serious.

I picked up my sweatshirt silently and headed to the door, zigzagging between cluttered desktops.

"Ulysses!" Afu called me when I was in the doorway. I stopped and gave him a dark look. The programmer was standing with a see-through tablet in his hands, a screenshot of Milos's sunken face on its screen. "Ulysses, I'm not your physician and I'm a dilettante in psychology, but... You're almost forty, you have an eye implant, you've had a drinking problem, and your virtual encounters disturb even me. And I've worked with virt-sims in prisons and rehabs, so believe me, I've seen messed-up things."

"You want to know why they've chosen me and not Hafiz or Den?" I asked.

"Yes. That experience thing—I'm sorry, I don't really believe it was the decisive factor." He shook his head apologetically.

"Think about what we did to Kovacs ten years ago and what we're doing right now. How would you sleep at night, knowing that you sent a healthy young boy on a mission like that, Afu?"

"I'm sorry, I shouldn't have started this...."

"Hurry up, you'll be late for lunch." I left the lab and slammed the door behind me.

The night before my flight I couldn't sleep. I imagined Milos spending days in a sealed spherical capsule, knowing that he'd already missed his exit point. After the first week of panic and despair, he would have started spending almost all of his time in the virt-sim, just to avoid complete isolation. He'd hope that the bubble wouldn't miss the other three emergency points we'd set up for him and eventually he'd be detected and saved. But time passes by, and nothing says his journey is over.

After months of living in the imaginary worlds that his consciousness and the AI have been building for him, Milos feels so lost in the layers of artificial dream that he quits simulation and swears to never return to it. He starts a journal and three days later deletes it. He wants to commit suicide, but the quantum immortality phenomenon has already excluded all chances for him to die until he is seen or measured by an external observer. He starts to understand the Bible.

He knows that as he was flying through the alternate universe, his capsule's mass quickly grew to an infinite number due to its speed, thus becoming a black hole. It will take it trillions of years to consume the galaxy, but inside of the bubble he will hardly be in his thirties by that time. Sometimes he wishes he could see the universe aging behind his window; but there are no windows and no sensors in the bubble, and he is trapped inside for eternity. He starts a journal and three days later he breaks his tablet to pieces.

Thirty years later he is a lonely madman still struggling to crack the capsule from the inside, although he knows that it's impossible. He keeps several journals and regularly deletes some of them. He knows he *is* a god.

In the morning just before my jump, they told me that Radzinsky had died of a heart attack. Somebody made a joke that they should've sent Radzinsky long-jumping instead of me: then Greg would have lived at least until the exit point. I didn't laugh. And not because I didn't hate Radzinsky.

When Hafiz was helping me into my suit, I asked him whether he wanted to swap with me. He didn't answer, just flashed a warm young smile at me, the one Kovacs was known for. Hafiz must have thought it was a joke.

"Never mind, boy," I said. "I already pulled off that trick once on Milos. Not this time." And I smiled too, my lips thin and dry. Hafiz just stared at me, his white smile slowly vanishing.

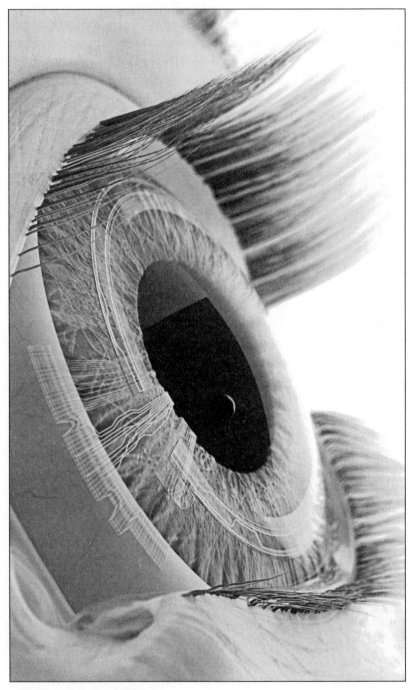

ADAM BREWSTER

There was no ceremony, no last words. Fists clenched to keep my hands from shaking, I stepped into the black bubble. The suit rustled in joints like crumpled paper as I lay down in the recliner chair and fastened the seatbelts tight around my chest, taming my aching heart. For half a minute I heard dull scraping and clunking as they sealed the capsule from the outside. I felt I was being buried alive.

Now, as I'm writing this journal, it's been seven Earth years, ten months, and thirteen days since I missed my exit point. Five of these years I'd spent together with Nancy, in the world I used to call virt-sim.

We first met on an underwater highway near Dubai City. I was a frequenter of that location in the sim, fond of taking long relaxing drives along the transparent tunnel that crawled down the bottom of the Persian Gulf. Depending on my mood, the deep waters above my head changed their qualities. After quarrels with the gestalt of Phoebe they were often dark and oily, full of garbage and dead dolphins; rarely, when she'd let me spend a day with Owen, the sea became azure and lucid, prehistoric armored fish apathetically staring with their giant round eyes at the racing cars.

But on that day everything changed. I was returning from a meeting with Owen, after he'd told me he just didn't want to have me in his life anymore.

"Why didn't you follow us to Earth? Why did you give up?" he'd said to me, adolescence cracking in his voice.

"But we *are* on Earth," I persuaded him, a Lunar Japanese fighting arcade flashing wildly around us.

"That's not it. It's a different place. And you're different!" he'd shouted, and I had gone offline, only to bite my lip and log back on to the empty dark dome of the arcade and a fuel-cell SUV waiting outside to take me to the undersea highway.

Owen's voice was still resounding in my head when I nearly hit the woman. She was just standing on the road, in the middle lane, cars sweeping past her and the frozen waters of the Gulf looming over the tunnel. She wore nothing but a purple silk nightgown and a yellow biker's helmet. Her hands were spread in a desperate acceptance of quick death.

My car stopped just an inch from her, the bumper slightly pushing her in the hips. She stood there for a second, honking cars flashing past us, and then collapsed on the SUV's hood. I immediately forgot I was in a virt-sim; I jumped out of the car and ran to her.

"Are you all right? How did you get here?" I was shouting. She did not answer, her back shaking from sobs and whimpers. Carefully, I took off the girl's helmet and lost my ability to speak. It was her. Nancy Ye, Milos's old girlfriend...

After that first meeting with her, I spent an unhealthy amount of time in the sim in one session, not noticing the artificiality of the places that surrounded us. I took her to one of Dubai's hospitals, but in the parking lot she wiped away her tears and asked me to drive her home.

"Okay. Where do you live?" I asked, as the black Arabian sky unfolded above the transparent roof of the car.

"Not my home. Yours," she said and looked at me with her dark Oriental eyes.

"Does Milos know where you—" She didn't let me finish.

"Don't mention him around me! Just...take me home."

I shrugged and brought her to a hotel by the plaza. A square-built Ethiopian greeted me in Arabic at the reception desk, his deep voice booming in the vast empty hall, and I led Nancy down the long corridors of the skyrise decorated with Babylonian statues and bas-reliefs. We entered a room without a number; Nancy went to a corner and collapsed, surrounded by bronze statuettes of scaly lions and winged bulls.

That night, curled in the corner, she told me Milos had changed after she'd given birth to a stillborn child, and now that he'd left her, nobody knew where he was. Touched by her Taiwanese accent, words were rolling down Nancy's lips like pearls, and I was just nodding silently, staring at a giant pyre blazing on the screen that covered an entire wall of the living room.

I knew where Milos had gone to. To the dark. The same dark which was consuming me now.

"Do you think Hafiz is smoking Indian cigarettes with my gestalt, back there on Mars?" I suddenly asked Nancy melancholically, and she looked at me in confusion, her bronze skin drawn tight around the sharp cheekbones. We both fell silent.

The first week Nancy didn't want to leave the room. She wasn't crying or talking; she just sat on the leather sofa in front of the TV, Al Jazeera news shows flashing on the giant screen on mute. Each time I entered the room, I was painfully aware of the sounds of my steps, the rustling of my jeans, the pumping of my sluggish heart. I would put a bowl of cereal with warm milk on a glass table before her, but she refused to turn her head away from the TV. Then I'd leave her alone, only to come back again ten minutes later to find the bowl empty and Nancy hugging her knees on the sofa, her brown face blank and cold.

I spent the whole week almost entirely in the sim, going offline only for food, sleep, and hygiene, until migraines forced me to take a two-day break. When I entered Nancy's shelter again after going back online, she just pounced on me from the dark like a hungry cat on a sparrow. Her nails plunged into the bulk of my back, and I felt a kiss of violent passion on my lips. More feverish kisses followed; she started untucking my T-shirt, and we stumbled deeper into the shadows like two struggling ghosts...

I was still inside her when Nancy fell asleep on me, our legs intertwined, cool sweat gleaming on our skin. We lay there on a Persian carpet, breathing quietly, two silver silhouettes under the voluptuous moonlight.

Going offline was like a drug crash after that night. My numb fingers would tear off the trodes from my head, and the picture would start blurring into focus: a dirty-gray blob of a capsule that was my reality, *all* my reality, all there was and would ever be. My eyelids would be itching and there'd be a throbbing pressure deep behind my eyeballs, but I would keep blinking until I could make out shapes. Screens, locks, microclimate panel, the soft padding of the bubble's innards. I'd rub my face long and hard, and it would bring back the smells; the air was filled with the sick sweetness of greasy hair, intermixed with old sweat. Gravity was not crushing me down, but every motion was still followed by an ever-present aching pain in my joints. With mouth open and face blank, I'd drift in zero gravity like a mannequin, and I would count the minutes until I could go back online again.

By the fourth year of my relationship with Nancy I was hardly spending four hours offline daily, even though the notion of "day" had completely lost meaning for me by then. I'd abandoned exercise trodes and workout machines for good, and seeing my muscles atrophy in zero G didn't bother me. Just like I wasn't bothered by the stench of piss and foul breath that followed me around the capsule. On the rare occasions when I did look in the mirror, I saw a gaunt-faced old man with a gray beard split into uneven dreadlocks. The only ritual I still fanatically observed was shaving my pale skull, for it was where the virt-sim trodes needed to be attached.

But in the sim, in the sim it all didn't matter. I was fresh and well dressed there; my skin was soft and tanned; I liked to smile and eat jelly beans. All thanks to Nancy.

First she and I were lovers, then we became soulmates. Together we traveled all around Earth (except for places she'd visited with Milos), and in the third year we took off for the Moon and Venus. Bitter memories of my past kept revisiting me once in a while, but in my mind I looked at them as if through the white film of a cataract. The past was eluding me, and with it the fear of immortality started to disappear too.

Until one slippery stair changed everything.

A long basalt staircase led to a neo-Buddhist temple on the flat top of Anala Mons on Venus. Numerous black bricks polished to a shine by thousands of weary feet clambered up the steep slope, weaving between volcanic rocks and shrubs of pale green ferns. Nancy had insisted on making the ascent, along with hundreds of others, half of them Tibetan pilgrims and the other half rich pan-European tourists in search of spiritual exaltation. I didn't mind joining her. All I had to do was whine and complain all along the way up to hide the fact that I couldn't feel fatigue in the sim.

After a two-hour climb, I saw the looming shapes of the temple as it came out of the gray clumps of clouds, and I rushed to the top past Nancy. A dozen steps short of the mountaintop I heard a scream behind me and turned. Nancy was falling down the stairs, slipping on some steps, rolling over others, her backpack bumping on her side and her slippers making impossible arcs in the air. A yellow-robed monk caught her by the strap a flight below, and I rushed down, still believing anything that happened in the sim could be miraculously fixed.

I leaned over Nancy's motionless body, removed strands of black hair from her bruised face, smudging rich red blood over the sweaty bronze skin. I was hoping that any moment she would open her eyes, look at me, shake her head and smile, like I'd seen in many virt-sims before, but seconds passed, and people were racing up the stairs for help, and the blood gushing from the split on the back of Nancy's head was all too realistic.

"How do I reverse it?" I babbled, tearing a sleeve off of my shirt to put it over the wound. "There must be an autosave or something. How do I fix it?"

The monk that'd caught Nancy just looked back at me with a frown and then turned away his wrinkled face, his yellow robe now smudged with red.

Ten minutes later I was shaking in an emergency helicopter, watching medics try to do the impossible. Before the vehicle landed, I tore off the trodes from my skull, but the picture kept floating before my eyes for half a minute: three white backs bending over Nancy's still body and her bloodless hand hanging down the side of the stretcher.

In blind anger, I pounded on the soft walls with my veiny fists, propelling myself across the capsule with every punch, howling like an animal, scraping my face to blood.

I had lost Nancy, and I couldn't follow her to the afterlife.

It took me a month to figure out how to use the console in the sim, and another half a year of fanatical research to master it. I still don't know whether Afu consciously left it there for users' access or his program was just too raw. Either way, for me it became a source of occult knowledge and divine power. Without it, I was just an immortal prisoner in my capsule. With it, I could change virtual reality by wish. I could bring Nancy back to life.

My heart was racing when I opened the door to her hospital room for the first time. There she lay, still pale and weak, her bed facing a giant sunroom window with a view of the snow-capped peaks of the Himalayas. I crossed the room and sat on a chair near her bed, but she kept staring into space, as if not noticing me. I cleared my throat, waited, and cleared my throat again. Finally, I opened my mouth to call her by name, but she spoke first.

"Why did you come?" Her voice crackled, as if she hadn't been using it for quite a while.

"I wanted to see you after you came out of the coma." I touched her hand, but she hid it under a blanket, her eyes still fixed on the mountain ridge.

"I wasn't in a coma. I was dead, buried, forgotten, and you just... undid it all. Proud of yourself?" Still her mind was there, among the gray peaks under a serene blue sky.

After a second of uneasy silence, I laughed and stood up to pour myself some water from a decanter.

"At least you're not saying you saw the light and some bearded old man in Heaven," I managed with a forced grin.

Just as I said so, a doctor entered the room without knocking: a Caucasian woman with a buzz cut.

"Enjoying the company?" she asked briefly, tapping a button on the wall touchscreen. The Himalayas gradually dimmed as the windows darkened and, finally, turned into mirrors.

"Of course. Nancy thinks I resurrected her, though. Tell her it's all post-coma talk." I sipped water from a plastic cup.

"'Resurrection' would be a rather poor word choice." The doctor's voice sounded cold, almost mechanical. "But something did bring her back from the dead, and placed her into this hospital. I would say we came into contact with a power we are yet to understand."

The plastic cup almost slipped from my fingers as the water went down the wrong pipe, and I forced myself not to cough.

"What kind of metaphysics is that?" I hissed, knocking myself in the chest to let the spasm pass.

"*You* did it to me, Ulysses. We already know it," said Nancy, finally turning her sickly birdlike face to me.

"We? We who?" I blurted.

"We, the people of this world," the doctor was talking again. "The only question left is, who are *you*?"

"Who *are* you, Ulysses?" Nancy echoed, softly.

"Who *are* you?" they repeated in chorus, both staring at me.

Before the plastic cup fell on the floor, I was already offline, my hands shaking, cold sweat licking my skin.

"What have I done?" I kept whispering. "What have I done?"

After a day of restless work on the console, I staged another meeting with Nancy, this time in a car. I thought a ride along the Persian Gulf highway would calm both of us.

"Stop playing with me! I'm not your toy!" Nancy shouted right away, furiously smearing the makeup I'd put over her face during the encounter setup.

"Nancy, listen to—"

She didn't let me finish, but opened the door and jumped out of the car to land under an oncoming tourist bus. There was a short screech of metal and a rough bump as the bus tore off the side door and smudged her body all over the side of my SUV.

Next time I was smarter choosing a place for the encounter. I brought us together in the middle of an empty football stadium.

"This is how you envision our date? How desperate are you?" Nancy said as soon as she found herself standing in front me. Her words echoed among thousands of empty plastic seats, spotlights bombarding us with blinding beams.

"Nancy, please, let's talk." I stepped back, my hands raised in submission.

"That's what Milos liked to do before he disappeared: talk." She kicked off her sandals and headed toward the nearest stand across the field.

"Nancy, dear, I'm not gonna be like Milos...." I pleaded, following her.

"Of course you aren't. He was just your gestalt, just like me." She suddenly stopped and turned, observing the effect her words had on me. "I wish I could meet the real Milos and compare him to your image of him." She continued her angry pace toward the edge of the field.

"It's impossible...." I muttered, looking after her.

When I caught up with Nancy, she'd already reached the stand and was halfway up the stairs.

"You're not a gestalt, Nancy. To me, you're real," I managed.

"If you thought I was real, you would've let me die back there, on Venus. Now, it's up to me to prove how real I am." Even though she was breathing heavily, there was grim determination in her voice.

"Prove how?"

"Kill myself. Unlike me, you're deprived of that option in this capsule of yours, aren't you?" She reached the edge of the stadium and turned to me, ghostly lights of a great city shining behind her. Only a low green railing separated her and the dark street below.

"How do you know all of this?" I babbled.

"I wouldn't, if you hadn't resurrected me. But each time you use the console, I know a little more about myself, about my world, about you." Her black hair fluttered in a warm June wind. "You want to know why? Because I am a creation of your mind, and your mind is sick and tired of lying to itself. You just have to accept the truth, Ulysses." She stepped closer and touched my cheek.

"What truth?" I forced myself to meet her eyes.

"That you have to let things go and endure your fate."

She gave me a short kiss before she sat on the railing, spread her hands, and fell back over. I didn't see her body hitting the ground, nor did I hear a sound.

After that session I spent hours floating inside the bubble with a small mirror in my hand. "Endure your fate," I kept repeating to myself under my breath.

That day I cut my beard with scissors, then shaved off the remains of it with a razor. Under that greasy facial hair, my pale skin was dotted with pimples and a rash, so I took a long shower and was surprised to see sharp rows of ribs where pectoral muscles once used to be. Within a week I returned to exercising, hoping to regain my shape, even though the damage to the joints and bones seemed to be permanent. I started reading instead of going online, but the temptation was too strong.

I resurrected Nancy again on the fifth anniversary of our first date. Before she got a chance to hurl herself out of the window, I told her I had changed and would leave her alone for good after a final date. She didn't say a word, just nodded silently. That night we went to an opera house, and on our way back to the hotel she asked me to stop by a gas station.

"You gonna kill yourself again?" I asked her.

"I thought it was a part of the deal," Nancy said, touching her golden necklace.

I pulled over to the side of the road, and we left the car. Stilettos clattering on asphalt and paving stone, Nancy slowly crossed the street toward the gas station, ignoring traffic as cars dodged her and honked. She swiped a credit card on the pump, took a hold of the hose, and made eye contact with me before splashing her black evening dress with gasoline. The station manager ran out of the building, shouting something at the top of his lungs, as Nancy lit a cigarette. Fire enveloped her within a blink of an eye, and before she threw up her hands in agony there came a blast.

That night I watched Nancy burn down to the yellowed bones and then went offline, tired.

I was surprised that I didn't feel the desire to see her anymore. That's why I broke my promise yet again. There was no conversation on that last date, no eye contact. Nancy just sat stiffly at the table in the boathouse restaurant, the tall figure of the Indian waiter looming behind her shoulder. With contempt, she watched me devour the dinner, first my meal, then hers. When I was done, I sent the waiter off with a tip, then wiped my hands and face with a napkin, produced a straight razor out of my suit pocket, and handed it to Nancy.

"Trust me, that's the end of it," I said, pulling my hand back as she reached for the blade. "Not here, people are staring at us. Go to the restroom and do it quick."

As she took the razor and quietly walked away, I ordered another steak. I was still working on it, when an old woman ran out of the restroom, shouting. I didn't stop eating. I had to vomit Nancy out of my life.

I haven't gone online a single time since then. I still remember Owen and Nancy, Milos and Phoebe, Radzinsky and Afu, but they're gone forever. If it means I have to live with my losses for eternity, so be it.

Now that I'm writing this journal, I keep hearing something scraping on the bubble's skin, an elusive, distant sound. Maybe it's a search probe docking with my capsule to carry me back to Mars. Or, maybe, it's madness....

These Walls of Despair

written by

Anaea Lay

illustrated by

BERNARDO MOTA

ABOUT THE AUTHOR

A natural city girl raised in deep ruralia, Anaea Lay currently lives in Madison, Wisconsin, where she sells real estate under a different name and collects jobs the way that the Internet collects cats.

When she isn't advising clients on how well a potential home could be defended during the zombie apocalypse, she can be found running the Strange Horizons *podcast, writing reviews for* Publishers Weekly, *waxing poetic on the virtues of well-designed resource management board games, or chasing a secret recipe for the perfect cup of hot chocolate.*

Her short fiction has appeared in places such as Lightspeed, Apex, Daily Science Fiction *and* Waylines. *Her long fiction is currently looking for a home.*

ABOUT THE ILLUSTRATOR

Bernardo Mota was born on February 5, 1996, in Setúbal, Portugal, and has had a fun ride so far. Interested in genetically engineering animals, convincing friends that the world was at stake and playing out more fantasies in his head than in retaining memories, his childhood was confusing and lacked drawing.

Growing up surrounded by books, movies, video games and the Internet brought out in him an interest in science fiction, fantasy and, eventually, illustration.

He started drawing at the age of thirteen, desperate to find out if it was an interesting path before having to choose a high school course, and it quickly became an obsession.

His short comic won the second place in the Amadora BD 2011 contest for work in his age range, and he was formally honored as a young talent by his hometown the next year.

He is now in his last year of high school, and is very excited about what the future holds for him.

These Walls of Despair

I loathe prison duty.

I pressed the small black button on the side of my case, then watched as its retractable legs unfolded, the top of the case sliding away as the sides expanded. In a moment the whole contraption had transformed into a passable chemist's table, the vials I would need displayed neatly in three rows. They were labeled in tiny script, painstakingly neat. Trust me about the painstaking; Master Nubeshai has exacting standards. Someday, when I have apprentices of my own, I'm going to cackle quietly in my closet while they write out hundreds of labels.

And I'll never take prison duty again.

My patient sat with her legs folded beneath her, staring at me with a true-calm face. People always try to look calm when they know they're being watched by a Sentimancer, but they do it by putting on a blank expression. Calm is a balance, not an absence. Even an apprentice Sentimancer knows that.

She was genuinely calm, though. In just a few short hours she'd face a hostile court that was certain to convict her, to execute her, and she was a portrait of serenity. Psychopath. That's why defendants are entitled to a pretrial consultation with a Sentimancer; they have the right to appear in court with the feelings they think they ought to have.

"There are just three emotions," I said, breaking into my bedside patter to hide my distaste for the garishly lit corridor and my reluctance to cross the force field and trap myself in a cell with her. "Fear, hunger and pleasure. Everything else is a combination of those fundamental elements. Before we can start tweaking your chemistry to create your desired emotional state, I'll need to take a blood sample and establish a baseline."

She was frightfully thin, her bones outlined by her skin as a series of sharp corners and sudden concavities. Her ears were too large for her head, jutting out from strands of scraggly hair. She was ugly. And calm.

"Did your lawyer have a recommendation or preference?" I asked, continuing blithely on with the standard patter.

"I have no lawyer," she said.

Right. She'd refused counsel, refused plea agreements, refused to give any defense. Five minutes into the interview I'd already forgotten everything except that this scarecrow of a woman before me had been caught trying to wake Dhalig Mora from his eternal slumber. *Very professional, Georg.*

"Of course. Just your thoughts, then. Remorse? Nervousness?" Fear. Unadulterated fear would be best.

"Thank you, but I won't be using your services."

"Oh. Well." Time to get out of there. If I was quick, I could catch a tram to the barrows and place bets on the urchins playing rat-catcher, Master Nubeshai none the wiser. I pressed the button on my case once more, let it fold back into its compacted form, then hefted it onto my shoulders. But I couldn't just leave it at that. Psychopath or not, what she'd tried was unfathomable. "Why did you do it?"

She smiled just enough to reveal a gap in her front teeth, more edges and crevices. "To end the world." It struck me then that as unattractive as her physical features were, her voice was stunningly beautiful. Rich and heavy, much more so than what I'd expect from anyone so scrawny, it resonated as if it tickled the strings of the universe.

I should have strutted on out of there, lost my pocket change gambling, then slipped back to the hall in time for supper and never seen her again. Well, Master Nubeshai has never accused me of being good at doing what I ought to.

"I know that. But why?"

She cocked her head to the side and studied me. "Show me your wrists."

I hesitated a long moment. Prisoners are entitled to consultation with a Sentimancer, but a first-day apprentice meets the legal requirements. Three years into my training, I'd earned four black circles around my right wrist. I was intensely proud of each of them, but all she would see were four lone marks where she expected an intricate network of bands. Still, I'd been impertinent, and she was entitled to see what level of Sentimancer she'd been sent. I pushed back my sleeves and held out my wrists for her.

"All from your master?" she asked.

"There was a man whose children were taken by the hollow people. He commissioned my fourth mark."

"Did you take away his grief?"

"I slaked his anger, allowing him to grieve."

"And how many patients have you treated who did not commission a mark for you?" she asked.

My ears burned a bit with that question. I'd started my apprenticeship at an age when most finished theirs. She assumed I was unmarked because I was incompetent, not because I was inexperienced. "He's the only patient I've treated, so far."

"Your master does not give you patients?"

"You are my tenth consultation. Most people I visit don't require my services."

"That stops you from providing them?" she asked, surprise plain on her features. "Interesting."

My impertinence balanced by hers, I repeated my question. "Why wake Dhalig Mora?"

"Do you think I can make you understand by explaining?" she asked.

"Perhaps," I said.

"Then tell me: what are the ingredients for despair?"

251

The bedside patter about the three basic emotions is true, but it's a truth we Sentimancers use to lie. You can, ultimately, break anything down to a combination of those three, but there's an alchemy to it, a series of subcombinations, of stopping points. Fear and hunger mixed in the right portions give you anger. Suffuse it with a hint of pleasure and it becomes rage. Layer it with another combination of hunger and fear and the rage becomes wrath. That's why a Sentimancer's case is full of so many vials. It could take days to generate some of the complex emotions we want if we start from the base elements.

I'd never been asked to explain that before, and continued my display of top-notch professional competence by fumbling as I tried to find a simple way to answer her question.

"I thought so," she said.

"It's very complex. Explaining it to a lay person..."

"When you understand despair, understand it truly, I will answer your question. I promise you that."

I could have told her about Kjolla, shown her that I might not know how to induce despair, but I knew the flavor of it all too well. Kjolla. Dead in a raspberry patch. Smiling. My fault.

I deflected instead. "I still have two years in my apprenticeship. What happens if you are executed before my master discloses the ingredients to me?"

"I make no promises I cannot keep." There was a smile in her voice, though none touched her features. It made the corridor seem marginally less horrifying. "You have somewhere else you want to be. Better go before you miss your chance."

The straps on my case were cutting into my shoulders. I nodded to her, pulled my sleeves back down to cover my wrists again, then trotted up the corridor, eager to put as much distance between the prison and me as possible.

I caught the tram, meaning to go to the barrows, but her question kept echoing in my head. *What are the ingredients for despair?* I knew the balances for countermanding it, but not the formulas for inducing it. As the tram clacked along the streets I mentally reviewed the inventory of my case, trying to pull out the subcomponents I would need, but none suggested themselves.

A good Sentimancer can work in both directions, starting from the basic elements of feeling to build up to the more complex ones, or breaking down a complex feeling into its component parts. I couldn't fathom the foundation of despair, so I changed directions and tried breaking it down. Inevitably, my mind wandered to Kjolla, to the flash of teeth behind his smile as he ran off, the misshapen, bloodied lump of flesh we found days later. Raspberries.

I missed the stop for the barrows. Instead, I got off at Market Street and went home to Master Nubeshai's.

I suspect everyone else living in Bubble spent the afternoon watching the preliminaries of the trial. They saw Prosecutor Mhed's opening statement as it was uttered for the very first time. "No motive, no excuse, no explanation could possibly justify the rash, selfish act of approaching Dhalig Mora with the intention of waking him. It is not just a matter of self-preservation that we keep the Moras asleep and apart; it is our sacred duty to our fellow beings, the world that nurtures us, and all that we hold precious." Before that trial, most people hadn't thought about Dhalig Mora in his filled pit or Vasik Mora in her stony keep since they were children listening to bedtime stories. After it, everyone was fired with a romantic passion to ensure that the sundered lovers were kept apart eternally, that we preserved the Sleeping Bubble that gave us all life.

Not me. I buried myself in my workshop, remixing each of my concoctions, relabeling them with a meticulous care Master Nubeshai would have to praise. It was well after midnight before he came to check on me.

"Everybody else slipped out to watch your patient on the broadcast," Master Nubeshai said. "They're just now trickling back."

"She's not my patient. She refused service," I said as I sealed a vial of ennui.

"She requested a second consultation, before the sentencing."

That didn't make any sense to me. She'd been so calm, and a little derisive about sentimancy. Why would she ask for me back? I tried to deduce an answer on my own—Master Nubeshai would not answer stupid questions—but came up with nothing.

"Was she so disturbing?" he asked after I'd been silent too long.

"I've no recipe for despair," I said as I wrote out the label for ennui. "I can't even pick apart its components."

"You know the process for balancing it, for countering it out of a patient's system."

"Yes, but I can't figure out how to induce it."

"Despair should never be induced. That is far outside the appropriate range of a Sentimancer's work."

"Grief was the first recipe you taught me."

Master Nubeshai pulled a stool over to me, its feet groaning across the slate floor of the workshop much too loudly. Then he perched on it, a tiny little man with thick clumps of white hair bunching in and around his ears. "Sometimes, people need to feel grief. They experience tragedy, but do not react to it as they think they should. The disparity can wound them far more thoroughly than the tragedy that sparked it. We give them protection from that."

It was a basic tenet of sentimancy, the first lesson taught to apprentices: there's no such thing as a bad emotion. People feel, and need to feel. It's our job to free them from the limitations or short circuits in their bodies that can miss one step or get stuck on another. And if Master Nubeshai was repeating that lesson to me, an apprentice of three years, it was because he was telling me something else entirely. I took a moment to turn it over in my head.

It's true that there are only three basic emotions, but we tell people that to lie to them, masking the complex with the illusion of simplicity. "Despair is a bad emotion."

"It is a dangerous one," Master Nubeshai said, "with no redeeming virtues. It damages, but does not teach. It's a counterpoint to calm, a balance demanding nothing, requiring nothing to maintain it, and crippling its victim until time wears out the chemistry fueling it."

"Or a Sentimancer intervenes," I said, thinking again of Kjolla. Of what was left of him. Of the police dragging me away from the morgue, and of a spry little old man with white tufts of hair jutting from his ears as he spoke quietly and stuck me with needles.

"You know despair, Georg. You remember its taste. That is enough for you to do a Sentimancer's duty. You do not need a recipe."

He squeezed my shoulder, then rose from the stool. But that wasn't enough; it couldn't be. If she wanted me back, then either something had changed in the hours since she'd refused my services, or she expected that something would have changed by the time of our next consultation.

I pictured her narrow, jagged features, the true-calm suffusing them, the rich beauty of her voice. The change hadn't come from her, wouldn't come from her. She expected something more from me.

"Did you watch the trial opening?" I asked.

"I could tell she'd refused treatment. She was calm," Master Nubeshai said.

"I can induce calm."

"Yes, but it was the wrong choice. They could forgive her for madness. They'll execute her for calm."

"What would you have given her?" I asked his retreating form.

"Fear," Mater Nubeshai said. "She needed pure fear."

That's what I'd thought, too.

That night I dreamed of Kjolla. His laughter echoed through the corridors of my sleep while phantoms of his small hands clutched my own, or held my shoulders, wrapped me about the waist in an embrace. All through the dreams I could feel the hollow people lurking in the shadows, waiting for my lapse, yearning to take him from me. I woke with the scent of raspberries and blood, both smells permanently mingled with my memories of Kjolla, though not both at once.

Predictable, Georg. You're so predictable.

Without turning on a light—there was no reason to tell the entire hall I was having nightmares—I went to my case, pressed the button on the side, and waited for it to unfold. I pulled a sampling capsule from a drawer on the side, pressed the needle to the pad of my finger, then fell back onto my bed while I waited for the results. Then I played beat-the-machine.

What are you feeling, Georg? Grief, obviously. Revulsion. Horror. Loneliness. There was a hint of rage under it. Weariness, too. Three years later, I was tired of mourning Kjolla, tired of running into reminders that set me brooding and sent me nightmares. Tired of wondering whether I'd really begun to heal, or Master Nubeshai had only sentimanced me into a too-old apprentice prone to brooding fits. What do these components make? What will the machine say?

Regret, of course. Raw and disjointed, but in the final reckoning, regret. I held the capsule up to catch streetlight through the window and read the display. It agreed.

Is regret the end state of despair? Sundered Moras, I hope so.

I couldn't go back to my patient with nothing more than I'd had before. She might or might not expect something new of me, but *I* would expect more of me. She was guilty and she was going to be executed, but I would not stand outside her prison cell unable to protect her from the inevitability of her fate. She might smile. Or smell of raspberries.

Master Nubeshai wouldn't give me the recipe for despair. He might not even have it, though I doubted that. But one thing any Sentimancer must learn before being sent to patients is that people do not always ask a question to get its answer. Sometimes, the question hides something else, a clue to their internal state, to the thoughts triggering it. The woman who'd tried to end the world asked me for the one recipe I would never have. I needed to know why she would do that.

Most of the reporting done during the night of the trial was biographical sketches of Prosecutor Mhed, and there were hundreds of those. I dug deeper, back weeks to when the first arrest was made. None of the articles gave any details—they didn't even give her name—but there was one clue. "Woman from Bernin caught breaking into Vedhalig Moreeum." "From Bernin" could mean she was born there, that she lived there, or only that Bernin was where she'd rented the car she took to Vedhalig Moreeum, Dahlig Mora's filled pit. Hopefully the article had been published before they found her gong, before they realized she'd been there not as a stupid prank or deranged stunt, but because she meant to end the world. Before she had become an official nonentity. Hopefully it didn't have her name because it was too soon to know it, not because we'd already decided she no longer had one.

I was in the pantry, gathering provisions for my trip, when Master Nubeshai found me. "Beginning your journeyman trek?" he asked.

I laughed. An apprentice could leave for their journeyman trek whenever they liked, but they'd receive no more training from their master. I was not about to walk out with two years of my apprenticeship left. "No. Just research for my patient."

"Going to Bernin?"

I turned to face the shriveled old man. His sleeping tunic was sleeveless. Even wasted with age, the intricate tattooing running from wrists to shoulders was impressive—black dots filled with bright colors in ever smaller, more detailed patterns. Would my arms ever bear a mosaic like that, a tapestry recording patients pleased enough with my work to commission a mark? "How did you know?" I asked.

"You are diligent, Georg. It's what I would do."

The compliment stunned me. And then, I wondered whether he'd actually meant it as a compliment.

"Leave your case," Master Nubeshai said.

"I could be gone for several days," I protested.

"An apprentice leaves the hall with his case for his journeyman trek, not before."

The smell of Kjolla's raspberries, of his blood, was still so strong with me that I could taste it. I couldn't be separated from my case for days.

"You won't need it. Trust me, Georg. Trust yourself."

I nodded my agreement, slung the satchel of food I'd gathered over my shoulder, then stooped to heave my case off the floor. "I'll take this back to my room, then go." I could tuck a few vials into my satchel. After all, I didn't need the whole case.

Then Master Nubeshai's hand was on my elbow, his muscles flexing under his tattooed skin as he took the case from me. "Borrow one of the hall's vehicles. I'll take your case."

Shame raced ahead of my fear. Predictable, and transparent. And about to follow a nightmare with nothing but my own chemistry to defend me. I stared at the patterns worked into the black ink of Master Nubeshai's arms. He knew what he was doing. "Thank you," I said. I let him take the case, and then I went out to the garage where the hall's vehicles were stored.

The sky swirled purple and rose above me as I drove, the skin of the Sleeping Bubble starting to glow with daylight. I went as quickly as I dared to Bernin, but still hadn't reached it when the glowing subsided and night fell. After sleeping so little the night before, I was exhausted, so I pulled off the road, threw down a sleeping bag, and called that camp. Five minutes later, I was fast asleep.

The black night sky shimmered faintly overhead when I woke to the scent of ozone and freshly turned earth. I froze instantly, too frightened to analyze my panic. My fingers clenched at my sides. My lungs burned, and it took me a moment to realize it was because I'd stopped breathing.

I was surrounded by the hollow people.

I didn't wet myself, and only a few tears slid from my eyes as I forced myself to sit up. There were eight of them, their charcoal gray skin reflecting the shimmer from the sky, their green eyes glowing. They were crouched low to the ground, hunched over their long limbs as they stared at me.

"It'll be fine, Georg."

BERNARDO MOTA

At the sound of Kjolla's voice, I turned. The one who'd spoken was a female. She was sitting up straighter than her companions, her glowing eyes with their slits of pupils making my skin crawl with every breath she drew.

"Don't...don't do that," I said.

"You worry too much, Georg," she said, still using Kjolla's voice.

"Just kill me and get it over with," I said, even as I pictured what they'd leave of my body for Master Nubeshai to claim. "Don't torture me first."

She cocked her head, the strands of wispy black hair she hadn't cropped into short spikes catching in a light breeze. Then she tasted the air, her black tongue darting out in short, quick stabs. I could just barely hear the low rumble that rolled from her throat. I blinked and they were gone.

"Sundered Moras," I cursed as I twisted around, looking for a monster from the night sneaking up with long fingers and a rock for my skull. Nothing. I bolted for the vehicle, locked the doors, then doubled over and wept. Some of it was relief. More of it was fear. And emptiness. No case, no vials to help me balance it, just aching, agonizing emptiness.

Kjolla.

He wasn't my son or my brother. As far as I know, we didn't share blood at all. But his mother took me in when my parents died during the Vasik rupture. I was twelve then, and sixteen when she died of the gasping sickness. Kjolla was just eight, and neither of us had anybody else. But I could find enough work to keep him in school and a roof over our heads, and that's what I did. The neighbors helped where they could. Everybody loved Kjolla. It was his smile.

The smile was still there, at the end.

When the sky glowed with dawn I was more exhausted than when I'd stopped. I darted outside long enough to retrieve my sleeping bag and to check the depressions where the hollow people had knelt and confirm it hadn't been a dream. There were no signs of a nest; *they'd* stumbled on *me*.

Bernin was only a few hours away. I was there by breakfast time and went straight to the shop where my patient had rented her vehicle. It was closed, so I sat down outside the door and fell asleep. I woke when the shopkeeper, a middle-aged man with a limp, swatted me with his cane.

"My doorway ain't a hostel," he said.

"I didn't spend the night," I replied. "I was just waiting for you to open."

"Well, I'm open now," he said, unlocking the door. I followed him in. It wasn't clear to me how he conducted any business inside the shop. Every horizontal surface save a creaking swivel chair behind the desk was covered in boxes and stacks of papers. The sheer height and instability of it all nearly left me claustrophobic. "Breakdown, robbery, or bad planning?" the man asked.

It took me a moment to figure out what he was talking about. "I'm not here to rent," I said when I processed it.

"You slept in my door to wait for a chat, then?" he asked.

"Yes...no...well," I absently pushed up my sleeves as I stuttered. I yanked them back down as soon as his eyes fell on my marked wrist. I didn't need this stranger assuming I was an incompetent, too.

"I see," he said, still watching my covered wrist. "Can't give you much help, I'm afraid. Girl wasn't from here."

"How do you know I'm here about her?"

"Everybody who's been here these last weeks but not for renting wants to know about her. You, I figure, might have a good reason to be asking, though."

I'd so hoped she was from Bernin. "Do you know where she was from?"

"Nope," the old man said as he settled into the open chair. His cane leaned against the desk, knocking a few papers off the top of a pile.

"How did she seem? Was she nervous or agitated?"

"Cheerful, I'd say. Seemed a little flustered, but I thought it was because of the accident. Guess it may have been nerves. I

261

wouldn't know." He shrugged with the pseudohumility people put on when describing other people's emotions to a Sentimancer.

"What accident?"

"She said that the hollow people had attacked her just outside of town. She stopped just before dawn to piss in some bushes and they pulled apart her vehicle. She bolted and didn't stop until she reached town. Found her sitting on my door when I came in to open the shop. *She* wasn't sleeping, though."

My disappointment compounded. Either the old man was lying, or he was credulous enough to have believed a truly incredible tale from my patient. "They attacked her vehicle, but not her?"

"That's what she said. I told her it weren't the hollow people if that's what they did. Might've been gesserack or flytings. There's some of them out there."

"Did you find the vehicle?"

"That was the strange bit," the old man said. "I was sure she'd run into flytings until we got to it. Now..." There was a grimness to his shrug this time.

"What?" I prompted.

"I seen plenty of those that come back from the hollow people. The bodies, you know. There's this feel to them, like it's been arranged somehow. You follow?"

All too well. I nodded.

"The vehicle, what was left of it, it had the same feel. I never heard of the hollow people sparing somebody, or of attacking machinery either, but there you have it. I haven't got the car, the investigators took it, else I'd let you see it for yourself."

"That's all right," I said. "Anything else?"

"Not as I can recall." He sent me off with another shrug.

I made it out of the shop before the shock hit me. *You worry too much, Georg,* rang in my head, glowing eyes in a night-gray face staring at me. The hollow people don't spare anybody they catch. But they'd spared me. And her.

Sundered Moras.

There were two days before the close of the trial and my

presentencing visit with her. I should have gone back to the apprentice hall, spent the time consulting with Master Nubeshai about the best way to serve my patient. Besides, I still had a pocket full of change yearning to be lost in the barrows. I should have run back to do my duty to my profession.

I pushed on, following the road to Vedhalig Moreeum.

It's not a pit. Everybody knows it's been filled, but that doesn't do it justice. It's been filled with prejudice, filled to overflowing, and then a small mountain built on top of it. Anybody who expects to drive up to the edge of a pit and peer in at the sleeping half of the Sleeping Bubble's creator has read too many kids' stories. I'm told that the pit used to be nothing more than a flat stretch of sand and gravel surrounded by untouched forest. That hasn't been true, if it ever was, since the repairs after the Vasik rupture. Now there's a two-ton block of iron over the pit, and that covered in a heap of gravel and sand that rises above the tree line. You can't see the block when you look at the mountain.

You can see the green fog, though. It rolled off the mountain, iridescent even as the day glow faded from the sky. There was a subtlety to the pervading sense of doom it carried, like a bitter aftertaste in something delicately sweet. I wanted to walk the perimeter of the mountain and examine every inch of it just as much as I wanted to run away and pretend I had more sense. What I didn't want to do was scale the mountain with a brass gong and wake up the buried god. I spent ten minutes staring at the mountain, opening myself to every insane urge that might present itself, and I didn't get so much as an inkling of that desire.

That settled one question for me. She'd definitely already planned to wake him when she came. I'd hoped that had been an influence from the place. It would explain her bizarre actions and her perfect calm in a way I could understand. None of my answers were going to be easy to find, it seemed.

I'd had to leave my car at the road and hike through the woods on foot. I meant to go back and sleep in the safety of my locked vehicle, or even to drive back to Bernin in the dark. Now that it was night, I realized there'd been a serious flaw with my plan; I'd never find my way back to the car. I wanted to blame that on stress and sleep deprivation but it was so much less stupid than coming here at all that even *I* didn't believe it. I settled down with my back to the mountain, crossed my arms over my chest, and waited.

The hollow people didn't disappoint. Only a female actually came out of the woods, but I could see the eyes from a dozen others watching me from the trees. She loped up to me on long, slender limbs, then crouched down just a few feet away. It wasn't possible for her to be the same female I'd seen the night before—even if the hollow people didn't stay near their nests, they'd never be able to travel as far on foot as I had with my vehicle. Still, she looked the same.

"We're sorry we frighten you, Georg," she said. It was still Kjolla's voice, but at least they weren't his words, this time.

"What do you want from me?" I asked.

"Protect the membrane. Stop the osmoid."

"I don't understand," I said. The breeze carried a whiff of her scent to me. Ozone and turned earth. I'd been resigned before, but that odor did me in and suddenly my heart was hammering against my ribs. Or it had been doing that the whole time and I just hadn't noticed. Hard to say which.

"The makers put us here to record their experiment. We take samples and save them. We must protect the membrane."

"You slaughter people," I said. "You're going to kill me."

"We must not, Georg," she said. Kjolla had never spoken with such gravity. She sounded like he might have if he'd had time to grow up, if he'd left the damn raspberries alone. I'd thought I'd never get to hear Kjolla's adult voice. "You must shackle the osmoid."

"I don't know what that is," I said.

She crawled forward, her long fingers reaching for me. I was scrambling up the mountain as fast as I could scream, but she was faster. She had me by the shoulders, pressed to the ground before the rocks I knocked loose finished falling. I stared up, her eyes glowing over me with the night sky shimmering faintly behind her. Her black tongue darted out, almost brushing my face.

"We can scent her on you. You know the osmoid. She has an obligation to you. She is like them."

"Who?"

"Your people have erased her name."

I was afraid she'd say that. "She's just a psychopath."

"She can fold the membrane. She could break it. We will lose our samples. None of you should be like the makers."

Anything that threatened the hollow people seemed like a good thing to me, but I couldn't talk. I'd forgotten to breathe. Again.

"You must understand," Kjolla's voice said.

Suddenly, I could hear it, the Bubble, humming—a minor chord echoing under my ribs. I could sense the entire curve of the universe in the sound. I knew I was still lying on my back next to the mountain over Dhalig Mora's pit, but I was aware of so much more. Our universe was a plaintive sound, vibrating against the edges of the multiverse, and at its core, the two imprisoned gods.

The sound of them, the tones of the Moras, reflected off the surface of the Bubble, reinforcing it, giving it structure, turning the single chord into a melody over time. In that moment I could hear the whole shape of our universe, from its inception at the height of our creators' passion to its eventual collapse when they join once more. I could feel myself drowning in it, the raw untempered emotion of it, my senses scattered with each beat, each progression. I went far enough to realize I was about to lose myself to insanity.

Then I found them, crawling over the surface of the membrane, a series of rests inside the chord: the hollow people. They were a stillness, a silence in the universe, a grip I could seize upon to take a breath. And I did just that, throwing myself into those gaps.

But I was wrong. They weren't silence at all. They were filled with voices, thousands of them, echoing across the surface of the membrane, playing counterpoint to the music of the universe that held them. Those voices sang, a choir of the dead and slaughtered, echoing from one end of time to the other.

"Do you hear it now, Georg?" Kjolla's voice said, and it was a crescendo, expanding across my awareness even as the world around me went quiet once more.

As the sound faded, I could hear notes from the ground, the trees, the mountain behind me, my own bones. My bones. I could hear my own notes across time, my resonance disappearing into the sound of the mountain, the membrane, falling out of tune when Master Nubeshai stuck his needles in me, but always veering back, disappearing into the chord as the hollow people spoke, lost until I heard their choir.

What's the recipe for despair? Suddenly, I could sing it.

My awareness collapsed completely, leaving me just me, alone in the woods with a nightmare creature hovering over me.

"We keep him safe with the rest," Kjolla's voice said. Kjolla's grown-up voice, a small window into what might have been. For a moment, it didn't seem so much like I'd lost him. I couldn't hear the choir anymore, but I still knew it was there, and his voice in it. "She will destroy him."

"You already did that," I said. But now I knew better.

"He was given to us. We will protect him until the end. You must protect the membrane."

Then she was gone, and the rest of the hollow people with her. I stood up, brushed myself off, and walked to the tree line. No sign of them. I knelt, bent over and heaved up everything I'd ever eaten, and half of what my mother had while she carried me. Then I went back to the edge of the mountain, stretched out and fell fast asleep.

Two tributes a year, and anybody who disturbs their nests. That's all the hollow people demand to keep them from raiding towns and cities. Two samples. Two voices to steal for their chorus. Two bodies returned, pulped and bloodied. Arranged.

Nobody had known that the hollow people were nesting near that raspberry patch. It was unfair to punish Kjolla for something when he couldn't have known better. The hollow people compromised by letting him stand as one of the mandatory tributes, though we usually gave volunteers who were old or dying. Everybody called it mercy. They looked me in the eye, before letting me see the body, and told me how grateful I should be for that mercy. I shouldn't take it so badly when Kjolla was so brave. After all, he was still smiling.

I had nine hours before my consultation when I arrived back at the apprentice hall. I spent them in a lab with my case. It was more than enough time.

Master Nubeshai took one look at me as I came in, then didn't say anything. No "How was your trip?" or "Did you find what you needed?" Master Nubeshai never wasted words by asking questions with obvious answers.

I arrived at the prison, my case slung over my shoulders, exactly on time. I was a bit disheveled, hadn't stopped even to shave since returning, but none of the prison guards who checked my pass noticed or cared. Why would they? I was only there to consult with the madwoman who'd tried to end the world.

She was still ugly, her bones just as jagged under her flesh, her hair just as limp and stringy, but I could see something else now, something telling in her calm poise as she perched on her narrow bench. It was faint, but something in her posture reminded me of the hollow people who'd spoken to me. I suspect they'd meant for me to see the resemblance. I suspect I knew what she would sound like to them.

Neither of us spoke as I pressed the button on the side of my case and let it unfold. I caught a whiff of raspberries as I pulled the new vial from among the rows. It was small, alone in the palm of my hand, unlabeled. Master Nubeshai wouldn't approve of the plan for this vial, no matter how carefully I labeled it.

"You found it," she said as I stepped through the force field of her cell.

267

I closed my eyes and saw Kjolla's smile.

"You met them, and found the recipe."

"They're frightened of you," I said.

"They should be."

"Why did you do it?" I asked.

I opened my eyes again and watched her. Her shoulders rolled as she shifted on the bench, and her voice, the one so beautiful it pulled at the strings of the universe, came at me like a slow trickle, easy and inevitable all at once. "They were lovers. Lovers and scientists and makers so passionate they formed our Bubble. And we took advantage of their exhaustion to sunder them. But we have no right to keep them apart."

"Dhalig Mora chose his pit. Vasik Mora her keep. They sundered themselves."

"We've put locks on the keep. And you've seen the pit. You know despair, Sentimancer. You've tasted it. You hold it in your hand. Can you truly accept existence at the expense of your creators' despair?"

Understanding came, the answer I'd gone to Bernin to find. "You lost your lover."

"And everything else in the bargain. But time heals, and I'd learned something once it did."

"What's an osmoid?" I asked.

Her lips turned in a small, sad smile that barely showed the gaps between her teeth. "Someone who understands the nature of the Sleeping Bubble. Someone who can control it, a bit."

"You have a way out of this cell," I said. "That's why you aren't afraid of the execution."

"True," she said.

"Could you destroy the hollow people?" I asked.

"I could."

I took a step toward her as I loaded the vial into an injector. Protocol dictated any treatment should begin by taking a blood sample and establishing a baseline, but I wasn't there to follow protocol. I already knew this patient wouldn't be commissioning a mark for me. Moras, she wasn't even going to consent to this treatment. "How can you leave the hollow people be, yet condemn us for locking the cages the Moras built for themselves?"

"If I reunite the Moras and end the world, that destroys the hollow people too," she said.

If I'd taken better care of Kjolla, if I'd watched him more closely, been able to feed him better, enforced more discipline… I don't know. If I'd done any of a thousand other things, he'd have never bothered that nest and he'd have grown up and finished school and become something great. He might have come to say some of the words the hollow people gave him when they spoke to me. But I didn't do any of those things and all that was left of Kjolla were my memories. And his voice. "They must preserve their samples."

Finally, a break in her calm. I could see the edges of alarm in her eyes, even as they started to glow. Her skin shimmered, like the night sky, and suddenly she was as beautiful as her voice, the sight of her stretching and melting into the world around her, unctuously enchanting. She was fading, escaping, bending the membrane that sheltered our tiny little constructed universe to put herself elsewhere. Melting into the chord of the universe.

I lunged and stabbed her with the needle.

She collapsed back into herself, the shimmer gone. Her eyes were wide and watering with fresh tears. Her bony chest heaved as she gasped, and she flailed against me. I took a step back, letting her come back to herself, letting her realize what I'd done.

She'd lost her lover and become like them.

"That's not… what did you do?" she asked.

There are no bad emotions. But there are dangerous ones.

"I gave you what the hollow people gave me," I said, stepping out of the cell. I closed my case and pressed the button on its side, letting it compact once more. "It's a bit of an overdose, but soon you'll agree you needed it."

As it turns out, there's a really good reason a Sentimancer should never induce despair.

"I can't… everything's gone flat again… won't let me pass…"

"You're cured." Not permanently, but they were going to execute her soon. I hefted my case over my shoulder and started down the hallway.

"What is it?"

I shouted her answer over my shoulder without breaking stride. "Hope." After this, I was definitely never going to take prison duty again.

What are you feeling, Georg?

Peace.

One ought to have some sort of transcendent reaction to the realization that the world exists because the gods are trapped in the same abyss you've occupied for three years. It should be inspiring or comforting or, I don't know, cathartic. Whatever the right reaction is, I wasn't experiencing it. I'd shackled the osmoid, and saved a piece of Kjolla. That was much more important than the metaphysical misery of the universe.

The urchins were just setting up the first rounds of rat-catcher when I arrived. I took up a post at the edge of the ring where I could see them as they prepped their dogs, riling them up by playing tug-of-war with bits of twisted rags. My change rattled in my pocket as I looked them over.

"Place a bet?" a stubby bookie asked, jostling my elbow.

"That one. The scrawny one in the corner," I said. He was even the right age.

"He looks lucky to you?" the bookie asked, skeptical.

"Yeah," I said. "I like his smile."

Synaptic Soup

BY VAL LAKEY LINDAHN

---

*Val Lakey Lindahn started working as a freelance artist in 1971
and went on to produce hundreds of illustrations for* Asimov's
and Analog *magazines. Then in 1983 she and her husband, Ron
Lindahn, decided to move to Georgia, where they formed Valhalla
Studio to collaborate on illustrations for books, magazines, videos
and movie posters. Their book cover illustrations have graced many
top science fiction and fantasy authors' works internationally.*

*Ron and Val are now collaborating on their own illustrated book
projects and have published* The Secret Lives of Cats, How to
Choose Your Dragon *and* Old Missus Milliwhistle's Book of
Beneficial Beasties.

*Twice nominated for the Hugo, Val has won the Chesley Award
as well as the Gaughan Award and, together with her husband, the
Frank R. Paul Award.*

*In addition to illustrating, Val also sculpts in ceramics and wood,
animates in pixels and is a gourmet cook. Her work and Valhalla
Studio have been featured in newspapers and magazines including
the* Atlanta Journal Constitution *and she has been named the
"Female Futurist" in* Southern Living Magazine.

*Val has been a judge for the Illustrators of the Future Contest since
its inception in 1988.*

Synaptic Soup

I was born blind, but I didn't know it. Oh, I could see broad blurry shapes and clouds of color, but it wasn't until I was well into the third grade that I discovered what the teacher was doing up at the blackboard, that trees had leaves and books could be read more than two inches from my face. That is when my eyes were finally tested and I received glasses with lenses rivaling those in the Hubble telescope. Being able to actually see was spectacular. But it was only the beginning. From somewhere within, a profound sense of wonder emerged. I was intoxicated discovering the world around me, and in my newfound delight I would ask "What else?" and "What if?" My already active imagination was sparked by my mother's love of science fiction and the stories she would share with me.

It was a narrow miss. I could have continued growing up frightened and paranoid; instead I became a happy explorer of what-ifs. Now, these many years later, I am often asked, "Where do you get your ideas?" After much consideration I can report with some authority that ideas come from "Synaptic Soup." Like stone soup, it is comprised of small contributions from everyone I meet and everything I experience. As I move through the world listening to music, reading voraciously, talking to friends, looking, seeing, touching and tasting the world, my soup becomes rich and hearty. Then when I ask the magic soup a question, my synapses snap erratically, synthesizing a bit of this and a morsel of that until, like the magic eight ball, an answer floats up to the surface of my mind. And it is usually a good one.

It is also useful to note that the quality of the question has a profound influence on the answer that emerges. Instead of simply asking myself, "Should it be red or blue?" I ask if there is a color that hasn't been invented yet. Asking hard questions and being willing to wait for the soup to finish cooking are critical to developing an outstanding product.

Any creator, maker, visionary, if they are honest, will report that having the idea is only a small beginning. Everyone has their own version of "Synaptic Soup"; in every mind ideas percolate to the surface as regularly as waves kiss the sand. The idea is merely a seed. It is what we do to nurture that seed, to feed it, to create a loving environment for it, to remove the weeds (obstacles to its full realization), that help it grow. Then we put in the time and energy to help it blossom and flourish. If we are doing it right, we invest ourselves; that is, our creation becomes an extension of us, our child. We are to be found in every brush stroke, each small decision, in every letter, word and sentence. In the process we reveal ourselves; our real selves shine through, leaving us naked and vulnerable. True creation requires the courage to be seen.

In the early 1980s, the Writers of the Future Contest was established by L. Ron Hubbard to discover and nurture aspiring writers in the field of speculative fiction. While a great investment of time, energy and financial support, it had a precedent: Hubbard had done this before with great success. However, creating the infrastructure for a contest aimed at identifying and supporting up-and-coming artists had never been done. At that time every existing art-related contest required an entrance fee, or loss of rights to created works, or attendance at one of the many genre-related conventions. The world of science fiction, fantasy and dark fiction artists was lonely and regional. It was a

Catch-22 world wherein one had to be published in order to get work and thus be published. This was the state of affairs when the question was asked: "How can new artists in speculative fiction be discovered and nurtured?" Eventually the answer surfaced: Set up a sister Illustrators of the Future Contest and enlist the aid of the best artists on the planet to assist in creating an international contest that has remained unchallenged in its achievement for a quarter of a century.

In February of 1988, Frank Kelly Freas was asked to help create the rules for entry and judging, and to select a world-class panel of judges to offer aspiring artists real-world guidance and feedback. The objective of the Contest: To identify new artists with potential and to make the transition to a professional level with their art rapidly and effectively. The panel of judges since the inception of the Contest has been stellar. Never before has a group of professionals at the top of their field come together to collaborate to insure that the future would be served by the best of the best. The seed was planted, nurtured, watered with energy and loving attention. Each obstacle, like a pesky weed, was removed. The idea grew from "What if?" to "What next?" What had begun as a simple desire to help, now blossomed into a most unique and productive means of finding talent and giving careers a jumpstart.

I was so honored to be selected for that first panel of judges. To be listed with the likes of Kelly, Frank Frazetta, Leo and Diane Dillon, Vincent Di Fate, Will Eisner, Paul Lehr, and so many of those who inspired and kept me motivated to do better, was a truly humbling experience. My heroes were now my virtual aunts and uncles in art. What a powerhouse family I found myself enjoying. And if that wasn't enough to dazzle a little blind girl, my sense of wonder has blossomed into a forest over the past twenty-five years of working with the amazing talent that has percolated to the top of our Contest. Each year at our workshop I am again humbled by the talent and aspiration of our finalists. An extra feeling of satisfaction comes over me when I hear about the extraordinary successes of many of our winners. Some have excelled so much that they have been invited to join our panel of judges.

Some of our dear friends who served selflessly as judges for so many years are no longer with us. They are greatly missed, but their legacy lives on in their contribution to the many careers they assisted in fostering. In the creation of the Contest Mr. Hubbard wisely made provisions for its continued service far into the future. New judges have been added from the best of the field, including Stephen Hickman, Cliff Nielsen and Stephan Martiniere.

After twenty-five years of delight in being a part of Mr. Hubbard's Contest, sharing his vision for a better future by improving the quality of the present, working with up-and-coming talent, having the opportunity to contribute from my experience, I find myself deeply grateful. It is with heartfelt thanks that I honor L. Ron Hubbard for helping to keep my sense of awe and wonder alive for so many years. His seed has spread to every corner of the world, and it is a better place for it.

Robots Don't Cry

written by

Mike Resnick

illustrated by

ANDREW SONEA

ABOUT THE AUTHOR

A native of Chicago, Mike Resnick is, according to Locus *magazine, the all-time leading award-winning author, living or dead, for short fiction and is fourth on the* Locus *list of science fiction's all-time award winners in all fiction categories.*

Mike has five Hugos (from a record thirty-six nominations), a Nebula and numerous other awards from the US and places as diverse as France, Japan, Croatia, Poland, Catalonia and Spain. He is the author of seventy-five novels, close to three hundred stories, three screenplays and has edited forty-one anthologies.

Mike was the guest of honor at the 2012 World Science Fiction Convention and is currently the editor of Galaxy's Edge *magazine.*

By way of introduction to the story that follows, "Robots Don't Cry," Mike had this to say:

"I was thumbing through a coffee-table book on East Africa in Barnes & Noble, and I came across a photo of Dr. Richard Leakey standing holding up a skull of what I thought said 'Australopithicus Robotus.' I did a double-take, read it more carefully, and of course it said 'Australopithicus Robustus.'

"But all the way home I kept wondering what an 'Australopithicus Robotus' would be like, and of course the only way to find out was to write the story.

"If I'd been enrolled in Writers of the Future the year I wrote 'Robots Don't Cry,' it's surely the one I'd have submitted. It's science fictional, with the trappings of an imagined future, yet it is a very human story, which I think is the key to writing a good story in any field."

Robots Don't Cry

They call us graverobbers, but we're not.

What we do is plunder the past and offer it to the present. We hit old worlds, deserted worlds, worlds that nobody wants any longer, and we pick up anything we think we can sell to the vast collectibles market. You want a 700-year-old timepiece? A thousand-year-old bed? An actual printed book? Just put in your order, and sooner or later we'll fill it.

Every now and then we strike it rich. Usually we make a profit. Once in a while we just break even. There's only been one world where we actually lost money; I still remember it— Greenwillow. Except that it wasn't green, and there wasn't a willow on the whole damned planet.

There was a robot, though. We found him, me and the Baroni, in a barn, half hidden under a pile of ancient computer parts and self-feeders for mutated cattle. We were picking through the stuff, wondering if there was any market for it, tossing most of it aside, when the sun peeked in through the doorway and glinted off a prismatic eye.

"Hey, take a look at what we've got here," I said. "Give me a hand digging it out."

The junk had been stored a few feet above where he'd been standing and the rack broke, practically burying him. One of his legs was bent at an impossible angle, and his expressionless face was covered with cobwebs. The Baroni lumbered over—when

279

you've got three legs you don't glide gracefully—and studied the robot.

"Interesting," he said. He never used whole sentences when he could annoy me with a single word that could mean almost anything.

"He should pay our expenses, once we fix him up and get him running," I said.

"A human configuration," noted the Baroni.

"Yeah, we still made 'em in our own image until a couple of hundred years ago."

"Impractical."

"Spare me your practicalities," I said. "Let's dig him out."

"Why bother?"

Trust a Baroni to miss the obvious. "Because he's got a memory cube," I answered. "Who the hell knows what he's seen? Maybe we'll find out what happened here."

"Greenwillow has been abandoned since long before you were born and I was hatched," replied the Baroni, finally stringing some words together. "Who cares what happened?"

"I know it makes your head hurt, but try to use your brain," I said, grunting as I pulled at the robot's arm. It came off in my hands. "Maybe whoever he worked for hid some valuables." I dropped the arm onto the floor. "Maybe he knows where. We don't just have to sell junk, you know; there's a market for the good stuff too."

The Baroni shrugged and began helping me uncover the robot. "I hear a lot of ifs and maybes," he muttered.

"Fine," I said. "Just sit on what passes for your ass, and I'll do it myself."

"And let you keep what we find without sharing it?" he demanded, suddenly throwing himself into the task of moving the awkward feeders. After a moment he stopped and studied one. "Big cows," he noted.

"Maybe ten or twelve feet at the shoulder, judging from the size of the stalls and the height of the feeders," I agreed. "But there weren't enough to fill the barn. Some of those stalls were never used."

ANDREW SONEA

Finally we got the robot uncovered, and I checked the code on the back of his neck.

"How about that?" I said. "The son of a bitch must be five hundred years old. That makes him an antique by anyone's definition. I wonder what we can get for him?"

The Baroni peered at the code. "What does AB stand for?"

"Aldebaran. Alabama. Abrams' Planet. Or maybe just the model number. Who the hell knows? We'll get him running and maybe he can tell us." I tried to set him on his feet. No luck. "Give me a hand."

"To the ship?" asked the Baroni, using sentence fragments again as he helped me stand the robot upright.

"No," I said. "We don't need a sterile environment to work on a robot. Let's just get him out in the sunlight, away from all this junk, and then we'll have a couple of mechs check him over."

We half carried and half dragged him to the crumbling concrete pad beyond the barn, then laid him down while I tightened the muscles in my neck, activating the embedded microchip, and directed the signal by pointing to the ship, which was about half a mile away.

"This is me," I said as the chip carried my voice back to the ship's computer. "Wake up Mechs Three and Seven, feed them everything you've got on robots going back a millennium, give them repair kits and anything else they'll need to fix a broken robot of indeterminate age, and then home in on my signal and send them to me."

"Why those two?" asked the Baroni.

Sometimes I wondered why I partnered with anyone that dumb. Then I remembered the way he could sniff out anything with a computer chip or cube, no matter how well it was hidden, so I decided to give him a civil answer. He didn't get that many from me; I hoped he appreciated it.

"Three's got those extendable eyestalks, and it can do micro-surgery, so I figure it can deal with any faulty microcircuits. As for Seven, it's strong as an ox. It can position the robot, hold him aloft, move him any way that Three directs it to. They're both going to show up filled to the brim with everything the ship's data bank has on robots, so if he's salvageable, they'll find a way to salvage him."

I waited to see if he had any more stupid questions. Sure enough, he had.

"Why would anyone come here?" he asked, looking across the bleak landscape.

"I came for what passes for treasure these days," I answered him. "I have no idea why you came."

"I meant originally," he said, and his face started to glow that shade of pea-soup green that meant I was getting to him. "Nothing can grow, and the ultraviolet rays would eventually kill most animals. So why?"

"Because not all humans are as smart as me."

"It's an impoverished world," continued the Baroni. "What valuables could there be?"

"The usual," I replied. "Family heirlooms. Holographs. Old kitchen implements. Maybe even a few old Republic coins."

"Republic currency can't be spent."

"True—but a few years ago I saw a five-credit coin sell for three hundred Maria Teresa dollars. They tell me it's worth twice that today."

"I didn't know that," admitted the Baroni.

"I'll bet they could fill a book with all the things you don't know."

"Why are Men so sardonic and ill-mannered?"

"Probably because we have to spend so much time with races like the Baroni," I answered.

Mechs Three and Seven rolled up before he could reply.

"Reporting for duty, sir," said Mech Three in his high-pitched mechanical voice.

"This is a very old robot," I said, indicating what we'd found. "It's been out of commission for a few centuries, maybe even longer. See if you can get it working again."

"We live to serve," thundered Mech Seven.

"I can't tell you how comforting I find that." I turned to the Baroni. "Let's grab some lunch."

"Why do you always speak to them that way?" asked the Baroni as we walked away from the mechs. "They don't understand sarcasm."

"It's my nature," I said. "Besides, if they don't know it's sarcasm, it must sound like a compliment. Probably pleases the hell out of them."

"They are machines," he responded. "You can no more please them than offend them."

"Then what difference does it make?"

"The more time I spend with Men, the less I understand them," said the Baroni, making the burbling sound that passed for a deep sigh. "I look forward to getting the robot working. Being a logical and unemotional entity, it will make more sense."

"Spare me your smug superiority," I shot back. "You're not here because Papa Baroni looked at Mama Baroni with logic in his heart."

The Baroni burbled again. "You are hopeless," he said at last.

We had one of the mechs bring us our lunch, then sat with our backs propped against opposite sides of a gnarled old tree while we ate. I didn't want to watch his snakelike lunch writhe and wriggle, protesting every inch of the way, as he sucked it down like the long, living piece of spaghetti it was, and he had his usual moral qualms, which I never understood, about watching me bite into a sandwich. We had just about finished when Mech Three approached us.

"All problems have been fixed," it announced brightly.

"That was fast," I said.

"There was nothing broken." It then launched into a three-minute explanation of whatever it had done to the robot's circuitry.

"That's enough," I said when it got down to a dissertation on the effect of mu-mesons on negative magnetic fields in regard to prismatic eyes. "I'm wildly impressed. Now let's go take a look at this beauty."

I got to my feet, as did the Baroni, and we walked back to the concrete pad. The robot's limbs were straight now, and his arm was restored, but he still lay motionless on the crumbling surface.

"I thought you said you fixed him."

"I did," replied Mech Three. "But my programming compelled me not to activate it until you were present."

"Fine," I said. "Wake him up."

The little Mech made one final quick adjustment and backed away as the robot hummed gently to life and sat up.

"Welcome back," I said.

"Back?" replied the robot. "I have not been away."

"You've been asleep for five centuries, maybe six."

"Robots cannot sleep." He looked around. "Yet everything has changed. How is this possible?"

"You were deactivated," said the Baroni. "Probably your power supply ran down."

"Deactivated," the robot repeated. He swiveled his head from left to right, surveying the scene. "Yes. Things cannot change this much from one instant to the next."

"Have you got a name?" I asked him.

"Samson 4133. But Miss Emily calls me Sammy."

"Which name do you prefer?"

"I am a robot. I have no preferences."

I shrugged. "Whatever you say, Samson."

"Sammy," he corrected me.

"I thought you had no preferences."

"I don't," said the robot. "But *she* does."

"Has she got a name?"

"Miss Emily."

"Just Miss Emily?" I asked. "No other names to go along with it?"

"Miss Emily is what I was instructed to call her."

"I assume she is a child," said the Baroni, with his usual flair for discovering the obvious.

"She was once," said Sammy. "I will show her to you."

Then somehow, I never did understand the technology

involved, he projected a full-sized holograph of a small girl, perhaps five years old, wearing a frilly purple-and-white outfit. She had rosy cheeks and bright shining blue eyes, and a smile that men would die for someday if given half the chance.

It was only after she took a step forward, a very awkward step, that I realized she had a prosthetic left leg.

"Too bad," I said. "A pretty little girl like that."

"Was she born that way, I wonder?" said the Baroni.

"I love you, Sammy," said the holograph.

I hadn't expected sound, and it startled me. She had such a happy voice. Maybe she didn't know that most little girls came equipped with two legs. After all, this was an underpopulated colony world; for all I knew, she'd never seen anyone but her parents.

"It is time for your nap, Miss Emily," said Sammy's voice. "I will carry you to your room." Another surprise. The voice didn't seem to come from the robot, but from somewhere... well, offstage. He was recreating the scene exactly as it had happened, but we saw it through his eyes. Since he couldn't see himself, neither could we.

"I'll walk," said the child. "Mother told me I have to practice walking, so that someday I can play with the other girls."

"Yes, Miss Emily."

"But you can catch me if I start to fall, like you always do."

"Yes, Miss Emily."

"What would I do without you, Sammy?"

"You would fall, Miss Emily," he answered. Robots are always so damned literal.

And as suddenly as it had appeared, the scene vanished.

"So that was Miss Emily?" I said.

"Yes," said Sammy.

"And you were owned by her parents?"

"Yes."

"Do you have any understanding of the passage of time, Sammy?"

"I can calibrate time to within three nanoseconds of..."

"That's not what I asked," I said. "For example, if I told you that scene we just saw happened more than 500 years ago, what would you say to that?"

"I would ask if you were measuring by Earth years, Galactic Standard years, New Calendar Democracy years..."

"Never mind," I said.

Sammy fell silent and motionless. If someone had stumbled upon him at just that moment, they'd have been hard pressed to prove that he was still operational.

"What's the matter with him?" asked the Baroni. "His battery can't be drained yet."

"Of course not. They were designed to work for years without recharging."

And then I knew. He wasn't a farm robot, so he had no urge to get up and start working the fields. He wasn't a mech, so he had no interest in fixing the feeders in the barn. For a moment I thought he might be a butler or a major-domo, but if he was, he'd have been trying to learn my desires to serve me, and he obviously wasn't doing that. That left just one thing.

He was a nursemaid.

I shared my conclusion with the Baroni, and he concurred.

"We're looking at a *lot* of money here," I said excitedly. "Think of it—a fully functioning antique robot nursemaid! He can watch the kids while his new owners go rummaging for more old artifacts."

"There's something wrong," said the Baroni, who was never what you could call an optimist.

"The only thing wrong is we don't have enough bags to haul all the money we're going to sell him for."

"Look around you," said the Baroni. "This place was abandoned, and it was never prosperous. If he's that valuable, why did they leave him behind?"

"He's a nursemaid. Probably she outgrew him."

"Better find out." He was back to sentence fragments again.

I shrugged and approached the robot. "Sammy, what did you do at night after Miss Emily went to sleep?"

He came to life again. "I stood by her bed."

"All night, every night?"

"Yes, sir. Unless she woke and requested pain medication, which I would retrieve and bring to her."

"Did she require pain medication very often?" I asked.

"I do not know, sir."

I frowned. "I thought you just said you brought it to her when she needed it."

"No, sir," Sammy corrected me. "I said I brought it to her when she *requested* it."

"She didn't request it very often?"

"Only when the pain became unbearable." Sammy paused. "I do not fully understand the word 'unbearable,' but I know it had a deleterious effect upon her. My Miss Emily was often in pain."

"I'm surprised you understand the word 'pain,'" I said.

"To feel pain is to be nonoperational or dysfunctional to some degree."

"Yes, but it's more than that. Didn't Miss Emily ever try to describe it?"

"No," answered Sammy. "She never spoke of her pain."

"Did it bother her less as she grew older and adjusted to her handicap?" I asked.

"No, sir, it did not." He paused. "There are many kinds of dysfunction."

"Are you saying she had other problems, too?" I continued.

Instantly we were looking at another scene from Sammy's past. It was the same girl, now maybe thirteen years old, staring at her face in a mirror. She didn't like what she saw, and neither did I.

"What *is* that?" I asked, forcing myself not to look away.

"It is a fungus disease," answered Sammy as the girl tried unsuccessfully with cream and powder to cover the ugly blemishes that had spread across her face.

"Is it native to this world?"

"Yes," said Sammy.

"You must have had some pretty ugly people walking around," I said.

"It did not affect most of the colonists. But Miss Emily's immune system was weakened by her other diseases."

"What other diseases?"

Sammy rattled off three or four that I'd never heard of.

"And no one else in her family suffered from them?"

"No, sir."

"It happens in my race, too," offered the Baroni. "Every now and then a genetically inferior specimen is born and grows to maturity."

"She was not genetically inferior," said Sammy.

"Oh?" I said, surprised. It's rare for a robot to contradict a living being, even an alien. "What was she?"

Sammy considered his answer for a moment.

"Perfect," he said at last.

"I'll bet the other kids didn't think so," I said.

"What do they know?" replied Sammy.

And instantly he projected another scene. Now the girl was fully grown, probably about twenty. She kept most of her skin covered, but we could see the ravaging effect her various diseases had had upon her hands and face.

Tears were running down from these beautiful blue eyes over bony, parchmentlike cheeks. Her emaciated body was wracked by sobs.

A holograph of a robot's hand popped into existence, and touched her gently on the shoulder.

"Oh, Sammy!" she cried. "I really thought he liked me! He was always so nice to me." She paused for breath as the tears continued unabated. "But I saw his face when I reached out to take his hand, and I felt him shudder when I touched it. All he really felt for me was pity. That's all any of them ever feel!"

"What do they know?" said Sammy's voice, the same words and the same inflections he had just used a moment ago.

"It's not just him," she said. "Even the farm animals run away when I approach them. I don't know how anyone can stand being in the same room with me." She stared at where the robot was standing. "You're all I've got, Sammy. You're my only friend in the whole world. Please don't ever leave me."

"I will never leave you, Miss Emily," said Sammy's voice.

"Promise me."

"I promise," said Sammy.

And then the holograph vanished and Sammy stood mute and motionless again.

"He really cared for her," said the Baroni.

"The boy?" I said. "If he did, he had a funny way of showing it."

"No, of course not the boy. The robot."

"Come off it," I said. "Robots don't have any feelings."

"You heard him," said the Baroni.

"Those were programmed responses," I said. "He probably has three million to choose from."

"Those are emotions," insisted the Baroni.

"Don't you go getting all soft on me," I said. "Any minute now you'll be telling me he's too human to sell."

"*You* are the human," said the Baroni. "*He* is the one with compassion."

"I've got more compassion than her parents did, letting her grow up like that," I said irritably. I confronted the robot again. "Sammy, why didn't the doctors do anything for her?"

"This was a farming colony," answered Sammy. "There were only 387 families on the entire world. The Democracy sent a doctor once a year at the beginning, and then, when there were less than 100 families left, he stopped coming. The last time Miss Emily saw a doctor was when she was fourteen."

"What about an offworld hospital?" asked the Baroni.

"They had no ship and no money. They moved here in the second year of a seven-year drought. Then various catastrophes wiped out their next six crops. They spent what savings they had on mutated cattle, but the cattle died before they could produce

290

young or milk. One by one all the families began leaving the planet as impoverished wards of the Democracy."

"Including Miss Emily's family?" I asked.

"No. Mother died when Miss Emily was nineteen, and Father died two years later."

Then it was time for me to ask the Baroni's question.

"So when did Miss Emily leave the planet, and why did she leave you behind?"

"She did not leave."

I frowned. "She couldn't have run the farm—not in her condition."

"There was no farm left to run," answered Sammy. "All the crops had died, and without Father there was no one to keep the machines working."

"But she stayed. Why?"

Sammy stared at me for a long moment. It's just as well his face was incapable of expression, because I got the distinct feeling that he thought the question was too simplistic or too stupid to merit an answer. Finally he projected another scene. This time the girl, now a woman approaching thirty, hideous open pustules on her face and neck, was sitting in a crudely crafted hoverchair, obviously too weak to stand any more.

"No!" she rasped bitterly.

"They are your relatives," said Sammy's voice. "And they have a room for you."

"All the more reason to be considerate of them. No one should be forced to associate with me—especially not people who are decent enough to make the offer. We will stay here, by ourselves, on this world, until the end."

"Yes, Miss Emily."

She turned and stared at where Sammy stood. "You want to tell me to leave, don't you? That if we go to Jefferson IV I will receive medical attention and they will make me well—but you are compelled by your programming not to disobey me. Am I correct?"

"Yes, Miss Emily."

The hint of a smile crossed her ravaged face. "Now you know what pain is."

"It is ... uncomfortable, Miss Emily."

"You'll learn to live with it," she said. She reached out and patted the robot's leg fondly. "If it's any comfort, I don't know if the medical specialists could have helped me even when I was young. They certainly can't help me now."

"You are still young, Miss Emily."

"Age is relative," she said. "I am so close to the grave I can almost taste the dirt." A metal hand appeared, and she held it in ten incredibly fragile fingers. "Don't feel sorry for me, Sammy. It hasn't been a life I'd wish on anyone else. I won't be sorry to see it end."

"I am a robot," replied Sammy. "I cannot feel sorrow."

"You've no idea how fortunate you are."

I shot the Baroni a triumphant smile that said: *See? Even Sammy admits he can't feel any emotions.*

And he sent back a look that said: *I didn't know until now that robots could lie,* and I knew we still had a problem.

The scene vanished.

"How soon after that did she die?" I asked Sammy.

"Seven months, eighteen days, three hours, and four minutes, sir," was his answer.

"She was very bitter," noted the Baroni.

"She was bitter because she was born, sir," said Sammy. "Not because she was dying."

"Did she lapse into a coma, or was she cogent up to the end?" I asked out of morbid curiosity.

"She was in control of her senses until the moment she died," answered Sammy. "But she could not see for the last eighty-three days of her life. I functioned as her eyes."

"What did she need eyes for?" asked the Baroni. "She had a hoverchair, and it is a single-level house."

"When you are a recluse, you spend your life with books,

sir," said Sammy, and I thought: *The mechanical bastard is actually lecturing us!*

With no further warning, he projected a final scene for us.

The woman, her eyes no longer blue, but clouded with cataracts and something else—disease, fungus, who knew?—lay on her bed, her breathing labored.

From Sammy's point of view, we could see not only her, but, much closer, a book of poetry, and then we heard his voice: "Let me read something else, Miss Emily."

"But that is the poem I wish to hear," she whispered. "It is by Edna St. Vincent Millay, and she is my favorite."

"But it is about death," protested Sammy.

"All life is about death," she replied so softly I could barely hear her. "Surely you know that I am dying, Sammy?"

"I know, Miss Emily," said Sammy.

"I find it comforting that my ugliness did not diminish the beauty around me, that it will remain after I am gone," she said. "Please read."

Sammy read:

"There will be rose and rhododendron
When you are dead and under ground;
Still will be heard from white Syringas..."

Suddenly the robot's voice fell silent. For a moment I thought there was a flaw in the projection. Then I saw that Miss Emily had died.

He stared at her for a long minute, which means that we did too, and then the scene evaporated.

"I buried her beneath her favorite tree," said Sammy. "But it is no longer there."

"Nothing lasts forever, even trees," said the Baroni. "And it's been five hundred years."

"It does not matter. I know where she is."

He walked us over to a barren spot about thirty yards from

the ruin of a farmhouse. On the ground was a stone, and neatly carved into it was the following:

MISS EMILY
2298–2331 G.E.
THERE WILL BE ROSE
AND RHODODENDRON

"That's lovely, Sammy," said the Baroni.

"It is what she requested."

"What did you do after you buried her?" I asked.

"I went to the barn."

"For how long?"

"With Miss Emily dead, I had no need to stay in the house. I remained in the barn for many years, until my battery power ran out."

"Many years?" I repeated. "What the hell did you do there?"

"Nothing."

"You just stood there?"

"I just stood there."

"Doing nothing?"

"That is correct." He stared at me for a long moment, and I could have sworn he was studying me. Finally he spoke again. "I know that you intend to sell me."

"We'll find you a family with another Miss Emily," I said. *If they're the highest bidder.*

"I do not wish to serve another family. I wish to remain here."

"There's nothing here," I said. "The whole planet's deserted."

"I promised my Miss Emily that I would never leave her."

"But she's dead now," I pointed out.

"She put no conditions on her request. I put no conditions on my promise."

I looked from Sammy to the Baroni, and decided that this was going to take a couple of mechs—one to carry Sammy to the ship, and one to stop the Baroni from setting him free.

"But if you will honor a single request, I will break my promise to her and come away with you."

Suddenly I felt like I was waiting for the other shoe to drop, and I hadn't heard the first one yet.

"What do you want, Sammy?"

"I told you I did nothing in the barn. That was true. I was incapable of doing what I wanted to do."

"And what was that?"

"I wanted to cry."

I don't know what I was expecting, but that wasn't it.

"Robots don't cry," I said.

"Robots *can't* cry," replied Sammy. "There is a difference."

"And that's what you want?"

"It is what I have wanted ever since my Miss Emily died."

"We rig you to cry, and you agree to come away with us?"

"That is correct," said Sammy.

"Sammy," I said, "you've got yourself a deal."

I contacted the ship, told it to feed Mech Three everything the medical library had on tears and tear ducts, and then send it over. It arrived about ten minutes later, deactivated the robot, and started fussing and fiddling. After about two hours it announced that its work was done, that Sammy now had tear ducts and had been supplied with a solution that could produce six hundred authentic saltwater tears from each eye.

I had Mech Three show me how to activate Sammy, and then sent it back to the ship.

"Have you ever heard of a robot wanting to cry?" I asked the Baroni.

"No."

"Neither have I," I said, vaguely disturbed.

"He loved her."

I didn't even argue this time. I was wondering which was worse, spending thirty years trying to be a normal human being and failing, or spending thirty years trying to cry and failing. None of the other stuff had gotten to me; Sammy was just doing what robots do. It was the thought of his trying so hard to do

295

what robots couldn't do that suddenly made me feel sorry for him. That in turn made me very irritable; ordinarily I don't even feel sorry for Men, let alone machines.

And what he wanted was such a simple thing compared to the grandiose ambitions of my own race. Once Men had wanted to cross the ocean; we crossed it. We'd wanted to fly; we flew. We wanted to reach the stars; we reached them. All Sammy wanted to do was cry over the loss of his Miss Emily. He'd waited half a millennium and had agreed to sell himself into bondage again, just for a few tears.

It was a lousy trade.

I reached out and activated him.

"Is it done?" asked Sammy.

"Right," I said. "Go ahead and cry your eyes out."

Sammy stared straight ahead. "I can't," he said at last.

"Think of Miss Emily," I suggested. "Think of how much you miss her."

"I feel pain," said Sammy. "But I cannot cry."

"You're sure?"

"I am sure," said Sammy. "I was guilty of having thoughts and longings above my station. Miss Emily used to say that tears come from the heart and the soul. I am a robot. I have no heart and no soul, so I cannot cry, even with the tear ducts you have given me. I am sorry to have wasted your time. A more complex model would have understood its limitations at the outset." He paused, and then turned to me. "I will go with you now."

"Shut up," I said.

He immediately fell silent.

"What is going on?" asked the Baroni.

"You shut up too!" I snapped.

I summoned Mechs Seven and Eight and had them dig Sammy a grave right next to his beloved Miss Emily. It suddenly occurred to me that I didn't even know her full name, that no one who chanced upon her headstone would ever know it. Then I decided that it didn't really matter.

Finally they were done, and it was time to deactivate him.

"I would have kept my word," said Sammy.

"I know," I said.

"I am glad you did not force me to."

I walked him to the side of the grave. "This won't be like your battery running down," I said. "This time it's forever."

"She was not afraid to die," said Sammy. "Why should I be?"

I pulled the plug and had Mechs Seven and Eight lower him into the ground. They started filling in the dirt while I went back to the ship to do one last thing. When they were finished I had Mech Seven carry my handiwork back to Sammy's grave.

"A tombstone for a robot?" asked the Baroni.

"Why not?" I replied. "There are worse traits than honesty and loyalty." I should know: I've stockpiled enough of them.

"He truly moved you."

Seeing the man you could have been will do that to you, even if he's all metal and silicone and prismatic eyes.

"What does it say?" asked the Baroni as we finished planting the tombstone.

I stood aside so he could read it:

"SAMMY"
AUSTRALOPITHICUS ROBOTUS

"That is very moving."

"It's no big deal," I said uncomfortably. "It's just a tombstone."

"It is also inaccurate," observed the Baroni.

"He was a better man than I am."

"He was not a man at all."

"Screw you."

The Baroni doesn't know what it means, but he knows it's an insult, so he came right back at me like he always does. "You realize, of course, that you have buried our profit?"

I wasn't in the mood for his notion of wit. "Find out what he was worth, and I'll pay you for your half," I replied. "Complain

297

about it again, and I'll knock your alien teeth down your alien throat."

He stared at me. "I will never understand Men," he said.

All that happened twenty years ago. Of course the Baroni never asked for his half of the money, and I never offered it to him again. We're still partners. Inertia, I suppose.

I still think about Sammy from time to time. Not as much as I used to, but every now and then.

I know there are preachers and ministers who would say he was just a machine, and to think of him otherwise is blasphemous, or at least wrong-headed, and maybe they're right. Hell, I don't even know if there's a God at all—but if there is, I like to think He's the God of *all* us Australopithicines.

Including Sammy.

The Shaadi Exile

written by

Amanda Forrest

illustrated by

VINCENT-MICHAEL COVIELLO

ABOUT THE AUTHOR

Amanda Forrest has slept beneath humming MMO servers, under the stars on the South China Sea, while strapped to the sides of thousand-foot cliffs, and (much to her waking surprise) along the morning migratory path of a Himalayan goat herd. While her many adventures provide inspiration for her stories, she wishes she could reliably nod off under more ordinary circumstances.

After many years away, Amanda recently returned with her family to her childhood hometown in western Colorado.

As a child, the quiet, empty landscapes of the Western Slope provided ample space for a thriving imagination. Her introduction to speculative fiction came before kindergarten when her mother read The Hobbit *to her, and while she reads widely, science fiction and fantasy have always been closest to her heart.*

Despite her love for literature, Amanda pursued another passion in college, studying computer science. Afterward, she worked as a programmer and manager in the video games industry. It wasn't until her daughter was born that she retired from software and turned her efforts to writing.

Writers of the Future gave her her fourth professional sale, and she has since had four more stories accepted at professional rates, including sales to Asimov's Science Fiction, Apex, *and* Upgraded.

ABOUT THE ILLUSTRATOR

Vincent-Michael Coviello is also the illustrator for "Carousel" in this volume. For more information about Vincent, please see page 162.

The Shaadi Exile

In the dark of the tea stall, men argued. Rise and fall of voices and glint of eyes and teeth. Daliya paused near the entrance, lured by the smell of flatbreads sizzling in ghee, the woodsy scents of dark-leaf tea. In the stall's front, a girl stomped on a bellows and the cookfire flared and popped, hot against Daliya's face.

"Chappati?" the girl asked. She offered up a brown-crusted flatbread with the butter still fizzing.

The girl's mother stepped from the dim recesses of the stall and pressed a kiss into the girl's hair. Daliya swallowed, abruptly swamped in memories of sandalwood incense and laughter and the faint creases of her mother's long-ago face. *Ammi.* Mama. So long gone.

Daliya shook her head at the offered bread and hurried on. She could miss her mother later. Alone.

A tram rattled overhead, and dust filtered down the narrow artisans' alleyway. Chickens squawked and ran, beaks jabbing the air with each footstep. She watched them, amused, while the retreating tram switched track lines to veer for the neathspace portal station.

Oh, Daliya, she thought. She'd dallied too long already. Tomorrow morning, a new bride would step through that portal. Alone, terrified, sent into an arranged marriage light-years from home. And instead of finishing the poor girl's memory box, Daliya'd let chickens distract her. She hurried on.

Her workshop door swung shut, wrapping her in silence. On her workbench, the unfinished box stood open, a rough-carved rosewood frame with a layer of nanites sparkling in the bottom.

She slid the *dupatta* off her hair, set the headscarf aside, and inserted a data capsule into a niche in the box's base, intending a quick review of the images of home that the bride's family had transmitted.

She ran a finger over the activation nub. The nanites rose in a cloud, swirled, and organized. An animated landscape coalesced inside the box and took on coloration. Mountains towered, crowned with cloud. Mud-brick buildings crusted the closest hill.

When the last group of nanites settled into place, Daliya clapped a hand over her mouth.

A dead man dangled from a heavy tree limb, noose tight around his neck. His face was purple, mottled. Open eyes stared out from the scene.

She cringed and advanced the image. Dirty teeth were bared in a snarl for the camera, close enough to show food trapped at the gum line. Thick veins like roots tunneled through the whites of the man's eyes. The only motion was a tremble in his upper lip.

In the next tableau, a dog limped in a circle. It dragged a mangled leg behind. Bone showed near the foot.

She clapped the box lid shut and ejected the capsule, held it away from her between thumb and forefinger as if it were poisoned.

Perhaps there had been a mistake. These scenes were supposed to provide comfort for a young bride sent between star systems. Daliya was used to seeing family gatherings with siblings lined up and clowning for the camera. Sunrise over the village lake. What kind of family would instead send these sorts of images through truespace while their frightened daughter walked the neathspace span?

Though it had been thirty years, Daliya's own journey echoed in her mind. She ached again, the black despair of abandoning everything she'd loved heavy in her chest.

302

There must have been some mixup with the data. She glanced at her watch—she'd be hard pressed to finish the lid's carvings already. But she needed to sort this out.

Quickly, she stuffed the capsule into her pocket and rewrapped her *dupatta* over her hair. She opened the door to the sounds of the street—goats, laughter of the street children, the whine of electric motors and clank of the tram overhead—and stepped outside.

A boy leaped in front her. He jangled jewelry on a stick, lapis lazuli and hand-worked silver. Dirt filled the lines on his knuckles, and his nails were cracked and split, but his eyes remained bright with hope.

"Tomorrow, Keef. I don't have time to look today." She laid a hand on his ratted hair.

A smile cracked his smudged face. "I'll be here waiting." He scampered off, and she smiled sadly after him. Sweet boy.

Shaadi. Marriage. It is for the women to carry our culture between the stars. To bind us as one people, even as we scatter across the galaxy like salt spilled on a table.

That's what they'd told her. Daliya was important. An emissary as well as a wife, picked for her wide range of achievements. Her coursework in the sciences, her mastery of the arts of woodcarving and inlaying. The volunteering she did for charity. It was an honor to be chosen as a bride.

But all those years ago, as she sat with her mother and her sister in the dark-draped room and submitted her fingertips and palms to the woman who marked them with henna, the words were nothing. The brush tickled her skin, cool where the henna stained her.

One more day. Breakfast, tea, and one last evening feast. And then she'd never see her mother again. She'd be cast out onto the neathspace span—a silver ribbon slicing the universe's ink-blank substrate—with just a kilogram allowance for clothing and possessions. To journey, light-years passing beneath her stride, while true years passed outside.

Her mother dabbed rosewater behind her ears. "You look beautiful, *piyaara*."

How could her mother call her *piyaara,* darling, yet raise no protest that she'd soon be gone? Daliya wanted to rip her chest open, show everyone what a breaking heart looks like.

"These preparations are ridiculous, *Ammi*. We're playing make-believe. By the time I'm married, you'll probably be..." her throat seized up "...dead."

Wrinkles deepened in the corners of her mother's eyes when she smiled. "But for you, it will be just days. For you, I will have been part of your preparations. There to see you readied for your husband."

Daliya ripped her hand from the henna artist's grasp. "I don't want to be readied for him. I don't want to be some she-goat sent off for impregnation."

Her mother's gaze was stern, and then her face softened and she pulled Daliya close. Folds of cloth, soft beneath, smell of cookfires and sandalwood and love. "You chose this, Daliya. You could have refused the invitation. But you didn't. Somewhere down inside, you want this. You're going to a whole new world."

A tear wet the crown of Daliya's head, and her scalp itched where the damp melted into her hair. Her mother sniffed and backed away, smiling through the tears. "You have an adventure ahead. I take comfort in that."

Daliya stared at her red-stained fingers. "I made a mistake, and it's too late now to fix it."

Her sister, Qirat, propped a mirror in front of her. Daliya glanced up. Reflected was a young woman with shimmering dust brushed on high cheekbones. Kohl rimmed her eyes. In place of a headscarf, a net of delicate silver set with semiprecious stones lay over her hair, nearly weightless but somehow pressing down so hard.

She parted her lips to speak but no words came.

"You're leaving forever, sister of mine," Qirat said. "At least let us have this part in your marriage."

The interplanetary communications manager regarded her with a clenched jaw. He slid one of the viewscreens on his desk back and forth. "I don't understand. Are you accusing us of tampering with incoming messages?"

"No, of course not. I should know how faithfully you deliver communications."

The manager inclined his head at that, and his jaw softened. Of course he'd know that she referred to the messages from her mother, received every week since she exited neathspace. Thirty years of tears and smiles, stories about her nieces and nephews. The communications department hadn't messed up a single delivery.

She sat on the edge of the chair in front of the man's desk. "I'm just not sure what to do. The capsule contains scenes that are...unexpected. I thought that there might have been an inadvertent—"

"I can show you the data trail if you like, but frankly, Daliya, I think you're looking in the wrong place. If anything, we handle these packages from brides' families with more rigor than the ordinary comms."

"No, that's all right. Thanks for your time."

Daliya stood. As she walked for the door, the man cleared his throat. "There's one thing. The data packages usually come ident-stamped from a family member. A DNA tag. But the incoming bride's package had no origin declared, other than the source planet. We usually see protocol irregularities like this from worlds that are more than twenty-five light years or so distant. This girl's home is just fifteen, I think. Anyway..." He tapped his index finger on the desk. "That's all I've got. You might check with the groom. He received a package last week, meant to acquaint him with his bride."

Fahad stared at her over the rim of his teacup. His eyes were black stones. He'd only admitted her after half a dozen pleas.

She smoothed the heavy silk of her *shalwar* pants where they fell over her hips and down to brush the ornate carpet. Lamps burned on the small, shin-high tables set around the room, casting warm light on the man's rich furnishings. She remained near the door, a respectful distance from him as indicated by their unfamiliarity.

"Forgive me for intruding," she said. "I've come with a concern about your bride."

Those black eyes flashed, and he rose from his seat on a low, cushioned bench.

Daliya raised her chin to keep from taking a step back. "I'm afraid that there may be ill will towards—"

His hand shook and tea sloshed over the rim of his cup. Daliya recoiled instinctively upon seeing searing liquid hit his skin.

"How dare you!" Fahad said. "A cripple all her life, and you come here to poison my affection towards her? You should be ashamed."

A cripple? She backed closer to the door. "No, no. I'm..."

Fahad's shoulders drooped, and his clenched fists loosened, but his glare pierced. "Then what? You came to question the suitability of my marriage?"

Daliya licked her lips. This wasn't unfolding as she'd planned, not at all. "Fahad, let me start over," she said. "I create memory boxes. Personalized nanite viewers that display scenes of the brides' homes. We coordinate with the families and give them to the girls as surprise gifts when they arrive."

He returned to his seat on the bench. Daliya exhaled, relieved despite the tension in the man's body.

"I didn't mean to give the wrong impression," she said. "Fahad, the scenes sent for your bride were ... gruesome. I can't imagine why a family would do this to their daughter."

A direct gaze met hers. "You really aren't aware of the situation on her world?"

Daliya shook her head. "I was a shaadi bride, thirty years ago. When I spend too much time investigating the girls' backgrounds, it tends to unearth too many memories of everything I left behind." She cut herself off, surprised at having said so much.

He rested one ankle upon the other, a sign that her confession had put him at ease. Fahad's brows drew together, and he steepled his fingers beneath his chin. "Shaadi is hard for both genders. I was fourteen and in love with every girl that glanced at me when I was selected as a groom. But I had to save myself for a bride who wouldn't arrive for fifteen more years."

"My husband spoke of similar things." She smiled. "We were lucky, though. Love came easily."

"Spoke?"

"He died ten years ago. Pancreatic cancer that spread too quickly for the nanosurgeons to excise."

"I'm sorry."

"Thank you. I miss him."

"You miss your homeworld too, I'm sure."

She nodded. "But this is my home now."

He adjusted one of the cushions behind his back. "It sounds like your children were blessed with a happy household."

"I . . . we weren't able to conceive. Genetic difficulties."

Fahad looked to the side. An incompatibility that nanosurgery and fertility treatments couldn't correct was exceedingly rare. "Again, I'm sorry. It seems I've asked all the wrong questions."

"Don't be. There are plenty of children on every world who need love. I give it where I can." She thought of Keef's bright eyes, of the other orphans who laughed and played games in the city's alleyways. In a way, she did consider them family. The only one she had.

From outside, she heard the bleats of taxi horns and the shouts of the roving food sellers. Fahad's heavy drapes muffled the sounds, but down here in the city center, nothing could shut out all the noise.

He tapped his fingernail against the porcelain of his teacup. "Rabeea sent me messages. Each year from her tenth birthday until she entered neathspace at twenty-five."

Daliya raised her eyebrows. Most brides that were selected so young tended to hide from their future.

Fahad reached into a compartment in an ottoman that stood in front of him. "Let me show you."

He extracted a viewsheet and held it up for her. A pinch at the edge of the sheet, and a girl's image appeared. She sat shrouded in a heavy veil, and when she spoke, the silk wavered with her breath.

Her words carried a thick accent, common with the linguistic drift between planets. "I know you must hate me. You can't stand the idea of marrying someone you didn't choose. But I think of you fondly. I wonder who you are, what kind of things will make you happy."

Daliya stood and moved closer. She crouched in front of the viewsheet, glanced back and forth between Fahad and the girl in the picture. "Her voice is so young."

"Watch. This is her first message." He traced the line of her shoulder with a fingertip. "I wasn't even born when she sent these words off to our distant star. Hard for me to conceive of that sometimes."

The girl reached down and grasped the fringe of her veil. Her voice quavered. "This will make you hate me even more, but you'd find out eventually. Better to get it over with."

She lifted the silk and revealed a face that might have been beautiful if not for the obvious paralysis at the midline and the deep, deep sadness in her eyes. She smiled, and half her face rose into a grimace while the other sagged, limp.

Fahad pinched the sheet to turn it off and laid it face down on the ottoman. "She had a stroke when she was three years old. One arm curls across her chest, unusable. When she does walk, she limps and falls often."

Daliya shook her head, perplexed. "But nerve damage is one of the easiest nanosurgeries—"

"Not if you live on her backwards, intolerant, feeble-cultured rock of a planet." Fahad slapped his hand on the bench. "They claim that changing a body—no matter how broken—is sacrilegious."

"That's terrible." Daliya's knees cracked when she stood. She'd need to schedule an appointment for joint repair soon.

"I received this message not long after I was chosen for shaadi.

In those early years, I grew to respect Rabeea very much."
Fahad looked at his hands. "Love . . . I don't know. This girl"—
he tapped on the back of the viewsheet—"is not the woman
Rabeea became. She's bitter. Scarred and afraid. But it's my duty
to marry her and care for her the best I can."

Daliya felt more lost than ever. She fiddled with the loose
ends of her *dupatta*.

"Fahad, I would like to review the messages, with your
permission. Maybe just a selection of those that aren't too
personal."

He pushed the viewsheet toward her. "Anything to help her
start a better life here."

She tucked it into her knapsack. "Thank you. I'll bring it back
when I'm finished."

Daliya wore these things into neathspace: a thin gold ring that
had been her grandmother's, her finest *shalwar kameez,* and the
net of silver wire and gemstones that draped her head. In her
arms, she carried letters from her family, penned on tissue-thin
paper, and a lock of her mother's hair. Her pockets held three
smooth stones from the streambed behind her home and a
chunk of plaster pried from the wall of the family kitchen.

One kilogram for clothing and possessions. Because of the
massive energy needed to insert a body into neathspace, she
was allowed nothing more.

She shivered as she walked. A silver trail shimmered beneath
her feet, an illusion the hypnotist trained her to visualize lest
she become disoriented by the void around her. She tried to
speak only once; her words were eaten by the silence. When
she cried, her tears wobbled in the air and then arrowed off in
all directions.

After what seemed to be about three days walking, she
found the portal back to truespace, a curtain of black rain. She
stumbled through into a sensory swamp. Smells, noise, lights so
bright she retched. And then the realization. Deep down in the
crevices of her heart, she understood that her mother was dead

already. Forty light-years away, buried under a cairn in the rocky valley behind their home. Some things a daughter just knows, a defiance of the apparent laws of the universe.

She sank to the floor of the portal station and began to mourn.

Rabeea stared out from the viewsheet, twelve years old and foregoing all attempts at modesty. No *dupatta* draped her hair. A tattoo of a snake curled across the paralyzed side of her face. The older woman next to her had to be her mother. She cradled Rabeea's hand gently in hers.

"It was a birthday present to myself. They'll make me remove it, of course." Rabeea sneered. "The tattoo, I mean. Removal is one of the five allowable—sacred, they say—reasons for nanosurgery. My ugly face will—"

Rabeea's mother tugged a strand of hair behind her daughter's ear and whispered something to interrupt the girl's self-hate. Daliya was relieved to see that Rabeea'd had that much at least. Someone had loved her.

"Anyway, my father is in trouble because I did this and he won't punish me for it. The others, the shaadi officials, tell me that I was chosen in order to teach your world that the natural order must be respected. I must remain a cripple. But I tell you this, husband. I hate them more than you must hate me."

The viewscreen went dark when the message ended. Daliya stood and crossed her quiet apartment. She brushed aside the curtains and peered down at the bustle below. Why would a society do something like that to a child?

She thought of the regular messages sent from her home. So different. *Ammi*'s words were compressed love shipped forty light-years across the galaxy.

Though she knew her mother had been dead by the time Daliya stepped out of neathspace, *Ammi*'s first message arrived just a week after Daliya, bound by the speed of light to give the illusion that the words were fresh, just spoken. Over the years, Daliya had watched her mother age. She'd learned of Qirat's marriage and the birth of her children. And now, although the videos showed an old woman speaking to a daughter who left a lifetime ago, time had not dulled the love in her eyes.

As always when she thought of the news from home, Daliya had to swallow back the knowledge that someday the messages would just stop. The woman on the screen spoke with a querulous voice. She squinted dimming eyes. Daliya could only hope that, once her mother passed, another relative would send the news of how she died. And even though it made her feel unfaithful, she hoped that once she finally knew, she might be able to finish her grieving. Maybe she could stop living for a weekly illusion of family.

She returned to Rabeea's messages, flipping forward. At sixteen, the girl hid behind a veil again. A toddler sat on her lap, tugging at the cloth. "My brother, Jari," she said, inclining her head toward the boy. "Anyway, there's not much to say. The government deleted the database of nanosurgery programs, even the five sacred ones. Whatever hope I had that I might arrive on your world as a whole person is gone. I'm sorry."

Eighteen-year-old Rabeea simply sat and cried beneath her shroud.

Daliya stopped the recordings. They weren't giving her any insight as to how she should proceed. She drummed her fingers on her knee. What if the memory box images *were* intended to comfort Rabeea? A reminder of how terrible her old situation had been. But that didn't seem right. The family had to know that Rabeea would never forget the horrors of her world. Reminding her just seemed cruel.

There was, of course, the irregularity with the package's origin. Perhaps it hadn't come from the family at all.

Daliya rewound to Rabeea's first message and advanced the video to show the girl's uncovered face. Above intense green eyes, the girl's brows arched high and delicate like the wings of a bird. A precious face that deserved so much more than she'd been granted.

Just as she was about to power off the viewscreen, the

resemblance hit her. She pulled a nanite viewer out from a storage drawer in the base of her divan and inserted the data capsule.

She flipped quickly through the scenes sent from Rabeea's homeworld. The other panoramas she hadn't yet viewed were similar to the first three. Violent. Grotesque. Daliya's mouth was dry when the final scene coalesced.

A man stood in front of the camera, badges on his shirt shining. He raised a hand-drawn sign.

Remember your duty, Rabeea. We will know if you forsake it.

She flipped back to the beginning and peered closely at the man who swung from the limb. Yes, there was something about the line of his jaw, his high-arched eyebrows. A similarity, if vague, to the girl in the messages.

The scenes were a threat of violence upon Rabeea's family, sent by her oppressors, meant to control her even after she arrived at her new home. But how could anyone know, from fifteen light-years away, whether she was faithfully executing her so-called duty? Any information sent back to her homeworld could be falsified. They must be counting on twenty-five years of conditioning to their oppression to keep her in line.

Daliya cradled her head in her hands. She would not inflict these images on the girl. That was an easy choice. The more difficult challenge would be convincing Rabeea that the zealots on her homeworld no longer had a hold on her.

Rabeea limped out from the neathspace portal, empty-handed and clothed in simple linen. Daliya hustled forward. She placed the memory box in the girl's hands and then cupped her cheeks in her palms. A copper plate with an inscribed poem sealed the empty data capsule port.

"You are free," Daliya whispered.

Rabeea stared back, silent. After a few moments, Fahad stepped from the circle of attendants who monitored neathspace exits and moved to support his bride. Though she refused to lean on him while she walked, Daliya thought she saw a flicker of relief on the girl's face.

She joined the pair on their journey back to Fahad's home. He'd insisted that Rabeea have a chance to relax away her first afternoon in peace. She could retire to her temporary housing at dusk, waited upon by the flock of attendants granted to shaadi brides. In the meantime, a single chaperone—Daliya—sufficed to ensure propriety as they were yet unwed.

The rickshaw jolted on cracked pavement. As they moved between the city's districts, the smells changed from cookfires to the tang of textile dyes to the ozone scent of the electric trams speeding upon rails as they whizzed above. Though the journey by tram would have taken a quarter the time, Fahad wanted Rabeea to have a chance to feel the texture of her new world.

Once inside Fahad's apartment, Daliya watched the awkward but beautiful moments of the pair's quiet courtship. He reached out and tucked the hair behind her ear. She knocked a pillow onto the floor and his hand covered hers when they both reached down to grab it.

Perhaps they'd be as lucky as she and her husband had been. Daliya sighed, realizing it would be better to confront the issue of Rabeea's homeworld now so that the developing mood would have the rest of the afternoon to thrive. "Rabeea," she said. "I told you that you were free when you exited neathspace. Do you believe me?"

The girl dropped her gaze and tugged her *dupatta* forward. It was already wrapped tight around her face, well past her hairline and showing no neck. Daliya wanted to reach out, but she stayed herself, choosing instead to adjust her own headscarf. She cherished the garment for the way it enveloped her like a hug, the way it connected her to a culture and religion that spanned the stars. Rabeea hid within hers.

Fahad met Daliya's eyes and then touched his bride's hand. "We know about the threats to your family."

The half of Rabeea's face that wasn't paralyzed twisted. "Then you know that I'm not free. I love them more than anything. They were punished enough each time I rebelled at home."

"But you're not home anymore. We're not like the people of your world. No one here will betray you to them." Daliya laid her hand on the girl's knee.

Rabeea's lip quivered, but she grasped a handful of linen trouser leg and spoke. "Look outside."

Daliya moved to the window and nudged the heavy drape aside with her shoulder.

"They'll be across the street," Rabeea said. "Two or three. Just watching."

Indeed, a pair of young, mustached men stood in front of the apartment building opposite. They wore drab clothing and angry stares.

"They call themselves Soldiers of Sanctity."

"How...I mean, why are they here?" Fahad joined Daliya at the window.

"Free, private access to interplanetary communications is one of your freedoms that my *people*"—Rabeea spat the word— "hate. It doesn't stop them from using it to recruit. The recruits then use it to send information back. It's been fifteen years since I left...my brother will be old enough to wed soon. I'll have nieces and nephews someday. Innocent children. And they'll have babies of their own. No matter how long it takes for word to reach my home, someone will suffer if I do not obey."

"We can hide...leave the city for somewhere more private," Fahad said.

"No, they'll assume that a disappearance is an admission of guilt. My father spent a year jailed as punishment when he wouldn't condemn the school paper I wrote attacking the nanosurgery restrictions. What would they do to my family if I disobey my entire purpose?" Rabeea looked down at her palms.

Daliya turned aside to give the couple a moment's privacy while Fahad wiped a tear from his bride's cheek. She smoothed the folds of her *dupatta* and pinched the fabric between thumb and forefinger, thinking. Those fanatics couldn't be allowed to continue to hurt the poor girl. But Rabeea was right about the flow of information. It would be impossible to screen outgoing messages for harmful information if these so-called soldiers were determined to report.

No matter what, the soldiers would want evidence that Rabeea remained handicapped. Daliya's eyes defocused while she considered an idea. Perhaps it could work.

"Rabeea, will you tell me about your family?" she said. "I would like to know about Jari and your mother and this man who would go to jail for his daughter."

It was as if a lamp kindled in Rabeea's eyes, sending the dark tones of Fahad's living room recoiling for the corners. "They are the most wonderful people."

The intercom crackled. "Are you ready, Rabeea?"

Daliya swallowed. She opened her mouth to speak, but didn't trust her voice and settled for nodding.

"I suspect you know this process better than I, but you only need to step through the portal. Do it quickly, so that you aren't too disoriented by the moments you're only halfway 'neath."

Another nod, and Daliya took a faltering step forward. She nearly collapsed when her weak leg took her weight—after two weeks of practice, she couldn't yet maneuver confidently with her new paralysis. While she walked, she recited the details to herself: Jari's favorite toys, the spice blend that Rabeea's mother favored with lentils, the address of the father's workplace. By the time she arrived on Rabeea's world, thirty true-space years would have passed since the girl first left. Jari would be grown, the parents changed. She hoped that any gaps in her knowledge would be smoothed over by the decades.

Daliya wore eight hundred grams of clothing, and carried zero point two kilograms in her hand—a long, long letter that declared Fahad's profound disappointment with his bride's handicap and her refusal to undergo corrective treatment.

VINCENT-MICHAEL COVIELLO

She caught a glimpse of her reflection in the stainless steel frame around the portal. Green eyes—the nanosurgeons had made them as striking as Rabeea's. High-arched brows. Half a face that looked like candlewax, frozen midflow. A DNA test would expose her, as would an exacting measurement of height—Daliya was one tenth of a centimeter shorter than Rabeea. But Rabeea believed that testing of genomes was one of the technologies swept away in the wash of zealotry. And who would think to take a measuring tape to her?

Fahad looked on, his expression wooden. By his side, Rabeea wore Daliya's face well. Though the surgery had added years to her skin, turning her from young to middle-aged, she stood straight. Daliya's heart lifted when she recalled Rabeea's first timid steps after the surgery, the wonder that crossed the girl's face when her once-weak leg took weight without buckling. Perhaps down the line, once the eyes of the soldiers turned elsewhere, Rabeea would undergo another treatment to restore the appearance of youth. At least now she was free to choose.

Shaadi. Marriage. It is for the women to carry our culture between the stars. To bind us as one people, even as we scatter across the galaxy like salt spilled on a table.

No, Daliya thought. Marriage did not keep them whole. Shaadi was an ideal, like so many, that failed in execution.

She stopped before the portal. *Ammi.* She closed her eyes. Once she stepped 'neath, there'd be no way for her to receive the last few years' worth of her mother's messages. This was a last goodbye.

Daliya took a deep breath and stepped into neathspace. A new family stood on the other end of the span, ready for her love.

The Pushbike Legion

written by

Timothy Jordan

illustrated by

CASSANDRE BOLAN

ABOUT THE AUTHOR

Timothy R. Jordan grew up in Essex, England, a healthy bike ride from London, surrounded by a loving family where science and fantasy were always part of their evenings and games.

His passion for fantasy and fossils led to an early love of Tolkien and a childhood spent with his head stuck firmly in the clouds, inventing stories and fantastical worlds.

While studying electronic engineering at the University of Leeds, Tim stumbled across Frank Herbert's Dune *in a secondhand bookshop—an event that awakened a lifelong interest in sci-fi.*

Tim's mind traveled far, but his physical form never left England until his mid-twenties, when a career as a software engineer sent him chasing across the ocean to Alabama and California before he settled in Florida with his family.

He is an avid science fiction fan and futurologist who explores transhumanism through the lenses of science and fantasy. When not working or writing, Tim enjoys playing the guitar, building robots and creating artificially intelligent computer programs. He often collaborates with faculty at a nearby university on AI and human cognition projects, helping to bring these topics to a wider audience of students and the public.

*This is his first publication, although he's just finished writing the second novel in his sci-fi series—*Glow.

ABOUT THE ILLUSTRATOR

Cassandre Bolan is also the illustrator for "Beneath the Surface of Two Kills" in this volume. For more information about Cassandre, please see page 66.

The Pushbike Legion

Late again, thought Aleck, rising up off his bike's wooden saddle to push down hard on the pedals. The ancient contraption skidded and skittered along the dirt road, pebbles shooting like bullets as the leather tires rolled over pits and potholes, shattering their icy crusts like eggshells.

His feet spun faster as gravity eased him downhill into a tree-lined gully and around a hairpin bend, breath trailing like clean smoke in the frosty morning air. A river, a ford, bumping across slick rocks, knees flying up past his elbows as momentum carried him across the riverbed and up the bank where his feet reengaged with the pedals, and he began the tough haul up Church Hill to the Legion's marshaling ground.

Tattledale Church loomed out of the mist. Aleck sped past the gaunt stone walls, weaving a course around the jutting porch with its woodwormed door. He sped out across the cemetery, fighting the long grass between the gravestones that seemed to reach up like tiny fingers, slowing his progress.

Ahead, the other legionaries were poised on their bikes, spears and shields at the ready, awaiting orders.

"Ah—tent—shun!" Praetor Jones's gruff voice barked out through the thick air, reflecting back off the nearby hills like the bark of a dog. "Shun! Shun...shun..."

"I'm here," Aleck gasped.

"Move...out!" With a clank of chains and armor the pushbike legion of Tattledale Town headed out on morning patrol.

Aleck crested Cemetery Hill as the sun broke through, and for a fleeting second he saw the entire Land, a perfect circle of green hills, fields and cottages surrounded by the stark brown and yellow of desert dunes. Blinking hard at the morning sun, he tagged onto the back of the legion as it wound its way downhill toward the perimeter road. There, it would circle the entire six-mile circumference, before returning to the town center and the Sheep and Shearer pub for ale and breakfast.

"Morning, Fossy," Aleck hissed as he swept past the rearguard. Old Foster Mason was already falling behind the other nine soldiers. It wouldn't be long before bad health forced his retirement. Aleck was his intended replacement, in training for a full week and late every day. He knew how much Praetor Jones frowned upon such tardiness.

"Morning, lad," grumbled Fossy, his eyes heavy and sad. His wife had died three months ago and his own health had gone into rapid decline.

"How's your leg?" Aleck asked his routine question to the old man who walked with a profound limp.

"Got a bone in it," was Fossy's usual reply.

Aleck concentrated on keeping in line, focusing on the broad back of Centurion Sheppard, who started weaving from side to side as they descended the hill. None of the bikes had brakes; those had all worn out decades ago, and replacement parts were hard to make. Weaving, boot jamming and plain old falling off were the only available methods of slowing down or stopping, and since they all carried weapons and armor, misjudgments often led to calamitous pileups and a group effort to fish at least one legionary out of a ditch or thorn bush.

"You're late, boy!" Praetor Jones said, dropping back along the line to Aleck's side.

"Yes, sir, sorry, sir, it won't happen again, sir."

"You said that yesterday." He glanced sideways at Aleck, his eyes leaving the road long enough to make him wobble and almost run off into the ditch. Jones had a weak chin, caused by his complete lack of teeth. His face was grizzled leather with piercing, authoritative eyes that glared out from beneath his imposing but bizarre-looking helm. The helm had once been a huge can, probably for beans, carefully stripped and beaten into shape with twisted cow horns fastened on either side to give it a barbaric appearance. Aleck's own helm was a simple basin held on with a chinstrap and painted military green—specially made for the new recruit. It had been over ten years since the legion last had a new recruit.

"Sorry, sir," Aleck hung his head.

"And could you run some sausages out to the Mannings' farm this afternoon?" Jones said in a hushed tone. "My delivery boy's not been well the last few days."

"Yes, sir." Aleck perked up as Praetor Jones returned to the front of the line. The day was young and so were his legs. It seemed he wasn't in too much trouble after all, but he vowed to try and get out of bed at the proper time tomorrow morning.

The legion pushed on toward the perimeter, passing Bill Trotter's pig farm and the ramshackle residence of Martha Seamstress and her ever-clucking chickens—the only birds left in the Land. They passed through the last remaining oak grove, then up and over Pilot Hill, pausing occasionally to retrieve a fallen bike part or to let the older soldiers catch their breath.

The exhilarating plunge down Pilot Hill ended at the Land's perimeter: a perfect cutoff where the grass and road turned to sand, its edge as sharp and defined as if freshly cut with a scalpel that very morning. Long ago, the road had continued out across green hills and valleys to the next village. A village whose name was lost in time, along with the road, the hills and, for all they knew, the whole of England and the rest of the world.

There had been no sight or sound of life, human or otherwise, for over sixty years. Few remembered the night the desert came, silent and unexplainable. Now, only stories of the old world remained, stories Aleck soaked up eagerly from the few old books and newspapers that remained. That lost world of planes and cities and spaceships seemed so fantastic, so unreal, he wondered if it had ever really existed at all.

After a sharp right turn onto the perimeter road, the legion paused at the flint farmhouse for their daily arms drill. As the rest of the troops caught up, Aleck inspected the old building. Cut clean in half along the perimeter line, one half of the building had turned to sand and vanished into the desert, and the half on his side of the perimeter stood like a sentinel, a poignant reminder not to take a single step farther.

He jabbed playfully with his spear at the gaps between the flints, watching the ants whip into a combat frenzy at the inexplicable attack coming from outside their realm of understanding.

A shout echoed through the still air, interrupting his daydreams of cloud-cities and motor-driven bikes. "Fossy, no, man, stop!" Aleck turned to see the old man speeding downhill toward the perimeter. For a second, Aleck thought Fossy was out of control, unable to defeat gravity with the toe of his boot, but then with a shock, he noticed that Fossy was still pedaling, his legs churning feverishly, face set in a determined grimace.

"Fossy?" Aleck barely had time to speak as the old man flashed past, crossed the perimeter line, and shot out into the desert. He kept going for a fraction of a second before the bike's front wheel bogged down in the sand, sending Fossy flying over the handlebars. As he went airborne, he came apart, exploding like a clump of bees going in different directions, then the bees broke up into smaller bees and on until he became just dust.

Fossy never hit the sand. He simply vanished along with his bike and his pain, no sound, no scream…nothing.

"Silly old goat," someone said.

"Waste of a good bike," muttered Praetor Jones.

"…and then he was just gone…nothing. Why? Why would anyone do that to themselves?" Aleck prodded a small chunk of meat around the edge of his bowl. His stomach rumbled with hunger, but he still felt sickened by what he'd seen earlier. In his mind, the bowl was the Land filled with a stew of people, all bounded inside the perimeter, and the chunk of meat...?

"Old Fossy had been sick for a long time. Sometimes people just can't take life anymore." Aleck's mother was a thin, nervous woman who never stood still. She whirled around the kitchen, cleaning and rearranging the few pots and pans they had left. She fussed over a vase of fake roses, placing them on the side table, adjusting the stem angles and leaves, then standing back to inspect the view. She was clearly trying to make the place look special, which could mean only one thing—Martha was on her way over. "Eat up now, no waste. We're not made of food, you know."

"Yes, we are, actually." He winced, waiting for the crack of knuckles across his ear that generally followed such flippant remarks. It never came; instead she chose to lurk uncomfortably close to his side, just in his peripheral vision, a large wooden spoon raised threateningly.

"You're a legionary now, and soldiers don't cry, and that lovely Martha girl is coming over soon, and we don't want her to think we're crybabies, do we?"

"I guess not..." Aleck mumbled into his stew. He had heard all the rumblings at the town meetings, the shrinking population, not enough young people coming along to do the work. Arranged marriages were the answer; get them all married off and breeding fast before the population died out. That had been the general sentiment at the last meeting, an idea first proposed by Father Haslop, and wherever his thoughts went, the whole town generally followed like sheep. "Baaah!"

"What?"

"Nothing..." He swirled the meat around his bowl until it flipped over the rim and onto the table. He stared at it, half expecting it to disappear into a puff of dust, but it just stayed, staining the tablecloth with brown juice.

It wasn't that Martha was a bad girl. Two years older than Aleck, and a lot taller and more adult-looking, she had bumps and curves that the girls his own age just didn't have. Not that there were many girls, or boys, for that matter. They all fit comfortably into the single-room schoolhouse, where Mrs. Rattlebee divided the lessons and her attention across the spectrum of ages from toddler to near adult. Soon, he'd have to leave that classroom and take on work and a wife, even though he still felt like a kid, and really didn't know what a married person was supposed to do.

A loud knock popped him out of his reverie, and the kitchen door swung open. Martha stood twiddling her thumbs and looking down at him through thick eyelashes.

"Well, chop-chop, Aleck...let the lady in. We haven't got all day."

"Yes, we have." He refused to move or meet Martha's gaze. He saw the spoon twitch toward his ear, and winced.

Instead, his mother scratched the top of her head with the spoon and rushed to the door. "Do come in, my dear. Excuse Aleck; he's a bit upset about that Fossy thing earlier today. He's a legionary now, you know, so he gets to see all sorts of horrors and things in defense of the Land."

"Yes, I heard about that...terrible really." Martha was in and at the table, eyeing Aleck's stew before his heart could manage another beat.

"Now you two sit and have a nice little chat. Aleck can tell you all about his new adventures. I'll just be in the next room making lots of noise, so excuse me, won't you..."

Saved by the sausages, thought Aleck as he viewed the town from up on Pilot Hill for the second time that day. Mr. Jones's sausage delivery had made an excellent excuse to escape the forced rendezvous with Martha. As he sat astride his bike looking back toward his home, he couldn't shake the thought that she was still there, lurking in the kitchen, eating and awaiting his return.

On a whim, he rode down a different dirt track and past the pig farm out onto a small flat plain lined with rows of vegetables.

CASSANDRE BOLAN

He hovered next to a rickety wooden water tower that leaned as if about to topple. Usually there was a mule tethered to a lever-and-screw mechanism that lifted water from the underground reserve to fill the tower. A branching network of pipes and ditches carried the water out across the acres of vegetables. Today must be the mule's day off. It stood off to the side in a small paddock, chewing carrots from a string basket.

Aleck meandered through the rows of beets and potato heads, leaving a winding tire track in the dirt behind. Nearer the perimeter, he saw the familiar sight of old Charlie Potato sitting on his bench, looking out over the desert.

"You're not thinking of riding out as well, are you?" he said bumping over the broken paving to where Charlie sat.

"Not today." Charlie was not one for words. Old and supposedly wise, he was one of the few left alive who remembered the coming of the desert.

"What do you mean...not yet?" Aleck sat on the bench next to him and let the bike flop into a nearby hedgerow.

"One day, but not yet." Charlie turned to look at Aleck. His face resembled his crop, a great, blighted turnip with a tuberous nose, fingerling ears, and skin like loosely scrubbed peelings mottled with the blemishes of time. A wide floppy hat kept the sun off his bald patch, and a thin gray mustache twitched across his upper lip like a roving caterpillar.

"You were a legionary once, right?" Aleck asked.

"Long time ago, but nothing happened."

"Nothing ever happens. Why do we even have a legion?"

"In case something does happen, I suppose." Charlie stared out onto the shifting sands and chewed thoughtfully on a parsley leaf. "We saw a fox once."

"I didn't think there were any foxes."

"There aren't, not anymore. He was the last one. Came out onto the road and just sat there as we all passed him by, gasping his last breath. We stood around and prodded him with the blunt ends of our spears."

"What happened?"

"He died, just sat there and died. No more foxes now. That was about the time I decided to leave the legion and join the Dusters."

"My Dad was a Duster."

"I know. I was there when he rode out."

"I was too young to remember, and Mum never talks about it. She gets angry if I ask about such things."

Charlie shifted uneasily. He was indeed a man of few words, but one who believed in the narrative; always tell the story even if it was in as concise a manner as possible. "I was there on that morning, early, cold, and clear as a newborn's eyes. Twenty of us were going, all on our bikes back then. Now they frown on that. 'Waste of good bikes,' they say. They all just rode over the perimeter and blew apart, not a sound, nothing, just following Clarence Elsby—the cult leader."

"You survived though," Aleck said, wide-eyed with amazement.

"I didn't go. I pulled up at the line and watched them all vanish."

"Why?"

"Didn't feel like it was my time, or maybe it was simple cowardice. Now I just grow potatoes and wait for the end." As if to emphasize his impending demise, Charlie coughed furiously and spat something nasty onto the ground.

"Waste of a good bike. That sounds just like Praetor Jones." Aleck looked over to his own decrepit contraption slung across the bush. "He says the bicycle chain's the most valuable bit. A rare commodity, he calls it."

"Bike chains are hard to make. Still we patch them together, carefully preserving each link, stringing together new chains out of bits of the old. Each link has probably been on a dozen different chains by now, but we're still running out. Young people should be learning to make new chains, not just patching up old ones."

"Why ride out? Can't people just die and end up in the cemetery?"

"Cemetery's full."

"Mum says that if someone rides out, they don't become a wisp, like the ones that haunt the churchyard."

"That's true enough. Fill the land with wisps, and there'll be no room left for the living."

Aleck shivered at the thought of wisps. Everyone kept away from the churchyard after dark when the wisps came out. Even seeing one brought sickness and bad luck. But wisps didn't only appear at the church, Aleck had seen one when coming home late from a friend's house. It rose from a hedgerow down by a cluster of deserted cottages called the Lowdown. It looked like a curl of lightly glowing mist, twinkling in the starlight. It came up through the gnarled brambles, reaching toward him. Aleck still saw it in his nightmares, like the floating image of a severed forearm with a hooked hand, fingers streaming off into nothingness. He'd run and screamed and never stayed out after dark again.

"Besides..." Charlie said, "there are plenty other reasons to ride out. Nothing much to live for these days—no medicine, no future. Growing old is real uncomfortable."

"It seems a terrible way to die though." Aleck shook away a vision of being the last person left living in the Land...cold and alone and surrounded by wisps.

"The Dusters never believed they were going out to die. No, they believed they were being reborn as part of the living desert. As the sand pulled them apart, they were absorbed into its mind, a mind as big as the world itself." He paused and chewed thoughtfully on his lower lip. "Charismatic man, that Clarence Elsby. Have you believe anything, he would."

"A great mind in the desert?" Aleck gazed out across the sand, eyes full of wonder. "Could that be possible?"

"Don't rightly know. Something's out there, and it eats you alive if you cross the line. It watches, sits and studies as if we're some preserved scene from the past, a museum exhibit like one of those paperweights you shake and make the snow fall. Perhaps there are other bubbles out there, all intriguing little examples of early twenty-first-century England. Except we're not really preserved, more like just hanging on and slowly going under, like the foxes did. Once there were two thousand of us living here. Go count the stones in the cemetery; they outnumber us all now."

Aleck moved to the edge of the Land, his toes coming close to the sharp perimeter rim. A soft breeze came over the boundary, but nothing else. At night the sand made sounds; it sang its sublime seismic symphony, deep, mournful notes that warbled up and down some impossible scale. So faint was the music that even a birdcall or a light breeze smothered it. Once, in a moment of exploratory madness, he had leaned far out, his toes crossing the boundary. He watched the tips of his shoes dissolve and felt a tingling on his feet just before he quickly withdrew. His mother had been furious. "Your shoes are ruined," she had cried. "We're not made of leather, you know."

"Yes, we are," he'd said, his chin thrust out belligerently as her hand cracked into the side of his head. His ear smarted for days after.

"What do you think caused it, Charlie?" he asked, backing up from the edge.

"No one knows."

Aleck tried to stare him down, willing him to reveal a truth with the power of his gaze, but Charlie's narrow eyes could outstare a rock, and Aleck looked away. "But you know...don't you? I've heard them talking, and they think you know what happened."

"People think all sorts of stupid things. How stupid we get is inversely proportional to how many people there are in the world, Aleck. Always remember that."

Aleck pondered the new fact, plotting a little graph of stupidity against population on the chalkboard inside his head. "What was it like? You know...when it happened."

"It was quick. We just woke up one morning and everything outside this little circle was desert, everything else was gone. No sign, nor sound, no radio, no TV, not a plane or a bird or a bug flying over us. We've not seen or heard a peep from the rest of the world since that day...nothing."

Aleck hopped to his feet and retrieved his bike. He stretched out a hand and gauged how far the sun was above the sandy horizon, around an hour of daylight left. Maybe it was safe to go back home now. "We should get home, Charlie, wisps will be coming out soon."

"Wisps never hurt no one," Charlie said.

"Why do you think the Romans didn't invent the bicycle?"

Charlie scratched his ear and gave Aleck a sideways look. "That's a funny question for any time of the day."

"They built long, flat roads. You would think they'd invent the bicycle to go on them."

Charlie chuckled. "A lovely image that is, legions of armed soldiers sweeping across Europe and North Africa on their pushbikes."

"I mean, it's not like a bike is that hard to make. We manage to keep them going without a forge or plastic or anything really technical." Aleck shrugged and mounted up. As he looked back, Charlie was still scratching his head and looking at him with amused bewilderment. Aleck enjoyed the feeling of leaving someone with a mystery to ponder.

Ambushed!

Aleck's mother was waiting as he came back from morning patrol. There was no time for protest, or breakfast, as she grabbed his arm and led him out the house and through the center of town to one of the abandoned estates on the Westside.

"Where are we going?" He whined, trying to free his captive wrist.

"It's a surprise." She tightened her grip and forged onward.

A small group had gathered by the side of one of the ramshackle houses, tools in hand; they appeared to be waiting for someone to tell them what to do next.

"It's your new house, Aleck. It's all yours."

"But..."

"The nice folks here have volunteered to help fix it up. It's been decided that you can have it as nobody has lived here for so long."

"But..."

"You'll be the first, then we'll move some of the other young folk in nearby, a right jolly little community you'll have. Just think, Aleck—independence at last!"

"But..."

"It'll take a few days to fix up, and then we'll get you settled. You can do the legion patrol in the morning and the rest of the day, we've decided, you'll take over some of the beehives from Jack Honeywell. He's not getting any younger, you know. You can start a new apiary right here near the middle of town, away from the dangerous perimeter edge."

"Bees? But..."

"Very important business, bees. Without them, we have no honey and the plants don't pollinate. This is a big responsibility. I'm so proud of you, Aleck." She dropped his wrist and wrapped him in a hurried embrace.

"But..." The number of objections was just too overwhelming. Aleck could only really focus on the single issue that had plagued him since he got up late that morning and missed breakfast. "But...who's going to feed me?"

He looked up and saw Martha standing by the edge of the gathering. She turned away coyly, then peered back, meeting his eye with an expression of determination. "I'll bring you food, Aleck," she said, attempting a friendly smile.

"There, you see, lovely Martha will stop in and bring food, and if she can't, then I'll be just up the road."

The tiny world swam before his eyes. He could see it all now, like an avalanche on the dunes. Once it started rolling, it was impossible to stop. The house, the food, the wife, the... whatever happened next. It was all arranged, all taken care of by Father Haslop and his committee. All he had to do was play along, and here, in the Land, there really was nowhere to run.

Aleck skulked around the northern perimeter, throwing stones and rocks out into the desert. They fizzled and vanished before hitting the sand. The game was to see how far you could throw a stone before it disappeared. It was a game that could get him in trouble if he was caught, as wasting the Land's limited resources was a crime punishable by imprisonment—or at least a good thick-ear and detention from your mother.

No one usually came to this part of the Land. The smell of fermenting cattle waste kept visitors away. Jackson Cowherd, the cattle farmer, called it his Sherbet; he inhaled it in great loving lungfuls, as if it were the smell of fine roast beef.

Aleck flopped belly down amongst the fodder-beets growing next to the cattle pen and looked out over the desert, watching the shimmering heat distort the distant hills of sand and the fuzzy patches of dust devils skimming across the open plains. A steady stream of small clouds wafted over the Land. "Suspiciously regular clouds," as Mother called them. "Someone sends us rain; they keep the heat out and the cold in."

Someone, but who? wondered Aleck.

The last few days had been busy and his new abode was almost complete. There was very little glass in the Land and no one knew how to make it anymore, so they built wooden shutters and fitted them over the window openings. They patched the leaking roof with stone tiles reclaimed from other abandoned houses, then set about reboring the water well, shoring up its sides, and capping it with a new bucket-and-winch mechanism, all held together with wooden pins and cow-hair ropes.

Several cats, borrowed from neighbors, were shut inside the house to cull its resident rat and mouse population. In only a few more days it would be fit for habitation, and Aleck could begin his new life as a soldier-bachelor.

With a hiss and a whistle, a large dust devil whipped past only feet from the perimeter. Startled out of his malaise, Aleck watched the dust devil change direction, moving along the perimeter as if scouting along its razor-sharp edge.

Another seemingly random spurt of motion sent the spinning

vortex straight toward Aleck; then, with a quiet *pop*, it crossed the boundary and hovered, stationary, in the cow pasture, as if waiting.

Frozen in fear, Aleck realized that this was something new, something that probably shouldn't be happening. He wondered if the desert was about to come alive and destroy them all, turning the Land and everything in it to dust in a single breath of wind, as many had long speculated must happen.

The devil shifted shape, winding down to solidify into a crude four-legged form that looked like a small table. A bland spherical knob extruded from one end, then widened until it resembled a head and neck. Its blunt footless limbs stumbled around on the loose dirt like a newborn calf taking its first steps. After a few seconds, it gained stability and stood still and upright, then the head started scanning from side to side, as if peering around.

Aleck almost screamed, he almost ran, but instead he lay there trembling. His fingers gripped the earth so tightly they pierced the ground, grubbing up handfuls of roots and pebbles. The sand-colored quadruped stumbled toward one of the cows. The beast looked up, only mildly startled, as if unable to distinguish the new arrival from the natural surroundings. The devil closed the gap and a nose-like protrusion extended from its head toward the cow's snout. The cow simply stood there, chewing its cud, eyes blank and uncomprehending.

At the instant of contact, the cow startled backward as if seeing the creature for the first time. The sand-figure exploded into a cloud of dust, and reformed back into a dust devil as it fled for the perimeter, making a louder and more urgent whistling noise as it crossed over and skipped away into the desert.

Aleck jumped up and ran, leaving the bemused cows staring at his back. The whole of Tattledale could hear him yelling, long before he reached the town hall.

The invasion bell tolled loudly in the church tower, but was unable to drown out the shouts and mutterings of the gathered villagers.

"Liar!"

"Malingerer!"

"Any excuse not to take on responsibility or go about his duties."

"I saw it, I tell you," Aleck stuttered. "A thing made of sand. It came out the desert and moved around like it was alive."

"Someone's been at Father Haslop's grog stash, by the sounds of it."

Aleck hung his head in despair. He was beginning to doubt his own mind under the heat of cross-examination from the village elders. His mother and Martha stood off to the side, their eyes full of concern for his sanity.

"And you say this thing looked just like a cow?" Father Haslop wore his church robe and flat black hat, but his face was bright red, either from tension or from a healthy premeeting dose of grain alcohol.

"It turned into a cow, but it was still made of sand." Aleck's voice trailed off, realizing how absurd it sounded, even to his own ears.

The frightened murmuring of the crowd grew louder and Father Haslop shook his head, clearly on the verge of passing some judgment.

"I've seen them, too." The quiet voice came from the doorway.

The crowd kept babbling, and no one except Aleck heard the voice. He turned and saw Jackson Cowherd leaning on the door frame with a long stalk of grass protruding from the corner of his mouth.

"I've seen them too," he said louder. Slowly the crowd stopped talking and turned to face him. He just stood chewing the stalk, like one of his docile ruminants.

"Tell us more, Jackson." Father Haslop silenced the people with a wave of his hand.

"Couple of times now, I've seen 'em come over and try to talk to my cows."

There was a stunned silence, made even more palpable by the sudden stilling of the church bell.

"And you never thought to mention this to anyone," shouted Father Haslop, a furious red vein pulsing on his forehead.

"Not really. You'd all think I was nuts or drunk, like the young fella there." He nodded at Aleck.

"Well... it sounds like the Devil has been walking amongst us," said the father, crossing himself feverishly with a long, pointed index finger.

"They probably think the cows are the smart ones," said Jackson, rearranging his hat and flipping the grass stalk to the other side of his mouth. "Because they don't go riding off into the desert to die... not very smart, that." He turned away and sauntered out the door as if nothing profound and lifechanging had happened, leaving behind a stunned audience.

People hugged and fussed as they stared at Aleck with wide, fear-filled eyes and wondered just how long before the sand devils came churning in from all directions and turned them all to dust.

Morning patrol was extra somber and serious the next day. Everyone, even Aleck, turned up on time, fully armed with spears and shields. Praetor Jones instigated a regime of warmup exercises and mock combats before the legion set off on extended patrol.

By full sunrise, over half the perimeter had been scouted and individual soldiers left at strategic guardposts as lookouts. Aleck suspected that the choice of strategy was more due to the aging soldiers' health concerns than any tactical advantage, as they always left the older men behind in areas of plentiful shade with convenient clumps of bushes. The younger blood continued on to complete the full perimeter, before heading back uphill to the square, where they disbanded and went home to their wives, their shuttered windows, and their ale rations.

Praetor Jones suspended all post-patrol pub outings, regarding them as too frivolous for a time of war. Not that Aleck had been allowed to attend anyway, deemed too immature to be of drinking age by town law. It was really just a way to keep the number of drinkers down, Charlie told him, a way for the elders to eke out the limited supply.

It took a month for the fuss over the sighting to die down. The legion spent a full week constructing a new watchtower on Bluebell Hill to the south, a small hut with a covered pyre. The intention was to have the station manned all the time...even at night. The pyre would be lit at any sign of invasion, giving the town plenty of time to rally into action. So far, no volunteers had come forward to man the post. Jones had suggested that they recruit new blood from the younger folks in town, but none of the children were really ready for such active service.

Aleck didn't feel like going home even though it was his last few days of living with his mother. Early next week, he would move into his new home, but the thought of the echoing, empty house all to himself left him cold.

Instead, he went searching for Charlie Potato. The old man had not been well lately, but they had spent some good time talking about the old days before the desert. Aleck learned about TV and cars, and how people had strange jobs typing and playing cards with each other over a vast planetwide communications network.

Unable to find Charlie, Aleck returned home, a route that took him past the deserted lane and the creepy hedgerow of the Lowdown. He paused and stared into the hedge, wondering if there were a dead body hidden under the thick hawthorn. How had the wisp gotten there? Who was it? There were other wisp sightings reported over the years, a small cluster down by the dried-up lake, and others in some long-abandoned houses, but this was the only wisp Aleck had ever seen.

He sped past the hedge, for a while running backward so he could keep his gaze on the bush so nothing could sneak up behind. As he topped the hill, he turned and ran down to the main village, never quite able to escape the feeling that something was following him.

He passed his new house on the way into town and stood

gazing up at the repointed brickwork and the brand-new solid plank front door. He pushed the door open, went inside, and stood still as his eyes adjusted to the dark. He could see a single chair in the center of the room, a few pots and pans arranged around the kitchen, and the freshly cleaned fire hearth awaiting its first installment of wood.

He brushed passed the chair in the darkness, hands touching the arm and setting it rocking back and forth. The place smelled of soot and cat urine. He wondered if there were any wisps in the house, ones that would rise up through the floor after sunset and suck his soul dry as he slept in bed. He trembled at the thought. There had to be a reason no one lived here ... what other reason could there be?

He turned to sit in his new chair and something huge and dark stirred in the corner. He yelled and stumbled across the room to the door, heart jumping so hard it almost burst. As light flooded in from the open door, he stifled another scream as a familiar figure emerged from the shadows. "Charlie! You scared the sherbet out of me."

"Sorry, lad. I was just passing by, and thought I'd check out your new place."

"What do you think of it?"

Charlie stood and looked around the meager room with his hands on his hips. "You should be very comfortable here."

"I would offer you something to drink, but I don't have anything."

Charlie tried to talk, but instead burst into a tirade of coughs and splutters. Aleck helped Charlie into the seat, where he rocked gently until the gurgling in his throat subsided and he was able to talk again. "Sorry, lad. I actually came by to ask you to help me with something."

"What do you need?"

"I want you to help me steal something."

"Steal something?" A prickle of fear ... or was it excitement? ... jangled his spine.

"Yes, lad. I need you to help me steal a bicycle."

But why do you want to ride out? Why do you want to die like that?" Aleck's eyes flooded with tears. He looked back at Charlie, whose face was full of pain and desperation; his usual nonchalant calm had gone.

"I've not long left, lad. Whatever is eating my insides shows no mercy. I'm afraid, Aleck, afraid of the pain. It's not like in the old days, when we had medicine. There's barely enough grog in the Land to knock me out for a single night. This is the best way, trust me."

The two of them teetered through the night, bumping along the western dirt road out of town, using the thin sliver of moon as a guiding light. Aleck stood on the pedals, working hard to keep the bike moving as Charlie sat perched on the wooden saddle, one hand around Aleck's waist and the other holding his hat on his head.

Aleck's eyes searched every hedgerow, peered around the shadowed corners. It wasn't safe to be out at night; everyone knew that. He took some comfort from the fact that Charlie didn't seem scared, but then by the sound of it, Charlie had nothing much left to lose.

"I've also been thinking about those Romans and their bikes." Charlie's voice took on a musical vibrato as they juddered down a steep hill and over some particularly rough ground. "Things tend to be invented in a strict sequence, the spear before the arrow, the steam engine before the petrol engine, and the car before the airplane. There's just an order to things, but sometimes, maybe things get invented out of order. How would the world be different if those Romans had invented the bicycle?"

"I don't think much would have changed," Aleck said. "Others would have copied them, and we'd all have bicycles and everything would even out."

"You may be right, my young friend, or maybe the Romans would have become too powerful and we'd still be living in ancient Rome."

"Praetor Jones thinks we still are." They both chuckled into an uneasy silence.

"You don't believe any of that Duster nonsense, do you, Charlie?"

"I doubt any of the Dusters are alive out there. I suspect they were all pulled apart, dismantled and examined. There's curiosity in that desert-mind. Why else would we still be alive? It wants to know us; it just doesn't know what 'us' is."

"I heard someone talking once when they thought I wasn't listening, and they said the desert is made of millions of tiny machines."

"You seem like a lad that's interested in the truth, Aleck."

"I am. I really am. One day all the old people will be gone and it'll be just me and Martha and a few others. . . . How are we going to survive if we don't know what happened?"

"Most folks nowadays don't like remembering history or discussing the truth. They hide from it, pretend that this is the way everything is supposed to be." Charlie let out a short, loud laugh that degenerated into a long, loud cough.

"You can tell me, Charlie, you really can." He felt the prickle of anticipation. Was he really going to learn something scary and new?

"I believe it's true, the desert is made of tiny machines, trillions of them and we made them years ago, a great big experiment and an even bigger mistake. It's almost a living thing, Aleck, a single mind, but a confused young mind, one with no mentor, no references, and no history. It lashes out, devouring. Playing, if you like, it's all the same, just destruction until there's nothing left. . . just us, a tiny bubble of something different and then comes the fear, the same fear we have suffered with for years: the fear of being totally alone, the only thing left alive. That's why it keeps us, Aleck, it watches, tries to learn, tries to understand, but is afraid to touch in case we go away and leave it all alone."

Aleck's head reeled with thoughts, shocking, terrifying, but so intriguing—a living thing out there watching them like God. . . but a childish, scared God.

"And that's where I believe I might be able to help."

"By riding out and dying?"

"It's worth a try, lad! Better than sitting around here in agony until I become another wisp. Maybe I can let it see into my mind, see something that's not full of fear and superstition, but something that's curious, that knows the past and where we all came from. I'll fill my head with images of humanity, of everything we ever did and loved to do. At the very least, I hope it sees me as something worth knowing, and realizes the cows are not the intellects around here." His chuckle turned into a long rolling cough, forcing them to stop while he recovered.

"Okay," said Aleck sadly, realizing he was not going to change Charlie's mind. "You can take my bike."

"No, you're young. You need your bike for legion patrol and visiting young ladies." Charlie slapped him playfully on the shoulder. "I'll pinch old Farthing's bike. He can barely ride it these days. It'll take a month for him to notice it's missing."

"Why do you even need a bike? Just walk out there, if that's the way you feel."

"There's a kind of resistance as you cross over. It stops the sand coming in, and at least some of our bees and bugs escaping. It slows you down as you pass through. The early Dusters tried walking out, and they got chopped and diced as if walking slowly into a mincing machine. Some tried to come back through in pieces and had to be thrown back. They screamed bloody murder, they did—horrible. The fastest thing we have is a bicycle, so it gets you in there and gets it over good and quick."

Aleck fell into thoughtful reverie as they approached old Farthing's dark house. He forced the tears back and considered not helping. He was fond of the old man and couldn't bear to see him go like this. In the end, he knew he had to help. Without a bike, the man would be forced to take that final journey on foot.

The Farthing house was as quiet as death and nearly as dark. Charlie rested while Aleck took off around the estate, looking for the bike. He stumbled over roots and old fence posts, seeing shadows and imaginary sand-monsters lurking around every corner. He eventually found a shed with a corroded padlock on the door. He followed the chain through the wooden securing loops and found some links that were so badly rusted he could snap them with his fingers.

Inside, he stood and let the trickle of moonlight filter in. The bike stood in the corner, no locks here, just coils of rope and knots that took a long time to pick through in the darkness.

As he wheeled the bike outside, he saw just how close to its own end the bike was. A frame so rusted it looked like a honeycomb, with wheels buckled into polygons by time and wear. The tires were leather straps coiled around the rims, and the crossbar was made of string and bone. Aleck wondered whether he had found the bike that proved his own theory wrong: was this an actual Roman bicycle?

He sat cautiously on the wood-block saddle, expecting the bike to collapse under his weight. It creaked and settled under him, then stabilized and miraculously held.

They headed back into town, Charlie following along on Aleck's bike, choking and wheezing as he went. Aleck looked up at the scrap of moon, wondering if it were made of tiny machines as well, or whether there was a lonely astronaut still orbiting the silent Earth, looking down, wondering where everyone had gone. Around him the Land felt dark and desolate, a little bubble of preserved life. What would it take to pop that bubble and expose them all to whatever lay outside?

The rattling of the bikes couldn't drown out the sound of Charlie's rasping breath as they trundled over Long Meadow and down into the Dell. "Let's go this way." Charlie suddenly veered off down a side lane instead of continuing straight back into Tattledale.

"But...that's toward the church....No, Charlie, the wisps... it's dark...."

"I thought you were in the market for some truths, lad?"

Aleck followed, but suddenly his legs felt heavy with dread. Church Hill seemed steeper and more dangerous than ever before.

They propped the bikes up by the stone porch and rounded

the side of the ancient building, passing by some of the oldest graves. Aleck stared at the great stone slabs and crosses that adorned them, but saw no wisps until they rounded the corner and stood looking out over the newer part of the cemetery.

"Charlie, no, please..." Aleck thought he was going to wet his pants, or faint. He felt blood pounding through his veins.

A few dozen wisps floated high above the graves, like ethereal kites bobbing in the breeze. They sparkled and shifted shape as they moved, sometimes winking out of view or burning brighter as they caught the light from the Moon or Venus that glowed low and green in the west.

Charlie lurched forward until he was directly under the wisps. They seemed to pause their delicate motion and began to drop slowly back down toward him. "Charlie..." Aleck stammered, trying to follow, but his legs wouldn't move.

"It's okay, lad. I come here all the time." Charlie reached out a finger and poked it through the body of a wisp. They began moving around him, clustering like slow-motion dust devils. Aleck came to Charlie's side, curiosity overcoming his fear. The wisps ignored him, seeming to focus their attention on Charlie.

"They like you," Aleck muttered, reaching out a hand. A wisp passed through his arm. He felt nothing, no heat or cold...no tingle of energy.

"They know there's a wisp inside of me, one that'll be ready to leave soon."

"But I have a soul too. Why don't they see me?"

"I'm sure you have a soul, lad, but you don't have a wisp. Only us old ones have those, but not anyone before the mid-twenty-first century. That's why the wisps are all over this side of the churchyard and not the older part."

Charlie eased himself onto a comfortable stone. Aleck sat beside him, and they watched the circling spectacle; maybe a hundred had gathered now. Aleck realized that they had no light of their own. The wisps just sparkled in the borrowed rays. "So what are they?"

"Before the desert came, nanotechnology—that's those tiny

machines again—was the new and scary thing. What's the first thing humans do with anything new they invent, Aleck?"

"Kill people, make war..."

"Smart lad, so the military had it first, and the whole world feared the end was coming, that we'd all be consumed into some gray goop as the tiny machines ate the planet."

"I guess they were kind of right, then?"

"Kind of. It didn't quite happen that way, though. The world was pretty stable by this time, no real big wars or terrorist outrages, so the new technology found its way into the medical field. People put these little things inside of them, clusters that formed into smart networks. There, they monitored and adjusted a body's DNA, metabolism... all sorts of useful stuff to make it live a long and healthy life."

"That's why I don't have a wisp inside of me!"

"Exactly. I'm afraid you were born after the desert came along. All of us old ones have these networks. That's why we've managed to last as long as we have."

"So the tiny machines keep you healthy?"

"They used to, but they age and need to connect to a master network for updates and tuneups. When all that went away, they started to lose their functionality. But the machines are pretty much immortal, and after we die, they live on, tiny little confused minds, hanging around without a purpose, latched on to the DNA of the corpses. They all come out after sunset; they rise up and touch and mingle, like a little social gathering, then they fall back into the earth and rest."

"Why after sunset?"

"Not sure... I suspect that they didn't do much other than watch during the daytime. Their real work started at night, while we slept, and the healing and rejuvenation all took place. Old habits die hard; with no bodies to fix, they just float around... looking."

Aleck suddenly felt the sadness. It came from each of the tiny, lost minds. "They're alive," he said quietly, reaching out to let one pass through his fingers again.

"Kind of. I guess they think, react...Some of them look bigger than others. I wonder if they find ways to merge. Maybe the bigger they get, the more complex and the more intelligent they grow."

"Until they are gigantic...like the desert?"

"Maybe."

"How do you know so much, Charlie?"

The old man shifted uneasily on the cold stone, sending the wisps fluttering up into a spiral around his head. "I worked for the company that made them. I was pretty low down in the ranks, just an observer really. Whenever they made a big software update, people like me were sent out to watch and monitor populations, make sure nothing funny went on during the changeover. It was just after a really big update that the desert came. Someone did a spectacular hack on the software, or something unthought-of just happened. I guess we'll never know the whole truth."

"Devilry!" The yell echoed out across the hills. Aleck jumped to his feet and Charlie rolled over backward and knocked his head on a grave stone.

From way across the hillside, Aleck could see a rectangular light. It shone from the window of the rectory where Father Haslop hung out the window, yelling. Aleck looked around and realized that a perfect ray of moonlight filtering down through a gap in the clouds now illuminated their guilty party—the man, the boy, and a thousand circling wisps.

"Devilry!" came the anguished cry again as Aleck tried to raise Charlie, but the old man just stared straight up. The wisps buzzed closer, as if poised to enter his head in one great swirling mass.

The rectory door flung open and Father Haslop raced across the moonlit hills, a bell clanging in his hand. "He's heading for the church...going to ring the big bell..." Charlie struggled awake, but was unable to sit. "Go save yourself, boy, or he's going to cause you all manner of trouble."

"But the bikes...the ride out...the truths?"

"I'll be okay, lad. What can they do to me now?" He winked, and Aleck found himself stumbling away through the gravestones. He looked back, feeling like the lowest of traitors, but Charlie waved him away and flopped back onto the dirt. Aleck watched the church door open. Oil lamps flickered on inside, and the main bell began its incessant, morbid clang.

In his mind, he saw Praetor Jones falling out of bed and donning his ridiculous helmet as the legion stumbled out from various doorways, grabbing their pikes and shields and teetering out on their bikes. Would they dare come into the churchyard at night? Would they risk seeing a wisp or having their souls drained?

He decided that they probably would. After all, didn't at least some of those old men know the truth about the world?

A light halo lit up the sky over Tattledale Town as everyone became abruptly wide awake. Aleck grabbed old Farthing's bike and ran it into a thick hedgerow, then retrieved his own and scooted it out and onto Church Hill. Halfway down, his rump managed to find the saddle and he was pedaling.... He prayed he wouldn't meet the legion on the way up the hill to the church.

What were you thinking, hanging out with that crazy old man in such a dangerous place? You're lucky you didn't lose your mind completely." Aleck's mother had cried a lot since the legion escorted him back home after he collided with them coming downhill. Some of the soldiers were over at Nurse Ellen's place receiving treatment for their cuts and bruises. Aleck had bowled them over like a bowling ball, sending many into the ditches and thorn bushes.

Aleck hung his head as his mother scolded. Praetor Jones and several trusted centurions hovered around the kitchen, as if ready to pounce or skewer him if he showed any signs of corruption.

Father Haslop sat at the same table, his face bright red and nose a deep shade of purple. Several mugs of strong tea had been required to sober him up, but his eyes held no drunken frivolity. They smoldered with fear and rage. "How do we know?" he asked the sky above him. "How do we know this young lad's soul has not been taken or corrupted into an instrument of the devil?"

"He's fine, just misguided and a little shaken." His mother suddenly came to his side, acting defensive. "It was that old man, dragging him out to the cemetery, polluting his young mind with fairy tales and ideas."

"In the old days we used a ducking stool and submerged—"

"No!" she yelled, silencing Haslop's slurred tirade. "No one is ducking or punishing my boy. If anything needs doing, then I'll decide what it is and I'll carry it out."

Aleck felt a twinge of relief. "Where's Charlie?"

His mother shouted, "I forbid you to ever go near that evil man again."

"He's in the jail," Haslop said. "We should have burned that evil warlock years ago."

"He's not evil—" Aleck stopped himself, sensing anything he said would only make things much worse for both of them.

"I saw his foul corruption last night." Father Haslop clutched his hands in prayer and closed his eyes. "Now all we can do is pray that he hasn't destroyed the soul of this innocent."

Aleck's mother dropped into the chair and grabbed his hands, pushing her face close to Aleck's. "Promise me you'll never see that man again. No one even knows where he came from. He just appeared here, out of thin air."

"What are you talking about?" Aleck pulled his hands away. Charlie's population-versus-stupidity graph was currently replotting itself across his mental blackboard.

Haslop snapped alert and stood up, arms waving wildly. "He just appeared here twenty years or more past. Said he had been hiding, but that's just not possible! Some devilry bought him here. I knew it all along, but no...the people accepted him, even forgot where he came from, until I saw him cavorting with the dead last night."

Rants and shouts broke out between the father and the legion troops. Aleck saw the graph rising up exponentially as the stupid level crashed on through Victorian to medieval...on its way to the dark ages. He found himself staring at his mother and she kept staring back. *No wisp inside of her,* he thought; *she's too young.* He felt quiet now, almost calm, as if the tiny bit of knowledge he did possess gave him some mystical power over those who chose to bury their heads in the sand.

He spoke quietly, so no one other than his mother heard him above the clamor. "I'm old enough to marry, old enough to fight, old enough to bleed and die defending the Land. I'm old enough to live on my own, to fend for myself, to breed...to multiply. So now I'm old enough to make my own decisions, to think for myself...and if I want to, I'll see whoever I damn well wish to see."

Her face registered no shock as Aleck stood, touched the backs of her hands, and walked out of the room.

Grog didn't taste quite as bad as Aleck thought it would. In fact, after several brimming mugs of the cloudy brown fluid, he was starting to feel quite good. His mood swung between seething anger and oddly flippant joviality as his attention struggled to stay focused on the people around him, rather than wander up and over the hills to the lonely jail where he knew Charlie was coughing up his last breaths.

His homesteading party was going rather better than he could have expected, although only handfuls of people had turned up. Most of the legion stayed away, and the children had been dragged off earlier by concerned parents who didn't want their offspring being tainted by his presence.

Father Haslop had reluctantly parted with a barrel of grog, as was the Tattledale tradition, although he remained noticeably absent himself. Aleck used the barrel as a seat on which he sat and watched proceedings. With very few drinkers present, he was rarely disturbed and felt really quite drunk.

The fires were lit around the perimeter at dusk. Supposedly

wisps were scared of fire and wouldn't come near the gathering. His house had been dressed in a large ribbon, and after a variety of unmemorable speeches the ribbon was cut, and food and drink appeared on the tables set inside the fiery ring. Music came from Tattledale's small folk band that strummed and banged on their patchy collection of homemade instruments. They were songs Aleck grew up with, old classics like *Tattledale Fair* and *Turnip Fields Forever*.

As the night darkened, the singing grew louder, and people danced and played games. The food really was good. Martha and her friends had prepared a spectacular beef stew with roasted potatoes and mushrooms, and there were honey biscuits and thick clotted cream for dessert.

Aleck led the dancing, but only when forced into the open by his mother. Martha showed him a few elementary steps to a basic jig, and after a few more mugs of grog he practiced the steps around the girls, much to their amusement, before returning to his barrel. He left Martha and her young friends clapping and skipping around the ring; fun to watch, it was an easy distraction despite his troubled mind.

His new house held no dread anymore. The wisps and ghosts he'd been brought up with were harmless fairy tales, and he quite looked forward to having a place of his own. Gifts of new furniture arrived throughout the evening. He was now the proud owner of four chairs, a table, a suspiciously generous-sized bed, and various gardening and cultivating tools that he had yet to investigate.

Three beehives arrived on a wagon and were unloaded around the rear of the house. Empty and silent, they sat awaiting the arrival of their first queens. More would come if he proved himself a competent beekeeper, something he still had huge doubts about, although his newfound fascination with tiny machines had raised new curiosity about hives and swarms and the way such things worked.

The fires flickered lower, and only a few people stayed around—only his real friends, the people who cared and mattered. He glanced across at Martha, seated at an empty table. Her mother and father sat off to the side, lost in their own conversation. Martha's eyes were downcast, sad, as if focused on something far, far away.

Her sadness suddenly touched him. She'd worked hard for this evening, and he'd hardly spoken to her. For the first time he really studied her, not as a child looking at another child, but as a friend, an adult ... as the future. She really was quite beautiful. In a world made of sand, somehow she was here for him, and he was probably the luckiest man in the world and didn't even know it.

Why so sad? What future did she see here? Her friends were all younger. They just wanted to play games, but she was a young woman, thinking ahead to a world that was poised on the edge of destruction, inside a bubble. There was only one man a few years younger than Aleck who was a possible suitor, the next two older men were married and living nearby in this new community. He and Martha were going to be together whether they wanted to or not.

With a sudden rush of emotion, Aleck lurched to his feet. No one seemed to notice, so he cleared his throat loudly. The small band stopped playing, and the singers went quiet. For a few seconds he hovered, suddenly a terrified little boy again. A lone cricket chirped from a nearby bush, as if urging him back into action.

"I have something to say," he blurted, surprised at the volume of his own voice in the chill night. "It's to Martha." He raised his mug toward her, but she couldn't seem to pull her eyes away from the fire. "I just want to say that...I really don't think..." the cricket chirped again, and he felt everyone taking a deep breath. "I really don't think that I've appreciated how much care and attention and...love... Martha has given to me. I'm sorry for that...so sorry. I promise to grow up.... I guess I've been lost, a bit confused really about ... things." He felt the collective wind of everyone breathing back out in mild relief. He also knew he should probably stop now before he said something

351

really stupid, but he blundered on. "Anyway, I promise to grow up and appreciate you more, Martha, and to become worthy of you, as much as I possibly can."

He dropped back onto the barrel, leaving a slop of grog hanging in the air where he had stood. It splashed down, soaking his crotch, and he sat rigid in the painful silence as everyone leached whatever meaning they could from his words.

The applause came and grew. He saw Martha's face lift and light up in the firelight. She smiled and mouthed a "thank you" at him.

They danced some more. He forgot the grog and food and just enjoyed being with her. The music became loud and the fires were restoked to see them late into the night.

People tired and drifted away. He waved them off, and Mother smiled proudly as she left him to his first night in his new house. He went around dousing the remaining fires, rolled the still half-full barrel of grog into the house, and positioned it strategically next to the rocking chair.

He sat and gathered his breath for a moment. The night was still young, and so was he. With no fear of the darkness and a fierce and newly acquired sense of independence, he knew one more thing needed doing tonight.... There were probably several, but one thing in particular just had to be done.

He spent only a short time watching the wisps wafting over the cemetery. He hid in one of the surrounding gorse bushes until the lights went out in the rectory and he felt sure no prying eyes watched.

He recovered Farthing's bike from the hedge and headed away, riding his own singlehanded and guiding the other gnarled machine alongside.

The legion's prison building was an old barn, reinforced with heavy timbers from trees that no longer existed in the Land. There were three individual cells. Aleck could never remember more than one ever being occupied, and that had been a long time ago. The end cell was used as the guardhouse. He heard snoring coming from inside as he propped the bikes, pointing downhill for a hasty getaway, and tiptoed up to the door.

His luck was in tonight since Mills Gilbert was one of the oldest legionaries and one of the deafest. He lay almost flat across his chair, feet on the desk, mouth wide open. His door was barred on the inside, but Aleck propped a stout log from the wood pile under the latch to ensure that he wouldn't escape anytime soon.

He tiptoed along the row of cells. "That you, Charlie?" he whispered through each door.

"Aleck? You'll get yourself in all sorts of trouble, lad." Charlie sounded weak, his voice a rasping reed that took all his effort to play.

"Good!" he replied, rather too loudly. He slapped his hand across his mouth, realizing that the grog was still affecting the way he functioned. "I'm getting you out of here, and that's that!"

The cell door had been secured with ropes wound around a large oak crossbeam. He fiddled and picked at the knots, but stronger hands than his had tied them securely. He heard a snort from the guardhouse and the sound of someone rearranging their body in a creaking old chair. Aleck froze in silence until the snoring began again.

"You still there, lad?" Charlie whispered.

"Never was any good with knots." The ropes finally gave, and with blistered fingers, Aleck pulled the coils off and stood back triumphantly to examine the crossbeam.

In seeming slow motion, the hunk of wood dropped from its mounts and crashed onto the ground. "Shit!" he muttered.

"Who's there?" Mills snapped awake in the guardhouse.

Charlie's cell door creaked open and a fetid waft of bad air came out. Charlie lay on the floor; he had fallen off his straw bed while trying to stand and now struggled to find his feet. Aleck heard Mills jiggling his guard door, harder and harder as the fact that he was blocked in started to dawn on him. "I'm coming out there," he yelled. "I'm armed...and dangerous!"

Aleck hauled Charlie to his feet, and the pair limped out and down the hill to the waiting bikes. Behind them he could hear Mills bashing something heavy into the door. The ancient hinges wouldn't hold out much longer.

"You got to ride, Charlie."

"Not sure I can, lad," he wheezed.

"You can do it. I have something special for you." Aleck gave him a small bottle of grog he'd tapped off of the barrel, and Charlie guzzled it down, nearly choking.

"Woah! Father Haslop'll be mad at you for stealing this, even though it's hardly the good stuff."

"He gave it to me for my homesteading party." Charlie straddled his bike as the door burst open behind them. He saw Mills silhouetted in the doorway, light from his fireplace radiated out around him like anger. His pants seemed to have dropped down below his knees, but he wore his metal helmet and brandished his spear. "Hey, you! Stop!" He surged forward, catching his foot on the door jamb and falling flat on his face.

Aleck gave Charlie a push and the old man began pedaling, the bike taking on a frightening zigzag motion as he fought for balance. Aleck hopped into his saddle and pulled alongside. The pair collided but managed to grasp each other rather than fall over, and together they headed off down the hill as a single stable four-wheeled unit.

It was an exhilarating ride. Aleck had heard stories of things called roller coasters. He imagined that they felt much like this ride. Careening downward, with little control, they navigated the dark lanes by instinct and impact, occasionally parting and then crashing back together and rejoining into a single force. Only once did they fall completely after a midroad collision sent them off to either side and into the bushes. It took a while to pick their way out of the thorns. By the time they had resaddled and creaked off across the meadow, the guardhouse bell was tolling, and Aleck guessed the legion was forming up in Tattledale Square, getting ready to head up to the prison.

They rolled into Aleck's new house, taking the bikes inside

with them and securing the door. "They'll come here looking," Charlie warned.

"I know, just not yet. I want you to be my special guest, the first guest in my new abode." He eased Charlie into the rocking chair and found his largest mug. "Here, drink." They clashed glasses in a toast and Charlie's pain seemed to ease as he settled back. The chair's gentle rocking motion sounded like an old clock ticking away the final moments of a life.

"Time for one more truth, Charlie?"

"Anything you want, my lad." Charlie raised the mug high.

"Father Haslop told me you came from somewhere else... that you just appeared here. I guess they are just being real stupid... right?"

Charlie's brow took on extra wrinkles as he internally debated exactly what he should tell. "Well, in truth... I used to live somewhere else, somewhere kind of like the Land, but quite a bit smaller."

"There are other places like this out there!" Aleck jumped to his feet in excitement.

"There was... one, at least. I was the youngest there, a young man living in a village full of the old. Everyone died, leaving me alone. Don't remember everything... just that your mind kind of goes away when you're that lonely... that frightened. I lived like that for years... just me and a handful of wisps and pigs... a few chickens, until I noticed the Land was shrinking. It had never been that big, not as big as here, but it seemed to close in around me, eating up the buildings, pastures, animals. Soon it was just my house, then the walls went away, and I was just sitting on my chair on a little patch of tile, surrounded by desert and dust devils."

He paused to refill his mug. Aleck didn't speak, but just stood in openmouthed amazement.

"That day, I just stood up and walked. Didn't expect to survive as I crossed the boundary... maybe I didn't. I always figured I was some kind of ghost, wisp or dust devil that just thought I was a human, but I walked away, just me and the sand for days on end. The dust devils seemed to guide me; I felt them nudging, corralling me along as if they had somewhere for me to be and I wasn't in any position to object....I just walked.

"Then, one day I saw the lights of Tattledale, like a fiery dome in the sky, and heard the church bell ringing. It sounds dull and muffled when you're on the outside, I do remember that much. I was so tired, thirsty, hungry beyond anything you can imagine. I stumbled across the barrier and all the sights, smells and sounds of life just overwhelmed me. I walked a while and fell into a hedgerow. I survived there for some time, living off berries and ditchwater, until I ventured out into town and stole some food from others."

"So they caught you eventually."

"Eventually. Haslop never liked me right from the start. He wanted to burn me, like in the old days—said I was a warlock when I told him I came from outside. Luckily others were not so dumb, and after a long trial and plenty of time locked up in those cells, I was let go. I took over old Charlie's potato patch that was left empty after he vanished a year or so earlier."

"There was another Charlie Potato?"

"The one and only, the original. I never really remembered who I had been. Something was lost from my mind when I crossed the barrier and left my town, so I took on his identity and became someone new."

"How did you survive crossing the perimeter?"

"Don't know. I've lost a few fingertips testing to see if I could cross back to the desert. Seems whatever watched over that town decided to let me go. I like to think there is something different about me; maybe the software in my wisp is special, as I worked for the company that made it, or maybe it just wanted me to come here and check you all out. Perhaps I'm some kind of snooping device to record what happens in here, and I'm expected to check back into the collective sometime."

"Do..." Aleck's jaw began to quiver. "Do you think you'll survive riding out?"

"I doubt it." He waved his stubby fingers in the air. "My

fingertips never survived the trip. Bodies probably don't survive, but the wisps might...kind of a homecoming for them. I've made a point of learning everything I can about you all, of filling my head with positive thoughts and ideas, so if they take a look inside my head, just maybe they'll find something useful, something that can help you all out. There are problems with the Land, you know, problems others don't talk about."

"What problems?"

"Water. You don't really think those tiny desert clouds keep our wells full, do you? We're lucky the Land is over a large underground reservoir. The boundary is actually a spherical bubble, so it goes under the reservoir, leaving it intact for us to drink, but it's running low; maybe a few more decades of water left."

"I didn't know that—"

"No, people try not to think about it. What can they do? Everything that evaporates goes up and out across the boundary. Then there's the loss of nutrients, of living diversity...of people. How many people are there going to be in your coming generation, Aleck? You and Martha better get real busy, or you'll be very lonely."

Aleck blushed. "Now you're really scaring me."

"Sorry, but it's important that you know the things that you face, lad. Knowledge is power. It's passed on like those bike chains, but you have to keep using them, fixing them, finding new ways to survive; otherwise they just turn to rust and everything is lost."

The loud bell from the church began tolling. They sat and listened to it for a few seconds, as if it meant nothing. "Guess the word's out." Charlie eased to his feet. "They'll come here next. I should go hide somewhere where a bunch of superstitious old men will never dare to look."

"Take some more grog." Aleck reached for his mug.

"I'm grogged well enough, lad. In truth, speaking with you has been the best pain relief I could have wished for."

They embraced in the firelight before dousing the flames

and pushing the bikes outside. "You watch out for that Father Haslop, lad, he's a dangerous man."

"He just seems kind of angry all the time, not really dangerous."

"Let me tell you one last thing about wisps. They're complex networks that were designed to live inside a human and monitor and control their biology. That meant they watched and listened and felt the world through our senses. They remembered the things we did, and what we became. There's a trace of the actual person inside each wisp, and sometimes they can connect with each other or even with you. You can learn a lot from just sitting and letting the wisps come to you, lad. There's much wisdom in those little minds. I was in that ditch a long time when I first came here, that ditch over by Lowdown."

Aleck felt that old familiar shiver of fear at the name Lowdown and its single, haunting wisp.

"Of course, the most painful, poignant memories are the ones most likely to get encoded in the wisp and passed along to anyone around long enough to listen. I learned a lot from the original Charlie about potato farming and the simple life he'd led, but the most vivid memory was of being beaten nearly to death by a red-faced, drunken Father Haslop for trying to steal some of his grog. I almost made it home in a terrible state...but the ditch seemed a comfortable place to rest. The real Charlie is still there, but a lot of his memories are in here." He tapped his temple with a stubby, half-length finger.

"Father Haslop is a murderer?" Aleck could hardly believe the words leaving his mouth.

"Bones are still down there in the mud if anyone cares to look."

A rattling calamity crashed down the lane toward the group of dark houses as Praetor Jones and his legion hustled along in a torchlit procession. Aleck could hear the shouts of orders and clanks of armor and shields suddenly dangerously close by.

"Looks like we'll be going the other way," Charlie chuckled as their pedals turned and the ancient bikes creaked off onto the lane.

They watched the sunrise from Pilot Hill, its splendid array of colors lighting up the sky and the tops of distant dunes.

"It looks like bacon," Charlie said, gazing up at the streaks of color, licking his lips.

"Bacon? But it's got blue bits in it."

"Old Trotter's bacon has blue bits in it."

"Yuck!" Aleck said, although at that moment his stomach would have been happy with any sort of bacon, with or without blue bits.

"Time to go," said Charlie, creaking to his feet. "People will be heading for church this way soon. Best not scare them any more than I have to." He picked old Farthing's bike out of the hedge and gave it a final inspection before easing himself onto its saddle.

Aleck sensed that this was the moment for a great speech, an inspiring outpour of emotion drenched with hope and meaning, but no words came and instead he found himself silently repeating his mother's words, "Legionaries don't cry. Legionaries don't cry...."

"Well...goodbye then, look after the Land won't you, and..." Charlie gave Aleck a huge slap across the back, sending him staggering into a juniper bush. "Be good to that nice young lady of yours."

As Aleck picked himself out of the bush, he saw Charlie teetering down the dirt road on his way to oblivion. For a few seconds the bike and the road seemed to resist, the wheels spun in the grit, and he fought for balance, but gravity came to his aid, and Charlie began to roll down and along toward the sunrise.

"Goodbye, Charlie..." Aleck was up and running, almost catching him, but Charlie's legs started working the pedals. He hit a smooth patch of road and lurched forward and careened off downhill.

Charlie glanced back, waving, his face alive and smiling. "Goodbye, lad."

Aleck kept running, but Charlie was bouncing along so fast

that his legs couldn't keep up with the pedals. A second before the perimeter, he took his hands off the handlebars and flung his arms over his head as if to greet the rising sun.

Aleck covered his eyes, but kept running and stumbling downward.

There was no sound, no cry of pain...nothing...followed by silence.

When Aleck looked up, the desert was empty, still, with a puff of dust where some minor disturbance had occurred.

He stopped at the edge and looked outward, hoping for a sign, anything. The dust settled, and through the utter desert silence, he heard the soft music, the sound of the breeze playing the dunes like an Aeolian church organ.

In the sand, he saw an object; it looked like a small black snake, just curled there on top of a miniature dune. He strained for a closer look, his toes creeping nearer the fatal edge, but dust wafted up and obscured his view. He watched as the sand twisted and circled into a small vortex that revved up and darted toward him.

He backed away, trembling with fear as a dust devil crossed the perimeter. Aleck's eyes widened as it coalesced into what looked like a stubby human figure.

The creature stumbled on, its stout cylindrical arms waving as it tried to balance on two legs, seemingly for the first time. The legs grew longer as it gained in confidence, taking on more human proportions. Bumps and pits appeared on its face in a childish parody of human features.

"Charlie?" Mastering his fear, Aleck stood his ground and let the figure approach until they stood face to face. He searched the sandy features for any sign that Charlie Potato was somehow still in there. The face rolled and swam as it mimicked his expressions: fear, concern, wonder, and then a smile.

The sand creature reached out a hand, and Aleck realized it was holding the snakelike object from the desert. It was Charlie's bicycle chain.

"Thank you," Aleck said, taking the gift.

The desert music grew suddenly louder, as if the barrier

between the Land and the sand had vanished. The creature turned and walked back onto dunes, dust billowing around its feet. Suddenly it was a dust devil again, spinning away, parting the sand in a wide, shallow furrow across the plain. The new pathway solidified, the grains of sand melting together into a solid sheet—a road.

It joined onto the truncated Pilot Hill road, snaking out through the desert like a memory of some long-forgotten highway.

Aleck watched as the sand road curved away over the horizon, cutting a path between distant dunes. He found himself wandering after the dust devil, reaching out, wanting to know more. Where did this road go? Was there another town out there? A new water supply?

With a shock, he realized he'd stepped over the perimeter. He winced, waiting for the pain of destruction, but nothing happened, just the flinty air rustling his hair.

Alone, he stood, maybe the only living thing in the entire desert. As he turned back, he saw the Land as never before—from the outside, and even though only a few feet away, it looked so different, so precious and vulnerable.

He turned and walked a few steps along the road, the new road to a new understanding. Many problems needed overcoming, but maybe this strange intelligence was talking to them now, or at least understanding what they were. A great adventure lay ahead, stretched out before him, right now.

No...not just yet.

He turned back and stepped into the land he knew so well. Ahead and back over the hill, he had a lot of explaining to do, but after that there was a new home, and a new life, and maybe...even a wife and family. Now that the world felt huge and full of possibilities, he needed that security, that anchor—a base to work from. Before, he had been confined, caged with everything predetermined, but those boundaries had fallen, and now, everything just seemed right.

He turned, smiled at the sun, and breathed in the freedom, "See you soon, Charlie."

He headed back toward home, and with the greasy chain swung rakishly over his shoulder, he began to ascend Pilot Hill. Soon, Father Haslop would open the church and the pushbike legion of Tattledale Town would gather for their morning patrol. A new life lay ahead for them all, and the unbroken chain of knowledge would pass down through the ages, driving the growth of civilization ever forward over bumpy, frosted roads.

Memories Bleed Beneath the Mask

written by

Randy Henderson

illustrated by

VANESSA GOLITZ

ABOUT THE AUTHOR

Randy Henderson was born in the states of wonder, awe, and Washington. He quickly learned the joy of escaping to fantasy worlds, from Middle-earth to Earthsea, from Amber to Pern, from Valdemar to Midkemia. He took some amazing vacation photos of these places (in his head) that he shares with all the friends he made (also in his head). His head has become rather cluttered.

After toying with such impressive creative pursuits as latch hook and recording really clever answering machine messages, Randy realized that what he wanted most was to write. It was not as easy as it looked.

Many years of dabbling followed, during which Randy studied social sciences and worked at a variety of jobs, such as weight-loss counselor, Alaska factory-boat worker, and writing tax sob stories for CPA clients (his first paid fiction), before he finally settled into IT.

Randy decided to get serious about his writing, and attended the Clarion West writing workshop where he learned things... dark and mystical things about the art of fiction, things best left unspoken. Ask him, and he'll gladly speak of them.

Randy then wrote new stories—faster stories, stronger stories—and began to publish in wondrous places such as Realms of Fantasy *and* Escape Pod *before winning Writers of the Future.*

He has since sold additional tales to editors with excellent taste in fiction, as well as a humorous urban fantasy series to Tor. The first novel in his series Finn Fancy Necromancy *is forthcoming in February, 2015.*

363

ABOUT THE ILLUSTRATOR

Vanessa Golitz was born in 1988 in a small town in Germany. As a child she sometimes watched her mother draw and paint with pastels and watercolor as a hobby and continued to draw and paint into her teens.

At age 16 she received her first graphics tablet and started to learn digital painting in Photoshop Elements. Some personal issues during that time, including bullying and the divorce of her parents, led her to give up painting a few times, but she eventually went back to it.

After graduating from high school, she considered attending art school, but as there are no art schools in Germany that teach the classical art fundamentals needed for mastering realism, she decided to enroll in English and Spanish courses at the university instead, since she has always enjoyed learning languages.

At the same time it became clear to Vanessa that the market for fantastical realism and fairy tale illustration is a very small niche, where only a handful of artists make a living. (Most do not, and the pay doesn't even come close to the equivalent of minimum wage.)

She struggled with personal problems and dropped out of university, working small jobs, and today holds a steady day job while working on her painting skills in her spare time.

She plans to soon make a portfolio website for her work. Her goal is to become a better artist and to reach a skill level like that of her favorite artists, such as Donato Giancola, Cynthia Sheppard, Boris Vallejo, Julie Bell, James Gurney and others.

Memories Bleed Beneath the Mask

Grandfather lay in his giant bed like a rescued baby bird tucked into a shoebox full of towels, his frail body swallowed by blankets and pillows. Machines of brass, glass and steel whirred and clicked and chimed, and yellowed tubes and braids of wire ran from them to Grandfather's nose and arm. Mother stopped me just inside the bedroom door, and leaned down to whisper, "Say your goodbyes, Trystan, and remember what we practiced. You're twelve, and need to be a man now. Your future depends on this." She nudged me forward as my aunts, uncles and cousins all watched from the edges of the room and whispered among themselves.

Grandfather's bedroom, like every room in his mansion, was more than twice the size of any room in our apartment and reflected the wealth he'd earned as a Supreme Justice of Ameriga. But it smelled of dust, urine and bleach. Like the entire mansion, it had the stuffy feel of a room too long closed up. Once Grandfather had become a justice, I doubted he'd ever set foot outside the mansion, except to tour the Federation courthouses in a Ministry airship. There were too many citizens who'd do a justice harm if given the chance.

I eased close to the bed. A nurse stood near the head, her attention focused on the machines.

"Come...closer," Grandfather said in a wet, rattling whisper. His skeletal hand twitched in a beckoning motion, causing the tube running from it to snake across the silk sheets. My eyes filled with tears as I leaned forward, the mattress top pressed against my stomach. I rested my hand on his. I had few memories of Grandfather, but every one of them was good, and in all of them he was smiling and full of life. Now, he'd become a shrunken, fevered ghost of that man.

"Ask," he said.

I glanced back at my mother. She had coached me on what to say, and how to say it: about my father and his unexpected death, how I'd not inherited his memories like my cousins would inherit their parents', how my father had always said that I reminded him of Grandfather. And that my father's dream had been to follow in Grandfather's footsteps, and for me to follow them both.

I was not to mention that she'd bought my Core Competencies illegally off junkies who'd traded their memories cheaply for drug money. Mother worked hard to keep us constantly one step ahead of being Plebs, but we couldn't afford the sanctioned memory auctions.

I turned back to Grandfather. "Father always—" My voice choked. In Grandfather's face I could see the face of my father, stiff and waxy in his casket. "I want to remember my father, when he was alive," I said. "I want to remember what he was like growing up. And I want to remember that family trip to your lake cabin when I was a little kid." That was one of the last happy moments I'd had with my father. And the last time I'd seen most of the people in the room with me now.

I heard the sharp intake of breath through my mother's nose, and the chuckle of one of my cousins followed by a harsh whispered admonition. I felt sure the reprimand was more from fear of looking bad than any concern for my feelings.

Grandfather squinted, and focused on me. "What do you want to do with your life, Trystan?"

I could feel Mother's intense stare on the back of my head. I knew what I wanted to say, but it was not what Mother would want. I looked back at her.

How many hours had she worked on her hair this morning, crying and yelling at the mirror? How many different dresses had she tried on at how many stores before finally picking that one? How many times had she fretted over her makeup on the way here, the makeup that failed to hide the exhaustion lining her face and shading her eyes?

She'd put everything into raising and educating me since Father died, without any help from Grandfather. Now was the moment that all the work and sacrifice had been for—as she'd reminded me a thousand times.

I turned back, and hunched my shoulders as I said, "I want to be a justice, like you. And I know it's what Father wanted too, before he died, even though I didn't get his memories."

Grandfather sighed, and closed his eyes. After a second of complete stillness, the relatives started edging close to the bed. "Grandfather?" one cousin asked. Grandfather didn't stir. "Oh God," another cousin whispered loudly. "If he's dead, does that mean—"

"I'm not dead," Grandfather said. "I'm just thinking." The words launched him into a coughing fit. My two aunts swooped in and fretted over him, offering tissues and bottled drinks.

"Enough," Grandfather rasped, waving them away. "Everyone, please leave. I want to be alone for a minute."

I started to turn, but Grandfather clutched my hand. "No, you stay."

That caused a ripple of confusion and anxious glances among the rest of the family.

"Why does he get to stay?" a sour-faced cousin whined.

"Grandfather," Auntie Louise said, "I really should stay, in case you need anything."

"I'm the one with the nursing experience," Auntie Eleanor said. "You go ahead, I'll stay with him."

"You have great-grandmother's nursing experience, Eleanor. I don't think he needs leeches."

"Leave! Now!" Grandfather said, and began coughing again. My mother stepped up and put her hands on my shoulders as everyone fled the room. Grandfather shook his head weakly at my mother. "No. You too."

"But—okay." She squeezed my shoulders. "Remember your manners, Trys." And by manners, I knew she meant the reason we'd come. My mother left the room, closing the door behind her.

"Now," Grandfather said, and his words rushed between wet breaths. "What do you want to be? And tell the truth."

I looked at the door. Even if Mother pressed her ear to that thick wood, she wouldn't be able to hear me, I hoped. "I...I want to be a mind healer."

"A mind healer? Why?"

"Because then I could help people."

"And you don't think a justice helps people?"

"I guess. Yes, sir."

Grandfather smiled, yet he looked sad. "You're so like your father, so like Daniel." He looked to the chessboard on his bedside table, and his eyes appeared unfocused for several heartbeats. He coughed, and said, "Speak honestly, Trystan, it's okay. You guess we help, but?"

"But...a justice punishes people to help them, because they did something wrong. And there's a lot of people who wouldn't even have to be punished if you helped them, so they didn't ever have to do something wrong in the first place."

"Didn't *have* to do something wrong? People have a choice, you know, Trystan."

"Sometimes." I picked nervously at the edge of the wool blanket hanging over the bed. "But...sometimes, doing something wrong is...not the right choice, maybe, but the best choice. Or better than anything else. And sometimes, it is the wrong choice, but it's—they just don't feel like they have any other choices, or don't really believe any exist."

Grandfather's eyes narrowed. "You're how old, Trystan?"

"Twelve, sir."

"And you didn't receive your father's memories?"

"No, sir."

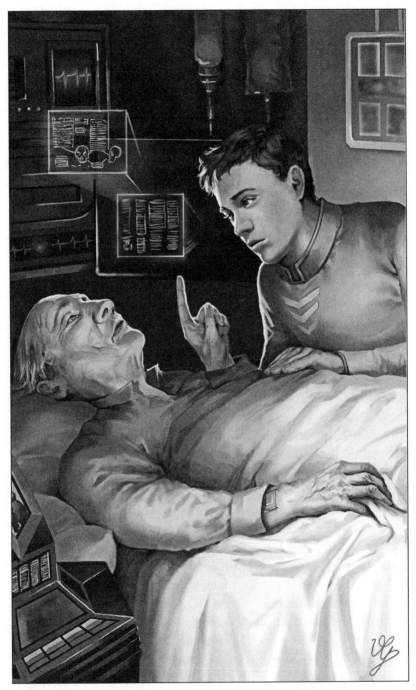

VANESSA GOLITZ

"Hmm." Grandfather closed his eyes and breathed deep rattling breaths for a minute before saying, "Those are strange thoughts to be hearing from anyone these days, but particularly a twelve-year-old. Especially when you talk as though you know these things from experience."

I opened my mouth to give an excuse, and realized it was too late. I'd said too much, and he knew I had tainted memories.

If I'd gotten my Cores from sanctioned donors, then the memory bleed—the connections and context needed for the other person's memory to be cohesive and make sense in my brain—would have still been there, but controlled, minimized, and sterilized. Instead, I'd gotten raw dumps of memory clusters from people for whom the important bits of knowledge I needed were interwoven with personal experiences and feelings that, given the nature of the donors, were often unpleasant. Memory Mike, the guy who'd done most of my transfers, had tried to convince me that this was a good thing, because I was getting "life lessons" in addition to the Core Competencies.

But Grandfather, whose job had been to put men like Memory Mike away for a long time, would not see any upside to me having illegal memories.

"Mother says I'm mature for my age."

"I see. And what does that maturity tell you we should do differently then?"

"I—I guess I don't know. If I was a mind healer, maybe I'd know what to do, though. I mean, that's part of being a mind healer, knowing how to help people, right?"

Grandfather chuckled, which sent him into a fit of coughing that grew loud and forceful. The nurse and family rushed back into the room. They were joined by Grandfather's personal lawspeaker, a woman in a black suit with a bright orange and scarlet flower pinned to her chest. Auntie Eleanor grabbed me by the shoulders and pushed me toward my mother. "I knew I shouldn't have left you in here alone. Out! Now!"

"Actually, everyone back out, please," the nurse said.

"I'm not going anywhere," Auntie Louise said.

"And unlike her, I can actually help," Auntie Eleanor said. "You heard the nurse," she said to the rest of the crowd. "Everyone out."

We all shuffled out of the room as Grandfather's coughs eased into gasping breaths. The lawspeaker closed the door behind us.

The room outside the bedroom was part library, part den, and filled with souvenirs—flintlock pistols and rifles, a display case full of coins from pre-Federation Ameriga, the bicentennial flag, a collection of law books used by famous lawspeakers and justices of the past, a marble chessboard covered in fallen pieces, and a handful of clockwork curiosities shaped like animals and birds. Most of the items were decades old at least and blanketed in a fine layer of dust.

A bald man in a black suit sat waiting in a chair in the corner, a large trunk on rollers sitting beside him. Mother spoke to him, and though I couldn't make out her words, she was trying to work her charms on him judging by her tone and sweeping gestures. But he just stared ahead silent and stoic. He shifted in his seat, and a silver infinity symbol flashed on his lapel. A memory doctor.

I looked back at the door to the bedroom, and my eyes burned with fresh tears. Why had Grandfather waited so long to give up his memories? He should have transferred his law memories to Uncle Blaine or Uncle Tagg years ago, should have kept his wealth and other memories and lived a happy retirement. If he had, he might not be dying now, worked to death, surrounded by these greedy, selfish people.

Or even if he'd become a clean slater years ago, given my uncles everything and they'd refused their obligation to care for him after, he couldn't have feared the life of cheap food, inadequate nursing, and mindless labor most found in a public retireage. He would have had his choice of the best Federal Retirement Communities in the nation. He could have finished his life as he started, a happy child, free from obligations except to learn and play.

I suddenly remembered him laughing like a child when I splashed him in the lake. Him and Father both.

I turned away from the door before the threat of tears turned to actual crying.

"But I'm the one he bought it for," Uncle Tagg said, drawing my attention. He and Uncle Blaine stood beside a small clockwork statue of Lady Justice, a blindfolded woman wielding a sword and balance scales. Uncle Tagg flicked one of the dangling scales with a finger. "I played with it whenever I visited. I'm sure he'd want me to have it."

"He bought it as a symbol of his job," Blaine said. "I'm sure when he passes his law knowledge to me, he'd want me to have the symbols of his office as well."

And I was sure that their argument had absolutely nothing to do with Lady Justice's skin being made of real gold.

Mother approached, a questioning eyebrow raised, but Cousin Sour Face rushed up and loomed over me first. "What did he say? Did he gift you any memories?"

Uncle Tagg glanced over from his argument. "Why would he get anything? He barely qualifies to be called family."

Mother's face flushed, and her hands gripped the sides of her dress. "If being an ass is what it takes to qualify, then maybe not. But he's your nephew, and he has as much right to his grandfather's memories as anyone here."

"He can have whatever he wants," Uncle Blaine said, "after Father's gifted me and Tagg, and our sons. And you should watch how you talk to your betters."

My jaw clenched. I'd felt out of place since the minute we'd arrived, but I knew how to deal with bullies at least. I took a step toward Uncle Blaine—

The door opened, and everyone fell silent. Grandfather's lawspeaker stepped out. The aunties were still at Grandfather's bedside, talking to him. Though I couldn't make out what they said, their voices had a hysterical edge to them.

"Justice Blakely is ready to bequeath his memories," the lawspeaker said. The memory doc stood, and wheeled his trunk into the bedroom.

Uncle Blaine also strode toward the door, but the lawspeaker raised a hand. "He has granted Trystan Blakely first request. Trystan, please come with me."

My mother burst into tears. I looked up surprised, but she was smiling, practically giggling. She nudged me forward. "Go. Go!"

"What? No!" Blaine stepped up to the lawspeaker. He glanced past the woman at Grandfather, and lowered his voice. "I want...I want a competency review. He can't just—"

"Denied," the lawspeaker said. "Justice Blakely is showing no signs of dementia or rapid memory loss. Now, Trystan, if you will please—"

"I protest on religious grounds then," Uncle Tagg said, moving to stand beside his brother.

The lawspeaker shook her head. "Denied. Religious exemption applies only if the memory donor is unable to communicate, and has no living will. Your father has made clear that he approves of the memory transfer. And, may I point out, a religious exemption would prevent you from receiving his memories as well."

Uncle Tagg blushed, and took a step between me and the lawspeaker. "I don't know how a woman was made lawspeaker. But I'm not going to take—"

Uncle Blaine put a hand on his shoulder. "Tagg! There's nothing we can do. Yet." He glared at me.

I understood perfectly well what he meant by "yet." As soon as Grandfather passed, they would appeal and try to get the memories pulled from me. If that failed, I might find myself kidnapped and hauled to some back-alley mem doc. They could claim afterward that I'd given them the memories voluntarily— after all, I wouldn't remember. Possession is everything when it comes to memory.

"Trystan," the lawspeaker said, showing no reaction to Uncle Tagg's outburst, and motioned me forward again. I edged past my uncles and followed her back into the dark and musty bedroom. She waved the aunties toward the door. "Ladies, if you will please excuse us?"

From my aunties' pale expressions, you would've thought the lawspeaker had announced a prison sentence. I suppose if they thought their family might end up in a pleb neighborhood, it wasn't much different, from their perspective.

The servant closed the door behind my aunties, and the lawspeaker guided me to the head of the bed, to stand beside the memory doc.

Grandfather rested with his eyes closed.

"Grandfather?" I whispered.

He opened his eyes, and after a second they focused on me. "Trystan. I'm about to grant you my memories of the law. Do you understand what that means?"

I nodded, and glanced at the memory doc as the familiar fluttery feeling swelled in my stomach and chest. I would not be the same person in a few minutes. Who knew how Grandfather's memories would change me, change how I felt, how I acted, what I liked or feared, what I believed was right or wrong. I used to have a dog, Max. I loved him. Then I got dumped a memory of being attacked by a dog as a young child, and we had to get rid of Max because I would break down crying whenever he got close.

But that wasn't what Grandfather was asking.

"It means I'll be a lawspeaker," I said. "And maybe a justice someday."

Grandfather's head wobbled back and forth on his too-thin neck. "Not a justice. They'll never allow it with your past."

"Then why me? Why not Uncle Blaine?" The words burst from me, and I snapped my mouth shut. Mother would be furious if she learned what I'd said. "It's just—I don't even want to be a lawspeaker."

"It is for the same reason I never sent your mother money. And I hope you'll forgive me for both decisions."

"I don't understand."

"Not yet. But you will. And you'll have twelve years before you're of age, free to do as you wish for most of that time. Think of that."

Twelve more years. I'd expected to be assigned a labor post next year, but they didn't assign decision posts until twenty-five, when the brain was fully developed.

"And I shall grant your wish," Grandfather said. "You'll receive all my memories of your father."

Tears welled in my eyes, and I rubbed at them roughly with my wrist. "Thank you."

"Are you ready then?" Grandfather asked.

I nodded. The lawspeaker handed me a document, and I signed. The memory doc opened his roller trunk, revealing a memory box, the design virtually unchanged since Newton and Hartley created the first one. Memory Mike often ranted about that, said the Elites kept the design from changing because their power depended on their control of knowledge, on keeping everyone in their place.

I was strapped into a chair. Both Grandfather and I had our heads immobilized, and memnets placed on them. Then they pumped in the drugs, and I fell asleep.

Mr. Blakely?"

I opened my eyes. I lay in one of Grandfather's guest beds. Mother sat in a bedside chair. The lawspeaker—Jennie, her name floated to the surface—stood patiently awaiting my response.

"Yes."

"Please state your full name."

I pushed myself up into a sitting position. "Trystan Xavier Blakely."

Jennie nodded, and commenced with a series of questions about the current year, and my own past, questions prepared by me to make sure my own memories weren't lost in the transfer. Full memory overwrites were illegal, but that didn't mean that there weren't people rich or ruthless enough out there to attempt immortality, who believed they deserved to live more than the next person.

I must have passed all of the questions, because Jennie nodded, and said, "That's good. Now, please open this." She handed me a small wooden box.

I took it, resting my hands on the polished surface, and looked at Mother. "Grandfather, is he—" I couldn't finish the question.

Mother leaned forward and placed her hand over mine. "He passed in the night."

My eyes teared up, though I didn't know why. Grandfather would not have been afraid. With so many of his memories gone, he probably didn't even know he was dying, or what death was.

Would he remember me in the afterlife without his memories? Would he recognize Father when they met? I felt a sudden pang of guilt. I should have thought to refuse at least some memories of Father.

"Trys, he left you everything," Mother said, her hand trembling. Tears welled in her eyes as well. "This house is yours now."

Jennie nodded. "It's true. Now—"

A shriek from outside. Startled, I almost flung the box from my lap. "What—?"

Jennie glanced out the window. "Your family is not being very cooperative in leaving the premises, I'm afraid. But security is handling it. Now, please, Mr. Blakely, if you will open the box?"

I ran my hand across the smooth top one more time, then lifted the lid.

Inside rested a stack of black-and-white photographs with yellowed edges, on top of a worn clothbound book. And on top of the photos rested a gauzy bag filled with leaves. Their green spicy smell wafted up to me...

"...Trust me, Geoffrey" Alice said. "This is the best thing to drink when cramming for exams. Won't leave you all jittery or wiped out like coffee." She held the cup under my nose, and the spice-scented steam washed over my face.

"Fine, I'll give it a try." I took the cup and set it down beside the criminology textbook. "But first, why don't you come sit right here?" I patted my lap.

"Sure, I'll sit there, if you can tell me the two main criticisms of social learning theory."

I sighed. "Right now? My main criticism is that learning inhibits our social interactions."

"Uh-huh, that's what I thought. Get to work, rich boy."

I scowled at the book. "What's the point? I'll learn all this when Father gives me his memories."

"Sure. Because Lord knows you wouldn't want to form your own opinions, or learn something your father doesn't already know. Or maybe you agreed with me about our cultural stagnation just to get into my bed?"

I glared at her. I hated when she was right. But for some reason I hated it even more when she was disappointed...

"...in me, Father," Daniel said, and leaned back from the chessboard, arms crossed. "Why can't you be happy for me?"

"Because," I said, studying the board. I had him in six moves, but only because once again he'd tried some wild, improvised strategy rather than following any of the dozen or more established responses to my opening moves. "She's a pleb with a record, Son. You marry her, and you'll never pass a justice nomination review."

"There's more important things than being a justice," Daniel said. "Especially when the name has become a joke."

I looked up sharply. Heat climbed my neck and burned my face, but I'd learned on the bench—over several lifetimes—to maintain control and an even tone during an argument. "And that is a perfect example of what I said. She's already filling your head with plebian nonsense. If you hadn't inherited your mother's rebellious nature—"

"Actually, Father, I got my opinions from you. Before you took Grandfather's memories. Before Mom left. Do you remember reading The Scarlet Pimpernel to me when I was a kid and—"

"So you think my time would be better spent playing a fop by day, and by night wearing a mask and rescuing aristocrats?"

"No!" Daniel stood and began pacing. "That's not what I meant. I—"

"Then you should choose your examples better. If you wish to win an argument—"

"This isn't a legal case, Father, or a debate! I'm not trying to win. I'm trying to make you understand."

"Then make me understand. What point were you trying to make? If the Pimpernel is a bad example, then give me a good one."

377

"Father, please. I just—"

"How about Robin Hood? Perhaps justices should act like some kind of thief, and undermine our whole system?" I shook the chessboard, causing pieces to tumble and crash into one another. "Should we redistribute wealth from the people who keep this nation working to..."

"...so-called plebian deviants," Miss Ginsberg said to the students gathered in her basement. Every single pleb there listened intently. I couldn't imagine how their families found the money to get them into this private class, but clearly they intended to make the most of it.

"Mr. Blakely." Ginsberg looked at me. "I believe your father just tried a theft case where he refused even to hear arguments of extenuating circumstances. Perhaps you'd like to share with the class your view on this, using the section on strain theory to make your argument?"

I looked around the room at all the faces turned to me now. Nobody enjoyed receiving Ginsberg's focus, but there was little sympathy...

...in their faces as the three justices listened to my client make his statement. My client was a pleb, and a dago wop to boot. He was as good as convicted given the doubly delinquent tendencies inherent to his kind. I glanced at Anthony. He looked rough, to be sure, more likely to be facing assault charges than conspiracy. But I'd seen his inventions. They were ingenious. If I could just find a way to make the justices see the benefits of the man serving his sentence through work release, or community service. I just needed to find the right...

...argument. It seemed like Alice and I were arguing every day now, every day since I'd received Father's memories. She was so afraid they'd change me that she now imagined seeing changes that weren't there. Why couldn't she just...

"...understand," I said, staring down at Daniel's gravestone. "Please forgive me, son."

I received no response, not even a sudden stirring of the cherry blossoms that I could take as a sign. Daniel would never answer me again, never again hear me tell him I loved him. All because some pleb *kid I'd sent to prison for stealing medicine, that I'd sought to make an example of to all the druggies, emerged ten years later as a hardened killer seeking payback for the death of his father that the medicine was meant to prevent.*

"What can I do?" I asked the cold marble. "My hands are tied by precedent, by the votes of the other justices, by my choices. I—"
I sounded as if I were writing a legal response. I rubbed at my eyes.
"Maybe you were right. Maybe we need a Robin Hood, someone dealing true justice."

The cherry blossoms whispered...

The memories unfolded with increasing speed, as though my mind raced down a tunnel filled with lights. Memories of classes, of tests, of cases. Grandfather's memories of my father laughing and crying, playing and sleeping, as a child and a young man. Memories of Father alive. Memories of his death. Then I burst out of the tunnel, and bright daylight flooded my mind's eye.

I understood. I understood the laws, and the system they supported. I understood its strengths. I understood its weak points.

I understood my grandfather.

And I understood why he'd never given us help.

"He'd wanted me to live as a pleb," I muttered, my eyes squeezed closed.

"What?" Mother asked.

"Nothing." I opened my eyes, and slid the book out from beneath the photos. An old copy of *The Scarlet Pimpernel*.

My eyes were drawn to the flower on Jennie's lapel, then to her face.

A League of the Pimpernel, Jennie. But with a different purpose. My son's purpose.

She smiled, seeing my understanding. "When you're ready, I shall give you a tour of the estates. I think you'll find your grandfather left you many interesting...toys."

Anthony's toys.

I saw my father's face then, my father as a young boy while

Grandfather read *Robin Hood* to him—grinning and eager for the next adventure.

"Actually," I said, "bring me Tony. We need to talk."

Grandfather's vision was to go after those who oppressed the plebs, those who treated people like disposable pawns, by knocking down the worst kings and queens of society one at a time. But I had a better idea.

I would find a way to transfer memory without destroying the original. I would become a mind healer to the world.

And then, we'd shake up the whole damn board.

A Word on the Art Direction

BY STEPHEN HICKMAN

Stephen Hickman has been illustrating science fiction and fantasy for four decades. His work is inspired by the masters of fantasy and science fiction writing—J.R.R. Tolkien, H.P. Lovecraft, A. Merritt, Edgar Rice Burroughs and Clark Ashton Smith.

His illustrations have been used as cover work for many contemporary writers: Harlan Ellison, Robert Heinlein, Steven Brust, Hal Colbatch, Tom Cool, Gordon Dickson, David Drake, Neil Gaiman, Mark Van Name, Anne McCaffrey, Larry Niven and Jerry Pournelle, Andre Norton and Steve Stirling, among others.

Stephen's work has earned him critical acclaim, including a World Science Fiction Convention Hugo Award and six Chesley Awards from the Association of Science Fiction and Fantasy Artists.

Stephen has been a judge for the Illustrators of the Future Contest since 2005, and this year he art directed each of the winning illustrators on their pieces appearing in this volume.

A Word on the Art Direction

Though I've made art my living for forty years, and have been asked for advice times beyond counting, this is my first official gig as an art director. However, as soon as I was asked to take this on, I knew how I wanted to go about the task.

My career arc has been unique in that it so happened that much of the time I was completely on my own as far as coming up with the ideas for the work I was getting paid for—from T-shirts to book covers and private commissions... In retrospect, I feel like I was a sort of Mowgli in the jungle of illustration. But I learned that I did by far the best work when I really put my heart into what I was doing.

So—my plan became simple: first, I would refrain from selecting the worst sketch that was submitted to me (two of my early art directors invariably did this, until I started sending in one sketch at a time).

Second, wherever it was at all possible, I would let the artist go with whichever idea they felt most strongly about.

As it happened, the artists made this plan easy to put into effect. Most of them knew just what they wanted to do, and in every single case these artists responded positively to any advice that I offered.

So my first stint at art directing turned out to be a good, even a novel experience—it was interesting for me to be able to watch how these vastly different artists evolve their illustrations from the first sketchy beginnings to the finished pieces. Now I can retire in contentment, and get back to my own work.

And to the artists in this book, it was a pleasure working with you on these illustrations!

LIST OF ILLUSTRATIONS BY ARTIST

CASSANDRE BOLAN
Beneath the Surface of Two Kills

CASSANDRE BOLAN
The Pushbike Legion

ADAM BREWSTER
Beyond All Weapons

389

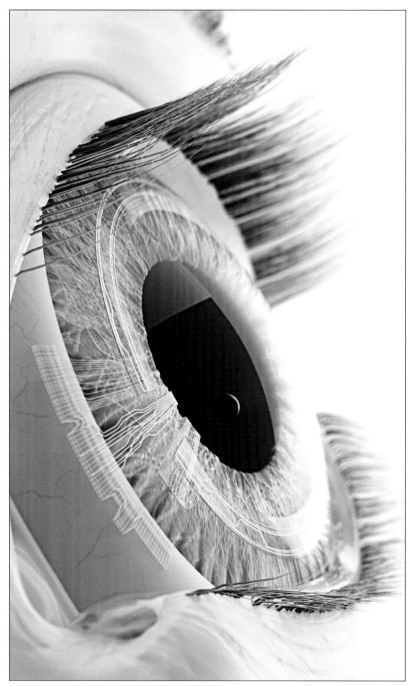

ADAM BREWSTER
Long Jump

VINCENT-MICHAEL COVIELLO
Carousel

391

VINCENT-MICHAEL COVIELLO
The Shaadi Exile

KIRBI FAGAN
The Clouds in Her Eyes

393

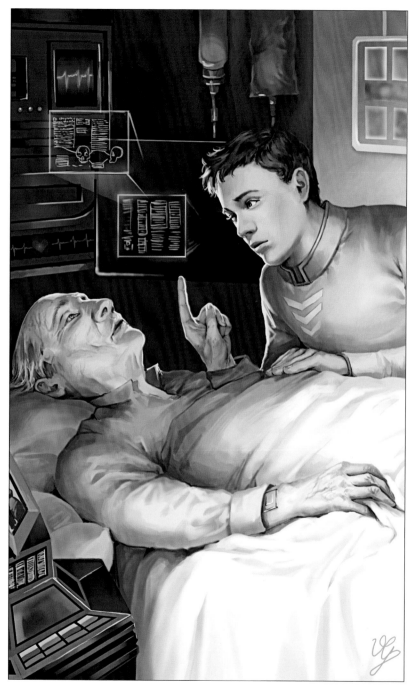

VANESSA GOLITZ

Memories Bleed Beneath the Mask

KRISTIE KIM
What Moves the Sun and Other Stars

395

SEONHEE LIM
Animal

BERNARDO MOTA
These Walls of Despair 397

ANDREW SONEA
Rainbows for Other Days

ANDREW SONEA
Robots Don't Cry

TREVOR SMITH
Giants at the End of the World

MICHAEL TALBOT
Shifter

401

SARAH WEBB
Another Range of Mountains

The Year in the Contests

In 2013, the Writers and Illustrators of the Future Contests continued their broad growth, with both Contests receiving more entries than ever before. Entrants to the Contests came from over 168 countries, and our actual winners, including honorable mentions, are represented by writers and illustrators from more than three dozen nations.

From the very first volume of *Writers of the Future,* past winners have distinguished themselves in ongoing careers. In just the past year, those winners have published 45 novels and more than 200 short stories. In addition, they—along with past artist winners and Contest judges—have racked up an astonishing number of awards, honors and nominations.

From the earliest winners to the most recent participants, including artists and judges, here is the impressive array of honors.

Karen Joy Fowler (Vol. 1) was nominated for the 2013 Nebula Award for Best Novel. Also from Vol. 1, winner and Contest Judge Nina Kiriki Hoffman was under consideration for the Locus Award for Best Collection, as was Contest Judge Robert Silverberg.

Robert Reed (Vol. 2) took third place in the 2013 Sturgeon Awards, while Contest Judge Frederik Pohl won the Sturgeon Award for Distinguished Service. Reed also competed with himself in the category for Best Novella in the Locus Awards, with three of his novellas under consideration, and in addition joined the already crowded field of nominations for the Locus Award for Best Collection.

Mary Turzillo (Vol. 4) was a finalist for the Bram Stoker Award for Best Horror Poetry Collection.

The 2012 Goodreads Choice Award for Best Science Fiction went to Stephen Baxter (Vol. 5), in collaboration with Terry Pratchett, for the novel *The Long Earth*. Baxter was also nominated for the Locus Award for Best Collection.

Winner and Artist Judge Shaun Tan (Vol. 8) was a finalist for a Locus Award for Best Artist. In addition, Tan was a finalist for the Aurealis Award from Australia for Best Children's Book and for the 2014 Spectrum Fantastic Art Award, along with Omar Rayyan (also Vol. 8).

Alan Smale (Vol. 13) was among the nominees for the Locus Award for Best Novella.

Contest winner Tobias Buckell (Vol. 16) was nominated for the Locus Award for Best Novel for his *Arctic Rising,* while artist winner Frank Wu (also Vol. 16) was nominated for the Locus Award for Best Artist. Other nominees in the category of Best Novel were Contest Judges Gregory Benford and Larry Niven, who collaborated on *Bowl of Heaven* and Larry Niven and Edward M. Lerner, also in collaboration, for *Fate of Worlds*.

Lee Battersby (Vol. 18) was a finalist for the Australian Aurealis Award for Best Horror Novel for *The Marching Dead*.

Ken Liu (Vol. 19) won the Nebula for Best Short Story with "Mono no Aware," and was nominated for a Nebula for Best Novelette as well as a finalist for the Locus Award for Best Short Story. Ken additionally won the WSFA Small Press Award for his story "Good Hunting." Jay Lake (also Vol. 19) was nominated for a Hugo for "The Stars Do Not Lie" and was a finalist and nominee for the Locus Award for Best Novella. The 2013 Lifeboat to the Stars Award was won by the novel *Tau Ceti,* written by Contest Judge Kevin J. Anderson in collaboration with winner Steven Savile (Vol. 19) and edited by Judge Mike Resnick.

Aliette de Bodard (Vol. 23) accumulated an impressive array

awards and nominations, including the Nebula Award for Best Novella for her short story "Immersion." She was also a nominee for the Hugo for Best Novella and Best Short Story. She also won the Locus Award for Best Short Story, was finalist for the Locus Award for Best Novella, nominated for the Locus Best Short Story Award and was recognized by the British Science Fiction Society in the Best Short Fiction category.

Ian McHugh (Vol. 24) was a finalist for the Aurealis Award for Best Fantasy in Short Fiction.

Artist Douglas Bosley (Vol. 25) was the first-place winner of the 2013 National Society of Arts and Letters Printmaking Award.

K.C. Ball (Vol. 26) was nominated for the Locus Award for Best Novella. Jingxuan Hu (also Vol. 26) won the Public Choice Prize in the final awards to winners of the ArtGemini Prize 2013.

The 2013 Apex Magazine Story of the Year Winner was Brian Trent (Vol. 29). And last year's grand prize-winning author Tina Gower won the 2013 Daphne du Maurier Award for Excellence in Mystery/Suspense for her story "Identity."

Contest Judge Tim Powers was a finalist for the Locus Award for his fantasy novel *Hide Me Among the Graves,* while Contest Judges Vincent Di Fate, Bob Eggleton, Frank Frazetta, Leo and Diane Dillon were all nominated for the Locus Award for Best Artist. Contest Judge Stephan Martiniere was nominated for Best Art Book for *Velocity* and a finalist for Best Artist.

The 2013 Scribe Award for best adapted novel was won by Judge Kevin J. Anderson for *Clockwork Angels.*

The winner of Canada's Aurora Lifetime Achievement Award went to Judge Robert J. Sawyer, who was also nominated for *Triggers* for Best Novel in English.

For the Chesley Awards, Illustrator Judge Bob Eggleton was nominated for Best Cover Illustration for hardback, Best Magazine Cover and Best Interior Illustration. Judge Larry Elmore was nominated for Best Monochrome and for the Lifetime Achievement Award.

Awards are not all the honors reaped by our winners. For example, Patrick Rothfuss's (Vol. 18) bestselling Kingkiller Chronicle series was optioned for film by Twentieth Century Fox, while Jason Fischer (Vol. 26) is the first Contest winner to have his story written as an opera libretto.

Robert Castillo (Vol. 24) was storyboard artist for the documentary "Kids for Cash" and "The Angriest Man in Brooklyn," a film releasing later this year. Ty Carter (Vol. 26) is working on the upcoming Peanuts movie, which is scheduled for release during the 2015 holiday season. He also recently published a book *Musings and Wanderings*.

The just-released 2014 Campbellian Anthology included ten past winners. Of these, two are from Vol. 28 and eight are from Vol. 29. Included in the anthology from Vol. 28 were David Carani and Gerald Warfield. Those from Vol. 29 were Alisa Alering, Tina Gower, Marina Lostetter, Chrome Oxide, Shannon Peavey, Christopher Reynaga, Stephen Sottong and Brian Trent.

Sadly, this past year, our longtime friend and Judge Frederik Pohl passed away.

The Science Fiction and Fantasy Writers of America named Pohl a Grand Master in 1993. In 2000, he was honored with the L. Ron Hubbard Lifetime Achievement Award for Outstanding Contributions to the Arts. He became a judge for the Writers of the Future Contest in 1985 and was one of the instructors at the first WotF Workshop in Taos, New Mexico.

The Contests continue to grow in size, while our past winners continue to grow in artistic stature and gain wider recognition. We look forward to seeing what exciting changes this coming year may bring.

For Contest year 30, the L. Ron Hubbard Writers of the Future Contest winners are:

FIRST QUARTER

1. *Terry Madden*
   ANIMAL

2. *Amanda Forrest*
   THE SHAADI EXILE

3. *Anaea Lay*
   THESE WALLS OF DESPAIR

SECOND QUARTER

1. *Randy Henderson*
   MEMORIES BLEED BENEATH THE MASK

2. *K.C. Norton*
   WHAT MOVES THE SUN AND OTHER STARS

3. *Liz Colter*
   THE CLOUDS IN HER EYES

THIRD QUARTER

1. *Leena Likitalo*
   GIANTS AT THE END OF THE WORLD

2. *Shauna O'Meara*
   BENEATH THE SURFACE OF TWO KILLS

3. *Paul Eckheart*
   SHIFTER

FOURTH QUARTER

1. *Megan E. O'Keefe*
   ANOTHER RANGE OF MOUNTAINS

2. *Oleg Kazantsev*
   LONG JUMP

3. *C. Stuart Hardwick*
   RAINBOWS FOR OTHER DAYS

PUBLISHED FINALIST

Timothy Jordan

THE PUSHBIKE LEGION

For the year 2013, the L. Ron Hubbard Illustrators of the Future Contest winners are:

FIRST QUARTER
Vincent-Michael Coviello
Seonhee Lim
Kristie Kim

SECOND QUARTER
Adam Brewster
Trevor Smith
Sarah Webb

THIRD QUARTER
Kirbi Fagan
Bernardo Mota
Michael Talbot

FOURTH QUARTER
Cassandre Bolan
Vanessa Golitz
Andrew Sonea

Our heartiest congratulations to all the winners! May we see much more of their work in the future.

NEW WRITERS!
L. Ron Hubbard's
Writers of the Future Contest

Opportunity for new and amateur writers of new short stories or novelettes of science fiction or fantasy.

No entry fee is required.

Entrants retain all publication rights.

ALL AWARDS ARE ADJUDICATED BY PROFESSIONAL WRITERS ONLY

Prizes every three months: $1,000, $750, $500
Annual Grand Prize: $5,000 additional!

Don't delay! Send your entry now!

To submit your entry electronically go to:
www.writersofthefuture.com/enter-writer-contest

E-mail: contests@authorservicesinc.com

To submit your entry via mail send to:
L. Ron Hubbard's Writers of the Future Contest
PO Box 1630
Los Angeles, California 90078

WRITERS' CONTEST RULES

1. No entry fee is required, and all rights in the story remain the property of the author. All types of science fiction, fantasy and dark fantasy are welcome.

2. By submitting to the Contest, the entrant agrees to abide by all Contest rules.

3. All entries must be original works, in English. Plagiarism, which includes the use of third-party poetry, song lyrics, characters or another person's universe, without written permission, will result in disqualification. Excessive violence or sex, determined by the judges, will result in disqualification. Entries may not have been previously published in professional media.

4. To be eligible, entries must be works of prose, up to 17,000 words in length. We regret we cannot consider poetry, or works intended for children.

5. The Contest is open only to those who have not professionally published a novel or short novel, or more than one novelette, or more than three short stories, in any medium. Professional publication is deemed to be payment of at least six cents per word, and at least 5,000 copies, or 5,000 hits.

6. Entries submitted in hard copy must be typewritten or a computer printout in black ink on white paper, printed only on the front of the paper, double-spaced, with numbered pages. All other formats will be disqualified. Each entry must have a cover page with the title of the work, the author's legal name, a pen name if applicable, address, telephone number, e-mail address and an approximate word count. Every subsequent page must carry the title and a page number, but the author's name must be deleted to facilitate fair, anonymous judging.

   Entries submitted electronically must be double-spaced and must include the title and page number on each page, but not the author's name. Electronic submissions will separately include the author's legal name, pen name if applicable, address, telephone number, e-mail address and approximate word count.

7. Manuscripts will be returned after judging only if the author has provided return postage on a self-addressed envelope.

8. We accept only entries that do not require a delivery signature for us to receive them.

9. There shall be three cash prizes in each quarter: a First Prize of $1,000, a Second Prize of $750, and a Third Prize of $500, in US dollars. In addition, at the end of the year the winners will have their entries rejudged, and a Grand Prize winner shall be determined and receive an additional $5,000. All winners will also receive trophies.

10. The Contest has four quarters, beginning on October 1, January 1, April 1 and July 1. The year will end on September 30. To be eligible for judging in its quarter, an entry must be postmarked or received electronically no later than midnight on the last day of the quarter. Late entries will be included in the following quarter and the Contest Administration will so notify the entrant.

11. Each entrant may submit only one manuscript per quarter. Winners are ineligible to make further entries in the Contest.

12. All entries for each quarter are final. No revisions are accepted.

13. Entries will be judged by professional authors. The decisions of the judges are entirely their own, and are final.

14. Winners in each quarter will be individually notified of the results by phone, mail or e-mail.

15. This Contest is void where prohibited by law.

16. To send your entry electronically, go to:
www.writersofthefuture.com/enter-writer-contest
and follow the instructions.
To send your entry in hard copy, mail it to:
L. Ron Hubbard's Writers of the Future Contest
PO Box 1630, Los Angeles, California 90078

17. Visit the website for any Contest rules updates at:
www.writersofthefuture.com.

411

NEW ILLUSTRATORS!
L. Ron Hubbard's
Illustrators of the Future Contest

Opportunity for new science fiction and fantasy artists worldwide.

No entry fee is required.

Entrants retain all publication rights.

ALL JUDGING BY PROFESSIONAL ARTISTS ONLY

$1,500 in prizes each quarter.
Quarterly winners compete for $5,000 additional annual prize!

Don't delay! Send your entry now!

To submit your entry electronically go to:
www.writersofthefuture.com/enter-the-illustrator-contest

E-mail: contests@authorservicesinc.com

To submit your entry via mail send to:
L. Ron Hubbard's Illustrators of the Future Contest
PO Box 3190
Los Angeles, California 90078

ILLUSTRATORS' CONTEST RULES

1. The Contest is open to entrants from all nations. (However, entrants should provide themselves with some means for written communication in English.) All themes of science fiction and fantasy illustrations are welcome: every entry is judged on its own merits only. No entry fee is required and all rights to the entry remain the property of the artist.

2. By submitting to the Contest, the entrant agrees to abide by all Contest rules.

3. The Contest is open to new and amateur artists who have not been professionally published and paid for more than three black-and-white story illustrations, or more than one process-color painting, in media distributed broadly to the general public. The ultimate eligibility criterion, however, is defined by the word "amateur"—in other words, the artist has not been paid for his artwork. If you are not sure of your eligibility, please write a letter to the Contest Administration with details regarding your publication history. Include a self-addressed and stamped envelope for the reply. You may also send your questions to the Contest Administration via e-mail.

4. Each entrant may submit only one set of illustrations in each Contest quarter. The entry must be original to the entrant and previously unpublished. Plagiarism, infringement of the rights of others, or other violations of the Contest rules will result in disqualification. Winners in previous quarters are not eligible to make further entries.

5. The entry shall consist of three illustrations done by the entrant in a color or black-and-white medium created from the artist's imagination. Use of gray scale in illustrations and mixed media, computer generated art, and the use of photography in the illustrations are accepted. Each illustration must represent a subject different from the other two.

6. ENTRIES SHOULD NOT BE THE ORIGINAL DRAWINGS, but should be color or black-and-white reproductions of the originals

of a quality satisfactory to the entrant. Entries must be submitted unfolded and flat, in an envelope no larger than 9 inches by 12 inches.

7. All hard copy entries must be accompanied by a self-addressed return envelope of the appropriate size, with the correct US postage affixed. (Non-US entrants should enclose international postage reply coupons.) If the entrant does not want the reproductions returned, the entry should be clearly marked DISPOSABLE COPIES: DO NOT RETURN. A business-size self-addressed envelope with correct postage (or valid e-mail address) should be included so that the judging results may be returned to the entrant. We only accept entries that do not require a delivery signature for us to receive them.

8. To facilitate anonymous judging, each of the three photocopies must be accompanied by a removable cover sheet bearing the artist's name, address, telephone number, e-mail address and an identifying title for that work. The reproduction of the work should carry the same identifying title on the front of the illustration and the artist's signature should be deleted. The Contest Administration will remove and file the cover sheets, and forward only the anonymous entry to the judges.

9. There will be three co-winners in each quarter. Each winner will receive an outright cash grant of US $500 and a trophy. Winners will also receive eligibility to compete for the annual Grand Prize of an additional cash grant of $5,000 together with the annual Grand Prize trophy.

10. For the annual Grand Prize Contest, the quarterly winners will be furnished with a specification sheet and a winning story from the Writers of the Future Contest to illustrate. In order to retain eligibility for the Grand Prize, each winner shall send to the Contest address his/her illustration of the assigned story within thirty (30) days of receipt of the story assignment.

The yearly Grand Prize winner shall be determined by the judges on the following basis only: Each Grand Prize judge's personal opinion on the extent to which it makes the judge want to read the story it illustrates.

The Grand Prize winner shall be announced at the L. Ron Hubbard Awards Event held in the following year.

11. The Contest has four quarters, beginning on October 1, January 1, April 1 and July 1. The year will end on September 30. To be eligible for judging in its quarter, an entry must be postmarked no later than midnight on the last day of the quarter. Late entries will be included in the following quarter and the Contest Administration will so notify the entrant.

12. Entries will be judged by professional artists only. Each quarterly judging and the Grand Prize judging may have different panels of judges. The decisions of the judges are entirely their own and are final.

13. Winners in each quarter will be individually notified of the results by mail or e-mail.

14. This Contest is void where prohibited by law.

15. To send your entry electronically, go to:
www.writersofthefuture.com/enter-the-illustrator-contest
and follow the instructions.
To send your entry via mail send it to:
L. Ron Hubbard's Illustrators of the Future Contest
PO Box 3190, Los Angeles, California 90078

16. Visit the website for any Contest rules updates at
www.writersofthefuture.com.

Launch your career with the
WRITERS & ILLUSTRATORS OF THE FUTURE PACKAGE

With this book package you receive 7 *Writers of the Future* volumes (Volumes 23–29) for the price of 5 and you automatically qualify for FREE SHIPPING.

You will find essays on how to become a successful writer or illustrator from Contest judges and professionals including: *L. Ron Hubbard, Kevin J. Anderson, Robert Castillo, Larry Elmore, Ron Lindahn, Judith Miller, Rebecca Moesta, Cliff Nielsen, Nnedi Okorafor, Mike Resnick, Kristine Kathryn Rusch, Robert Silverberg, Dean Wesley Smith, Shaun Tan* and *Stephen Youll.*

These books contain the award-winning short stories as selected by a distinguished panel of judges. Witness the unleashing of the power of dreams and unlocking of the secrets of the universe. Experience their vision and find out for yourself how good you have to be to win the Writers & Illustrators of the Future Contests!

Find out what it takes to be the best.

ORDER NOW!

Get this package—a value of
$59.95 for only $39.95

Call toll-free: 1-877-842-5299 or visit www.GalaxyPress.com
Mail in your order to: Galaxy Press

7051 Ho.   **32953011986546**   ł, CA 90028